A Man of Quiet Conviction

Kelley's apprehension about the show was summed up in his own unique style when he told Roddenberry, "This is going to be the biggest hit or the biggest miss God ever made."

Roddenberry knew there were a few lines that could not be crossed with Kelley, and one small instance dramatized this. DeForest recalled: "I had great trouble when we started *Star Trek*. Roddenberry said no jewelry, and I had my mother's ring on, and he said no jewelry, and I said no jewelry, no DeForest." That's all there was to it. Just like that, everyone knew he meant it. Clora's ring became part of Dr. Leonard McCoy.

"Everything to do with McCoy we did with Kelley's input. We created McCoy with Kelley right there," Dorothy Fontana remembers. "Roddenberry was the creator of *Star Trek,* but DeForest Kelley created Dr. McCoy."

From Sawdust to Stardust

From
SAWDUST
to
STARDUST

The Biography of DeForest Kelley,
Star Trek®'s Dr. McCoy

TERRY LEE RIOUX

POCKET BOOKS
New York   London   Toronto   Sydney

An *Original* Publication of POCKET BOOKS

 POCKET BOOKS, a division of Simon & Schuster, Inc.
1230 Avenue of the Americas, New York, NY 10020

Library of Congress Cataloging-in-Publication Data

Rioux, Terry Lee, 1961–
    From sawdust to stardust : the biography of DeForest Kelley, Star trek's
Dr. McCoy / Terry Lee Rioux.—1st Pocket Books trade pbk. ed.
        p. cm.
    Includes bibliographical references.
    ISBN 0-7434-5762-5
    1. Kelley, DeForest, 1920–1999. 2. Actors—United States—Biography. I. Title.

PN2287.K45R56 2005
791.4502'8'092—dc22
[B]

                                                            2004051063

First Pocket Books trade paperback edition February 2005

10 9 8 7 6 5 4 3 2

Cover photo courtesy of Greg Jein

Manufactured in the United States of America

For information regarding special discounts for bulk purchases,
please contact Simon & Schuster Special Sales at 1-800-456-6798
or business@simonandschuster.com.

For Carolyn, Anne, Bette, Aileen, Kris, Tony, Don, Phil,
H.G., R.W., J.S.,
Katherine, Kelley, Samantha, Callie, Amy, Myrtle,
and the *real* Captain Kirk, with love.

From Sawdust to Stardust,
or How I Got from Hell and Damnation
to Star Trek *and the Federation*
—DeForest Kelley, 1999

For De:
Real love stories never have endings.
—CAROLYN M. KELLEY, 2003

The Actor's Prayer

Oh God, here in my dressing room with the door shut, I am alone with Thee. . . . Can not an actor be God's man? Convention classes me and my fellows among the loose and thoughtless. So Thou art my secret. I triumph inwardly to find Thy presence and taste the mystic joy of Thy friendship. While the world suspects not, Thou teachest me subtle ways to resist despair, to master my passions, to heal unworthy weakness; the rare medicine of Thy presence is for me, too, as well as for the cloistered monk or meditating scholar. Teach me to be great among the many who are content to be called great. Let me be an unusual person because of that simplicity of heart and lovableness of nature that I learn from Thee.

—DR. FRANK CRANE,
The Kelley Home Archive

Contents

A Foreword
Harve Bennett

I am not especially religious, but I do believe in the Hand of God. And never was His Handiwork more evident than on the day DeForest Kelley got his star on Hollywood Boulevard.

The selection of which hunk of blank sidewalk shall be dedicated to which "Walk of Fame" inductee is a mysterious process known only to the Electors of the Hollywood Chamber of Commerce and their chairman, my good friend Johnny Grant. Little consideration seems to be given to the building or business that abuts the sidewalk, often resulting in the most glorious of stars being cemented in front of the most inglorious of establishments. Since Hollywood Boulevard over the decades has gone from riches to rags to urban renewal several times, it is not now, nor has it ever been, the Fifth Avenue of the West. So of all the gin joints, lingerie boutiques, and pawnshops available, only the Hand of God could have selected the most perfect of venues to honor Jackson DeForest Kelley, one of the most perfect of men to ever walk this boulevard, or, for that matter, this earth.

De's star site was located on the sidewalk directly in front of a glittering new multi-story theater and shop complex. The centerpiece of the architecture was an endless escalator which seemed to come down from the clouds themselves. Or was it from somewhere even higher

than the clouds? The huge electric sign at the top of the escalator answered that question.

"The Galaxy," it proclaimed.

There are as many differing memories of DeForest Kelley's Moses-
like descent down that "galactic" escalator as there were people in the
crowd below waiting to honor him. Some swear he was in his *Trek*
series costume, the long-sleeved blue T-shirt with the black crew
collar. Others remember him in the maroon tunic he first filled so ele-
gantly in *The Wrath of Khan*. A few romantics saw him in the doeskin
look of *Star Trek: The Motion Picture*, and more than one person has
argued with me that De was in some kind of a frock coat looking
either like: 1) a preacher, or 2) that embodiment of the Southern Gentleman, Ashley Wilkes in *Gone With the Wind* (a part he would have
played brilliantly).

My own memory, of course, was the most accurate (if only because
it was mine). My DeForest, youthful, radiant, was top to bottom in
fringeless pale buckskin, the long-legged pants worn, John Wayne
style, over reptilian cowboy boots. He had a cowboy string tie round
his neck, and above it all, a narrow cream-colored Stetson. I would
have bet money on the accuracy of this memory. Then I saw the video
record taken by Kris Smith on that day, December 18, 1991. Roll
tape . . .

The escalator was only two stories high. De was wearing black
slacks and a blue and black argyle sweater with a black turtleneck. Around his neck, there was a Croakie chain, holding his
bifocals on his chest. He wore no hat. Reptilian cowboy boots,
his favorites, were protruding, John Wayne style, from under
his pants. He looked a little thin, a little tired, a little frail. He
smiled gently. He waved somewhat shyly. And then, with a
little effort, he managed the Vulcan Salute.

Why do our memories conflict? Why, on that day, did we each see
a different DeForest? The answer seems clear to me now after finishing the book you are about to read.

DeForest Kelley was all the things we saw in him—and so much more. But because he was, above everything else, a private man, the antithesis of The Actor, few if any of us saw all the pieces of his mosaic. Each of us saw in him the piece we found most comforting; but in taking that comfort, we missed the full sum of the man.

Now, as a gift to those of us who knew him and the millions who wanted to know him, Terry Lee Rioux has painstakingly put the mosaic together. She has dug meticulously not only into the story of the man, but into the Georgia soil from which he sprang and the time and feelings of what Tom Brokaw has called "The Greatest Generation," that noble group in which De unquestionably deserves a front row seat. In the process, she has provided a perspective on a lasting contribution DeForest Kelley made to American culture, a contribution I had not fully appreciated until Terry illuminated it for me and for those who read this.

Star Trek, which began in the turbulent '60s, will forever be remembered as the first major breakthrough in ethnic and gender diversity on television. Gene Roddenberry's ensemble boldly went where no TV show had gone before. It included an African woman of intelligence and authority, an Asian clearly destined to captain his own ship, a humane and lovable Russian (a daring statement during the height of the Cold War), and a humorless alien whose pointy ears, green blood, and intellectual superiority would not normally have made him what he became, the most popular kid in class.

So where, we might ask, was the boldness or diversity in Kelley's "Bones" McCoy? Was he not a television cliché, "the wise country doctor"? Had we not seen this character on *Gunsmoke* and *Welby*, and in much of American literature? Rioux's answer, like many of her insights, makes us appreciate "Bones" all the more for the statement he made, and the time in which he made it, when America was in its mid-century spasm over the emergent Civil Rights Movement.

No "country doctor," but a homeboy scientist wielding a magic tricorder wand of the future, and the promise of a better life for all of us. Cantankerous, opinionated, funny. Yet the red clay in his voice and his dignity made a very specific statement: He was a humanist with a Georgia accent. Atticus Finch with a medical degree. And this at a time when television itself had helped stereotype Southern Whites as bigots and Southern Gentlemen as demagogues or Grand Dragons.

Dr. McCoy's function on *Star Trek* may have been to heal the sick, but his presence on the bridge of the *Enterprise* did much more. It set a tone of decency, humanity, and reconciliation amid ethnic and planetary strife. He took it upon himself to heal the Universe, and that is why the character of "Bones" McCoy is so universally loved.

Or is it just the character?

One of the joys of reading this book is that you will come to know that there is no line between "Bones" McCoy and the actor who played him. The man and the part were one. What "Bones" was, DeForest was, a Healer. He brought that healing spirit to his audience. He brought it to his friends.

May that spirit live to the twenty-third century, and beyond.

Part One

The Sawdust

Chapter I
The Preacher's Son

"It was a hard row to hoe, to be perfect."
DeForest Kelley, 1992

Reverend Ernest David Kelley began his ministry to the congregation of Conyers, Georgia, on January 12, 1930. At first meeting, the new shepherd made a mild impression, fine-boned with smooth skin, spectacles, and a bald head. By surface appearances, he was a timid man, but his quick, sharp eyes and the fire of his sermons revealed that he was not. His greatest gifts were the content of his sermons and the strength of his presence in the pulpit. His own soul knew the bitter taste of daily trials, and so he was a genuine witness in his mission to frail humanity. His was a constant litany, crying out about the perfect soul-gathering rescue of Jesus Christ and the joys to be found in him.[1]

Reverend Kelley could speak directly to the souls of these Georgia people. His heritage was close to that of his congregants. The Kelley family origins were proud, Irish, and Southern. From Virginia in the 1750s, the Kelleys found their way into Georgia, to Franklin County and the small hill town of Toccoa. Theirs was the rugged earth of north Georgia hill country, a land of Cherokee people and hardscrabble settlement. A century later, the region became a favorite highway for the mean ruin of Union forces during the Atlanta campaign. Two young witnesses to the Civil War, Mary Emily Payne and Emory Jackson Kelley, later married and raised nine children surrounded by the deprivations of Reconstruction. Ernest David, born in 1883, was called to ministry in 1911. Ordained through the Broad River Baptist Church, Reverend Kelley chose to serve the common man on the sawdust trail. He met and married Clora Casey of Cedartown, eleven years his junior, and his first son, Casey, was born in 1917. Jackson DeForest came along in 1920. In 1925, Reverend Kelley earned a graduate degree in theology from Mercer University. He served churches with names like Zebulon, Attica, County Line, and Penfield. With Clora at his side, he ministered all over the interior of Georgia.[2]

Now at the height of his physical and spiritual strength, Reverend Kelley shared the gospel in Conyers. Educated and poor, after nearly fifteen years of preaching, the Reverend knew the hearts and minds of men and the dangers of a worldly life. His call for unswerving Christian faith was mixed with Christian warning: he made it very clear to his congregation and to his children that there were grave consequences for sinful yet ordinary behaviors such as going to dances and movies and drinking and smoking. The saved and those yet to be salvaged were invited to find and renew their spirit in a Baptist way of life with the Kelleys. While the Reverend ministered with his sermons and mastery of the Bible, his wife ministered by loving example and gentle touch.[3]

Reverend Kelley kept his boys, Ernest Casey and Jackson DeForest, close to the church. He made them learn the responsibilities of the elect; the boys knew they were representing something far larger than their own small lives. The mission of the father was the mission of the family. As a preacher's kid, DeForest was bound to the sawdust trail of his father's ministry. Athens, Woodville, and so on, they moved from one Georgia mill town to the next. Reverend Kelley shaped his sons with an eye on the promise of heaven and the literal existence of hell. He ruled with the steady hand of the righteous, while Clora worked to soften that hand with humor and diplomacy. However, the traditional round of Bible study, quotation and recitation, psalms at supper, Wednesday evening prayer meetings, and Sundays filled with classes and multiple services challenged the obedience of even the most respectful child. DeForest's brother, Casey, chafed under the restrictions of the household and seemed quite unable to please anyone completely. He was already a teenager, vexed by many things his little brother couldn't begin to imagine. DeForest, like his mother, sought to keep the peace. DeForest's first role was his portrayal of the Good Son.[4]

Sometimes DeForest spent long hours playing outside, and when it was time, from deep in the shadows of the porch, Clora would call out, "DeForest! . . . DeForest!" and the boy's name rang out all around the big house and yard. DeForest loved that sound of his mother's calling. Other times, the little boy stayed close to his mother to keep her company as she worked. While she did her chores, his eyes were often drawn to her only finery, an ice-bright diamond ring. Clora wore it always, while washing, ironing, and scrubbing, "and it was all smooth . . . and the prongs wore down slowly," the boy remembered. She cherished that ring, and so did her son. Her brother, the mysterious Herman Casey, won the ring in a card game in France and gave it to her. Her boy DeForest wanted to give her something, too; he wanted to give her the world. As young as he was, he knew her life was hard, and he wished to make it easier for her somehow, and so he became her sunshine.[5]

DeForest was immersed in the Reverend's mission in Conyers. There his sermons were thundering appeals delivered in lightning. He called all to a worldly mission to "seek and save the lost." To join him, one must be filled with the Holy Spirit, and for that to happen, one must surrender. "Are you willing to crucify self?" the Reverend challenged every member. He promised them that failure would mean "wreck and ruin."

Ten-year-old DeForest began to think that there could be only hellfire and damnation for someone as weak and selfish as he knew himself to be, and his father gave no indication otherwise. DeForest worked ever harder at being the good son. With some resignation, he recalled, "It was a hard row to hoe, to be perfect."[6]

2 Before their first year in Conyers was over, Reverend Kelley introduced the congregation to DeForest's musical talents. In the words of Erskine Davis, DeForest's friend during those years, the boy had a "very good voice for singing. He often sang a solo at the morning church service. Two of his favorites were 'Living for Jesus' and 'Jesus

Is All the World to Me.' While DeForest sang, Reverend Kelley would beam with pride and joy. Sometimes he would stand by DeForest while he sang." The Reverend made good use of DeForest's gifts and seemed determined to forge the boy into an instrument of ministry. For the holidays, the Reverend presented a Christmas exercise. DeForest received "a great hand, the solo work of this 10-year-old boy being especially good," according to the local paper. DeForest's uncle, Dr. Luther H. Kelley, "slipped in and took a back seat just like most doctors do at church and grand opera."[7]

DeForest's performances, his manners, and his charm made him popular in Conyers. He was a sensitive boy who appreciated neatness, process, and order; messes and contrariness disturbed him. Contrariness, indeed! One grandmother drove DeForest to distraction by insisting on calling him Forrest, as in Nathan Bedford Forrest, the Civil War hero. When he tended to her, she would look at whatever he might bring her and say, "Set it down here, Forrest." And he'd put her tray down. Finally, he brought her a gift and told her if she would say his name right, he would give her his gift. Smiling, she agreed. He gave it to her; she admired it and handed it back to him: "Set it down here, Forrest." Everyone knew, and she did, too, that he was named for Lee DeForest, the genius of the new century who made the radio possible, as well as talking movies and all kinds of things. Dr. DeForest traveled the country, promoting his work and inspiring the common man to look forward to the new world just taking shape in the early twentieth century. Reverend Kelley was very impressed with the mind and inventions of Dr. DeForest, and his second son was given a name fit for the future.[8]

But the present times were hard. To help out, DeForest hunted squirrel, rabbit, and possum—anything that might fill the family table—but he had no taste for killing and never hunted unless he had to. Reverend Kelley took on a second church, the Rockdale Baptist Church a few miles west of town, for the small sum that congregation could offer. While the Reverend preached, DeForest hunted and sometimes hosed down the coal laborers at the Conyers rail depot for a coin or two, but these small amounts could not do much to relieve the Kelleys' ministerial poverty. There was no shame in their lack, and it was no sin to do without.[9]

In Conyers, one of DeForest's favorite playmates was the small son of Emma Banks, who did some day work for Clora Kelley. Emma's house was little more than a shack in West Conyers, but her yard was interesting, with an outdoor laundry kettle, chickens, and a woodpile where DeForest and sometimes his brother Casey would go to play and be with Emma. She made a deep impression on DeForest, and he took her into his heart.[10]

DeForest took pleasure in his life in Conyers, trapping rabbits, fishing, wading in the water to catch tadpoles and bugs. He loved Sandy Kelley, the little brown dog that kept close tabs on the young master, waiting for him while DeForest was in school. Toward the end of every school day, DeForest would go near the classroom's open window and sharpen his pencil, signaling Sandy that dismissal time approached. He remembered, "That little dog's tail would raise up, and off he'd go, down the street, through the window without the screen, and all around the house; then he'd come back and lead me home."[11]

School lunches could be dreary, but Erskine Davis's mother baked a yeast loaf for his sandwiches. Erskine's father was a dairy farmer and grew wheat for the family bread, taking it to the local mill to be ground. The smell and taste of the bread were just wonderful. "DeForest would come around at lunch recess and swap two of his sandwiches for one of mine," Davis remembers. A boy who knew quality had to be willing to pay up for it, and DeForest was such a boy.[12]

DeForest's elementary-school teacher, Mary J. Cowan, gave him stellar reports for neatness, promptness, attendance, and conduct. He did very well in agriculture, grammar, geography, and reading. He earned B's in physiology, history, spelling, and writing. Arithmetic never meant very much, though he did fairly well. In 1932, he was advanced into high school.[13]

It was easier to express high spirits among the children, teachers, and staff at school than in the company of Reverend Kelley. And DeForest's angelic sweetness had a good touch of Tom Sawyer salt in it. It seems he was just the boy for the role of Tom, in something he vaguely recalled later as "Tom Sawyer Paints a Fence," apparently his first experience onstage. He enjoyed cutting up for his classmates; Tom Doyle especially appreciated young Kelley's efforts. The principal of Conyers High School was a tall, stern man with a bald head, rather like the

Reverend Kelley. Doyle recalls that the principal would, whenever he passed their classroom, go up on tiptoes to peer at them through the window at the top of the door. When he did that, DeForest would croon, "The moon is rising! The moo-ooon is risiiing!" Muffling the laughter would be half the battle, stifling admiration for DeForest's nerve the other half.[14]

One of DeForest's favorite classes was Miss Bedenbaugh's French class. She was "a tiny, pretty, dark-haired lady," Doyle recalls. "Each French class, DeForest would tell her, 'My, you look pretty today!'" All sugar and snowball, DeForest flummoxed her with charm. He didn't let up. She was so dazzled, "we didn't learn a lot of French," Doyle admits.[15]

DeForest and Tom were far outnumbered by the girls at school. The boys soon realized their sublime situation. Often, they hid in the cloakroom for a kiss or two or three, with one or two or three of the girls. Estelle was an especially pretty girl, and one day she got a pass to go to the library. DeForest and Tom decided to go, too, and all three headed arm-in-arm to the library in the basement. In the stairwell, Tom and DeForest each gave Estelle a big smooch, and just then they looked up and saw the principal at the top of the stairs. The boys dropped their books and ran for it, Tom crying out, "Excuse me, Professor!" All three skedaddled back to the classroom.

After school, there were hours of precious freedom. I. G. Ellis's dad was the manager of the Coca-Cola plant just across the street from the Baptist church. Often after school, three pals—Tom, DeForest, and Flip Cook, the sheriff's son whom DeForest christened "Flip Flop Floyd the Flea"—would go with I.G. to visit his dad at the plant, "and he would give us a free ice-cold Coke . . . a big treat."

Toward dusk, it was time to see Tom to the depot for his ride home on the Dinky. Tom's father ran the quarter-sized locomotive from Milstead to Conyers for the Callaway Mill; his last run was at the end of the day, and Tom had better be on it or walk miles to get home. Often the boys would hear that whistle blow, and DeForest and friends would holler, "The Dinky's waiting for you! The Dinky is singin'!" and they would race to the depot.

Sometimes there would be a sleepover. Tom, DeForest, and Flip looked for adventure on those nights. One Saturday, the musketeers slept over at Flip's. The Cook family lived downstairs in the jail, with prison cells above. The cells were generally used only for drunks on Saturday nights. "After everyone was asleep, we went upstairs. We took an empty Prince Albert Pipe Tobacco can and raked it across the prison cell bars, waking the drunks and tormenting them!" Doyle says. The sheriff finally woke up and put an end to it, and they got an earful from prisoners and sheriff alike.[16]

DeForest treasured his memories of schooldays and friends in Conyers. Other idyllic memories came from travels during summer break. The Kelleys would make their way back to Toccoa to enjoy the family reunions. DeForest met up with his cousins and many aunts and uncles. "Tons of good food and watermelons later taken from the cool water," he recalled. The boy was especially close to his dear Aunt Gladys, a loving, centralizing force in the Kelley clan. And DeForest was very proud of his uncle Dr. Luther Kelley, a highly respected surgeon and veteran, who brought DeForest into the world with his own hands. Luther was the most successful and respected of the Kelley clan.[17]

To follow in the footsteps of his uncle would have been a great and noble thing, but the Great Depression meant that higher education was already out of the question for Casey and DeForest. DeForest had all the usual youngster's aspirations of the day, such as being an aviator or a cowboy. He wanted to be a cowboy more than anything. He dreamed all kinds of big dreams, but there was no money and no sign that things would ever change in the Kelley household. His father and mother strongly impressed upon their sons that expectations must be held in check. Humility and spiritual rewards were paramount. Their teachings may have been the kindest lessons they could impart, for the 1930s were not conducive to lofty goals such as higher education or the arts.[18]

3 DeForest looked forward to seasonal events, family reunions, and the traveling wonders that came and went. He particularly enjoyed the evangelists T. W. Tippett and Gypsy Smith, but his world was small indeed. Practicality and drudgery might have been the boy's future, except that DeForest's much storied and mysterious uncle, his mother's brother Herman Casey, came to visit and took the town of Conyers by storm.[19]

Reverend Kelley set down an account of the Caseys' visit for the church bulletin: "Mr. & Mrs. W. H. Casey, of Long Beach, California, arrived in Conyers this week, following a six-day tramp across the continent to visit Mr. Casey's sister, Mrs. Ernest D. Kelley." Herman and his wife, Shorty Casey, were part of a team driving with Ernest Stuht, a "Speedmotor and gasoline technician," out to record their driving experiences in their Willys-Knight six-cylinder. Apparently, the only trouble on the entire trip from Long Beach by way of Phoenix, El Paso, Shreveport, and Birmingham was a right rear tire that failed six times. The reverend wrote that Stuht "recommends that tourists leave [the] right rear wheel at home." Apparently, the Caseys and Stuht were involved in oil exploration and speculation in Long Beach. They were high rollers on the road for a good time.[20]

"I thought he was the greatest guy in the whole world. When he smiled at you—you just laughed all over," DeForest remembered. The Caseys kept everyone in stitches, with jokes and stories, filling the Kelley house with delight. Clora's brother had the wonder of life, the love of adventure, and the wit of an Irish hero. To DeForest, he seemed to be a big man, "a broad-minded . . . tremendous guy . . . he looked like a sort of a dashing Noel Coward." And for DeForest, nothing would ever be the same.[21]

Herman Casey was extraordinary, even down to his handwriting. DeForest had him do some samples on sheets of paper, and later he showed Erskine Davis the beautiful script that belonged to that life-loving man from California. And DeForest began telling Davis that he would go to California someday, and he would try to get into pictures.[22]

His parents encouraged DeForest's performing talents. His singing aroused such interest that Reverend Kelley decided to take his son over to the big Atlanta radio station, WSB. The local paper welcomed the preacher's son to the airwaves and proudly reminded its readers that Mrs. Kelley was from Polk County. The press agreed with the Reverend that DeForest was a popular singer and an appealing talent. DeForest was featured in a WSB broadcast from the Sunset Club at the

Biltmore Hotel. The boy's solos were good enough to keep him coming back. He performed duets with a young lady named Miss Margaret Perrin.[23]

In January 1934, shortly before his younger son's fourteenth birthday on January 20, DeForest's father departed the Conyers congregation and moved the family to the Atlanta community of Decatur. Good-bye to country life and the friends of Conyers, where DeForest came to the age of responsibility, self-awareness, and dreams. He could take nothing of Conyers with him except what it had taught him and the memories. The curtain drew closed on his sweet youth of Tom Sawyer adventure and simplicity.[24]

4 At Decatur Boys High School, DeForest discovered a natural talent for sports. He was one of the proud Decatur Bantams, champions of the 120-pound Sandlot League, who were, as the press reported, "Undefeated in their march to the title." Ever careful with his appearance, DeForest was the only boy on the team to pose for the news photographer in a sweater and tie.[25]

Reverend Kelley was without a church. He and DeForest were compelled to work for the Roosevelt agencies designed to lift the country out of economic crisis. Reverend Kelley went to work for the WPA, the Works Progress Administration, and DeForest went to work for the NYA, the National Youth Agency. The federal government taught him to be a janitor, cleaning bathrooms and lockers and scrubbing floors at a local school after his own day of classes.[26]

In addition to baseball, DeForest played football and some other sports, and he dabbled in all the activities of a large boys' high school, including dating: "I remember when my brother was old enough to date, there was constant disapproval from my parents." He kept the peace living by his father's law. He dated young ladies under the Reverend's strict eye, and therefore not very late, not very often, and not very successfully. He did manage to enjoy female company, however, acting in the Decatur Girls High School production of *He Couldn't Take It,* a comedy in three acts by Austin Goetz.

In June 1936, DeForest was sixteen and preparing to graduate in the midst of the Great Depression. At the time, it seemed he would spend his adult life as a janitor or laborer.[27]

Just before graduation, Uncle Herman Casey visited them again. The Casey magic hadn't faded; in DeForest's eyes, he was the complete opposite of the Reverend, with his clothes and dash and "million-dollar personality." Uncle Herman told DeForest to come visit him in California. The nephew seized on the idea, making it the central purpose in his life. Graduation came and went in a fog of daydreams. The typical high school senior events, such as signing yearbooks, didn't hold much significance. He hoped that he was just passing through Decatur and Atlanta. He was on his way to California and unnamed possibilities.[28]

Sometime before graduation, DeForest got a job as a drugstore's car hop, and he made sure he kept it. He spent weekends working at the local theaters. He did not falter in his determination to get the bus fare that would take him to Long Beach and the Pacific Ocean. His mother brokered the deal; if he could get the money, he could go to California for a few weeks, where Herman and Shorty Casey lived in sunshine and excitement.[29]

As an usher at the Paramount in Atlanta, DeForest soaked in the movies. He continued singing at church and on the radio. He was chosen to sing with the Lew Forbes Orchestra at the Paramount. DeForest remembered the event as "my first real contact with an audience, and though I was dreadfully nervous, I found the experience exhilarating." He sang with the orchestra, and the experience lifted him up and out of himself.[30]

In 1937, his father returned to the ministry at Atlanta's Woodland Hills Baptist Church. Reverend Kelley and other leaders made a leap of faith and established a new church building on the corners of Woodland and Confederate Avenues. The Reverend was restored to the pulpit, and he resumed teaching through passionate sermons. He forcefully recounted the labors and trials of the men and women of the Bible. Everyone knew that the Prodigal Son was the most cherished in his father's sight, and perhaps this father did not yet know which son was which. He appealed, "Christian mothers bar the way to hell!" Yet Clora knew it was time to let her Good Son go.[31]

DeForest finally had the bus fare saved. Clora saved the small notice in the local paper that announced the event: "Dr. Forest Kelley left Thursday for California to visit his uncle Herman Casey in Long Beach." Oh, that name again! Well, another doctor in the family couldn't hurt.[32]

5 Finally, Long Beach, California! In 1937, DeForest stepped off the bus into a world of sunshine and palms and beaches so white as to blind a boy. This new world was astounding, enlivening, beyond daydreams, and without limits. "I was an innocent young thing—just a white-cheeked kid—living a sheltered life as a minister's son," DeForest recalled. He presented himself to Herman Casey, occasional oilman, welder's foreman, entrepreneur, and, mostly, professional gambler. Uncle Herman was a card player in private clubs; he played dice, and he played on his great charm within the community. He was a fellow who relied on his way with people, his knowledge of the odds, and his mastery of the game at hand. He and his wife, Shorty, were never well off. They accepted the cards they were dealt and played them with relish and good cheer. They loved having DeForest as their guest. In just a few weeks, Herman Casey determined that the young man should stay and try to become a part of his world. DeForest needed little prompting to slip into the part of the high roller.[33]

When a cousin from New Jersey came through some six weeks later, DeForest's descent into the nightlife accelerated. The kid was a gambler and "a tough guy, who talked out of the side of his mouth," DeForest recalled. They soon became partners, setting up their own gambling den. "A poker game would start Friday and continue on through Saturday and Sunday. . . . My job was to serve booze, help drag the game, and wipe [the players'] foreheads with a wet rag when they got sleepy," DeForest recalled. Herman Casey made sure his sister's son did not play cards, since card playing was a sure ticket to hell for a Southern Baptist. And DeForest himself developed a dislike for gambling; however, the smooth, cool lifestyle was appealing enough. Soon, though, the boys found out that their little business had come to the attention of the police; the cops were on to DeForest and his cousin. They left the apartment in a hurry, scared witless. They found a hideout in a building with some very rough characters, seamen and longshoremen and women who matched them. One night during a domestic quarrel, his cousin went to the defense of a friend and wound up beaten terribly and in the hospital. Aunt Shorty was enraged with the whole adventure, and DeForest was mortified. "I can't believe I was really involved in such things," he later confessed. Lessons learned, DeForest moved back into Casey's house and began looking for wage work.[34]

A healthy young fellow could find work among the steel mills, shipbuilders, canneries, and cleaning crews. The hardest work and the best wages were found in the oilfields, doing the grinding work of roughnecking on the rigs. DeForest worked the platforms, the drills, and the dangerous derrick assemblies that were covered in mud, crude, and sweat. The boy's natural physicality was honed and tempered in labor and heat. He lived among rough working people, exposed to vice and sickness.

If DeForest were to stay in Long Beach, he would have to become streetwise, and his Uncle Herman tried to teach him. DeForest had to find the fine line between raising hell and risking real damnation.[35]

Away from the oilfields and the seedy interior of Long Beach, DeForest discovered the tonic of beach-bumming in 1937. It was a pure way of life—body surfing, hanging out, and all the while surrounded by girls. His labors and swimming defined his long muscles and darkened his skin; his hair bleached blond. The Pacific rolled in to embrace him. He became enamored of the ocean and the people who were drawn to it as much as he was.

Occasionally, DeForest treated himself to a meal out, and one day, he recalled, "I was sitting in a restaurant when this guy named Ronald Hawk came up and asked if I'd ever worked in theater. I told him I hadn't. . . . He asked if I'd come to the [Long Beach Little Theater] and try out for a play he was going to direct. And then he heard my thick Southern accent . . . but decided I should read for the part anyway, as he felt I was just right for it." He didn't take it very seriously. "I'm sure I joined originally to meet people—because I'd absolutely no designs on Hollywood at all." He had forgotten his comment to Erskine Davis about making pictures, and now the desire to perform was borne to consciousness through the social banter of Ronnie Hawk.

Ronnie's girlfriend, Valerie, was popular in the clique of performing artists in Long Beach; she saw DeForest and brought him into that circle. Sure enough, he got the part in a small one-act production of *Holiday* for the Little Theater. He was kidded and coached by his new friends about his mush-mouth drawl. He tolerated their jokes and accepted their instruction over several weeks. With *Holiday*, DeForest became aware of the motion-picture talent scouts who prowled the small theaters and amateur productions for their studio contract players. DeForest recalled, "This guy came from backstage. 'I'm from Metro-Goldwyn-Mayer, a talent scout. . . . I just want to tell you you're too young for us to do anything with you right now, but stay down here and keep working.' Well, I was floored."[36]

Herman Casey was "in violent disagreement" with his nephew's new pastime. As DeForest later recalled, his uncle was so determined to steer DeForest away from the addictions of greasepaint that he invested in a string of gas stations. Casey knew how to cajole his nephew: DeForest just had to come in with him and do real work, and he would find a real occupation with a real future. DeForest did not want to do it, but he was a malleable youth, and his uncle was a persuasive and charismatic man whom he loved and admired. DeForest hated to say no. He couldn't explain why he was so drawn to acting, because he himself did not know. Without a position to defend, DeForest succumbed to his uncle's wishes.

In a matter of six months, Casey's chain of gas stations went under with hardly more than a gasp, and that was a great relief to DeForest.[37]

Once again, he was a free man, but with freedom came struggle and despair. DeForest would take the red car on the Pacific Electric rail line, north and east to the hills and to Hollywood, some thirty miles from Long Beach. On these small escapes from the realities of Long Beach, he would look for odd jobs and wander around the wonder of Hollywood.

On one occasion, he discovered Grauman's Chinese Theater, a veritable shrine to the movie industry. DeForest marveled at the odd Asian design. He studied the concrete slabs filled with signatures and imprints of hands and feet. All around were the impressions of the odd feature, prop, or symbol associated with the glamorous celebrity.

With a soft lead pencil, he scratched into the waxed surface of a Chinese Theater postcard:

> Bud
>   *I am just before going in the dump. I have been up here all morning looking for work. "3 comrades" is playing. Sure is some place. I have been looking at all these footprints of the stars.*
>   *Write me,*
>   *De*

He addressed it to Mr. Casey Kelley of the Monroe Company in the Standard Building in Atlanta and posted it on June 1, 1938. Surely, brother Casey could sympathize, even though he was making his way pretty well in the world. Young DeForest was unsettled, restless, and aching for something. What else was there to say?[38]

Older brother Casey was at work selling calculating and adding machines, bookkeeping, and check-writing machines to the business-men of Atlanta. He made a good beginning in a solid and growing business sector. It seemed the rebel Casey would do very well.

What DeForest, the shining and talented boy, found so alluring in Hollywood was everything his father stood against, and damnation would be the price of such worldly seduction. Not even his uncle could understand what was growing in his head and heart. Could he dare say out loud what he had once told Erskine Davis? The talent scout's approval, the shadow and light of make-believe, and the actor's life enthralled him. And just as overwhelming was the guilt that came with knowing that he was the Prodigal Son and that such a life would shame his parents and torment his conscience. Though his untried dreams tasted like sawdust, he was only a kid struggling to get along in 1938, and he felt himself on the edge of despair. He held on as long as he could—but finally, he gave up and went home to Atlanta, to save his parents the worry and perhaps to save his soul.

DeForest returned to his father's house. The claustrophobia was horrible, especially after the freedom he had known. Sadly, he realized that he could never settle down into the life he would be expected to live as a preacher's son in the land of his ancestors. He wept for the peace a simple life might have offered. He wept, and within weeks he was on the verge of collapse.

Perhaps DeForest's chance to have a "normal" life was doomed from the beginning. His time in California had revealed a fundamental truth about his spirit: he was an artist. His upbringing and his conscience told him it was wrong not to be proud and satisfied as a working man, but the young artist within was desperate. "I cried each time I made the attempt to tell them I couldn't stand it, that I had to go back. . . . It was a whole new world for me. I had to return, or I'd be miserable the rest of my life." His mother was sympathetic and realized her son needed to be free from the shadow of his father to make his final decision. She insisted that he go with her to Cincinnati to visit her friends. If there in Ohio, where he could think clearly, he still felt so strongly about leaving, then she would have to let him go. Painfully, DeForest remembered: "I didn't change my mind. She and a friend showed me off. Getting on that bus was the hardest thing I ever had to do. We were very close." She loved him enough to let him go. His dear mother would have to return to her simple gray days without him.[39]

DeForest again rode toward the Pacific, this time heartbroken. Never an assertive young man, he was oppressed by the memory of announcing his emancipation from his father's harness: "When I told him I had decided to become an actor, he was sure my soul was lost forever. I was going straight to hell!" Guilt burrowed down deep in DeForest. He was filled with too much desire to be stopped, but he harbored an underlying fear that had been planted long ago deep in the pit of his stomach: damnation. Guilt and fear would not let him rest as he decided his own fate. He would have to be faithful to his understanding of right and wrong as he lived and worked among sin and excess. He would survive the contradictions by finding balance in his life. And if in truth he was doomed, well, then, in the meantime he would be an actor.[40]

Chapter II
The Young Artist
1939–1942

"He hung the moon."
—ANNE JOLLY, 1999

In the middle of February 1939, DeForest Kelley returned to California. Certainly free but possibly damned, he surrendered himself to the Long Beach nightlife. He danced at the Majestic Ballroom and in the music halls with plum print wallpaper, oval lacquer tables, cigarette smoke, and smart-looking gals. He mingled smoothly, dressed in a suit with stylishly wide lapels, a glass in hand, constantly smoking and charming his way through the nights. Vivian Laird's Bohemia, the Robinson Hotel, South Seas Dancing, and the Garden of Allah offered exotic partying, drinks, and music. There were Mediterranean and Asian faces and Catholic girls with beauty marks. DeForest saved the dance tickets as nights went by. He sent exotic-looking napkins and coasters home to Clora to enjoy and wrote "Scrap book Ma" on little trinkets that seemed from another world. He danced with girls like Orpha and Betty and Colleen and Margaret Ann Nichols and another Betty . . . and on and on. Luckily, a fellow could get lunch at a ritzy place like the Palms for thirty-five cents, or a real spread for fifty if he was flush, which was somewhere between rarely and never.[1]

Everything looked promising and glamorous, and surely DeForest made quite an impression on Long Beach, but he was still a "white-cheeked kid" adrift in a strange world. Grace Hartung saw the truth of the situation and cast him a line to hold on to. Grace and her husband opened their little restaurant, the Chat 'N Nibble, in early 1939 on Ocean Boulevard, across the tiny alley from the Fox West Coast Theater. Grace had the day shift, serving the theater ushers, matinee moviegoers, and students of performing arts teacher Oranne Day, until her husband took over for the evening. She remembers DeForest: "He was very shy. He was very broke. He sat at the counter stirring a cup of coffee. . . . I went out and sat down with him. 'Have you eaten today?' 'Noooo,' he'd say, and so I fed him." Her maternal care answered the loneliness just under the polished manners. Grace could see that he was a boy with serious intent, but he was sweet and lovely to talk to. From their first meeting, whenever he ordered only coffee and stirred too long, she knew that he was hungry. That's when she'd just go ahead and feed him. Grace always got her money, as soon as he could pay.[2]

Anything she could do for DeForest, she would, and while Grace forever grieved the loss of her first son, DeForest soon came to mean so much to her that he became the son of her heart. DeForest found comfort in her presence and called her "Ma."

Grace knew intuitively that DeForest was bound by a very strong sense of right and wrong. He couldn't bear to do anything unseemly, or so Grace observed. Once he came in to confess that he and another fellow had trespassed at a movie studio. Mike Hill, DeForest's buddy, instigated a trip up to Metro-Goldwyn-Mayer. On arrival, the boys found a huge lot, a big tent, stores and façades and sets, and a fence between them and all of that fascinating confusion. Mike climbed over the fence to have a walk around and see some real moviemaking. DeForest followed along. "We walked for what seemed like miles and finally saw the lights and all the action going on outside. And we walked up there, and we're standing around, and all the grips [were working], and I looked over, and there was Robert Taylor sitting there in a chair. I nudged Mike, and I said, 'There's Robert Taylor.' . . . Taylor looked up, and he said, 'You two guys slip in here?' " The boys admitted it. Taylor considered, and, as DeForest recalled, Taylor said, " 'Well, when these guys start to move around something, get over there and start pushing it with them so they'll think you work here, and they'll let you stay in.' . . . Barbara Stanwyck came on the set, and she had two beautiful horses with these blankets thrown over them trimmed in green and the initials *RT* on them."

For the price of a little nervous adventure, they got an eyeful of Hollywood. However, DeForest could not help but confess to Grace that he had trespassed, and he felt a little bad about the whole thing, as wonderful as it was.[3]

DeForest was a young man of deep sympathy. Grace remembers an occasion when she was so busy one Sunday that while DeForest was visiting, she decided to ask him to take her son Ronnie around to Mrs. Jordan's, who minded him while his mother worked. "Ronnie always cried when he first went to Jordan's—the first few minutes. When DeForest came back, he said, 'Don't ever ask me to do that again.'" He was nearly in tears himself, because he couldn't bear to see a little boy cry.[4]

Perhaps Grace's greatest gift to DeForest was her unswerving faith in his commitment to acting. "I was bound and determined that he would succeed. My father would not allow me to study music as I wished in Chicago, because it was Al Capone's time, the gangsters and all. . . . I was determined Kelley would make it." In Grace, DeForest found the understanding love he so needed, and "he knew I would always tell him the truth . . . and I was his first fan."[5]

2 DeForest's natural dignity and manners played well in California, especially after *Gone With the Wind* swept the country in early 1940. It made his Georgia style somehow exotic and intriguing. He perfected little social entertainments, such as having a coin crawl up and down the backs of his knuckles or nonchalantly performing a rather startling imitation of Clark Gable. He mastered the small niceties that pleased many a new acquaintance. His masculine grace, whether drinking a cocktail, smoking a cigarette, or tying his tie, belied the daytime realities of his menial working life and his very modest background. He may have worked every kind of dead-end job, from dishwasher to hospital orderly to janitor, but he acted the part of a Southern bon vivant. By all accounts, he was a gentleman, genuine, decent, trustworthy, and a hell of a lot of fun besides.[6]

The key to DeForest's new world in Long Beach really belonged to

Anne Jolly, a precocious fourteen-year-old actress who seemed made for a good part in a good story. After joining the Community Playhouse at First and Alamitos in the fall of 1939, DeForest fell in with Anne's gang. They could often be found next door at Friar's Café, crowded into a large circular booth, spending hours in animated discussions over cherry Cokes and French fries with catsup.

Anne and her mother lived in a small apartment at the Colony, 409 East 4th Street. When it was too hot to sleep, they'd grab towels and spend the night on the beach, listening to the Pacific under the stars. Although Anne was too young to frequent the joints and dens of Long Beach, other rendezvous were easy to find. The gang, now including DeForest, would often gather at the Merry Go Round Café or at the ocean near the foot of Linden Street, where Anne's mother would apply suntan oil to the guys and gals and enjoy watching the beautiful lifeguards who patrolled the shoreline.

Anne's mother, Wiltrude, called "Billee," was in her mid-thirties, vivacious, and born to party, a lover of life and good times. She was an original, an independent lady who played piano, sang, and participated in the Long Beach nightlife, often wearing chiffon gowns accessorized with a .45 automatic. Her brother was a well-known Long Beach policeman who also lived at the Colony. Billee was young enough to enjoy the gang's games and beach-bumming yet old enough to keep things well in hand. Anne sometimes suspected that her friends really came to see Billee.

But Anne's relationship with DeForest was much more than casual friendship. Anne recalls that just after DeForest joined the Playhouse, "Mother and I went to live in North Long Beach. . . . I got sick with some childhood disease where you have to draw the curtains [probably measles]." With her mother working, Anne was all alone in her illness. Well, not quite alone—DeForest often made the trip to see the girl he considered his little sister. "Of all the people [we knew], only one came to cheer me up. . . . We played like we were going on a sleigh ride. . . . Oh, he just did all kinds of things" to help her spirits through her illness, without care for himself. "It was a nickel to get there, so a dime both ways on the bus. That money was hard to come by. . . . I was the baby. . . . He knew I was alone out there. I'll never forget that." Although Anne's true love was Greg Baker, a big, handsome boy who had captured her heart earlier in 1939, she knew her relationship with DeForest would be special. They were marked for each other by an odd crossing of veins they both had on the backs of their hands that looked like anchors. Yes, she was quite sure they were anchored together forever.

3 The time and place were ideal for a young actor. There were magazines and movies to dream by and the local paper to plan with, and there were always jobs, because Long Beach was the Navy capital of the United States. Before long, the Jolly gals were back where they belonged, in a little apartment at the Colony once more. DeForest and the gang converged on the one-room apartment for rehearsals and charades. On school nights or when Anne was just worn out, she would say her good nights and make herself a nest in the bathtub as the gang went on without her.[7]

As was the custom of the times, DeForest became known as Kelley, or K. He was a young man devoted to "nothing but laughs, and no regrets!"—a quote remembered as his signature declaration, regardless of the circumstances. Somehow Kelley discovered that Fay Warmack, one of the Playhouse gals, was very ill; in truth, she was dying. She spent her last weeks in Southern California in a tiny room a few doors down from the Playhouse. If you were a friend of K's, you went to Fay's, because that is where you would find him, making the best of the last. There would be games and good times, even though the gang knew Fay was dying, a lovely girl otherwise alone in the world. The young man's pastoral compassion was a matter of fact and his natural reaction to the situation. With an inborn authority, he assumed the watch at Fay's side. He was not bound by judgment and trepidation. DeForest was his mother's son. There would be more laughter than tears. He said so, and it was so. There would be poetry readings and verse writing:

Largo
I can forget quite well his face . . .
When one is gone so long!

I can forget both time and space . . .
I can forget a song
I don't know how to hold a dream
Or how a rhyme should start
But I do know that words can cling
Like tear drops on my heart!
— FAY WARMACK

Before the end came, Fay's folks found out and carried her home, never to be heard from again. K went on, seemingly without a backward glance, and moved the good times back to the usual venues. He was barely twenty then, and in his private heart, he remembered Fay all the rest of his days.

DeForest did all manner of work trying to make this world his own. By late May 1940, he was part of the scenery at the Playhouse, while Robert Cornthwait and Anne Jolly acted in *The First Mrs. Fraser*.

All around him, peacetime militarization swelled the population of Long Beach. At oceanfront in Bluff Park, there were anti-aircraft guns. The threat of war was in the streets and the parks, on the beach, and on the airwaves. As war preparations accelerated, Kelley and his friends clung to their normal lives.

One night, he went to the Playhouse with Larraine Day, a promising local actress, in September 1940. Anne Jolly portrayed the "hysterical, baby-faced trouble-maker of the show" in *No Interest in Women,* under the direction of Oranne Truitt Day, by then something of a legend on the local theater scene. Playhouse veteran Joe Laden brought down the house with his performance. As Laden remembers, first he was stabbed, and then he staggered around the stage for about ten minutes; then, with a heart-rending dramatic crash, down he went onto his face. A standing ovation, thank you very much. Laden asked himself, "Should I get up and take a bow?" He meditated on his predicament while the applause roared in his ears. He was supposed to be dead, he decided, so he lay there and listened. "Genuinely histrionic," critic Herbert Wormser commented in his Long Beach column.[8]

Laden vividly recalls: "A while later, I'm looking at the marquee of the Fox West Coast on Ocean [Boulevard], and I look up. . . . This six-foot bleach blond, blackened in the sun, blue-eyed fella. 'Are you Joe Laden?' he asks. And once assured, [he] asks about the death scene and the ovation. He admired the work and wondered about the performance. He was so interested." Kelley wanted to know all about it. "Oh my," Joe thought, "this guy must sleep on the beach, he was so interesting to look at. No one looks like this." Joe asked if he were interested in the theater. " 'Yes, uh, Joe, but ahm nervous about it.' " So Joe set up a tryout for him down at the Community Playhouse, when all the girls would be there. "They were all over him, oh my God. So I figured I'd go take a break," because no one had eyes for Joe the day Kelley took the stage.[9]

They were very young, barely twenty, and now and again something would remind them of the fact. "I had a car, my folks' car, but I had one," Joe recalls. "We thought we were 'big fat.' We parked the car one day at the curb of the Depot Playhouse, smoking our cigs. Suddenly, out of nowhere, there is my mother! She wanted that car and was yelling at me, and the Southern gentleman next to me, you should have seen the look on his face! 'Both you bums—out!' " Two big boys standing in the street, flat-footed and smoking.

Even with such friends, life could be very harsh on DeForest, who was trying to scrape by on his own. Joe appreciated what DeForest was going through: "Kelley had it hard. Once he took a riveting job in the yards, with the rivet gun down in the holds. Oh, and one day he came back on Ocean . . . I saw him near the Fox West Coast, and he pulled a pint out of a pocket—'gotta have some'—and down it went, he was so tired . . . he didn't have it easy."

Money was always scarce. As Laden understood the situation, Kelley got to run a tab for his meals at the Chat 'N Nibble, and he could get one for Joe if they went in together. Joe figured the man who owned the Chat 'N Nibble must have thought DeForest was headed for the big time and wanted in on DeForest's good graces. Joe went with Kelley to the restaurant for a meal on tab. "Ma" Grace was Kelley's secret for reasons of pride and discretion.

While they were there, Kelley proceeded to preen and pose in the restaurant's mirror. Joe knew about Kelley's fixation with mirrors. He would play to them, compare his appearance in one, then another, and study the effects of different lighting or times of day on his features. He'd examine himself in every mirror he passed. Kelley knew he was pretty. But, Laden remembers, "The Chat 'N Nibble mirror was a horror. Every line, every fault was revealed in that god-awful mirror." DeForest was as fascinated as Joe was repelled by it. They looked like hell.[10]

The scrappy New Yorker and the courtly Southerner made an odd combination, but they were the best of friends. Laden took DeForest to the people who could give him the training he needed; the most important was Oranne Day. She took a particular interest in DeForest, singling him out and working long hours with him alone on the stage after everyone else had gone. DeForest was a devoted and determined student, greatly vexed by the voice that had to be tamed and trained. He made notes to himself, and sketches, little visual cues for his own reference on how to develop the diaphragm to control breath and tone and projection. He rehearsed Spartacus's speech to the gladiators and Hamlet's speech to the players. He practiced "hummmm" to develop head tones, "Ma za ska ahh" for voice range, and "please" drawn out over and over for the sustaining sounds. Mrs. Day taught him how to use his body's fluid movement and expressive hands for maximum impact on the stage. Years of memorization and recitation developed as a preacher's kid were put to use in theater. The dramatic arts won his soul, and so he began the real work of his calling and his craft in the fall of 1940.[11]

4 DeForest continued to live hand-to-mouth on a series of menial jobs, including swabbing floors, which he hated, and a stint as an orderly at Seaside Hospital, cleaning up after emergencies and surgeries. During this time, he teamed up with Harold Cleveland, who worked as a drugstore hash slinger. Harold had an apartment on the beach, and DeForest moved in with him. They could entertain the girls and live the high life without interference. It was never time for the girls to go home, there were never rules to follow, Kelley recalled. Freedom was good. But it brought trying situations for a minister's son. One day, Grace Hartung was surprised to find DeForest at her counter with a disgusted scowl on his face. By then, there were three boys at his place, and apparently they had hired a girl and had her in the apartment. "I got out of there," he told Grace.[12]

Soon after, DeForest got lucky with an elevator jockey job at the Cooper Arms on Ocean. It was a nice place, with massive ornamental urns in front and the Pacific just across the boulevard. "He got to sleep in the cellar," Joe Laden recalls, remembering how he crashed there on many a night himself. It was like living in an underground parking lot with just a bed and a chest of drawers and the whole length of the Cooper Arms stretched out into the darkness. And of course, there were women to date and romance in the subterranean expanse of the cellar. Those were good times for young men![13]

5 DeForest was taken with the stage, but when he discovered the Long Beach Cinema Club, it turned his head completely. When he arrived on the Fosholdt family doorstep in the well-heeled Alamitos Bay neighborhood to receive his first lessons in moviemaking, DeForest found himself in a world where his deep desire to be a movie actor was met with enthusiasm. At last, his ambition was allowed to rise to the surface. His airy, easygoing ways evaporated, replaced by hungry concentration.

Ray Fosholdt, the founder and heart of the club, was a cinema enthusiast and a skilled makeup man trained by Max Factor himself. People were invited to discuss and educate themselves about cinema; more than that, they were encouraged to write, plan, produce, act in, and edit their own films.[14]

Moviemaking was a vocation for Fosholdt, his hobby and his delight. He used his business fortunes to finance and share his passion. Ray and La Nelle Fosholdt's house was like no other. Most evenings, La Nelle's home was turned into a meetinghouse for her young cinema friends. The house was actually designed around the permanent projection room with a soundproof projection booth that held both the 16mm Victor and 8mm Bell and Howell projectors. Disc recording made sound films possible with synchronized music and dialogue through speakers placed strategically in the viewing room. Ray and La Nelle and their protégés processed film footage in the bathtub. The

Fosholdts also supplied the amateurs with reading material, film industry magazines, and periodicals.

Ray never held back when it came to sharing his joy in moviemaking. He was always ready to watch and dissect films, discuss the industry, and whet the amateur's appetite for it. Other evenings passed quietly, listening while Ray played classical music on the phonograph. The luxurious divans and big chairs, the detail and quality of the home, were well beyond Kelley's prior experiences of comfort and wealth. La Nelle and Ray introduced him to levels of art and culture he had never known before. Kelley frequently ate with the Fosholdts, but he balked at their diet of afternoon onion sandwiches. A Georgia boy should appreciate Vidalia onions, La Nelle thought; they were so sweet and nutritious. But Kelley just couldn't believe the Fosholdts could eat them and live![15]

DeForest Kelley was a fixture at the Cinema Club, serious, silent, and smoking. He won the male lead in *Susanna,* a maritime tale of love and adventure that was filmed along the shore. This silent short inaugurated Kelley's career in motion pictures. Ray Fosholdt used a floating barge both for his camera work and as a set platform. He and his mates slowly maneuvered along the shorelines and canals of Long Beach, changing the scenery at will. Kelley went along to study staging and production. He watched closely between his scenes, shirtless and wearing white-belted trunks. Little ten-year-old Stan Fosholdt later characterized Kelley as always very nice and preoccupied. Both Stan and La Nelle remember DeForest as aloof in a curiously attractive way. They knew that he was in the game for keeps and meant to succeed. In *Susanna,* he got to play the young hero; he beat the bad guy and got the girl. What more could a fellow want?[16]

6 On September 16, 1940, every male age twenty-one to thirty-five, was called to register for the peacetime draft, and the hard waiting began. No one could miss what was happening in Europe; it was in all the papers and on the radio. American broadcasters brought the war right into people's living rooms as they described the merciless German attacks on England. Through August and September, the people of the United Kingdom had fought against incredible odds during the Battle of Britain. Luftwaffe pilots declared an "ocean of flame" over London. The Royal Air Force managed to defy logic, down hundreds of German planes, and strike Germany itself with breathtaking courage and desperate resolve. Somehow the British people kept hanging on, awaiting the intervention of the United States. Then Japan joined the Axis pact on September 27, 1940. In Long Beach, no one could overlook what was happening, but the Kelley gang sure tried, even as all the guys went to the local draft board to sign up.[17]

The first Americans were drafted just before Halloween in 1940. The Japanese had invaded French Indochina, the U.S. Navy had called almost 28,000 reserves to man newly built ships, the Nazis advanced toward the Balkans and took Bucharest. The Vichy in France banned Jews from public offices just as Portugal banned Jews from traveling through the country, essentially denying a safe haven and blocking an escape route from the Nazis. By the end of November, German troops had forced the entire Jewish population of Warsaw into a walled ghetto.[18]

The world's realities cast shadows over everyone's heart, even as the Long Beach Community Players continued their work. Borrowing a little of Joe Laden's boldness, Kelley screwed up his courage and auditioned for *Our Town* after only about eight intense weeks of training with Oranne Day.

Anne Jolly recalls that there were "a bunch of us young ones . . . little smart alecks sitting in the audience . . . in the little audience chairs watching auditions. Kelley got up and read. Oh! Just blew everybody away, and of course he got the part of Emily's boyfriend in *Our Town*." Joe Laden didn't even bother to read for the part.[19]

Kelley's mentor, Oranne Day, continued her work of teaching the actual skills needed for stage and cinema. She taught adult continuing education programs in North Long Beach and along the coast. At no cost to her students, she taught a generation how to work for the stage through the reign of producer-director Herbert Yenne, a retired professor from the University of Nebraska.[20]

Yenne gave himself to the community theater project for the love of it. He let his young people concentrate on the preparation and performance of theater, while he reserved the most tedious chores for himself. Among the Community Players had been Larraine Day (who had changed her name to honor Mrs. Day), Hugh Beaumont, Bob Cornthwait, Van Heflin, and Joe Laden. Now there were the new kids—Robert Mitchum, Anne Jolly, DeForest Kelley, and so many others. With the production of *Our Town*, Yenne would focus on De-Forest Kelley, to see what he could do with such an unassuming and cooperative young actor.[21]

So, DeForest became George, the juvenile lead in *Our Town*, in late January 1941. During rehearsals, some of the veterans came in and out, watching, among them Robert Cornthwait. He observed Kelley working the scene in the ice cream shop at the beginning of George's romance. A nice boy, Cornthwait thought. Kelley's performance was good, solid, "eminently satisfactory," the local press concluded.[22]

The young entertainers were aware that radio was the most promising performance venue of their day. With war looming ever closer, it was obvious to everyone how important the radio was, both for news and for escapist entertainment. Kelley and his friends gathered for rehearsals at Anne's little one-room apartment. They would just take the shade off the lamp and pretend it was the mike. Young Long Beach writers Irving Ravetch and Barney Girard turned out the original skits for their performances. Before long, the rehearsals and rewrites paid off; KFOX and KGER were broadcasting Ravetch and Girard stories performed by Anne Jolly, Kelley, and friends all over the Long Beach area.[23]

Girard became a good friend of DeForest's. They shared gentle, sometimes pensive hearts and a deep desire to express themselves in the world. Barney was raised in the racial and social mix of Northern California. Throughout his youth, he was pulled from one town to the next by his frustrated father, a former vaudevillian. When he hooked up with Anne's gang, Barney was just discovering the power and the burden of his own creative genius. With Kelley, Ravetch, Anne and Billee, Barney found the refuge and encouragement he could find nowhere else.[24]

By 1941, Kelley had become familiar with the performing arts communities of radio, theater, and film. The Long Beach Cinema Club was the most ambitious outfit he worked with. The club kept tabs on its members and announced the screening of DeForest Kelley's new short film, *Happy Landing,* to be previewed at the Marine Room at the Hilton Hotel. The small story of a girl and two boys featured Long Beach itself and the sparkling young people who called it home.

Each month, they viewed short films, did screen-test exercises for the actors in their group, and brought in lecturers, agents, professors, and talent scouts to talk about the profession of film acting and the film industry as it really was, up the road in Hollywood. There were also presentations of documentary photos and film depicting the war zones in Europe. Larger meetings and screenings were often held at the YMCA, capped off with cookies and ice cream.[25]

The Cinema Club's newsletter informed everyone that member Orpha Olson had signed on with Earl Carroll's Revue, and a Hollywood director from Hal Roach Studio came all the way down to see *Happy Landing.* Through connections made with the club, Kelley was expecting an audition at a leading studio. He and other young aspirants would travel to Hollywood to try out or look for a break, and they'd return to the Fosholdts to bind up their wounds and prepare for the next opportunity with the studios.[26]

Cinema, radio, stage. Glamorous and tempting it may have been, but the gang was pretty square and held fast to a lot of traditional ways. In one instance, a boy they knew smoked marijuana, and Anne could have nothing more to do with him. The gang had a code of behavior that was unspoken but strong. They kept a protective watch over one another, and if one were insulted or in need, then all would rally around and come to the aid of their friend. Kelley seemed to lead the gang by example. In one memorable instance, he was shocked by a grown man's depravity concerning the deflowering of a young girl. He did not react, he was not even unkind; the fellow simply ceased to exist in Kelley's eyes. The young actor was shunned by DeForest and his gang. Their message was clear, and at the same time they kept the peace at the Community Playhouse. DeForest cultivated gentility and backed it up with an authority that took his young friends, and perhaps himself, by surprise. Though determined to be a success in Hollywood, the very womb of delusion and ruin, Kelley grew to maturity among his well-chosen friends in Long Beach.

As he found balance and strength in self-knowledge and self-restraint, his confidence grew. His mother seemed to know that her son would thrive even in a competitive and often cruel profession. Clora seemed to understand the strength of decency in her boy, to believe in his moral spine. DeForest remembered, "I was receiving excellent reviews in the local newspapers, so I'd cut these out and send them home. . . . I think my mother was quite proud of me." Clora seemed to know that the prodigal son wandered with a purpose and could survive almost anything.[27]

7 A dark Graham Greene story, *This Gun for Hire* had been kicking around Hollywood for four years. Peter Lorre had been considered for the lead role, with Claude Raines to play the killer—named Raven— back in 1936. The script wandered, hand to desk, until April 1940, when Anthony Quinn did some rewriting, rekindling some interest. Finally, in the summer of 1941, director Frank Tuttle and producer Richard Blumenthal got the green light for production at Paramount. Motion-picture and dialogue rights were settled for $12,000, and Tuttle signed on for $15,000. Robert Preston and Veronica Lake were set for the leads. William Meiklejohn, the lead casting director for Paramount, was brought in to find the murderer, Raven. The role, they decided, called for an unknown actor to send a chill through this film noir.[28]

Milton Lewis, Paramount's talent scout, knew of DeForest Kelley from Long Beach, and Bill Meiklejohn had him called up to the studio. Through June, July, and September 1941, DeForest used the gate passes Meiklejohn sent him for interviews at Paramount. Expectations and excitement kept DeForest on a roller coaster of nerves as he proceeded through thirteen interviews for *This Gun*. Meiklejohn seemed really confident about Kelley with Paramount. A contract player! It was hard to hope, hard to breathe, and hard not to believe.[29]

The producer, the director, and Meiklejohn all seemed sure that Kelley was their Raven. But DeForest was unaware of the frantic behind-the-scenes lobbying by actress-agent Sue Carroll on behalf of her lover, Alan Ladd. Carroll was a strong-willed executive hustler with every intention of getting her man a studio contract. Carroll had Tuttle's ear and introduced him to Ladd, seven years Kelley's senior, small, blond, and stoic. Ladd had something distant and edgy in his eyes and manner. Here was a man more suited to the icy killer image of Raven. Perhaps this temperature was closer to the Raven persona than Kelley's heat; perhaps Kelley's Raven was not the remorseless killer, rather more the tormented soul. In essence, young DeForest was more likely prey than predator. Raven was a cold-blooded killer— Kelley wasn't cold, and Ladd was.[30]

Meanwhile, DeForest, believing he had the role, celebrated with his Long Beach friends and champagne. The next morning, he reported to Blumenthal's office to finalize the deal. Kelley vividly remembered, "While I was waiting for the producer in his office, I happened to glance over at his desk. There I saw a slip of paper and a penciled line through my name. Underneath was written another name—Alan Ladd."[31]

DeForest went back home to the beach. It hurt too much to want and to hope and to believe. There was not a thing he could do about it; everything had been out of his hands. He did not blame Carroll or Ladd for their luck and in fact soon believed it was his own draft status that finalized the decision against him.

The draft was hanging over everyone's head, and Kelley certainly appeared to be draft material. Ladd, with a chronic back problem, did not. Indeed, it was the studio's consideration, even in the peacetime draft, that a young man could be plucked out of production by the government, costing time and money. The practice of inquiring about a man's draft status was soon incorporated into the interviewing process and appeared in the paperwork of both agents and studios.[32]

This Gun went into production without Kelley. The screenplay had been reworked to focus on Ladd, with the lead played by Preston nearly forgotten. *This Gun* became Ladd's movie, and it made him a star. "After seeing what a wonderful job Ladd did, I've often wondered what I'd have done to the part," Kelley said later.[33]

DeForest went back to his Community Players, to Anne's radio gang, and he continued to engage stubbornly in the cycle of audition, hope, and rejection in Hollywood. His scrapbook grew with the accomplishments of his short time as a performer in Long Beach. On the surface, there appeared to be a steady march toward success, yet the Hollywood auditions could be spirit-breaking. He described the process later on. He'd arrived at a studio hope-filled and excited. He would learn a scene and perform it in a specially made glass box. He performed blind; he couldn't see the director or anyone else. The pressure was maddening and the dread crushing. "Then, finally, the critics compare notes," he recalled, "and say, 'Sorry—you're just not the type.'" And he would go home. Rejection was something a fellow had to learn to live with. He also learned to keep a little emotional distance from the process of rejection, even as he grew in devotion to the work. There would be other days, other chances; he was young and handsome, with as good a chance as anyone. He continued to study his art, and himself, ever mindful of the temptations that could fester inside and make a man hollow. "Before you are five and twenty, you must establish a character that will serve you all your life." He pasted Lord Collingswood's quote into his scrapbook alongside the snapshots of his work with the movie crew on Long Beach. He was not yet twenty-two. There was still time, wasn't there?³⁴

8 Meanwhile, the buildup for the war effort pulled thousands into the California work force. At home in Long Beach, the *SS John C. Fremont* was launched after 126 days in terminal, with 1,500 "Miss Americas" or "Rosies" involved in the production lines. Terminal Island became the womb of the U.S. Navy. Agents, talent scouts, and studios were interested in Kelley. The longer he remained a civilian, the more opportunities there would be as other young males were drafted as the nation moved steadily toward armed conflict.³⁵

President Roosevelt prepared his young countrymen to offer up the last full measure of devotion, not for the sake of a nation's survival, as they had been asked to do two generations before by Abraham Lincoln, but this time for the cause of humanity itself.

In June, the Nazis began their mad roll across Europe and into Russia. By the fall, Hitler's troops surrounded Leningrad, determined to starve the people to death. Meanwhile, the Jews in Germany were forced to wear the Star of David on their clothing. People were dying by the hundreds of thousands in Europe and in Asia.³⁶

Clearly, the world was at stake, and war was coming for the youth of America. The children of the Depression were called by their country, and they answered the call by the thousands.

Fellow Playhouse member and radio personality Robert Cornthwait shared Kelley's aspirations to be a fine actor, but with a 1A draft status, agents just wouldn't sign him. He joined the Army Air Corps in the fall of 1941, and Cornthwait made the rounds of Long Beach to bid farewell to friends and colleagues. When he went to the Playhouse to say good-bye to everyone, Kelley was not around. "Apparently, just as I was getting to my car, he must have come in from the other side, and someone must have told him, 'Bob is just leaving—into the service.' And he came running . . . running to catch up with me in the car, you know, down Alamitos . . . to say good-bye." The memory of the lanky young man he barely knew running through traffic to wish him well and safe return always stayed with Cornthwait. He had not worked with Kelley but recalled the young man's concern as typical of DeForest. "I remember him . . . that he was one of the nice ones in our calling, in the game."[37]

Rehearsals for Samson Raphaelson's *Skylark,* a sophisticated comedy, were soon under way, and Kelley had top billing. In November 1941, it opened to audiences. On November 10, Ivan Kahn, a talent scout for 20th Century Fox's Lew Schreiber, memoed his boss in Hollywood that he would be taking in the new play in Long Beach: "From this show I will interview DeForest Kelly." Meiklejohn was also coming to see his young man. But a letter arrived at Kelley's new digs at 38 Altoni Place. The news was deflating: Meiklejohn was under the weather and could not preview "Mr. Kelley." With all apologies, he promised to attend one of the actual performances.[38]

With *Skylark,* the Community Playhouse opened its doors at its new location, the old Lime Street church, and Kelley soared in this new open forum of a theater. Joe Laden came to see him and was taken with the kid's laid-back, easy style. Laden enjoyed his friend's performance thoroughly. It hardly seemed possible that Kelley had only one solid year of acting under his belt. *Skylark* drew crowds and critics, particularly because it was performed in the round. Critics were agreed; the play was enlivened by the "remarkable poise and easy nuances of expressiveness by DeForest Kelley. Too high praise cannot be given his performance."[39]

The review was carefully clipped and placed in a Kelley scrapbook. As a poignant counterpoint, "The table you left to go to California," Clora wrote on her picture of a plain board table set with biscuits, coffee kettle, spoons, and saucers. It was a picture of somnolence and shadow at 1290 Woodland Avenue, Atlanta. Sunshine struggled through the rippling leaded windowpanes and through the thin curtains to spill over the table and onto an empty chair. Darkness swallowed everything else in Clora's composition. But DeForest did not appear, at least outwardly, to dwell on the past. He often gave the impression of having simply appeared to the world in 1939. To many, the young actor had no past; he lived among friends for the day and worked at his profession for the morrow.[40]

Kahn followed up on his hunch about Kelley and reporting to Schreiber again: "I wrote you a note about this boy, having seen him at Long Beach in *Skylark*. I think he would be worthwhile your interviewing, and Bill Woolfenden will contact your office regarding making an appointment to bring him in." On November 19, 1941, 20th Century Fox called DeForest Kelley for a screen test and interview. Kelley later explained, "The expense of a screen test is one reason why it's difficult to crash Hollywood. Each test costs a movie company about $10,000, so directors are awful prone to cast established actors rather than spend so much trying out new ones."[41]

On November 27, DeForest held his interview passes tightly and reported to the makeup department at four P.M. "A gloomy day," he scribbled on one of them later. The passes went into the scrapbook with the notation, "The day I made the test—my first and hope not the last."[42]

The past year had been both astounding and frustrating for DeForest. It seemed he could do no wrong in Long Beach, and yet he could not get a break in Hollywood. He had two major plays with his name at the top of the credits, and he had two short films to prove his potential in motion pictures. He was something of a radio personality around Long Beach. He counted his blessings, particularly his wealth of friends: Walter Truax, Wally Jordan, Jimmy Workman, Irving Ravetch, Barney Girard, Anne and Billee Jolly, Joe Laden, Grace Hartung, the Fosholdts. After a childhood as a transient preacher's kid uprooted and planted again and again from one mill town to the next, he knew he was fortunate. His young friends looked to him for "nothing but laughs and no regrets."

And then, on Sunday, December 7, Grace Hartung was getting her restaurant ready for the day. She told her helper, a young girl with dark red hair and big brown eyes, to go and get her some change from the liquor store across the way. The girl was gone for a while, and when she came back, "her eyes were as big as dollars. 'We're at war,' she said." Meanwhile, Anne Jolly had decided to take in a Don Ameche and Alice Faye movie matinee. She walked home in the afternoon and was soon troubled by the empty streets of her beautiful city. Then she found out—Pearl Harbor.[43]

Perhaps everyone was in shock. Would Long Beach and the Navy base be the next target of Japanese planes or warships? The waiting began and lasted through the holidays and into the new year. Kelley took his exams for Officer Candidate School and awaited his fate.

In the dark of February 25, 1942, the reality of war approached the Southern California coast, when the horrible droning of plane engines filled the night. Dread filled Long Beach hearts as swarms of airplanes thundered overhead and the *aack-aack* boomed. Then papers and radio reported. No, these were friendly planes, an incident, oh, an accident. . . . Then, after weeks, the authorities finally spoke. There had been no planes at all. It was a Long Beach community hallucination, and that was the end of it. But that night, so vivid in the memory of Long Beach residents, there was indeed a confirmed bombing of the U.S. mainland—San Francisco area oilfields were bombed by Japan. So, no one knew, or could guess, when their Navy base, ship terminal, and shoreline would be attacked by air or water, but the terrible promise was there, all the time.[44]

Diversions became increasingly important. Anne Jolly attended a play, a costume drama called *Bittersweet*, across from the Chat 'N Nibble. In the middle of a scene, the house lights came up, and a man in uniform took the stage. "All servicemen report to your stations immediately," Anne remembers—there was a stillness. Is this it? Are we all about to be bombed or crushed by invasion? Now? Then sailors, marines, soldiers—literally half of the audience, beautiful young people in uniform—with an intake of electrified breath rushed for the doors. Anne and the other half of the audience were stunned a long moment, then shattered the silence with a great torrent of applause. "You know the roar of an audience. I never heard applause like that before and never, ever . . . ever again like that, as these young men were rushing to their stations." Sometimes the exquisite beauty and sadness of it all brought tears to her eyes. Once recovered, Anne went to the Chat 'N Nibble, and some of the guys from the radio station came down and told her the Japanese had shelled Santa Barbara.[45]

The Community Playhouse productions hit the road to entertain at the military bases. But inside Kelley's gang, you wouldn't know war existed. Anne recalls, "We never talked about the South Pacific or Europe. We were having as good a time as we could as long as we could." There was a concerted effort not to allow the upsets of the world in. Maybe you could discuss the war with people you didn't love so much, but not Kelley. The war and Kelley could not—would not—be allowed to occupy the same place in Anne's mind.[46]

Chapter III
Her Innocent Young Man
1942–1945

> *"To have and to hold, and in time to let go.*
> *There is always tomorrow, Cherie!"*
> —DEFOREST TO CAROLYN, 1944

On Long Beach in the spring of 1942, the performing artists determined that the show must go on, now more than ever, and auditions were set for their next production. DeForest Kelley took the supporting part of beachcomber Bill Hogan in *The Innocent Young Man*. Anne Jolly took the role of Annabelle, and a new arrival to the Players, Carolyn Dowling, got the lead role of Fay Phipps. Oranne Day, as instructor of dramatics, gathered her players around her and set to work again with director Herbert Yenne.[1]

Mrs. Day had worked with Mrs. Dowling before, in her North Long Beach adult education classes in the late 1930s. Of Carolyn's first performance with the players, a critic wrote that she "plays her role conservatively and with the proper amount of restraint that makes her an actress who understands good theater." Kelley turned in "an experienced performance and he gives the best characterization in the play." The production was light fare for military and local audiences, and it worked well for nine performances, an unusually long run by Playhouse standards.[2]

By this time, DeForest was used to being surrounded by women, and he was quite conscious of the effect he had on them. Grace Hartung recalls that he sometimes came to her restaurant all dressed up for his roles so strikingly that she swooned. "Oh, Clark Gable!" Kelley never lacked for female attention. But in *The Innocent Young Man,* the tables were turned. He was the one smitten; during the run of the play, he lost his heart to Carolyn Dowling.[3]

He recalled, "I was playing a beach bum. At the end of the play, he's broke, you know, and that sorta thing, and we were using [Carolyn Dowling's own] money for stage money, and she hands me the five-dollar bill at the end of the play and says, 'Here take this and do something with it.' One day, I was sitting at a bar shortly after [a performance], and I realized that I had walked out of [the playhouse] with her five-dollar bill. So I went to the telephone, and I called her, and I told her I was in a local bistro and that I had her five dollars, and would she come down and help me spend it?" The mutual attraction had been undeniable from their first moments at the Playhouse, and now this. Carolyn and DeForest were in something of a quandary. What would this five-dollar meeting at the bistro mean?[4]

Before her marriage, Carolyn Meagher Dowling had made quite a name for herself from San Francisco to Los Angeles. She worked the movie theaters and posed for promotions of movie houses and city-wide events. She was acquainted with singers, bandleaders, and actors. With her knack for meeting and impressing creative people, her vivacity, and her native humor, she became a favorite of local newspapers and a featured subject of photographs. But after a few years of marriage in Long Beach, it became evident that she was only an afterthought in Jim Dowling's life. Carolyn's one close friend in Long Beach was her neighbor Olive LaFata. She was a new mother tending a toddler named Tony. These ladies were so close that Carolyn was named the boy's godmother, but it looked as if the LaFatas would be moving on at any time. So she joined the family of the Community Players.

Anne introduced Carolyn to the gang in Jolly fashion. Anne's mother, Billee, and Carolyn hit it off, and Anne loved Carolyn, that was for sure. The feeling was mutual.[5]

Carolyn loved animals with complete abandon, and in turn they loved her without reservation. She introduced new friends to her cherished Stardust Melody, her dog named after the Hoagy Carmichael song. Stardust was the warm center of their home at 5525 Pine.

One day and just because, a corsage box with a big blue bow arrived for Anne at the Colony. The box said "Meow." A sweet white kitten was snuggled inside. She was named Caranne, for Carolyn and her dear young friend Anne.

Carolyn found success in plays such as Dorothy Parker's *Here We Are*, in September 1942. She toyed with entertainments, thought about dancing in a chorus line, and dabbled in dramatics, but she had no particular ambition.

DeForest got a message from his man at the Bender and Ward Agency on Sunset, letting him know he had appointments at MGM and 20th Century Fox. Once again, he was traveling the corridor between Long Beach and the studios, still without good results.[6]

Jolly, Ravetch, Girard, and a rotating cast of players kept working the craft of radio entertainment. They were a good team, though Irving Ravetch recalls that DeForest was not always with the radio group, preferring to pursue acting opportunities wherever he could find them. Ravetch remembers that for all of DeForest's ambition, he was not in the least theatrical; even though swept up in creative intensity, DeForest was sweet and so very straight and steady.

As a group, they called themselves Modern Theater. DeForest Kelley, Irving Ravetch, and Barney Girard were simply passionate about their work, the go-getters of the group, and they were very fortunate as doors began to swing open for them. Ravetch and Girard took the lead in writing original radio plays, which Anne, Sally Golner, Dick Hamilton, Ronnie Hawk, DeForest, and sometimes Girard performed. These half-hour dramatic broadcasts were carried by KGER Los Angeles. Anne kept some of the skits written by Girard, such as "Misadventures of the Gory Fellers," "The Dandelions," "The Law of Ugliness," and "Judge B. Nutt," which was broadcast on KGER on the evening of August 25. Ravetch mused that for some reason, major radio stations allowed him and the "young hellions" to perform every week. With talent like this, DeForest was satisfied to make suggestions and collaborate just a little bit. He never tried his own talents for writing. Under Girard's direction, the team captured the attention of an ever-widening audience. They knew they were good. They were really "big fat" now.[7]

2 Even among such warm friends, Kelley was quiet about his background and his family. But as much as he might have wished to keep his life prior to Long Beach to himself, his past caught up with him during that summer. The Reverend Mr. Kelley had grown restless in his retirement and traveled west to see his son and the Caseys. Before anyone knew it, DeForest's father was living with him, and they were preparing for Clora's arrival. Joe Laden was invited to a nice lunch with the Reverend and DeForest. DeForest thought the suit Joe wore was marvelous, and the Reverend agreed. Later on, DeForest let Joe know the minister thought Joe was a good fellow, with good common sense. Joe figured the minister just didn't know him well enough yet and, given the opportunity, would surely change his mind.[8]

Once Clora arrived and settled in with DeForest and her husband, Joe came to lunch again, this time at their new place at 2107 Atlantic. At one point, Joe was talking seriously to the minister, so earnestly that his New York *dees, dems,* and *dozes* were coming on fast and furious into the Reverend's face while DeForest laughed. "The minister didn't understand why he was laughing like hell at me." Joe explained later that DeForest looked for moments when Joe's careful diction slipped. In turn, when DeForest slipped, everyone enjoyed that, too. Except for their fondness for Joe Laden, the elder Kelleys seemed most comfortable in the social circles of Herman and Shorty Casey. Grace Hartung saw Reverend Kelley a few times at the Chat 'N Nibble, but he hardly ever said a word. Grace never heard a word from Clora, and DeForest never spoke of her. Casey Kelley visited the restaurant at one point, and Grace found him to be a pleasant man, nearly as quiet as the father.

Clora loved California and the Pacific. She modeled bathing suits for the camera. She posed with her spectacles and dark curls and soft white features, motherly and radiant with happiness. When she got hold of the pictures, she wrote funny things about herself on the borders and backs of the prints. Clora was having a ball in the salt air and sunshine.

Relations between the Reverend and his son remained guarded and formal. DeForest's churchgoing days were long over, but his father would always be the Reverend to everyone who knew him. In one snapshot, DeForest sits down in his denims, a little tired, addressing the camera with the light of confidence on his face. His father, posed behind him in his traditional black suit, appears as he always has, but now there is a trace of uncertainty in his eyes. It seemed that while DeForest was finding his way in this new world, the future had no place for the Reverend Mr. Kelley. In the captured moment, it seemed as if it were he who had the second sight, as his wife was said to have, and he could sense the coming burdens draw down upon him.[9]

The old gang was swept away as Girard and Ravetch were called up and drafted, essentially ending their radio careers. Kelley's resolve to volunteer for Officer Candidate School at Fort Jackson, Mississippi, continued to be frustrated by paperwork and Army contrariness. While awaiting his orders, Kelley learned that Walter Wanger, independent film producer and Hollywood maverick, was interested in him. Apparently, Wanger had considered his options and called Kelley's agent to offer a term contract for the young man.[10]

Kelley's euphoria was short-lived. The very next day, March 3, 1943, his number finally came up, and he was called to Army service as an enlisted man. The big break in Hollywood was snatched away once more. His "luck" was a harsh discipline, but it was consistent; nothing the young actor ever really ached for had come to him. His "luck" was more like blind fate that could only be made palatable by blind faith. But at that moment, there was little chance to reflect on his career aspirations.[11]

As Kelley went through his induction process, he discovered his real name was Jackson DeForest; the first name honored his grandfather. Within the week, along with about eighty Long Beach fellows, "Jack" Kelley reported for service. On March 10, a little lady from the induction board greeted and thanked the fellows as they climbed onto the train bound for the induction center at Arlington, as the Long Beach Municipal Band played martial tunes. She had performed this role before, yet the press noted she was nevertheless "visibly shaken by her duties." The press also mentioned that Kelley was a prominent inductee among his fellows, the leading man in several productions and a member of the board of directors for the Long Beach Community Players. No one could guess what would happen to Kelley from there.[12]

It was a dreadful time. Anne's mother, Billee, decided it was party time for the war effort and left her daughter behind to serve as a WAAC. There were horrible, heartbreaking stories in the paper, on the radio, from the mouths of strangers. Young men were missing from the streets, the theater, and the oceanside. "We were living in an armed camp," Grace Hartung recalls. Her Chat 'N Nibble was rarely, if ever, closed while the war was on. It became a favorite hangout for young men awaiting their scheduled flights or movements. Equipment, armament, and jeeps paraded up and down Ocean Boulevard as Grace watched and wondered if the world would ever be the same again.[13]

One of the gang, Walter Truax, an electrician and prop man for the Community Playhouse, was dead. He had once posed for snapshots with the Jolly girls and Kelley on an Easter Sunday, beautifully dressed and ready for fun. Now, he was lost at sea, on a ship torpedoed by a Japanese submarine. The full truth of Walter's death really stunned Kelley. He protected Anne from the knowledge that the submarine had circled the wreckage of the Navy ship and hauled the survivors out of the water. The Japanese had tied those sailors to the conning tower of the sub and submerged again as the sailors struggled to get free—Walter Truax among them. In order to spare his loved ones harsh truths, DeForest denied himself the comfort of shared grief.

In spite of her friend's efforts to shelter her, Anne did know that with Kelley, Billee, Irving, Barney, and her beloved Greg Baker off to war, the life she had hoped for was gone.[14]

The home front got behind war bonds and war stamps in a big way, and Jim Dowling headed his area's efforts. He ran the popular Burt's shoe store on Pine, and from there he helped manage huge sales of stamps and bonds, as well as the Victory show at the auditorium. Dowling then decided to attend Officer Candidate School by the end of the year. Carolyn stayed behind, working for the war effort at Terminal Island's shipyards and participating in the entertainments at the Community Playhouse. The separation was welcome.[15]

Anne joined Carolyn at Terminal Island's major shipbuilding facility, Calship. She was assigned to the same building as Carolyn, who was the secretary of the training department. Since Billee was in uniform, Carolyn became all the more important in Anne's young life. With all the rationing, it was an adventure to get cigarettes, a pair of shoes, gas, stockings, makeup, and liquor.[16]

3 Kelley's basic training lasted the usual month, and then, as if sent from the heavens above, his classification arrived: Army Air Corps 274, public relations writer, and Army Air Corps 552, control tower operator. He was now a private first class of the Signal Corps. Perhaps the heavens had a little help; indirectly, it was Anne's doing. Because of his background in radio, DeForest was selected out of the thousands of unskilled and modestly educated draftees sent into combat.

He was assigned to the 91st Air Base Squadron, Roswell, New Mexico. He was stateside, among friends, and safe for the moment. That, apparently, was Barney Girard's doing. As Joe Laden explains, Girard managed to go to Roswell's flying school. He was Special Services, Signal Corps, and Girard wrote for newspapers, for entertainments, and performed his duty as a radio tower operator. Quite a few of the Long Beach radio announcers, writers, and musicians somehow got out to New Mexico. Joe recalls, "And how they all got there to Roswell, you tell me—but here I am thinking about getting into combat or going out there to the old gang, and Barney lets me know he could arrange something for me."[17]

As control tower operator at Roswell, Kelley made full use of his radio skills. He was trained so that he could direct aircraft and vehicles in the landing area, guide approaching and departing aircraft, issue information and instruction to pilots, and use International Morse Code at a rate of ten groups per minute. He learned to use radiotelephone procedures according to the rules and regulations of tower operation and knew the blinker light equipment and the system of codes used with such equipment in the control tower.

The flying school was spartan and meant for serious business. The control tower itself was a spidery-looking thing, with five flights of stairs and a big platform on top with a shack on top of it. A railing around the shack made it possible to go out and have a look, stretch, smoke, and catch a little New Mexico breeze. Barney Girard hated heights and climbed the stairs with trepidation, only to find Kelley at the top ready to question him six ways to Sunday about which Hollywood agent he should pursue once all this was over. It seemed to Girard that Kelley never stopped thinking about his acting, no matter what he happened to be doing at the time. Even there, atop the rickety control tower with its sparse interior and tables of fresh lumber tacked together, metal chairs, headphones, mikes, wires, and papers everywhere, Kelley's head was full of the actor's life.[18]

Kelley's capacity for memorization, his voice control, and his precise recitation and diction were well used on a minute-to-minute basis, as pilots relied on his voice and his judgment to land them safely. Kelley sent Clora a public relations article that featured a grainy picture of himself and others at work with a small note: "Maybe the next Mother's Day will be different." Kelley was justifiably proud to be fully qualified as an "aerial traffic cop," as the public relations writers labeled him and his kind. This was a real job by anyone's standards.[19]

Roswell Army Air Field had been established just before the war to meet the needs of a 30,000-pilot training program under the Western Flying Training Command. Roswell's focus was on producing bombardiers.[20] A big college fellow, R. G. Armstrong, worked in the map room and kept charts on the progress of the flight school trainees. As he recalls, the program turned out airmen fast and furiously, but chances of surviving the results of their training were miserable. Army Air Corps crews were required to complete twenty-five missions in 1943; their life expectancy was no more than fifteen. Morale-building entertainments were an important factor in the face of such grim reality. Special Services, courtesy of Long Beach, California, answered the challenge. After his watches, Kelley went to work with Barney Girard and friends to entertain their captive audience.

On the mess deck, Armstrong remembers, would be Arthur Goldstein, Barney Girard, and "Jackson D. Kelley" working on skits and plays and talking art, drama, and theater. These were the kinds of things Armstrong wanted to hear.[21]

Very quickly, Kelley and Girard cowrote a script with a former Long Beach radio announcer, Frank Tessinger. The musical comedy, *Jodie,* was scored by Long Beach musician Paul Masterson. The ranking base officers determined that the play was fit for an air base tour after a full production at Roswell. As a reward for the play, Kelley, Tessinger, Girard, Masterson, and newcomer Artie Goldstein got a furlough in July, complete with shuttle priority seating on General Scanlon's plane all the way to Long Beach.[22]

For a few precious days and nights, Kelley's Army Air Corps contingent stampeded all over Long Beach. Ample time was made for visiting Mr. and Mrs. Kelley and the Caseys. Pictures were taken of everyone seated at a full table near the windows, with coffee, meat, mashed potatoes—the whole spread laid out for the hungry boys. Kelley leaned into the camera frame with a great sunburst over his shoulder. The light of youth was on all the GIs' faces, just beside themselves with glee. Girard was soon so much at home with Clora Kelley that he dubbed himself her number three son.[23]

At one point, Clora paid her respects to the boys in the service by donning Kelley's uniform and marching out into the street. Kelley couldn't stand up, he laughed so hard. Admiring folks gathered as she saluted the camera. She had an extra shot taken to send to her Casey, who was determined to serve his country in airborne combat. The picture seemed to convey her heart. "This is your mother saluting you, my dears," she seemed to be saying, a whimsical smile just touching her lips.[24]

A few streets away, the Calship girls had taken over 5525 Pine. Kelley made sure he spent some party time with Anne and the lady of the house, Carolyn Dowling. Already, Carolyn knew she would never figure out DeForest Kelley. How could a man move so slowly and still be early everywhere he went? He didn't seem to have a nerve in his body. But the girls sure did, especially on a morning like this. There were frantic gyrations, because there were three girls to one bathroom, and the shipyards were crazy about punctuality. Nevertheless, Carolyn, housemate Charlotte See, and Anne simply could not go to work without stockings, or at least the appearance of them; so, even with Kelley in the house, they went through their ritual of creating the illusion of stockings. They applied the special Helene Curtis makeup to their legs, then took turns standing on the toilet, while one girl drew a "seam" of eyebrow pencil on the back of another's legs. The result was rather convincing. All three girls were wedged into the bathroom, doing their legs, and Anne recalls Kelley came sauntering through after his coffee, sauntering and shaving at the same time— and he slowly breezed by their chaos in the powder room. "Weeeahve gottah huurrayy gihrls," he crooned sweetly over his shoulder. The girls stopped their frenzied chirping for an embarrassed moment and then fell down in a heap of giggles. Kelley lived for moments like that.

As always, the Calship gals made it to work on time. By then, they were turning out Liberty Ships in thirty-five days, keel to delivery, topped out at fifty-three ships in four months. "That the whole world may be free again!" the *Calship Log* proclaimed.[25]

Only days later, Anne's world came to a crashing halt when Greg Baker was killed in a flight training accident off Windsor Locks, Connecticut. Anne was devastated. Barney Girard tried to be the white knight. He was working for a few days with Ravetch, who had already been discharged for medical reasons, in Los Angeles. Barney took the train down to Long Beach, but he could not find Anne. Later, back in Roswell, Barney wrote to Anne: "I called frantically and found no answer." He wanted to comfort her. He wrote that she was a proud and noble girl, with a beautiful life ahead. He even made friends with the kitten, Caranne, while calling for Anne. That was some token of his esteem, since once before, he'd seen her kiss the cat and then would not kiss her good night. But Barney made the mistake of making his letter to her about him rather than her loss. He apologized for not using all of his furlough to win her, or at least to comfort her. He confessed he wanted to be something more to Anne than old Mr. Girard, but, he said, "I'm probably landing on the wrong runway."[26]

4 On the evening of July 10 at the Uptown in Long Beach and later at the Venetian Room, DeForest and Carolyn made those connections, those electric exchanges, that tell some people that their lives are no longer their own, that they belong to each other fully and without definition. Carolyn was a goner, a mature woman completely "whango whango," as they liked to say in those days, about her young man. She recalls, "He wasn't as goody two-shoes as he made out to be . . . he was not an innocent. He had innocence." Hers had been a hard life, and at almost twenty-seven, Carolyn knew she had finally found her man, her love, and her mission. He was free of bitterness and disappointment, and she would "grow him up right," as she says. This was it. She found him smooth and gentle, with a catlike grace that entranced her. Finally, they could not deny the strength of their attraction and the allure of wartime romance. They made their way to the only private quarters they could find, the little apartment at the Colony, where they "made beautiful music together" for the first time, as DeForest remembered. "I wasn't there!" Anne says.[27]

As innocent as DeForest was, Carolyn was worldly, a product of frontier savvy: "I was born in Montana." She was raised in Nevada, a gambler's daughter. As a girl, her father was wounded in a gunfight, and upon his recovery, her parents separated. Carolyn was carried off to a Catholic academy in Colorado, where both parents visited; then Seattle and another convent, where she was alone and drenched in the rains. She had an aunt living in the sunshine and began to dream of brighter days. "When I grow, I go!" to Southern California, she promised herself. She smoked and drank as a child and rebelled whenever she could; alternatively, she wrote sparkling letters filled with heart-rending appeals to her father. She was a good, bright, smart girl. Come and get her, she pleaded. He did not. And so, for all of her life, she had tried to outrun the convent, the rain, her mother. Finally, she found a man who could become her sunshine, and she had no doubt that this love would be her life.

At the end of July, Carolyn wrote to the boys back in New Mexico. With a "Howdy Barney," she made sure to include everyone, but to Kelley she wrote an aside: "If clocks could be turned back, I'd turn mine back two weeks ago tonight—July 10, 8:30 at the Uptown, then the Venetian Room. Remember? C'est le guerre. Cherie."

A flurry of exchanges ensued. A few had dark undercurrents as Kelley came to appreciate the rather helpless and near hopeless position he would be in should he be called for overseas duty. He seemed lost, uncertain of his fate or his romance: "Sweetheart, you've led me this far, should we go on? Love anyway . . ."[28]

Carolyn kept busy. She took the lead in *Cry Havoc* with Anne Jolly, an all-women play directed by Herbert Yenne. But all the plays and entertainment could not heal Anne's grief over Greg's death. She began to have trouble getting through the weeks. Anne feared she was desperately ill, but finally a doctor acknowledged the sorrow she bore. He told her to leave town and surround herself with a new life.[29]

In the late summer of 1943, Caranne the cat and Anne Jolly moved to Hollywoodland. In September, she found employment with Hugh Harmon Productions on Santa Monica in Beverly Hills, "Harmonizing" animation for the war and for entertainment. They drew nice things for her, such as Caranne's cartoon portrait, and she appreciated their kindness. She tried to fight off depression and bitterness as best she could.[30]

Also in September, Carolyn did the damn near impossible and somehow got a flight from Los Angeles to Roswell, New Mexico. As a civilian woman traveling for love, Carolyn was very low on the seating list, and therefore she had plenty of time to collect matchbooks and swizzle sticks along the way. Finally, she arrived and settled into the Nickson Hotel in the town of Roswell. Private Kelley showed her the sights, the army flying school, and the Norton Bar. Tessinger, Girard, and the troops were around for party time, but no one forgot little sister Anne Jolly. On the back of a napkin, Kelley sent her a token of love and remembrance, though he was clearly silly with burgeoning romance and booze:

Roses are red, bourbon too, Carolyn's here, where are you!! DeForest.
P.S. We always drink three taps to you—the Good Kid Club is now in session!

Another napkin, another bar:

sorry Anne no literature for this bar, this is war, Baby ooo—words cannot explain how we miss you . . . life could be so complete with you.[31]

Carolyn picked up a pretty color postcard of their hotel. She indicated where they stayed on the second floor, with the Nickson neon sign flashing into the room. Carolyn wrote, "Well cookie this is really It." She reported that they were all sore from laughter. That was one treasure Carolyn and DeForest knew they had; they found each other incredibly funny. She had a deep, throaty laugh that was warm and pleasing. His was like a cold engine trying to turn over. Somewhere in his chest, the laughter would make its way toward the shy smile and drop back, and sometimes he'd just have to throw back his head and let the laughter pour out loud from deep inside. So they were sore.

All too soon, it was time for Carolyn to get back to Calship, but that was easier said than done. As a civilian, she was bumped again and again from flight after flight. Finally, on September 22, Carolyn telegrammed her housemate Charlotte to have someone pick her up in Burbank. The trip back had taken nearly a week.[32]

With Carolyn gone, the Long Beach boys returned to their labors. Poor Barney Girard began his anxious creative misery over *Nuts and Bolts,* an original play scheduled to open October 4, yet he had not written the first word as of September 24, the date of his letter to Anne. He wrote her that he and Kelley were promised three-day passes in return for the work, so he asked Anne and Carolyn to pray for help from his muses. He was sure he had lost all chance with Anne, now that "real writers" in Hollywoodland surrounded her. He signed off, "Regards to the Cat."[33]

As if in a different world, Kelley also went to work on *Nuts and Bolts* and considered himself one fortunate son of a gun, about love, about his career, and about his prospects. He told his tale about *This Gun for Hire* to R. G. Armstrong and the boys on the mess deck. He had lost the role because of his draft status, and there was no blame or anger in his story. It was simply the way things were. When the war was over, he knew he would have to start all over again, but there was no bitterness in him.[34]

On the other hand, Barney once wrote to Anne, the "dynamo had not enlisted with me. I returned to find it, but Anne it's either stolen or lost." He had built his identity on his capacity to dive deep within himself and come up with a play. Now that alchemy seemed to be failing him. Nevertheless, Barney and the Long Beach boys pulled off *Nuts and Bolts* on time and with great success. Musician and artist Roy Knott joined their crew and found Kelley a magnetic personality and a true friend. Knott did the artwork for *Nuts and Bolts* in the spare moments the Air Corps reluctantly granted for the task. The brass liked to keep everything humming and worked everyone to near exhaustion. According to their own write-up for the play, *Nuts and Bolts* originated in the rec hall from the "true art of Kibitzing." It was mostly written after taps in the wee hours by the light of the shower room. Everything—all the staging, backgrounds, script, and scoring—was done by the Long Beach boys. Barney shouted himself hoarse, pushing the cast through six hours of rehearsals each night after a full workday. Yet no one went to sick call, though there was some talk of nervous breakdowns. Kelley took the stage to play the bombardier in the chorus and sang a solo. The program for the performance was tongue-in-cheek and noted, "Any living persons showing similarity to characters in this play should be dead."[35]

Most of the entertainments were light comedies or musicals. Barney also wrote for the Roswell Army Air Field radio program. De-Forest got a good deal of air time, and on December 6, 1943, he performed *Overturned* by Barney Girard about three men trapped inside a destroyer. A harrowing tale of fellows in their last moments, the brief play opens with the sailors already in peril and banging at the hull of the ship in the black closeness of an upside-down compartment. They buck each other up and handle their doom differently but honorably. The three men slowly drown, gasping, finally going under water. It was a disturbing dose of reality-based radio drama. Barney wrote it to honor the U.S. Navy men. Once "Anchors Aweigh" was played by the band, the Army Air Force's "Song of the Ground Crew" followed. The announcer took over: "Take-off Time comes to you each Monday at seven through the facilities of KFGL. Next week, the same flying crew will be on hand, and until then, on behalf of the Roswell Army Air Force of the Army Air Force Training Command, we wish you a pleasant good night."

For the holiday, Kelley sent an ankle bracelet to Carolyn. He was wishing he was 4F; he was plain lovesick. He wrote of the bracelet, "Remember kicking it around would be kicking me around—oh to be chained my love. . . . There is always tomorrow. Love you . . ."[36]

Their furlough came through as promised, and the *Nuts and Bolts* boys came home at three A.M. on January 1, 1944. When the fellows flew in on furloughs, they came into Los Angeles airport or the Long Beach Air Force Base, then the bus to North Long Beach station, and then walked over the river to 5525.[37]

Anne knew she was always welcome at 5525, but she spent most of her days and nights up in Hollywoodland. She rented a little room with a fireplace in a woman's home. It was in a good neighborhood, on Woodhaven in Hollywood, with flagstone steps up to her side of the house.

One night, she recalls, "I'm asleep, and a bump, and a noise, and somebody removes the window at the front." Billee had left her the .45 to defend herself, and she knew how to use it. Anne kept it under her pillow. "I was just a little girl. I was still a virgin." A man was at the window; she could hear him. Anne reached for her .45 and pulled it from under the pillow. She got a good grip on the heavy automatic, "and I sat up and took aim, remembering what a kick it had—so I got it braced and aimed for the window . . . then I hear Carolyn's giggle, and I hear De drawl, 'Honnay be quiiyut.' "[38]

They said they tried the front, then they tried to wake Anne gently, then they decided to come on in. To visit. Just climb through the window. They came within an inch of getting themselves shot. They just laughed. But if she hadn't giggled and he hadn't drawled, Anne could have killed them both.[39]

5 Just after St. Patrick's Day of 1944, Carolyn and a girlfriend made the front page of the *Los Angeles Times* with a curiously upbeat article about wartime divorce. Judge Beardsey had found that marriage was a burden to Lieutenant Jim Dowling and released him from it. The separation was permanent, and Carolyn was free to have her De forever, if the war and the fates would allow it. The Dowling home at 5525 Pine now belonged to Carolyn and Stardust Melody. Carolyn stayed on the job at Calship.[40]

Aileen Pickering of San Pedro recalls meeting Carolyn on her first day at work. While Carolyn held the training department together as executive secretary, Aileen went to work as a draft and design engineer, with electrical plans and diagrams. She had dreams of flying and a passion for horses. Even standing still, she gave the impression of light and speed and fearlessness. Aileen remembers how impressed she was with Carolyn's laughter and her wit and how Carolyn inhaled cigarettes down to her toes. One of the funniest women alive, Carolyn was. Really, she was a laugh riot. Then Carolyn told Aileen all about her dog, Stardust Melody, and she had pictures. "This is my boyfriend," Carolyn simply said of Kelley.[41]

As Aileen found out, nothing but DeForest really seemed to matter very much to Carolyn. Almost reluctantly, Carolyn told Aileen that Paramount's casting wizard and Kelley's benefactor, Bill Meiklejohn, wanted Carolyn to make a screen test for the studio. On March 30, 1944, Carolyn and Aileen quit Calship to go to the screen test Meiklejohn had arranged. Aileen was confident that this would be something big. Carolyn had beauty, a great speaking voice, and a way about her that suggested star material. That's why Meiklejohn wanted Carolyn.[42]

Of course, they had to have drinks in Long Beach the night before, and the next morning it was off to Paramount with Carolyn and Aileen. "I had this Desoto I used to drive," Aileen recalls, and it took a lot of time and a lot of gas rations to get up to the old center of Hollywood on Melrose. "At 11 ayem we get all the way up there, and she says, 'No I can't. What will De say?' and she's like 'What will De think?' . . . What? Oh shut up! . . . Who gets a chance like this? Christ."

Carolyn was sure she couldn't, she wouldn't . . . she said she wanted De to have the career. It was all for De, not for Carolyn. She froze in the car, wouldn't even get out. Aileen begged, "But Carolyn, we have an appointment. Go do the thing, then say no." Maybe she just couldn't bear a rejection, but Aileen admits, "I was sure mad, parked there at the Paramount gate." Aileen stewed sitting there at stalemate with a friend of equal stubbornness and as different as the sun from the moon. Finally, they drove back to Long Beach, having stood up Bill Meiklejohn of Paramount Studios.[43]

Kelley found such devotion and longing to be irresistible. Carolyn's all-encompassing love made their wartime relationship a poignant celebration of romance, separation, and desire. In his letters, De would exclaim, "To have and to hold, and in time to let go. There is always tomorrow, Cherie!"

For Carolyn, life without DeForest was emptiness. At Calship, it was hard to concentrate. Carolyn was organized and detail-oriented, very efficient, and thus had time to muse about things. Sometimes she typed letters, snatches of poetry, or bits of wit. Her collections grew, and she pasted them in her scrapbooks.[44]

The anxiety of separation was awful for Carolyn. Her depth of

commitment was troubling, expressed by a few lines she found somewhere and tapped out on her anvil of a typewriter: "Dear God—help
me to love him less."[45]

Though she seemed to find it hard to concentrate, her sense of
humor kept her from being overwhelmed by longing. She was very
good at employing her beloved animals to lighten the burden of daily
life, for herself and for others. For instance, on May 5, 1944, a telegram
from Western Union arrived for Pfc. Kelley at the 91st Air Base
Squadron: "One blonde and 3 brunettes had leading roles in Star's
four-star performance last night. Stardust Melody's Medley, Starlet,
Fluff, Purr and Eager."[46]

Everyone in Carolyn's circle received lovely cards and notes with
animal motifs or "from" individual pets. Each mailing was a unique
creation, an expression of caring attention.

She entrusted animals with her tender heart and used them to
convey her delicate feelings. She humanized the animal world and
made the human world more humane through her animals. In every
other respect, she was a shrewd realist. Her sphere of animals and
carefully selected friends created a refuge from the outside world. She
knew that outer world was both deceiving and chaotic.

6 Bette Creutze describes how she became part of 5525: "I was married, my husband was overseas, and I had this red convertible Buick
and an allotment, and so I did whatever I pleased." Bette moved into
5525. "It wasn't long before Carolyn decided I had a car and she
should go to Roswell to see De, but how were we going to get gas
during the war?" No gas. Rations. Bette recalls Carolyn's resolve: "She
asked if she could get the gas, would I go? Sure. And I have no idea
how she . . . but all of a sudden we had gas. So I got the car lubed and
checked for this big trek to Roswell." Stardust Melody was boarded
out with friends, and everything was going just fine.[47]

But they weren't finished yet. Bette explains: "This guy at the
liquor store was madly in love with Carolyn. [She tells him,] 'I'm
going to see my brother in the army, we wanted to bring some bourbon . . .' This guy falls for it . . . cases of bourbon, of scotch, and of

rum." Bette had to pick it up at the back of the store in the alley, where no one could see. "I had to load it—we had clothes everywhere, and cases of liquor."

Then, just before they left, Bette found a skinny little man in the living room of 5525 in his little black suit, like a little deacon. He was looking at them, at these scarlet women! Reverend Kelley had come to see about his son! "We were packing for Roswell—thank God he didn't see all the booze in the trunk!" After a while, he warmed up to Bette and Carolyn. He was so rail thin, so proper, and very concerned about his son, because, well, Carolyn was separated, a divorcée and De was so much younger, really. Once that little encounter was over, the gals made their final preparations. Bette recalls, "We didn't have any idea where Roswell was. I had never been to New Mexico . . . we just went." Carolyn remembers dryly, "We didn't have an idea in our heads."[48]

Out of Southern California, on Route 66, into the Great West, they drove on in their '41 Buick ragtop, the Red Bird. What a ride! Bette remembers. Sure, it might have been dangerous, but "Carolyn knew what was what." She had a nose for danger. For instance, they pulled in at a motel in Kingman and spied a roadhouse nearby, but Carolyn said, "We're not getting a toe caught in that bar." She just knew. Bette was eighteen and relied on Carolyn's senses to get her across the wild land in one piece. And she did.

Finally, they arrived at their destination of a Roswell motor court with frontier-style whitewashed stucco buildings and shaded overhangs of twigs and timber. They parked the Red Bird in a big yard of dust. Private Kelley called and had them meet him at the Roswell Hotel, in the one-block town nearby. He was bringing Barney for Bette to meet. "De was going to fix me up with Barney Girard," Bette recalls, but the place was filled with GIs, and for some reason Barney didn't come along. Instead, it was Tessinger. Back at the motor inn, the whole army came over when they found out that Carolyn and a friend from Long Beach had a car full of liquor. They had the newest car on the road, and the gals were stars—dark little Carolyn with sapphire-blue eyes and sultry voice and style, and long, blond Bette with curves and a smile.

Kelley took them up to his air control tower—not that he was supposed to, but one must see the sights—and then over into the Roswell graveyard, where Bette, Tess, De, and Carolyn goofed around among the headstones.

After only a few days of laughs, it was time for the girls to head back to California. On the way home, they pulled off the road and onto the shoulder and got stuck. A truck driver stopped to help. "We had no booze left, so we gave him a five-dollar bill, and he would not think of taking it," Bette remembers. In those days, men proved their strength and manliness by being well mannered, helpful, and gentle. Just how gentle they could be under trying circumstances, how civilized they could be in a harsh world, that was the measure of a man, and Bette saw that Kelley was all that. Thinking back on it, Bette knew she had never met such a strong gentleman as Carolyn's De.

Perhaps the most difficult event in Carolyn's wartime adventure was the day Jim Dowling came to take custody of Stardust Melody. Carolyn loved that dog enough to let her go to the home that would be best for her. Not long after their return to California, Carolyn and Bette decided to kick up their heels and shake the sand of Long Beach out of their shoes. They were off to Sunset Boulevard and all that might await them in Hollywoodland. Bette and Carolyn set themselves up in a room at the St. Moritz on Sunset, with the bowling alley across the street and the bar below. Party time commenced.[49]

Anne Jolly had now finished a year in the world of Hollywoodland. She picked herself up and took herself home, to a tiny place on Appleton in Long Beach. She went back to the Community Players and performed one play after the next and worked as a writer and performer down at radio station KGER. From Sunset Boulevard, Carolyn tried to get Anne to come out with her and get into the chorus line with Lou Carroll's Review. In fact, Aileen Pickering was already part of the Review. Anne begged off, preferring Noel Coward plays, and she couldn't even play hopscotch, never mind dance. Later, Tessinger reported that Anne seemed well and looking fine at the Venetian Room in Long Beach. Meanwhile, Private Jackson D. Kelley reported in at the St. Moritz on Sunset whenever he had furlough.[50]

With Carolyn, Bette enjoyed her best years. She was seventeen when she'd been brow-beaten into marrying a traditional boy in a soldier's uniform. She was expected to be a good, obedient girl, told what her life and options would be. The war meant freedom, and she was going to live every moment of it with Carolyn, De, and the gang for as long as she could. Of those years, Bette remembers, "Oh, hey, I've never been that free." And like so many women of her generation, never that free since.[51]

7 At Roswell, Kelley became a veteran of air traffic control, using cigarettes and doodling to soothe his nerves. One terrible day, so many planes were coming in under his guidance that Kelley believed he saw two approaching the same landing strip. "Pull up pull up pull up!" he ordered the pilot at higher altitude—and he got no response. He ordered the maneuver again and again as the two planes continued on their collision course. He chanted harder and harder, willing the planes to separate while they continued their approach, one on top of the other. Pull up! Were they intentionally going to ram themselves into the tarmac? Was it something he, the controller, was doing wrong? Frantically, he howled for the pilot to pull up while he considered that here Private First Class Kelley was going to kill them all, two planes full. With never a word, they finally came in, nearly one on top of the other, without explanations and without a peep to the tower. Were they just playing with him? Kelley was shaken to the core.[52]

The agony of those raw minutes scarred his nerves and his psyche. He would never know if he had made a near-fatal failure in judgment or if those flyboys thought the whole thing was funny somehow. Indeed, he was a young man more suited for cathartic artistry than for the chaos of reality. More than anything else, it was his Army Air Corps service at Roswell that told Kelley who he was and what he was meant for in this life.[53]

Meanwhile, the Allies continued the push toward victory at a very high cost to the American soldier. Mature American men who knew the consequences of war stepped up to volunteer. Casey Kelley continued to maneuver for combat duty. He would have preferred aviation, but things did not work out. Finally, he was assigned to an anti-tank company, 275th Infantry Regiment of the 70th Division, otherwise known as the Trail Blazers. By the end of 1944, Corporal Kelley was bound for Germany. Joe Laden also went into combat, as a tail gunner flying nerve-shattering missions over enemy territory.

Back in New Mexico, at the Roswell Army Flight School, they churned plane crews out as fast as they could—sent them to be chewed up by *ack-ack,* gremlins, and shock. Laden did not begrudge Kelley his peaceful little place in the Roswell control tower and on the stage for the morale of the Army Air Corps. No, he was glad his friend would be spared living through what Joe was determined to live through.[54]

In January 1945, Kelley was transferred to a place even safer than Roswell: all the way back home to Southern California. Ravetch got out on a medical discharge and went right into the Hollywood studios. Then Girard got out for nerves and right into Warner Brothers— very nice. Laden kept on with his combat missions, as tailgunner and formation leader, bombing the living hell out of the Germans, and he thought about Kelley and luck.[55]

By his own recollection, Kelley had been eyed to become an active combat crewman as the months dragged on and ready crews were depleted. As a control tower operator, he was also qualified to serve as a B-17 radioman. An inner ear problem developed on those furlough flights from New Mexico to California and kept him grounded, at least for a while. He did draw for a fellow looking for artists for training film production. The "Smoking GI" sketch was a Kelley standard.[56]

Perhaps his luck and drawing talent really were enough to get him a transfer, but before it was all said and done, Kelley did a very rare thing for him: he appealed for help. He wrote to Bill Meiklejohn. On January 3, 1945, Meiklejohn promptly wrote back on eye-catching Paramount stationery: "Received your letter. Please don't ever feel that you are imposing on me. I will call Capt. Kumin as soon as I get back."

In peacetime, Irving Kumin was the casting director for Warner Brothers, and in 1945 he was the casting officer for Motion Picture Unit One, Army Air Corps, at Roach Studios, also known as Camp Roach. In short order, Kelley was transferred to Hollywood to make movies for the war effort.[57]

Chapter IV
Cinderella Boy
1945–1948

"It turned out to be one big audition for me. It changed my life."
—DEFOREST KELLEY, 1996

On January 18, 1945, the *Atlanta Journal* reported that Private Kelley was "firmly ensconced" in Hollywood at the Hal Roach Studios to assist in creating the military's training films. Clora happily supplied the Atlanta papers and magazines with the good news about her son. Now the Kelleys knew that one son would certainly be spared the dangers of war. DeForest turned twenty-five safely inside studio walls as part of the 18th Army Air Force Base Unit, also known as the First Motion Picture Unit.

The First Motion Picture Unit (FMPU) had been created three years earlier, to turn out instructive shorts for training and to document actual combat. General Hap Arnold and studio mogul Jack Warner created the unit for the U.S. Army Air Corps. Their man at the helm, Owen Crump, initially enjoyed a direct enlistment policy which allowed him to reserve Hollywood's finest for the unit's efforts. FMPU was a kind of saving grace for Hollywood's image and for the leading men, because it gave them a way to serve, to save face, and to stay square with the American public. Even Alan Ladd, who suffered mightily with back problems, insisted on serving in some way. The FMPU gave him an important role to play. As well as his faithful appearances for patriotic entertainments, public relations, and acting roles, he was often observed on KP duty around the studios, signing autographs while picking up cigarette butts. Although Clark Gable was too old for active duty, he insisted on qualifying for combat. He did go on some combat missions. He then became something of a liaison and public relations man among Hollywood, the Army Air Corps, and the citizens who kept up with him through the FMPU shorts shown in the nation's theaters. James Stewart went into combat as a pilot and also worked for the FMPU as their first spokesman and premier pilot recruiter. Ronald Reagan, Lloyd Nolan, William Holden, and others became virtual soldiers, fliers, and sailors, as the concept of training through film expanded to benefit all of the armed forces.[1]

For the Hollywood types, there seemed to be three choices: combat, cowardice, or the First Motion Picture Unit. Hollywood answered the call of the nation with overwhelming courage and creativity. You could bring the Army to Hollywood, but Hollywood then could bend and seduce the military into its own devices and desires. For Kelley, it was a world of stars and glamorous artists united for a cause beyond their careers and beyond their lifetimes. He experienced the Hollywood industry as a powerful force for unity and good. And it made a powerful impression. He recalled that it was a family environment. They largely ignored rank and seldom, if ever, saluted. With guys like his new friend George Reeves, a popular actor who appeared as a romantic young Southerner in the opening scenes of Gone With the Wind, it may have seemed to DeForest as if he had awakened into a dream.[2]

Kelley served as motion-picture production technician, an artist's assistant among thousands of professionals. The unit addressed the broad subjects of training, morale, information, and military intelligence for the American fighting man. The GIs had to learn to survive, to fight, to identify the enemy, and to resist interrogation. Visualization, animation, and dramatization worked well with these young men who had grown up with movies. Kelley had already been impressed with the Motion Picture Unit's health and hygiene films, particularly the ones on venereal disease that scared him silly. Even so, he admitted that after a few drinks, a fellow could forget!

With Europe firmly in hand, the Motion Picture Unit turned its attention to the Pacific and Japan. The warriors of make-believe at Camp Roach began their most ambitious offensive of the war, and artist's assistant Kelley was part of it. Produced by Captain R. Goldstone, *Target Tokyo* took up two sound stages to create a virtual raid by the 20th Air Force on Tokyo. Models were made of the entire topography of Tokyo for the airmen to study. Magnificent execution was achieved with plastic, paper, paperboard, dirt, sand, and fabric. The crew created cities, mountains, roads, rivers, and railroad tracks. Exact routes, targets, checkpoints, and landmarks were meticulously laid out. Fresh to the FMPU, Kelley created many of the trees and shrubs from sponges and paint. Finally, a sophisticated camera doubled for the American pilot flying over water and land and onward to the approach and bombing of each industrial target. Personnel officer Captain Ronald Reagan narrated the training film that prepared American fliers for their part in the massive first raid into Tokyo. The mission's real flyboys watched *Target Tokyo* again and again until they memorized it.

Most meaningful to the Hollywood warriors were the comments they heard from the real air crews that had participated in the raid on Tokyo on February 25, 1945. They said that it seemed as if they had seen Japan and Tokyo before—that they had done it all before. Some 2,000 tons of bombs were dropped by 1,200 warplanes on this first Superfortress strike on Tokyo. While a few carrier planes did go down, none of the B-29s was lost. How many American lives had been saved by *Target Tokyo* and all the other work of the Hollywood warriors is unknown. The Hollywood guys were touched with pride and humility by the reviews and thanks of the American fighting men.[3]

Target Tokyo was the crowning achievement of the home front First Motion Picture Unit fellows. The world premiere took place at the United Nations conference at the Sir Francis Drake Hotel in San Francisco on May 15, 1945. The training film and the documentation of the actual B-29 bombing were featured. Dignitaries, diplomats, politicians, and military brass attended the conference; so did the men who made *Target Tokyo,* including DeForest Kelley. Photographs of the event were taken, and the GIs were given commemorative copies.

Target Tokyo was released to theaters and to the public on May 24, 1945, through RKO so that audiences could vicariously experience the Tokyo raid. The film ran more than a dozen weeks at 16,000 theaters. Victory was coming, and everyone anticipated a new lease on life. On

May 27, Kelley posed on the St. Moritz fire escape with friends and family, the haze across Sunset Boulevard behind them. Carolyn, Bette, and DeForest played hosts as Reverend Kelley and others passed through Hollywood celebrating.

Kelley's work at Camp Roach with the First Motion Picture Unit was an education in absolutely everything a full studio had to be, with sound stages, costumes, animation, script writers, special effects men, supply, drapery, art, and music. Although technically an artist's assistant, Kelley was picked to help as a warm body and appeared on camera for the military in *How to Clean Your Gun* and *How to Act if Captured*. Kelley and George Reeves went through makeup for a hideous moment together in a film devoted to first aid in case of nuclear attack.

Will Jason directed Kelley in *Yellow Ticket*. Jason was a well-regarded man in Hollywood known mostly for his musical compositions. Kelley's performance in the Navy film *Time to Kill* and in Jason's *Yellow Ticket* caught the eye of the film industry's civilian talent scouts.[4]

On June 1, Lew Schreiber interviewed DeForest once more to see how he was doing, and to evaluate him as a prospect for 20th Century Fox. During those two years and four months of Army service, Kelley had done training films, but he had also performed in some 150 radio shows and served as master of ceremonies for a series of fifteen-minute radio programs. Indeed, his earlier radio work had served him well, and he was a steady voice with Armed Forces Radio and Television Service out of Roach Studios. He had worked with Alan Ladd in radio, and the press noted that the casting choice for *This Gun for Hire* left no hard feelings between the two very different actors. DeForest also told Schreiber about the three musical comedies at Roswell and a number of other Army productions. Once again, Schreiber sent all this off to Ivan Kahn and others at Fox. Once again, DeForest waited for positive results. Once again, none came.[5]

The only documentation of Private Kelley's Hollywood education was his listing in the summer of 1945 on Major Owen E. Crump's personnel roster. It just happened to carry Jackson Kelley, part of the "Art Crew-detached." Indeed, he was such small fry that he did not even register on anyone's radar in Hollywood. Nevertheless, Kelley knew he had received an education like no other with instructors such as Reeves, Gable, Reagan, and a cast of thousands. He acquired "a great feeling of the picture business, because at least you know you could go on a set and see somebody working. . . . I hadn't even done that . . . it turned out to be one big audition for me. It changed my life."[6]

2 On August 10, 1945, DeForest smuggled Carolyn into the Hollywood Canteen to see musician friends of his play. While Carolyn loved to dance, DeForest preferred to watch from a table, talking, listening, and drinking with friends. While they lived the high life, the old gang was always in their hearts, and Carolyn wrote to Anne, "We had quite a V-J Day anticipation party." She noted that otherwise things were dull, and then dryly wrote, "Will probably do something desperate for excitement soon—like getting married!"

It seemed everything was falling back into some semblance of what it had been before December 7, 1941. Of course, nothing would be the same, but they were hopeful that perhaps their lives would be once again in their hands. Carolyn and DeForest found their first home together, a rental on Normandie in the center of Los Angeles. With peace in the air, they became engaged to marry.

Corporal Wiltrude came home from the Army and settled in with Anne on Appleton in Long Beach. Within two weeks, Mother's party time had them evicted and out in the street. Anne pasted the eviction notice into her scrapbook. Billee scraped and put a down payment on a small house for them. She then sent for the Great Dane Guinevere, an honorary WAAC she had adopted just before her discharge.

On August 15, the country celebrated V-J Day, and Anne got drunk for the first time ever on French 75s—and as she recalls, it was champagne, lemon juice, sugar, and gin.

Anne wrote and worked for radio and got married. Bette hardly knew her husband and soon got a divorce. The Fosholdts seemed to pick up where they left off, making movies and enjoying their Long Beach lives.

DeForest's brother, Casey, served with the Trail Blazers, and he swore that upon a safe return home, he would never leave Atlanta. The

Reverend Kelley and Clora returned to Georgia and their lives among the Kelleys.[7]

DeForest kept up his writing to Joe Laden, but no one had heard from him. Irving Ravetch and Barney Girard were working full tilt inside the studios, marrying and setting up new lives as grown men in Los Angeles. They seemed to be heading out on separate courses, independent and disappearing from view. Grace Hartung continued at the Chat 'N Nibble, wondering about all those boys and missing DeForest Kelley. He had come to visit her only once since he went into the Army, but he wrote a note or called now and then, and Grace went on with her life, wishing him well and keeping him in her heart.

Carolyn's friend from Calship, Aileen Pickering, was a vital presence, determined to live an adventure, a full, headlong dash into life for all the years she might have before her. She was often in Hollywood getting bit parts at the studios, jobs that paid better than a lot of other things a young woman could do.

Of all the gang, Aileen remembers that DeForest was the one who would become the actor, because the old boy was trying to escape the solitary person he was, that way he could escape the small world inside himself. Aileen saw through him, and DeForest knew it.

Sure, he smoked and smoldered, but he looked almost exclusively inward for answers, and he looked to his art for outlet. Sometimes charmed, sometimes confounded, Aileen recognized that she and Kelley were in a fix, because he was attracted to her kind of energy. Carolyn was an all-encompassing embrace, and Aileen was a shooting star. Before letting things go too far, Aileen decided for him. "Marry Carolyn," she told him. Even then, he went on for months, into the fall of 1945, head over heels in love with Carolyn but too tentative to make the leap.

Aileen thought it rather amusing, then, that he was in such a rush the morning of September 7, 1945. She tells the story: On the morning of September 7, she was getting ready to go to the beach when De and Carolyn called. "Stand up for us!" they shouted through the phone lines from their cottage on Normandie. At first, Aileen had to turn them down. She told them she was going to spend a few hours on the beach. She told them her uncle was visiting. He had been a prisoner of war in Germany for two years; before that, he had been a ball turret gunner, and he had been badly burned when his plane was shot down. "Bring him!" they shouted.

At the Los Angeles Municipal Court, they piled out of Aileen's car and went in pursuit of a judge they had heard of who would marry them for free. De and Carolyn had twenty-five-cent Indian wedding rings. No one was quite ready, and De seemed to be in an awful hurry. Aileen and her Uncle Donald and William Onstead, a boy De and Carolyn had picked up somewhere, made up the wedding party. They went in and found Arthur S. Guierieu. Aileen recalls: "I was going to the beach, so there I was in shorts, and the judge presiding looks up at us in the back of the courtroom and says, 'You young lady with shorts, you'll have to leave.' We all got up and left."

Outside, De and Carolyn had to choose their best man, and they couldn't decide how to be fair. So De flipped a coin, and the boy, William Onstead, became their best man. They returned to see the judge, who was by then back in his chambers and more welcoming to the young party, and the Kelleys were married in the blink of an eye, Aileen at their side in her red shirt and white shorts.[8]

Two days later, Mrs. DeForest Kelley wrote to Anne: "We were married Friday afternoon and are just getting settled in our little house 1203½ Normandie. I lost my job Friday, so we're really starting from scratch." Her trademark *CMK* was used for the first time, for Carolyn Meagher Kelley.

Aileen confirms that they were poor as church mice. She brought them sheets and towels stolen from the motel where she stayed on the nights she worked in Hollywood. As far as she knew, they didn't even have a change of shoes.

A lifetime later, Aileen reflected on the Kelleys and her life with them. She admits her nature was in sharp contrast with her good friends. Of Carolyn and De, Aileen says, "We just really loved each other in ways you don't get that often, you know." She loved their soft hearts, their loyalty and humor, but their cautiousness drove her just a little nuts. Their domestic lives she described as "boring as hammered owl shit."

They had it all planned out. They would live and eat off DeForest's pay as an Army private until Carolyn got a job. She was the head of their small household. DeForest would be her world, and she would be his. She wanted her man glued to her hip, heart, and mind, and she to his. "Oh, to be chained, my love," he once had written soulfully to her. To mean so much to one person was completely captivating for DeForest. And Carolyn was the ways and the means that would make his dreams reality. She could interpret a confusing world and intercept it before it became disruptive to his nature. With her shrewdness as a buffer, DeForest could develop as an actor in a rather sheltered environment. He trusted her instincts. She knew what was what. Carolyn was his foundation; she became the very Earth to him.[9]

3 With the war finished, the Army Air Force proudly and happily pulled the plug on the First Motion Picture Unit. So swiftly did production cease and the book close on the FMPU that before anyone knew it, the entire operation was being boxed up and taken by railroad from Culver City to Colorado. Private Jackson D. Kelley was now a carpenter among boxes and crates, materials and bracing made to freight the entire operation to storage. The nation moved its attention away from bloody war to cold war; government filmmakers turned to documenting nuclear testing and the second half of the twentieth century. Entertainments also dismissed the war, often in favor of the forbidding or ridiculous nuclear menace themes of B-movie science fiction. Overall, it seemed that the sooner the world war was forgotten, militarily, politically, and socially, the better.[10]

Finally, at the "convenience of the government," it was time for Kelley to be mustered out. The central command for that military function was clear over the Rockies at Lowery Field in Colorado. George Reeves, by then a great friend of DeForest's, was also assigned to Lowery field for his last weeks in the Army. It is uncertain if the fellows were on orders or on a lark, but Kelley and Reeves got hold of transportation and started off for the nearby town of Steamboat Springs. DeForest recalled, "We picked up another soldier on the way. [Then, late in the trip,] it began to snow, and we're crawling up in these mountains, and we had a bottle of bourbon with us in the car. It was a Ford coupe of some sort, and the three of us are riding along, and suddenly the car just froze in motion, and we had no idea . . . it was night, so we sat there, and we really thought we were gonna freeze to death." At the top of Rabbit Ears Pass in a blizzard, Kelley and Reeves faced facts. No one passed them, nor were they going to, because they were caught in a blizzard. Nature called, and one of the fellows walked a little distance from the others and saw the lights of Steamboat Springs. Reeves took the wheel and shouldered the front of the car. "We pushed the car. We were freezin' to death," DeForest remembered. Reeves's size sure helped, and with some desperate resolve, they pushed that car up over the ridge and topped it. "Man, I tell ya, we were pourin' that bourbon down to keep warm, and then we coasted all the way downhill to this little village." They found a small hotel but could rouse no one, so they broke in and wrapped up in the rugs on the floors of the lobby and survived. The sheriff came by and rousted them. He found them harmless but liquored up, so he put them in jail for the night.[11]

Not long after this brush with eternity, as DeForest recalled, "I was sitting on a bunk . . . at Lowery Field, when a telegram came through from Bill Meiklejohn at Paramount and said, 'We're prepared to offer you a seven-year contract,' and I almost fell off my bunk." Finally, DeForest had entrée to the big time in Hollywood. This was it.[12]

Six days after his twenty-sixth birthday, on January 26, 1946, DeForest telegrammed Carolyn on Normandie: "Will be a civilian Monday at 3 o'clock will wire place and arrival date discontinue correspondence I love you—de."

At Lowery Field, Army Air Force Separation Base, Jackson D. Kelley became a civilian. He was filled out at 165 pounds, five-foot-ten in his socks, with wavy hair and just the hint of creases under the eyes. A man ready to go home to a new wife and a future with Paramount Studios. From the disbursing officer, he got his mustering-out pay and travel allowance, totaling a little less than $200. He had his American Theater Ribbon and World War II Victory Medal. He pressed his right thumb on the inkpad and leaned hard onto box 34 of his discharge paper. He had no training or schooling to list on the papers, though he had some academic courses. When asked his civilian occupation for the record of separation, he responded, "Entertainer." He continued his insurance. He was government surplus after two years, ten months, and thirteen days. He was a very lucky man, and he knew it. He took back his name and identity and ran for it.[13]

DeForest kept up his letter writing to the silent Joe Laden. Joe couldn't believe this guy. An artist, right, then he made training films, right, then he's discovered, yeah, and now he's going home. And he's got a contract with a studio before he is discharged! Laden could only laugh in amazement and admiration for his friend and the sweetness of his life. Someone had to win at this game; if not Joe, then let it be DeForest. Joe stayed away from his old friends for a while. It seemed as if the war had done something to him, the world had changed in his soul, or his soul had changed in the world. Maybe he would feel better in a while; he'd get in touch with them when he was ready.[14]

4 On February 20, 1946, DeForest collected his Paramount identification card and signed the dotted line for another enlistment, this time with the studio system. A week later, the *Evening Herald-Express* carried the good news to Long Beach, that DeForest Kelley had finally made it into a real movie studio without having to scale a fence. The actual contract was less than seven years; in fact, it was a term of one year with the studio's option to renew for one or two years at a rate of $150 per week for the first year and then $200 per week in the second. In each case, there were forty weeks guaranteed. He would not get additional salary for wardrobe time or publicity outings and was subject to layoffs as Paramount determined. Modest, but Kelley was happy to get the deal. He understood the ways of the studio system and knew he could be groomed, trained, and cultivated toward ever larger roles, while paying his dues as a stock player. He could also be loaned out to other corporations. He knew as a stock player he would be part of an industry that saw him as a property that could be used to its maximum value—or ignored—and always at the corporation's convenience and for its benefit. That was the way of things as they had been for decades. Other actors had great or at least good success within the studio system, and in early 1946, Kelley had no reason to think he would not be one of them.

A few months later, he wryly observed, "I had to join the Army to make a Navy picture to become an actor," or so he told A. C. Lyles, a hungry young publicist for producers William Pine and William Thomas and Paramount Studios. Kelley was on his way.[15]

Fear in the Night was not an A movie or a B movie—it was rather more of a C movie. But it was heaven-sent for a young actor barely out of the Army for a few weeks, and DeForest was in the odd and enviable position of being not only in every scene but narrator and subject of the entire production. This was the low-budget tale of Vince Grayson, played by DeForest, a young man hypnotized and manipulated into an act of murder, tormented by insane thoughts, and in real jeopardy.

A William Irish story, *Fear in the Night* was directed and written by Maxwell Shane. It was Shane's first outing as a director. Paul Kelly, a veteran actor who was known for better productions but had done real hard time in prison for murder, was cast as the rough policeman who drives the confused Vince Grayson through a harrowing guessing game toward the truth.[16]

DeForest rose at five A.M. and was at the studio for makeup at six-thirty, then to work at seven. Around lunchtime, a station wagon would come around, and all the actors piled in for a good meal at the Brown Derby. For DeForest's drowning scene, they dunked him in Baldwin Lake in the dead of winter, and for his suicide scene, they dangled him from a tenth-floor window of a midtown building. The crowd below did not know it was a movie, and some of the expressions caught on film were the genuine reactions of pedestrians. Twelve days and $200,000 did the trick. DeForest had his first studio movie in the can.

During his time on *Fear in the Night,* DeForest made a great friend in A. C., or "Ace," Lyles. Lyles had been a junior reporter at fourteen for the *Jacksonville Journal* and somehow had managed to interview Hoover, Roosevelt, and other newsmakers—and he did so while working nights at the local Paramount theater. After high school, he traveled west to Paramount Studios and became the mail clerk. He quickly worked his way into the publicity department. During the war, he served three years as an Army Air Corps liaison officer for Admiral Nimitz. Now, back in Hollywood, he handled the publicity for *Fear in the Night* and wrote copy for the film's star, the new Paramount prospect, DeForest Kelley. By then, it seemed A.C. knew everyone, or everyone knew him; his idols were also his friends, among them James Cagney, Ronald Reagan, and, soon, DeForest Kelley. A.C. was pure Hollywood and unfailingly attracted to the genuine American. The kind that came to mind when A.C. looked at Kelley was "Boy Scout." A.C. was typical of old Hollywood, a schmoozer, a barker, and a man on the make; nevertheless, he was real in his love for his friends, and once pledged, he was loyal and true. Lyles was good for a new actor to have in his corner, and DeForest invited this big, ambitious man into his circle on Normandie. Besides, with A.C. around, Kelley could just relax and let Lyles do the entertaining.[17]

Grace Hartung remembers that the preview of *Fear in the Night* took place at a small theater in Los Angeles. It was the last time she saw DeForest Kelley with her own eyes. Grace got an invitation in the mail and decided to take her Swedish cook and her son. That night outside the theater, she was lost in the crowd when a big doorman told them to clear the way and let Grace through. It was the first time she felt that she had clout. They enjoyed the picture. Afterward, the cast came out to sign autographs. When Kelley found her and signed his autograph, he said to her quietly, "You know, you'll be able to sell this for a lot of money someday." Grace was beside herself with happiness for him.[18]

Some weeks later, Reverend Kelley and Clora, who were residing on Roswell Road in Atlanta, went to see *Fear in the Night*. "It's him!" they both exclaimed the first time his face came on the screen. The *Atlanta Journal* was there with the Kelleys to photograph their pride at their son's triumph. DeForest's parents had come around, his mother lit with joy. From this beginning, certainly DeForest would be marked for success by the studio system as he made his apprentice's way through films and exercises. There was no limit to what their boy could do now.[19]

The reviews of the film came in through February, March, and April 1947. At *Newsweek*, they characterized the seventy-one-minute melodrama as a "strange kind of movie . . . fairly interesting . . . it succumbs to choppy continuity and mediocre acting . . . a B picture on a subject [hypnotism] over its depth." Finally, "with more expert telling, it might have been a good picture." Another, more promotional review called it "the finest entertainment upon which Pine-

Thomas has ever placed a trademark." *Star Trek* producer Harve Bennett, who grew up during this era of filmmaking, agrees with that assessment, remembering that William Pine and William Thomas were known around town as the "Two Dollar Bills," famous for churning out low-budget motion pictures of questionable artistry. Most sources agreed the picture was carried on the broad shoulders of Paul Kelly. DeForest was characterized as promising and unpracticed and, rather hurtfully, as "dopey" by the *New York Times. Motion Picture Daily* commented that Kelley's Vince Grayson was a young hero whose "only distinctive characteristic is an extreme docility."[20]

In general, one could summarize from the reviews that DeForest was convincing as a gentle fellow who was bewildered, vulnerable, and tormented. Harve Bennett reflected on *Fear in the Night* and young Kelley, "I see the primary gears he learns to define and use later." Where Kelley went a little over the top in his characterization in scenes of fight or flight, those are the instances where the director is lacking, and not young Kelley. "I think he was told to pop his eyes. . . . This is not a well-directed picture . . . but it's priceless because it is so pure. . . . It is such a classic example of a cheap, low-budget B-picture of the period, of film noir or a bad imitation thereof."

Had he been a producer then, Bennett might have called DeForest in to read. "He has a quality, and if I were looking for that quality, I would say let's read this guy. . . . The quality is vulnerability—and sweetness. . . . The one great achievement of the role—and it's a very very difficult role to do this with—is to achieve audience sympathy while essentially doing nothing. And that, of course, is the essence of De on the screen. You like him. Likability never failed him. Even when he's asked to be this inexplicable, strange man."

Indeed, all of the characteristics of his first film performance as Vince Grayson were truly parts of DeForest Kelley. Just standing there, looking confused, he drew the eye of the viewer regardless of what was going on in the scene. He evoked a mysteriously maternal response in the feminine heart. Everything DeForest Kelley was or would be as an actor was there nascent in *Fear in the Night,* and Bennett wistfully concludes, "It's a joy to see him because he's so beautiful at that age."[21]

Women responded to the actor on film as they did to the young man in life. With his first film, DeForest established a pattern that ran throughout his career: he was more popular with the audience than he was with the critics or the industry. *Screen Romances* noticed his appeal with the ladies and presented a spread about *Fear in the Night*.[22]

The film was a sleeper, and in some places, it was more popular than the A movie it was distributed with. DeForest's contract was freshly renewed for another year at $200 per week. He was given promotional materials, Paramount cards, and head shots for his own use. Anne Jolly kept a clipping announcing, "DeForest is regarded now as Paramount's new bid for stardom."[23]

5 Kelley was quickly learning the protocols of good professional relations. At Paramount, he had wonderful examples of what to do and what not to do. While many young people fell victim to the excesses and temptations of the industry, DeForest seemed older than all that, and the studio people responded to his steadiness by welcoming him as a fellow artist on the lot. He enjoyed champagne with the great stars and coffee at the canteen with the rising and falling ones. He learned the ropes of the profession by observation, along with the manners and courtesies expected of a real professional. Small kindnesses, gifts of gratitude, and a genuine concern for his fellows went a long way with studio workers, crewmen, and the public. DeForest was a natural among celebrities and genuine screen legends.[24]

The Kelleys treated themselves to a well-earned vacation at Laguna and Will Rogers Park. The beach bums were Hollywood friends and industry people. De was such a devoté of the sea that the beach bums named a little shallow of gentle water Kelley's Cove. On one occasion, a shark sighting forced De to demonstrate just how good a swimmer he was as he frantically raced to make land before becoming lunch. Otherwise, DeForest and Carolyn managed to do nothing with great skill and style. These were some of the happiest days of the young marriage. De was as dark and bleached in the sun as he had been years before. Carolyn was a cool sophisticate in the shade of her bungalow.

On one occasion, DeForest found himself down on the Santa

Monica pier wandering through all the beachside entertainments. He came upon a palm reader and thought he'd take a chance. The seer examined his slender hands, and he confidently awaited her confirmation of his future achievements. He got something else. The reader said he would not accomplish much until after he was forty. Forty? Here he was with a motion-picture contract and stardom just around the curve. Forty? He would be retired by then! He tried to shrug off this new worry. He wouldn't—couldn't—believe such a ridiculous prediction.[25]

6 The Variety Clubs of America was a philanthropic organization that began with eleven showmen in the late 1920s. By 1946, it had raised some $12 million for poor children without consideration of race, creed, or color. The money was raised in a variety of ways, from stage shows to a new Paramount film effort. The production also served as a vehicle for its own talent, such as Billy DeWolfe, Red Skelton, Dorothy Lamour, and Alan Ladd. The show was a fast-paced mélange of skits held together by three young people who were written in to carry a mistaken identity theme throughout the production. Olga San Juan as the over-the-top star wannabe, Mary Hatcher as the talented Variety Girl, and DeForest Kelley as the handsome though flustered young talent scout.[26]

Kelley was called in for the Paramount film in the fall of 1946, "They told me it was a thankless role," DeForest said to the *L.A. Times*. It was, but the gracious young man kept the real heartache far away from reporters and fellow performers. Life in the studio system was tightly controlled. A young contract player was very limited in his right to refuse work. DeForest had already done so, to the point that he was threatened with contract suspension. "Several studios wanted to borrow me, but Paramount insisted on putting me into *Variety Girl*. I made a real beef." He could only make good through the studio's graces, and yet his studio was denying him the roles he needed to be their valuable property. There was desperation and frustration throughout the industry.[27]

As the entire studio assembled for director George Marshall's *Va-*

riety Girl, DeForest was assigned a significant supporting role. He swallowed his pride as a potential leading man and plunged into this broad comedy of celebrity, cameos, and silliness. At times, he seemed embarrassed to be there. He was uncomfortable with the lack of dignity surrounding the story and the silliness of the skits. He imbued his character with a little strength of integrity, through his voice, hands, or stance; somehow, he managed to communicate his personal truth through the nonsense. His fittings for wardrobe took longer than the whole shooting schedule of *Fear in the Night*. His salary was about equal to the cost of one of costar Mary Hatcher's costumes. Alan Ladd was paid $4,500 for one day's work; Bob Hope received $75,000 for two. Olga San Juan received $15,000 for working October through December on the film. Kelley was paid $1,400 for his entire commitment of the same length.[28]

DeForest was a diplomat and not inclined to express the frustration of his career to reporters. He focused on, and spoke highly of, the Paramount people, especially Bing Crosby, who put a sheltering arm around Kelley's shoulders. "I'll tell you, I was darned nervous until Bing Crosby and other troupers calmed me down helping me with dialogue etc.," he told an *L.A. Times* reporter. He posed with Bob Hope and other stars of the time. In late 1946, the work was mercifully finished; Kelley could move on to other roles and try to forget *Variety Girl*.[29]

On January 7, 1947, DeForest wrote his folks in Atlanta that he was hoping for a new movie right away. He expressed his continued gratitude to his parents and promised he would visit. Carolyn then sat down to write one of her many letters to her old gal pals from the Long Beach days. To Aileen, she declared that the Kelleys were on the wagon after a long round of parties—"sooo tired of it all truly." She reported that just a few days earlier, they had bid farewell to Olga San Juan, who was off to New York for promotional work. Apparently, De was not included in the buildup, for she said, "wish we had the same chance—we'd welcome with open arms." Earlier, they had been to one of Michael Harvey's poker parties—"the JDK's are shirtless, as gamblers we'd make a good song and dance team." Most recently, there was yet another party at Normandie with all the usual characters, including Tom Drake, who was an up-and-coming talent, known around town and everywhere else as "the boy next door" in Judy Garland's *Meet Me in St. Louis*. Tom was a handful. Carolyn wrote that he had spent the evening very drunk and rolling on the lawn, till five A.M. They tried to get him to go home, but he just wouldn't stop talking. Then, proudly, Carolyn wrote Aileen that things were getting better with De's success: "my darling husband . . . bought me a suede full-length coat . . . mighty lush."[30]

After seeing *Fear in the Night*, young Alice Meyers of California founded the DeForest Kelley Fan Club in April 1947. She wrote him long letters in tight teenage script. Her letters were encouraging. She wrote that she believed he was a great actor and obviously a very good man. The Kelleys found her devotion sweet, and they even met with her. They took pictures of each other and shared gifts. DeForest found such attention rather inexplicable but warming and pleasant nevertheless.[31]

Although DeForest had not been included in the preliminary buildup for *Variety Girl,* publicity plans changed in the summer of 1947, when the premiere of *Variety Girl* was held in Atlanta. DeForest and Carolyn were dispatched along with crazed bandleader Spike Jones to promote the film. Of course, the local-boy-makes-good story came off well in Atlanta. The *Atlanta Journal Magazine* dubbed him the "Georgia Cinderella boy" and described him as the romantic interest in the movie. He saw *Variety Girl* with his parents and Carolyn at the Fox Theater. He also spoke candidly to *Journal* reporter Olive Ann Burns about his time in Hollywood. He admitted that he was still a raw recruit and had his hands full learning all the movement and technique, along with the terminology of film craft. "You have to learn to walk chalk at the same time you're trying to remember lines." Then a director might instruct, "Don't step away from the inky-dinky." DeForest explained that the inky-dinky was "a beadlike ray which they shine on your face to make your eyes brighter." There were other things, like "Cheek to the right" which meant "I'm cross-eyed." DeForest chuckled. "Say the camera is aimed over the girl's left shoulder while I'm making love to her. If I forget and look into her face—the natural thing to do, you know—the director reminds me to cheek right [focus beyond her head]. [Otherwise,] from the camera's angle at such close range, the eyes look crossed." Also, "if the director detects the slightest trace [of Southern accent], it's death. I was lucky—I got kidded out of mine by theater friends."

Then DeForest shared a little of his inner heart, insisting the most important quality for success was "*Sincerity*, onstage and off." His professional and personal lives were both subject to his own code of conduct. Then, of course, there was doggedness: "Getting into the movies takes determination more than anything—except talent. You've got to set your mind on a goal and keep it there. To do that, you must have faith in yourself and what you want, because once you start back, you're lost." He believed his luck had changed when he married. However, "romantic leads in two movies don't put an actor in the ranks of the 40 stars I worked with in *Variety Girl*. . . . Already seven of the eleven fellows who got contracts through government training films have been given the brush-off, and that knowledge is enough to keep my feet on the ground!" Then he concluded that if he did reach stardom, he would not "go Hollywood," as long as he kept his old friends and made new ones who shared his cherished values.

On his return to Los Angeles, he was interviewed about his trip to Atlanta. "They treated me royally, but because my screen credit was so microscopic, I got nervous about personal appearances. However, they put my name on the marquee and had me sign souvenir programs and gave me a beautiful gold watch, so this was a big success." But his conservative nature eliminated any ideas of a big head: "The way they are laying people off these days makes one stop and think. At one time, they had thirty young actors testing [at Paramount,] but now I'm one of three newcomers left. So I'm not buying any Beverly Hills mansions. In fact, there is an automobile salesman's job waiting . . . just in case." On the other hand, he sheepishly admitted to reporter John L. Scott, "my fan mail is picking up . . . from 20 letters a week to 200."[32]

His kind of self-effacing humor was developed, DeForest said, during those shifts as clean-up boy in the surgery rooms of the Long Beach hospital. Gentle modesty and a quick wit came to his aid then and now at the cusp of stardom. DeForest seemed to enjoy sharing his experiences with reporters. He told one, "The other day I met actor John Lund near the studio . . . and he cracked, 'De, they sure must have been worried about your acting, putting in all those stars to help you out.' He sure had me there, didn't he?"[33]

7 Bette Creutze often came by to see the Kelleys on Normandie. She slept with Carolyn while De slept on the couch. Once she was awakened late at night by a rustling outside. She woke her friends. "Aw, we're kinda used to it," De explained, adding that the landlord had a habit of peeking in the windows.

He never said much about the time lost and damage to his career the war had caused. He just smiled and soldiered on. The little house on Normandie certainly benefited from De's abundant spare time. Spotless and orderly was the way he and Carolyn liked it. The tiny place was a refuge, a haven, and a place for the introspective actor to keep his mental and emotional house in order. DeForest's simplicity allowed him to take pleasure in the most ordinary things.

The war had taken so much away from De's career, but his friends recall that he never seemed bitter about it. Bette was awed by their love, as poor and happy as they were. She remembers well the depths of Carolyn's devotion. Carolyn wanted De to be happy more than anything in this world, and that meant he acted; that meant she worked the daily grind in a pink-collar workforce as a secretary, mostly pounding away on the stiff keys of black anvil typewriters, when all the while all she really wanted to do was stay at home and keep house and have party time.[34]

Anne Jolly was married for a short time, then she became Long Beach's first patrolwoman with lockups and paddy wagons and adventure on the Long Beach police force. Hers was a gentle heart, but she did right well among the uniformed patrolmen. They were gentlemen to her, and she was a friend to them as well as a competent fellow officer. DeForest and Carolyn often came and got her at night after her shift and brought her up to Hollywoodland for the weekend. Anne remembers one experience with a grimace: "I was seeing them all the time on Normandie. I got this terrible sore throat—I've got to go home," she told them. She knew it was going to be bad. They had her stay the night. Very early the next morning, DeForest got up and got dressed and went out and got her some kerosene she was supposed to gargle with. "If it had been anyone else but De, I would have said, 'Forget you!' He said do it, and I did it." She got on the Pacific Electric, and by the time she got home, she was so sick a nurse was sent for. It turned out to be scarlet fever.[35]

Once she was recovered, party time resumed with Anne, DeForest, Carolyn, and Tom Drake, the young and successful contract player. They had so much fun on those weekends—especially with Nick and Nora, the hamsters that Tom carried around with him. Carolyn loved to play with them. She'd let them loose in her sweater. Eek! But she loved it. The Kelleys thought Anne and Tom ought to hit it off, and all the while Anne thought Tom was a little in love with Carolyn. He surely helped them out often enough, when they were on their financial uppers. Tom was making big bucks, and Spencer Tracy thought he was the best on the MGM lot and was going to be the next great star. While Tom was the boy next door, a romantic star on the rise, DeForest was hoping to be something the same—to continue his youthful leads, to do good work as frequently as possible, and to make a name for himself while he made a living learning his trade.[36]

Tom Drake understood and played the old Hollywood game and played it well. He sometimes was able to drag DeForest to a gala or an awards ceremony, but rarely. The Kelleys kept pretty close to home. Even A. C. Lyles could not persuade the Kelleys to make the rounds of Hollywood. By nature, he was not a schmoozer or a go-getter; nevertheless, De needed to get out there and let more people know and appreciate him the way Drake, Lyles, and Reeves did. At least, that would help. Visibility in those days made people remember—a name could come up at casting time.

Kelley was well aware of all the things he was not doing to promote himself and his career. Carolyn worked a hard fifty-hour week for her small paychecks, and honestly, it exhausted her. How could he then ask her to play a game she didn't like with people she didn't know and would have to kowtow to? And he was reluctant to go without her— after all, she made it possible for him to sit at home waiting for the phone to ring. And besides, everyone knew the toll that the Hollywood lifestyle took on marriages. DeForest also knew full well that this schmoozing was no guarantee of success, and the happiness Carolyn found with him in her limited leisure time was worth the risk. So DeForest was unwilling to make a unified and prolonged push into the consciousness of Hollywood. Even as the trajectory of his career seemed to reach an early and disappointing apex, his devotion to his wife and to his marriage remained paramount.[37]

The realities of postwar Hollywood confirm his decision as truly wise, especially for such a young man. There was little he could do to improve his career, as forces beyond his control were gathering against his leading-man aspirations. As a good student of the industry, he knew the truth: after the war, returning GIs and their girls flocked to the movie theaters and 1946 went down as the best year ever. But in no time, those same GIs were settling down with their new families in areas far from the urban theaters, and ticket sales plummeted.[38]

Just as the doors of Hollywood opened to DeForest, the studio system failed. Paramount man Rolf Larsen recalled that those were the last of the Hollywood glamour days, and there was something of a war between the studios and the talent. Contract players like DeForest fought for their rights as performers and people. The end of the decade was bringing about a lot of changes in unions and in society. It was clear that the studio system was in reality a great and careless manipulation of people. On the up side, there was stardom and big money; but on the down side, there were so many talented people who were lost in the system. Johnny Johnson, for example, was a man whose talent rivaled Bing Crosby's. Rolf Larsen recalled that Paramount bought Johnson under a long-term contract and then kept him in cameos, where he would be fed and cared for but where he was no threat to Crosby or Paramount. Larsen recalls that there were many other stories like Johnny Johnson's.

The final blow was the inflation that rocked Los Angeles just after the war. By 1947, the cost of living was three times the prewar level and twice what it had been only two years before. Just making a living was a struggle.[39]

Unease in Hollywood grew as the government moved to dismantle the studio monopolies of film rights and distributions. After the Paramount Supreme Court decree, the studio system was broken up. Labor unions and strikes then became part of the Hollywood scene. The "Red Scare" sent tremors through the creative industry and the country. The House Un-American Activities Committee had been around since the 1930s, but now it was empowered as never before to pursue the Communist threat in Hollywood. The warmth and optimism that once had characterized the wartime film industry shattered, leaving careers in ruin and a pall of suspicion everywhere. De-Forest was as nonpolitical as a man could be, but he could not escape the changed environment. Arm-in-arm, the Kelleys faced the uncertainty of postwar Hollywood. Now the goodwill of Tom Drake, George Reeves, A. C. Lyles, and others was more important than ever, but they, too, were facing uncertain times.[40]

8 Joe Laden called on his old friend DeForest. De told him to come back out to California. Joe belonged in Hollywood, and he could help De out when he made it big, or so DeForest cajoled his friend. De had his contract, Carolyn, and a little house—and Joe could stay with them. Carolyn got him an Army cot to sleep on and crammed it into that tiny cottage she called the "outhouse." Maybe he had a chance if he could make Normandie more real than freezing flights through the *ack-ack* and flames.

Joe remembers that the Normandie parties included some glamorous people, who were beginning to annoy Joe with their la-de-da kissy-face nonsense. A lot of the guys were 4F studio contract players—and those trust fund whining little boys rubbed Joe all the wrong ways. And there was that kid who came to the party with Judy Garland's sister, the *Meet Me in St. Louis* boy, Tom Drake—with his $1,500-a-week term contract and his smart mouth. Laden lost it one night, threw Drake out of Normandie, and whacked him good. De came to Tom's rescue and pleaded with Joe never to do such a thing again at Normandie—ever.

Joe believed that De had a glorious future with the studios; if a guy like Joe stuck around, he would just make a mess of everything for De. Joe packed up and left the Kelleys for a life of wandering. Joe and De never really let go of each other. Through the mail, the phone, or an occasional visit, DeForest remembered and honored his friend. De's blood brother and his Long Beach brother were both living with the consequences of a war that no one wanted to remember.[41]

Part Two

The Actor's Life

Chapter V
The Cold Hunger
1947–1952

*" 'It is important to remember that Fred Astaire's Ginger Rogers
did everything Fred did, backwards and in high heels.' "*
—CAROLYN KELLEY, 1999

In late November 1947, DeForest was set to play Lieutenant Parker in
Sealed Verdict, a drama of political intrigue starring Ray Milland and
Broderick Crawford and directed by Lewis Allen. He did the testing
and lineups earlier in the month, but before shooting actually began,
DeForest was suddenly replaced by stock actor Dan Tobin. Other supporting actors were also replaced by less expensive stock talent. Each
replacement saved the production money. The Tobin switch saved a
little more than three thousand dollars.

With *Sealed Verdict,* DeForest's long trek of disappointments
began. The few heady months in 1946 and 1947 were past. He was in
a no-man's-land between character actor and bit player. The status of
featured player and the promise of another star billing seemed suddenly very far away indeed.[1]

While he was living on Normandie, a poem found DeForest Kelley,
probably by way of Clora. He kept "The Actor's Prayer" in his wallet
for years until it became nearly transparent. His prayers were private,
and his troubles were kept largely to himself. He was a curiosity even
to those who loved him.[2]

The Hollywood trenches were crowded with former contract players willing to accept virtually anything just to have work. True, the

Paramount Supreme Court decree and other antitrust cases demolished the old studio power and thereby loosened the bonds of an actor's servitude, but the ruling also destroyed the valuable system of apprenticeship so important to promising newcomers like DeForest Kelley. By 1948, one-third of the Hollywood workforce had been cut away.[3]

By then, George Reeves was a Normandie regular, and Aileen Pickering recalls him as pleasant, big, and quiet. He had troubles with his new wife, Eleanora Needles, and hand-in-hand with that, he found no alternative but to work in increasingly low-budget vehicles. Reeves was an established talent, and even this fellow was feeling the pain of the changes in the industry. For DeForest, it may have been helpful to know his career difficulties were endemic in the system and not in his focus, his craft, or his character.

In the public eye, Reeves was rather closed-mouthed and coolly distant. He did not seem to have the open personality that made Kelley a Cinderella boy with journalists. Reeves came from a much harsher world than Conyers, Georgia, and knew what gossip and Hollywood mean-spiritedness could do to a fellow. Kelley's own simplicity and "aw shucks" style seemed to smooth away sharp questions and gossip. He was new and without guile, and he was his own best publicist. Reeves seemed much older, wary and watchful of Hollywood machinations. Reeves was a veteran of the Pasadena Playhouse, a well-endowed sister of the Long Beach Community Playhouse. He was an established and talented actor, a man of good heart and genuine warmth.

Of course, everyone recalled his immortal few moments in *Gone With the Wind*, but that was forever ago in the mind of Hollywood. There were many other movies, such as *Smashing the Money Ring*, *Torrid Zone*, *The Fighting 69th*, *Border Patrol*, and the highly praised *So Proudly We Hail*. Toward the end of 1943, Reeves was on the edge of stardom, and then he was drafted. He did his time at Culver City with DeForest, on the stage, in radio shows, and in training films. He traveled with shows and did part of his service in New York.

Then, in postwar Hollywood and New York, Reeves pounded the pavement, trying to recover the promising career that had been taken from him five years earlier. He appeared for a moment in *Variety Girl* and began working for Paramount with fair success in B movies.[4]

2 In the late 1940s, the movies still belonged to older men like thirty-two-year-old Gregory Peck. A promising new actor appeared in 1947, with an Alan Ladd stoicism and a unique cold rage. Richard Widmark established himself in *Kiss of Death;* this newcomer was also years older than Kelley. Burt Lancaster, Kirk Douglas, even old Long Beach Playhouse actor Robert Mitchum acted older, tougher, more reckless, more dark. They were. Compounding Kelley's youth problem was the fact that he was not stoic or dark or brooding, and this was not a time for gentle young men or romantic heroes in adult cinema. Neither was this a time for young men with little classical training—for such men would have to compete with Broadway veterans as well as Hollywood's entrenched elite for the few roles worth fighting for. The industry had Martin and Lewis, Abbott and Costello, film noir, westerns, light comedy, and musicals. All told, Tom Drake was the best bet for success in the late 1940s. This darling "boy next door" kept working and drinking, and his prospects were still good. But it seemed that Reeves and Kelley had nowhere to go.

Thirty percent of the film releases in the late 1940s were westerns, mindless kid stuff, or adult action dramas, but they were all somehow morality plays. The westerns were an older man's venue, with bright, dominant stars and stock-company cronyism. Debonair young Kelley and westerns were an even less likely pair than Kelley and comedy. *Variety Girl* was a pale example of what he could do in humorous vehicles. Although most agreed that Kelley was a very funny man in a well-timed, understated sort of way, subtlety was not what they were looking for in 1948.

Kelley was loaned out for small religious films, then finally nothing. In 1948, Paramount let him know that his contract would not be renewed. He was the last of the Paramount bullpen, and with his dismissal the old studio system was dead. His glamour days were all history now. He was shown the gate with no more than a nod from the guard. He learned bitterly that once a contract was pulled, once a guy didn't have a going concern, the studio just forgot him—as if he never existed. He held tightly the memories of his champagne lunches with Marlene Dietrich, greetings with Gary Cooper, coffee with Clarke Gable, lunch with Bob Hope and Bing Crosby.

The semidocumentary was emerging as a new genre, and Kelley hoped he could find some success with this gritty style of filming. *Canon City* was a realistic portrayal of a contemporary Colorado jailbreak. Filmed on location, the Eagle-Lyon release starred Jeff Corey and Scott Brady. Kelley played Smalley and was billed fifth or sixth, yet his presence on the screen was momentary. Nothing else seemed to follow; the genre itself was weak and overtaken by big shows and cowboys.

It was stunning how quickly everything turned against Kelley in a matter of months. He began to cultivate a notion of fatalism about his career that empowered rather than weakened him. Perhaps that palm reader was right after all; certainly he could do nothing to change what was happening. He would have to endure and hope luck would smile upon him another day. Dogged optimism seemed stronger with DeForest than reason or despair—and with Carolyn beside him, he could not give up.[5]

The starving actor could always try radio or the stage, but these mediums paid half of nothing. Then there was the clumsy new medium of television. Friends such as Barney Girard were making their first inroads with television. Girard remained a loyal friend of the Kelleys and struggled along with them in Hollywoodland.

Girard and Kelley were young men ready to make a career in movies only to find the industry suddenly knocked to its knees. While the studios fought the spread of dreaded television with ridiculous campaigns and airs of superiority, some professionals recognized that the infant medium should be absorbed rather than resisted. Independents and industry giants made their first moves to establish television in California in the late 1940s. The B film studios were turned into television workhouses, and pioneers learned their craft on the air for all to see. The executives of Hal Roach Studios, Bing Crosby Enterprises, and Ziv Television all knew the medium would be a home entertainment power that would rival and overtake radio. Television eventually could reach the audiences the movies had lost. For guys like Kelley, television was a fighting chance to keep working in the profession.

DeForest Kelley crossed the line in 1948 and appeared on a fifteen minute skit series, *Public Prosecutor,* starring John Howard, at Fairbanks Studio for the National Broadcast Company. He played a naive kid, manipulated and dopey as could be. Actually, working the skit was nearly impossible; the technology, staging, and writing were so clumsy, it was hard for any actor to really perform. Soon, Frederick Ziv improvised and created a color dramatic program on film conceptualized for syndication. *The Cisco Kid* set the pace for the industry, and thus Ziv gave the medium the professional momentum it sorely needed. Even so, most of the television action was live in New York. DeForest had entertained ideas of trying Broadway, and television became another reason for the Kelleys to look east for a new lease on an actor's life.[6]

Finally, when even the likes of George Reeves could not catch a break in Hollywood, the idea of trying to make it in New York really took shape. In late 1949, Reeves was going to go to New York for radio, theater, and live television; so would the Kelleys and their darling Cherie Kelley, the parakeet. They decided to drive across the country together, Carolyn, Cherie, DeForest, and George.

Many years later, Kelley confessed that they saw an unidentified flying object while driving across country. He said he was riding in the back of the car; they were entering Alabama when they saw it. "This object came by at a tremendous rate of speed at a very low altitude—around 700 or 800 feet . . . it looked to be about 65 feet in length. It was a long, cigar-shaped object with green and blue flames coming out of its side." There was a soft sound like a missile, it had a red taillight flashing, and it had no wings. Once in Montgomery, the trio found a newspaper that carried stories of the sightings. Even when Kelley told the story decades later, he did not mention Reeves by name. He quietly guarded the old friendship, and, besides, some things were just too fantastic to believe.[7]

Once they got settled in Manhattan, Reeves went his own way into the city nightlife. Once again, being a devoted husband meant that Kelley was left behind.[8] Still, there were promising nibbles in New York. Kelley appeared briefly in *Duke of Chicago,* released by Republic. He played Ace Martin in the small film about boxing, reviewed as slow-paced and seemingly a lot longer than its fifty-nine minutes. More significantly, he worked for television in *Studio One* and *The Lone Ranger,* which became his bread and butter on a few occasions.[9]

DeForest was represented by the Charles Conaway Agency at 1576 Broadway. His working headshot portrayed a handsome, honest face. On the reverse, he listed seven years of stage acting in New York and Los Angeles. He claimed an equivalent of three years of radio experience, the two years under contract to Paramount, and four independent religious films. It all went nowhere. DeForest recalled: "You know, I was hustling around here running to agents' offices, and I was doing some live television and that sort of thing. Starving."[10]

The Kelleys met a tall, handsome, Italian-looking fellow by the Anglo stage name of John Walton. He had a smile that lit up a barroom and a way about him that was endearing to both Kelleys. John was a veteran of a summer stock company way out in the Pennsylvania territory, and he invited the Kelleys to jump on the bandwagon. There seemed little else to do, and tiny apartments in Manhattan were literally tiny ovens in the summer. DeForest, Carolyn, and Cherie packed up and accompanied John Walton to Pennsylvania for the summer of 1950.

In the area of Berwin, Pennsylvania, the Lakewood Theater scene was big doings. The Kenley Players assembled their young protégés, interns, and local talent and then recruited featured players such as Shelley Winters, Frank Sutton, and Victor Jory.[11]

Berwin locals housed an actor or a couple through the season, and everyone ate at the same boarding house with the little bar nearby. With the Kenley productions, everyone was used for everything, and the wives or girlfriends of the male talent were expected to step up. Carolyn walked right into the chorus line for a lot of numbers, occasionally allowing her acting talent to shine in small roles.

DeForest was such an easygoing fellow that some of the youngsters had no idea that he had been in any movies or anything. He seemed calmly pleased to focus on the work at hand. He and John Walton figured in *Finnian's Rainbow* and then one production after another. Often, they worked on three shows at once—the one onstage, the one in late rehearsal, and the one just going into production.

In September, the highlight of the season was Jack Kirkland's production of *Tobacco Road,* with none other than John Carradine to lead the troupe. Carradine would arrive for the show in his whiskers. His drinking never seemed to affect his performances, but the wine did flow. Most impressive to the Kelleys was not his capacity for wine but his gulping of Coke before he went on, so he could rudely belch at will throughout the play.

Carolyn Kelley recalls that Carradine was a stitch, and the four-some of Mr. and Mrs. Kelley, Cherie, and Carradine made for high times and rollicking laughter. It was nothing new to find all four of them in bed giggling themselves silly, Cherie perched on someone's head playing the straight man. Among such thespians, Cherie was taught to say things of no thespian consequence, such as "See De pee" and the bird's most famous line, "Fuck Hollywood," attributed to Car-radine. DeForest recalled: "John Carradine and a whole lot of actors got to know [Cherie] because we lived up over a bar in Pennsylvania. And we'd leave the bird with the bartender . . . in the evening, and she'd sit on his shoulder. . . . She became a real pet. We were very much in love with this little bird."[12]

Kelley's role in *Tobacco Road* was as Jeeter Lester's boy Dud. Carolyn went through makeup for her role as Grandma. The chemistry was good with that play. The papers celebrated his performance as a swaggering sensation, but DeForest was too modest to take curtain calls.[13]

The Chocolate Soldier was presented next. Kelley and John Walton were all done up as doll soldiers for the musical. Soon, however, it was time to pack up for the season and head back for the lovely fall and dreaded winter of New York City. By then, Walton was part of the Kelley ring of friendship, which to them was stronger than the bonds of kinship.

The Kelleys' adventurous friend Aileen Pickering went out and did what she always dreamed of doing: she learned to ride, and she learned to fly out in the Mojave Desert under the tutelage of pioneer flyer Pancho Barnes. So when she came to Manhattan to visit her rather boring friends, Aileen flew on in with one of her new gal pals. Even though she met wealthy and courageous people while racing around the country in Powder Puff Derbies and with the Ninety-nines (a sisterhood of fliers), she kept DeForest and Carolyn close to her heart. She found them in small circumstances but managing to carry on as they always had. Carolyn could walk to her secretarial work at Warner Brothers, and they had a favorite bar down the street from the apartment. Aileen listened to Cherie's new dialogue. They played and partied, and DeForest was hopeful about his theater prospects.

He had sporadic work, mostly in television, with the tinny black-and-white picture that took every nuance of his face and blurred it to a flat, rather moonlike mask. His live television credits in New York were on programs such as *Danger, The Web, Armstrong Circle Theater,* and *Crime Syndicated*.

3 Flat jumping was a New York City sport, and the Kelleys did their share of swapping one questionable domicile for another. As winter came on, they settled in a seedier section of Manhattan, on 44th Street, between 8th and 9th Avenues. DeForest often told a revealing tale: "We were very broke. . . . I was in the habit of going into the office with Cherie on my shoulder and paying the rent." He would go from his apartment to the lobby to pay cash. "So, this particular winter night, I walked in to pay the rent, and there was a little grocery store at the time right across the street, and I suddenly remembered that we needed a loaf of bread. So I walked out the door with Cherie. I had forgotten that she was on my shoulder, and as I walked out into the street, this little white parakeet flew up into the skies of New York City." He was panicked. "I ran back in and said, 'My God, Carolyn, Cherie has flown away,' and I ran back out to look for her. The first thing I saw on the sidewalk was a bunch of feathers." Stricken, he walked closer to the forlorn pile, only to discover that it was a paper bag full of chicken feathers.

He continued his search near the Martin Beck Theater. "It was a cold night. . . . There was a truck driver out front putting oil or something in a furnace in the sidewalk, and I said, 'Did you by any chance see a little bird?' He said, 'Yeah, I hoid a boid choip,' and he said, 'I think it flew up to that fifth-floor window.' So I went in and found the night man, and I pointed." The night man was sympathetic, and they searched for Cherie and investigated the most likely-looking apartment where the bird might have been taken in. Two old ladies in that apartment said yes, they had opened the window for Cherie, but she had flown up and away. So DeForest and the night man continued their search on the roof of the Whitby Apartments. In the frozen night, DeForest was making his chirping and squeaking noises for Cherie. He had the night man doing the same thing. "This wonderful guy is running around squeaking . . . I'm hysterical," DeForest admitted.

Soon someone called up to them. Cherie was down on 45th Street. There was a guy with a broom shooing Cherie off a canopy down into the street, and at each end of 8th and 9th Avenues a couple of policemen on horses had the block secured while Carolyn called Cherie from the street. The little bird flew down, Carolyn walked out and knelt down and put her finger out, Cheri got on, and Carolyn took the little bird to her bosom. DeForest always remembered and concluded that if New York was a cold city, then "it's got a warm heart." As Carolyn observed, DeForest was not an innocent, but he had innocence—his real gift was in bringing out that quality in people, even New Yorkers.[14]

Carolyn could beguile just as well as her husband. Her forte was imagination and expressions of kindness through her animal friends. To her mother's husband's bird, Chico, she wrote as Cherie Kelley. The letter was decorated with glitter and little white tufts of feathery down:

> *Dad is out. Mom is cooking turkey. We have so much to be thankful for. Our DeDe got a job in the Plainclothesman show for airing next Sunday. . . . And Fox will test him next week. . . . We got the turkey ready last night. . . . DeDe shelled chestnuts and we all three helped pick out the excess pin feathers. Yes, I got on top of that big ol' bird and helped too . . . he was dead so he didn't scare me.*[15]

Carolyn and the parakeet might put up a good front, but DeForest was scared. He admitted it then and in later years. He had been dropped from the only studio he knew, and he had been desperately scraping for two years. He was still leaning on Carolyn, who had become an executive secretary for Warner Brothers. Sure, five flights of stairs for the apartment, washing dishes in the bathtub, listening to garbage falling down the trash chute—all the charm of New York living wasn't lost on DeForest's sense of humor, but New York surely wasn't the fresh horizon he had hoped for.

In the summer of 1952, they finally got a nicer place and furnished it with the help of friends. Kelley found a great old table at the Salvation Army and refinished it to his very particular satisfaction. His hope a little refreshed, he went on pounding the pavement. Hard times kept coming.

In 1952, during a terrible hot spell, he came home at lunchtime disgusted by another promising offer that had just fallen through. He was hot and upset. Carolyn was also home at lunch. He said it first: California. "And Carolyn didn't say a word. She just got up and went to the closet and started packing. Until that moment, I never knew how unhappy she was, for three years. She never complained," DeForest recalled. She directed DeForest to go to the landlady and ask her to buy their furniture. He was in a daze, and he did as he was told. The landlady gave them fifty dollars for the lot, but he could not let go of the table. By the time he got back to the apartment, Carolyn had already called the airport, sent a wire to ask a friend to pick them up, and wired Warner Brothers to let them know she quit. The fifty dollars was used to ship DeForest's table home.[16]

Chapter VI

DeForest Lawn

1952–1956

> *"One day chicken, the next day feathers."*
> —CAROLYN KELLEY, 2001

DeForest, Carolyn, and Cherie flew home to California during the summer of 1952. Carolyn recalls that when they got back to Los Angeles, they were without a cent, poor and without prospects. Of course, Tom Drake came, picked them up at the airport, and took them in for six months. Tom drove Carolyn around and around and around looking for work. "Tom Drake was a real friend," Carolyn says with all the power she gives that charmed word.

DeForest's opportunities were no better than they had been before he left. In fact, they were worse. Carolyn recalls that the few years after their return to California were simply the hardest of their lives. Kelley's shy wit made the connection between the lovely Hollywood cemetery and his own career: "For a while, I was going to change my name to DeForest Lawn." It seemed no one remembered him, and no one gave a damn. He might as well have been planted over at Forest Lawn Cemetery for all they knew of DeForest Kelley. Now the Kelleys were dependent on the kindness of friends, the goodwill of strangers.

Their frequent guardian angel was an old friend who had lived next-door to Carolyn in Long Beach before the war. Olive LaFata had been like a sister to Carolyn since the late 1930s and although Olive had a hard row to hoe herself, she always seemed able to make room in her heart and at her table. Her son Tony grew up knowing Carolyn

Kelley was his godmother and that she and DeForest were important in their lives. Olive stood by Carolyn through her separation and divorce from Jim Dowling.

Over the years, Olive worked hard and served her community with compassion. She was "mother to the world," as Tony recalls. Moral support, making extra at meals, or growing a bigger garden were all ways she could tend to her friends and foundlings. Everyone knew that if she had one loaf of bread, she would give most of it to those less fortunate and then decide how to make the rest last for the children. The miracle was, there was always enough. Often a portion of the loaf went to the Kelleys. Olive worried that far too much of the Kelley budget was going to party time, but nevertheless she sent what she could to help them through the lean weeks and months and years. When she went shopping, she might buy extra cans of food and send it over to Carolyn and DeForest. There might be extra vegetables in the garden or a large pot of stew, and over to the Kelleys it went. Why?

Tony explains: "Mom and Carolyn were very close, and I'm sure they shared everything. . . . She did love them both a great deal. . . . I can remember clearly her talking about how Carolyn and DeForest were so close that they didn't want to be apart at all, and that they were truly meant for each other. . . . when Carolyn realized that De was the 'love of her life,' I'm sure that Mom saw how true it was." Olive did everything she could to help her friends, because she loved them both and because of the very rare love story they were living. In contrast, Olive's husband was a good-time Charlie, addicted to gambling. He meant well but could not do well. Everything the family built for themselves his schemes seemed to tear down. For young Tony, the little conversations and visits with the Kelleys touched his heart and whispered to his soul: this is how love could be.[1]

While the Kelley circle of friends surely appreciated the depth and preciousness of Carolyn and DeForest's devotion to each other, perhaps Olive knew better than most how hard it was for Carolyn to do what she was doing. Carolyn was the Kelley family security and anchor, but truth be told, her health was always precarious. There were internal troubles, peritonitis, female troubles, skeletal pains, weaknesses, and other chronic problems. There was no money to address these concerns unless there was a health crisis, and then she got only the most immediate and necessary care. They had always known that there would be no children; their world would consist only of the pair mated for life. DeForest tended to her in sickness and in health, and he jealously ensured her happiness and rest. She was one tough cookie for her man, and he took good care of her.

DeForest got some significant work, such as the lead role in the *Favorite Story* episode "The Man Who Sold His Own Shadow," a Ziv teleplay for Olympia Brewing Company. DeForest was the man who had sold his shadow for an endless supply of coins, a prelude to losing his soul. He had fair results at Ziv and took the lead in another episode for them in *Inside Out,* a tale of Cold War prisoners and a correspondent behind the Iron Curtain. This time, the correspondent himself is in the Russian prison camp. A reviewer quipped, "How you dig DeForest Kelley as the captive correspondent is preferential but there is no gainsaying that he himself is not a digger. He seemed always digging himself out of his jail cell."[2]

Hollywood was still ignoring him, and there seemed nothing DeForest could do about it. Defying logic and reason, he made a final leap of faith. In early 1953, the Kelleys moved to Beverly Hills, and Carolyn worked for an agent there. They hadn't been settled very long when Tom Doyle, the boy from Conyers, Georgia, found DeForest cooling his heels under the palm fronds and sunshine. Tom tells the tale: "I drove a bus for Greyhound Lines, and in July 1953, three drivers and I drove two busloads of Boy Scouts from Chattanooga, Tennessee, to the Boy Scout Jamboree at the Irvine Ranch south of Los Angeles, California. While there, I told the other drivers I grew up with a movie star. I looked in the phone book, and there was DeForest Kelley in the Beverly Hills phone directory. I called DeForest and said, 'Is this De from Conyers, Georgia?' "

Kelley knew it was Doyle, from his Tom Sawyer days. "DeForest told me how to get to his apartment by bus, and we spent a day together, remembering the good times at Conyers High School. DeForest's wife was away at work." De gave him an autographed studio photo just for himself and sent one for Tom's older sister, Myrtle, too. DeForest reminisced about the great biscuits she made for them when she was a classmate of Casey Kelley's. After a while, they went outside and took some snapshots. The photographs were a little blurred, but clearly DeForest was well dressed, classy, and urbane. He slouched a little, hands in trouser pockets or toying with something, a bemused grin on his face. Even in this casual moment between boyhood friends, he addressed the camera with energy and honesty.

Tom reflects: "DeForest asked me how much I made driving for Greyhound and told me to 'stay with it.' . . . 'It's much more secure than the acting business!' He said that he'd been in New York City, and in Beverly Hills now for six months with little luck. 3-D movies were popular at that time, and they said DeForest didn't have a good face for 3D!"[3]

In spite of the difficulties and uncertainties, Kelley remained one of the nice guys in the game. Bob Cornthwait recalls that there was a lot of hard competition as the film and television revolution in Hollywood created a two-tier system. An actor had an established price for film and another, much cheaper one for television. All the major studios continued to cut away talent, let new contracts run out, and lop off a few heads wherever needed. "So you had entrenched people in full competition . . . it was a tough era," Cornthwait recalls.

Cornthwait remembers that sooner or later, everyone dropped by the unemployment insurance office on Santa Monica Boulevard. "That's where you saw everybody, yes, sooner or later, and in those days, you had to stand in a line and get some sort of ticket to go and pick up at the cash window. . . . I went out the Las Palmas side exit, and there was an open convertible parked there with a young man at the wheel and a middle-aged woman seated in the back. There was De standing, leaning into it with his arms on the side of the car, talking to the man behind the wheel." Kelley looked up and recognized Cornthwait. "He said, 'Hey, Bob, have you ever met John Barrymore?' And then Barrymore looked up and said, 'I saw you last night' [in a recent film]. Now, that's one for the book, to be seen by a Barrymore. But that was typical of De that when he knows someone, he wants to introduce and share, a quietly social person, and this was true whenever I ran into him. . . . A very easy man, no pretension, no telling the grand things, no need to bolster his own ego."

Through 1953, the Kelleys lived simple, sheltered lives and enjoyed their way of doing things. Sometimes they would go to the movies, and something would come on about *Superman,* and the audience would roar—it was so exciting, as Carolyn recalls. A few years before, George Reeves had gotten mixed up with the wrong crowd, and the Kelleys lost him all together. But all that aside, the Kelleys enjoyed following Reeves's career and his triumph.[4]

When the television series *Superman* aired nationwide, the country was full of children, and the show became a phenomenon. The series cost Reeves artistic control and creative fulfillment. He had been an unselfish and mature actor; now he was a comic-book character.

Much to his relief, Reeves was cast for a considerable role in *From Here to Eternity,* a film with an A-list of talent. But during screenings, someone realized that there was Superman in the middle of their adult film. Cinematic disaster was avoided by cutting Reeves's part to an absolute minimum. Reeves was crushed. He resorted to drink and other distractions from the hurt.

He endured for the sake of the children, whom he adored. They flocked to him, even as he wished for such acceptance and respect from their parents and the industry. For public appearances, he wore the hated costume until he could no longer take the humiliation. But he went to hospitals as the Man of Steel and held the hands of sick and frightened children. He became what they needed him to be when they needed him the most.

The Kelleys had little knowledge of Reeves's difficulties, though some of his kindnesses were made public. He was in a completely different world. A generation later, when asked, DeForest always made the point that Reeves's life went a different way, but "that didn't mean I didn't love him anymore."[5]

2 It was Barney Girard who saved DeForest Kelley's hide one more time. *You Are There* was a creative and scholarly show. The little half-hour teleplays taught the American audience how to "see" history. The interpretation was done through a reporter who seemed to travel through time and interview historical figures and characters. Walter Cronkite narrated the events for the public of the 1950s. It started out in New York, but by the time it made the move to Los Angeles, Girard was a writer and the primary director on the show. A generation learned history from the television set, as presented by Cronkite and created by Girard.[6]

Girard never forgot a friend, and besides, he knew how Kelley worked. So, suddenly, there was Kelley portraying a lawman on the trail of John Wilkes Booth. He returned for "Surrender of Corregidor," "Spindletop," and other episodes, until he was considered a featured regular.

As *You Are There* veteran actor and director Larry Dobkin remembers, the show was shot in a dilapidated facility near the Los Angeles airport. "I remember once I was playing Napoleon for him at the beginning of the 'Hundred Days,' a challenging episode, and we were shooting in a little rat hole of a studio called Culver Studios . . . and we were in the flight path and there was a plane about every three minutes and forty seconds, and I had one speech that ran four minutes and ten seconds!"

Dobkin continues, *"You Are There* defied traditions for the actor. When you're working on camera—if you ever strike the lens with your eyes, you make contact with the audience—you break the fourth wall—it's a no-no." An actor was trained to keep the eyes away from the lens, but not so with *You Are There;* in a two-minute scene, one would flow in the scene with another actor, and the narration would come in, and then the actor would hit the lens to touch the audience.

Kelley excelled in those moments when he broke the fourth wall and touched the viewers. In an episode concerning Clara Barton's heroism at a field hospital during the Civil War, he played a Yankee soldier who was suffering a musketball injury to his face. Girard held the camera so close to Kelley's face that the fourth wall, in fact, disappeared, and while Clara Barton was the intent of the camera's eye, Kelley's profile became foreground as she tended to him. It was his suffering that made plain why she was there at all. At the end of the episode, Clara Barton's declamation on war and its costs was accompanied by Kelley weeping for his comrades, his country, and his own ruined life. It was one of his most effective performances.

Of the *You Are There* experience, Dobkin most vividly recalls his director, Girard: "In a profession that is extremely envious . . . the people who are generous and helpful can be numbered on the fingers of one hand. Once he had faith in you, the sky was the limit." Dobkin was a classically trained actor, a Broadway star, a voice of the Armed Forces Signal Corps on the East Coast during World War II, and a graduate of Yale's fine arts program. In the public eye, he was Dutch Schultz on the *Untouchables* with Robert Stack. And yet he had not found a man who would let him try the reaches of his craft—until Girard. "Ninety-nine out of any given hundred directors faced with a protégé would squash him like a bug," but Girard allowed Dobkin to work scenes with him. Then the day came, and "Barney said, 'Mr. Dobkin is going to take the crew and take the next scene. Take your orders from him." Dobkin was stunned, but Girard let him loose, and, much to Dobkin's relief, "that was okay with [the show's star] Lee Marvin."[7]

That kind of personal and professional generosity was what De-Forest knew and loved about Barney Girard. Through the years of uncertainty and struggle, Kelley and Girard managed to stay true to the professional and personal codes of conduct they had believed in as youths in Long Beach before the war. Now, Girard was doing very well in television, and to him it was only natural to make sure his friend DeForest came up in the world with him.

DeForest then worked on *Your Favorite Show* and *Cavalcade of America*. He still had the odd small appearances in film and even in radio. He did not let the medium get in the way of performance. He only wanted to act, the more roles the better. With Girard's doses of high-quality work, momentum was the key to a future of professional progress. Within a year Kelley, was a working actor. Talent and perseverance over a decade made it possible; love and friendship ensured it.[8]

Work was picking up, and somewhere along the line, Aileen Pickering got a call from DeForest; he was going to try for his first real western. He was a town and city Southerner, not a horseman, not a cowboy. He appealed to her to teach him. She told him she just didn't have time to train him in everything he was going to need in westerns. She had been riding competitively, playing polo, or riding for Roy Rogers in parades over the years, and she knew how long it would take to make a Hollywood cowboy of DeForest. But she thought she could teach him the basics. The two met over at Griffith Park in North Hollywood and got to work. Later, he got lessons and kept honing his skills for the western genre. "He got very good at it," Aileen concluded.[9]

3 Kelley played a variety of men, usually newly matured and earnest fellows or closed-mouthed tough guys. In each role, DeForest tried to give a unique interpretation. In early February, Kelley was picked up to play the innocent young man Ed Clary in *Illegal*, a Warner Brothers film about a professional and personal crisis in the life of a high-powered district attorney. As a man wrongly accused of murder and found guilty, DeForest's few moments opened the story. On March 15, from three to six-thirty P.M. on Stage 8 at Warner Brothers, DeForest did that opening courtroom scene. The brief performance as a young man hounded by fear and hopelessness was just the right mix of attractiveness and vulnerability. Later in the movie, he was led to his death, proclaiming his innocence to the end. The death-house corridor scene was shot on Stage 14 a few days before the courtroom scene.

Kelley was paid less than $500, and he was done with *Illegal* and for the week. The movie was a box-office dog, but Kelley was on to other things by then. Through 1955, he appeared on *Science Fiction Theater, You Are There, The Millionaire,* and *Matinee Theater*.[10]

Kelley later reflected that he never imagined himself playing bad-guy roles, never mind real villains. It was so foreign to his nature that a stiff-lipped gangster seemed to be the limit of his work as a heavy. That was as far as he thought he could go. "DeForest Kelley is okay in his brief appearance as the meanie," *Daily Variety* commented, which seemed to confirm his own thoughts about his performance as a bad guy in the *Studio 57* series. A meanie was not really the impression a heavy wanted to make.

Then, as Kelley explained it, a director for *You Are There* pushed him into the role of a villain. That director, of course, was Barney Girard, in 1955, who insisted that his gentleman friend could play Ike Clanton, the infamous cattle rancher who was the instigator of the gunfight at the O.K. Corral in the high-desert mining town of Tombstone in 1881. Girard persisted with such confidence that Kelley finally agreed to give it a try.

For Girard, Kelley created a living presence. With a stringy mustache, a wad of licorice in his mouth, and a viper's squint, Kelley made Clanton so dangerous that he seemed to unnerve Cronkite's reporter on the street. Perhaps most memorable was DeForest's turn and twist of voice and accent, from Southern cracker to Western psychopath. He was simply threatening standing there on a Tombstone sidewalk in the sunshine. He came on so strongly through that fourth wall of the camera's lens that he made a more villainous and lasting impression than many actors could have with weapons drawn.

In sum, Girard was right about casting his sweet friend as a villain. Kelley's antithetical portrayal of Clanton changed his career and his life.

Off the strength of his performance, Kelley was chosen for an odd little cowboy movie called *Tension at Table Rock,* for RKO. It featured Kelley as Breck, a hired gun sent out to finish hero Richard Egan in the last moments of the tale. Kelley was rather stiff in the western outfit, too new and clean, with the hat fresh from a dry goods store. It seemed Egan had talked Kelley into turning away to live another day. As they came out to the sidewalk, where a parting could have taken place, Kelley stroked his horse and turned to face Egan in the street. After a little eying back and forth, Kelley was killed cleanly and landed on his face.

While he worked this B-movie oater, he was well aware that he might be missing the chance of a lifetime. A producer of high-quality movies named Hal Wallis liked to watch *You Are There.* He was impressed with Kelley as Clanton, very much impressed. Beginning in February 1956, Wallis got to work on creating a big-screen version of the Earp-Clanton conflict in Tombstone for Paramount, to be filmed in VistaVision and Technicolor. The production budget was almost $2 million. John Sturges was assigned the direction of the picture for $60,000; Kirk Douglas had been cast as Doc Holliday for $200,000. The final script came from Leon Uris. Edith Head created the costumes and look of the film for $3,000.

Although Paul Nathan was in charge of casting, Hal Wallis wanted DeForest Kelley as Ike Clanton from the very first. Nathan wrote to Wallis: "For Ike Clanton you saw on TV and liked DeForest Kelly, and when you catch your breath, I want to bring him in." Casting proposals came and went. Wallis kept penciling lines through other names and writing Kelley's in. Lee Van Cleef, James Whitmore, no . . . no . . . Kelley, Kelley. The paperwork went back and forth. It seemed Wallis was trying to wait on Kelley, and Nathan was trying to convince him otherwise. On February 23, a guarantee of $1,000 went to Kelley for his portrayal of Ike Clanton and the same to John Hoyt to play Morgan Earp. The role of Morgan would be thankless, a presence, with few lines and a lot of time on camera. Whoever wound up with the role would have to do nothing—and do it very well. It seems there were insurmountable scheduling difficulties with Kelley, since he was committed to *Tension at Table Rock* while the Clanton scenes were to be shot. So, finally, on February 27, Wallis allowed Kelley's name to stay next to the role of Morgan Earp. In the end, Ike Clanton had six scenes and fifty-eight lines, while Morgan Earp had ten scenes and twenty-eight lines.

By March 2, 1956, the decision was final. Kelley was Morgan Earp, guaranteed at $1,000 a week. That was good money but hardly the memorable character among the supporting actors that a fellow would want. Martin Milner and John Hidson were the other Earp brothers, led by Burt Lancaster's Wyatt. Veteran heavy Lyle Bettger got the Ike Clanton role.

The production was highly professional, worked out in detail, and every aspect was first-class. After fourteen years of struggle, Kelley took his place alongside Lancaster and Douglas. At thirty-six, Kelley had just as many miles and just as many hours as many of his costars. Though he had never experienced anything like this level of production before, he was solid and mature on film, perhaps older and wiser than Wyatt and Holliday. He did his "nothing" with a sense of brotherly caring and incredulousness. He was as inventive as the confines of the role allowed him to be.

The exterior scenes and the gunfight took place on location in Tombstone and in Old Tucson, the favored western movie town of the period. Shots were fired on April 23, 24, and 25. Again on May 10, the Earps were assembled to film the gunfight as it left the O.K. Corral area and over a field of dust and into a ravine of sorts. Just before lunch, Morgan Earp and Doc Holliday were scheduled to film at the ravine.[11]

DeForest told the story: "I was doing a scene with Kirk Douglas. We were approaching the corral, and the shooting starts, and we jump into this ditch, and I was carrying this rifle, and when I jumped into the ditch, I fell the wrong way, and the rifle jammed my ribs. So in the movie, Kirk Douglas saves me by pulling me down this gully on my back, and he's flat out [running,] too. He's jerking me, and I'm going 'Ugh,' and he's pulling me, 'Ugh,' and we get up to the edge where the camera is, and John Sturges, the director, said, 'Gee, De, that was terrific. It really sounded like you were really hurt. You can get up now.'"

De couldn't, and he was taken to the hospital. "They found out that I had torn all the cartilage in this right side, so they gave me a shot, some kind of dope. I don't know what it was. I was up on this table, and the doctor got through taping me up and everything, and I started to get off the table." The doctor wanted him to stay in the hospital, but Kelley insisted on going back to the Tucson Hotel. "They allowed actors to stay there, but there was a very, very ritzy club downstairs, a membership club that we were not allowed to go in. But due to the fact that Burt Lancaster, Kirk Douglas, and all these prestigious people were there, they were going to allow us to have dinner there that night. It was a beautiful place. It was done in red leather upholstery, brass spittoons, and so forth.

"So I'm in my room. I took a shower, and I had on this kind of light shirt—Jack Elam came by, you know, the guy with the big crazy eyes, and he said, 'How are you feeling, De?'" Kelley was feeling no pain, and Elam talked him into coming out. "So I went downstairs, and I joined a table with Sturges and Burt Lancaster and John Ireland and Elam . . . we were all sitting there . . . and suddenly it got hot in there, and I started to perspire, and I said, 'I think I'll go upstairs,' and I said, 'I got this tape on,' and I could see that the perspiration was falling onto the shirt. 'Get this tape off.' So as I get up, I grabbed the check. I thought it'd be nice to pay the bill as long as the director was there, kinda ace myself a little bit with him . . . and walked toward the bar. And as I stood there, the bartender said, 'Can I do something for you?' The sweat was just pouring off me. I said, 'Yeah, you can catch me. I'm gonna faint.'

"So I passed out . . . and when I awakened, I was in this ritzy place, mind you, where they don't allow actors, and when I awakened, I awakened with Burt Lancaster sitting there with a brass spittoon, and I was throwing up." It was quite a welcome to the Hollywood big time.[12]

Chapter VII
The Reel Cowboy
1956–1959

*"Here comes Eddie Dmytryk, big cigar, looked over.
'You all right, De?' 'Yeah.'
He said, 'God, I'm glad I hired real cowboys.'"*
DEFOREST KELLEY, 1991

During the filming of *Gunfight at the O.K. Corral*, DeForest got the news. Perhaps there were intimations, letters, phone calls now lost in the privacy of grief, but with a surgeon's certainty, and a surgeon's insensitivity, Dr. Luther Kelley declared Clora's cancer too far advanced to do anything but wish for a merciful end.

DeForest had always wanted to make her life easier, to make her comfortable, to honor her labors and her sacrifices. Still, he was a fair success in a very difficult field. She had been so very proud of him. If only she had lived longer—if only he had done better—if only he had been better. Clora knew her son blood and bone and sometimes would call from Georgia "and tell me things I was doing in California, and there was no way she could have known." The loss he suffered was beyond expression. Decades later, very simply, DeForest disclosed, "When she passed away, they asked me what I wanted of hers, and I said I wanted nothing but that ring." And that was all he would ever say about the death of his mother.[1]

DeForest then embarked on the most successful period of his career as an actor. Role after role would be his to play—plain evil, pathological, tormented, cold-blooded, simpering, cowardly—all these elements that went into acting the heavy. But how would he know if he were losing himself in the part, in the roles of darkness? His answer was profound. DeForest acted symbolically. He wore Clora's ring; and in honoring her, he remained true to himself, his mother's son once and always.[2]

2 The Civil War romance of 1957 was *Raintree County*. The three-hour film was designed to rival *Gone With the Wind* in scope and personal story. David Lewis produced the picture with an estimated budget of $5 million. The reconstructed Edward Dmytryk, a target of the Red Scare days in the early 1950s, was named the film's director. This was to be the largest film mounted by MGM since *Gone With the Wind*. The romance was for Montgomery Clift and Elizabeth Taylor. The scope of the film was surely epic, but the story was not strong enough to carry the weight of melodrama and romantic memory, and the writing did not compare to that of *Gone With the Wind*. However, the supporting character roles were fleshed out, including Lee Marvin as Orville "Flash" Perkins and Tom Drake as Bobby Drake. On screen for only a few minutes, DeForest Kelley found his own heritage calling as a Southern officer, unnamed but dashing. His role was memorable for the falling stallion, a mustache, and the Rhett Butler kind of banter he had with his Yankee captors, Clift and Marvin, until he killed Marvin. Kelley enjoyed making the film thoroughly. Overall, though, Dmytryk was unable to pull the strengths of the film together. Critics considered the picture a disappointment.

A short time after the film's release, Kelley went to Georgia, mostly to see his father, who was living alone in the Briarcliff Hotel. It seemed that the death of Clora was also the living denouement of the Reverend in many ways. He grieved his loss so deeply that nothing could answer his pain and nothing could retrieve him from a living purgatory.

Casey Kelley was raising a family, working in sales, and doing all right, but he had the burden of taking care of the old man on top of his many responsibilities. DeForest tried to help with a little money for his father and moral support for his brother. There was, however, little he could do unless he was willing to change his life and care for his father, and he was not willing to do that.

While in Georgia, DeForest was compelled to step from a very private world into a very public venue as the Atlanta papers rediscovered their Cinderella boy. In fact, when he went to Atlanta, he talked with journalists there for the first time in a decade. Reporter Katherine Barnwell began by reintroducing him to the public: "An Atlanta-born actor visiting here said he has had to 'relearn his Southern accent.' Now a veteran of 150 movie and television roles the portrayal of a Confederate officer brought him back to his roots. 'I had lost my Southern accent,' he explained, 'but it wasn't too hard to pick it up again. . . . I'm trying to use soft tones like most Southerners do—not a broad ridiculous accent.'"

DeForest grew his hair long for the heavy roles and let the bangs grow even longer for the Confederate role. He told the reporter that the people of Atlanta "look at me on the streets as if I were an idiot" because of the long hair. He looked back over his career and told Barnwell, "If I were starting over, I wouldn't go to California first. I would go to New York and get a job in summer stock." It seemed he would never shake his awareness of his lack of classical training, and his lack of higher education. Modesty aside, this awareness had some sadness in it.[3]

3 He never took advantage of the GI Bill and was rather at a loss to explain why. Home study had become very important; he read widely as research for his roles and for personal enjoyment. He carefully went through the newspaper every day. But, as Aileen Pickering recalled, his lack of formal education undermined his confidence. He became a man of no public opinion, almost afraid to open his mouth for fear of being wrong or ridiculed.

In fact, DeForest rarely elaborated on the few opinions he did hold. Often, people were left with two explanations: he was either philosophical or ignorant. It was up to the hearer to conclude which; he was unwilling or unable to explain.

His friend Aileen saw him become a very passive man over the years, so much so that she didn't know what to make of him anymore. He could be bent and shaped and made to agree with just about anything; just keep after him a little, and he'd cave in to someone else's will, usually Carolyn's. The essential quality that made him so seductive—was that he could be seduced. Equally seductive and equally maddening was the absolute truth that in matters of profession, integrity, and especially spirit, he simply could not be pushed. Those who loved him knew he was at once the kindest and the toughest man they had ever known. He was the most private of men—no one ever seemed to know the depth of his family turmoil, his grief, or his aloneness. He was exceptionally aware of his limitations and of his calling. He felt keenly each disappointment and frustration.

While he addressed the world with warm detachment and goodwill, Carolyn had a fluctuating demeanor, like the phases of the moon. Light or dark, she never loved lightly, not her friends, not kin, and never De. Her pull waxed and waned—sometimes hypnotic and overpowering and sometimes more gentle than a brief caress.

But sometimes it all got a little trying if things didn't mesh well. If times were too hard, if party time went on too long, De's passiveness became melancholy, and Carolyn's sharper moods could become vindictive. It was during one of these downturns that Carolyn went on a jag of playing of Stan Kenton's "Eager Beaver" over and over again loudly on the phonograph, and it drove Aileen to the brink. It was time for a break from the Kelleys. She just had to get out of the circle for a while. These breaks came, empty periods when people moved in or out of the Kelley orbit. DeForest would be upset; he wanted Aileen in his life, but he learned to take her coming and going as a natural cycle of events. He was right; she always came back.

4 While they had no end of friends who were their contemporaries, the Kelleys had been making their way through life essentially without elders to guide them. This was true of their generation, the first to be mobile, diverse, and so changed by the twentieth century. America's veterans had severed family connections for a variety of reasons.

A lucky few had mentors, and the Kelleys found theirs in Palm Springs.

As Carolyn recalls, they had their beach-bum friends at Kelley's Cove, and then in the 1950s, they began taking weekends and holidays in Palm Springs, where they made their desert-bums friends. Carolyn was very friendly with the motel owner where they liked to stay. One day, the owner asked her to mind the front office for just a few minutes, and she agreed. Betty Daniels came in to pay her bill. Betty and Carolyn were an instant hit. That same day, Bill Daniels and DeForest connected. Just like that. There was no Hollywood nonsense, no airs, none of the preening of the rich and famous, all much to Carolyn's relief. The Danielses were old enough to be comfortable and comforting, a joy to be with. Then well into his sixties, cinematographer William H. Daniels was a highly respected man in Hollywood, and he enjoyed the fruits of his labors with Betty and their new friends Carolyn and DeForest. For Carolyn, it was like having a favorite aunt and uncle appear out of nowhere. The Danielses had a beautiful home in Encino, and, with Betty a gourmet cook, the Kelleys were made welcome and comfortable, like beloved children returning home. Carolyn recalls that the Danielses were people who made her feel that she could let her hair down and talk about anything she or DeForest wished. With Bill, De got to do regular guy things, such as looking at cars and hanging out.[4]

For years at MGM, Greta Garbo was the greatest star of her day, difficult and tempestuous as a woman could be. The suits and the handlers agreed William H. Daniels held the key to working with Garbo. He could not only photograph her to best advantage, but it was he who calmly worked with her over the years. He was responsible for the Garbo look, and he was her admirer, confidant, and guardian. He knew her better than anyone, and she knew it, too, and kept him close to her.[5]

Daniels also had a quality that Kelley seemed to like in his friends: he was a demanding professional who had no toleration for fools. Kelley was never combative, but he seemed drawn to passionate souls, such as Girard and Pickering. Something in him liked a fighter, and he enjoyed the role of counselor that gave these heroes strength and rest. With Daniels, especially, he could also be the reflective son discussing the ways of things with his elder.

From October through December 1957, Kelley left Carolyn at their new Castle Heights address to join the production of *The Law and Jake Wade,* to be filmed in the High Sierras and in Death Valley. Robert Taylor and Richard Widmark were teamed as adversaries, and Kelley broadened his interpretation of his western sociopath as Wexler, Widmark's wolf on a leash. Young Henry Silva, an intense Puerto Rican actor, was cast as Rennie. The film had strong production values, performers, and direction by John Sturges. Importantly, Sturges allowed the bad guys to become distinct and engaging in their own right.[6]

Of course, out of character, DeForest was amiable and a pleasure to have around the set. He seemed always ready for a little pleasantry or a laugh. On the first day of production, he broke the ice with star Robert Taylor. They were having coffee, and DeForest recalled that he said to Taylor, " 'You know, we met before, a long time ago.' He said, 'Oh, really, when?' I told him the story how I climbed over the fence and saw him and that he told us to push the lamp around to be able to stay on the set, and he looked at me, like, is this guy full of it or what? I said, 'Incidentally, Barbara Stanwyck came on the set, who you were married to at that time, and she had these two beautiful horses with a green blanket over each one and RT on it.' He said, 'I'm a son of a bitch. You're right.' . . . I thought it was kind of funny after all those years."[7]

On November 1, the wardrobe department finalized costumes. Kelley seemed to enjoy the rowdy cowboy environment, dressed in dirty denim and black leathers, looking big and mean at six feet and 160 pounds. The outfit consisted of a black hat, size 9 gloves, and 31x31 jeans. He was top-heavy and broad-shouldered with vest and coat. Guns and belts completed the look. He posed for the wardrobe camera with just a little obligatory menace on his face, while Henry Silva looked on, amused.

Everyone watched as Widmark went through his costuming. His intense and forlorn look never seemed to leave him even in wardrobe shots. He had an academic's sharpness and a gangster's toughness. For Kelley, working with Widmark was more than an experience with an accomplished and complex actor. In Widmark was that wild something that when called would change the look of his body, the color of his cheeks, and, as DeForest recalled, his eyes. Looking into his eyes was like looking through the gates of hell. Widmark was so very good at acting the dark, angry soul, for that is what he was. For Kelley, Widmark was the ideal subject to study, a man who might as well have come from the other side of the moon.[8]

The Law and Jake Wade was a "top-notch suspense western" the critics concluded, and Kelley was enjoying a marked escalation in television work. One day on the 20th Century Fox lot, he had a rather memorable meeting: "I came into the commissary, and this cameraman came by and said, 'I'm going to photograph the man that you were named for, Dr. Lee DeForest.' " Apparently, Fox was going to make a biographical film about the inventor. "And I said, 'Well, I really was named for him.' He was about eighty years old then. So I got up, and I went over, and I had the pleasure of having my picture taken with him." The inventor also seemed mighty pleased to meet a radio, film, and television actor who bore his name on the lot of 20th Century Fox.

"The father of radio" took credit when he should not have, but Dr. DeForest did work on sound for the movies, long-distance telegraphy, radar, television, cosmic-ray measuring devices, and the like. He considered television a stench and a misuse of a beautiful medium meant for communication and education.[9]

On the other hand, television was paying the rent with a steady stream of roles for Kelley. In fact, his appearances became so frequent that the Kelleys had trouble keeping track of it all. Dick Powell's *Zane Grey Theater* explored group psychology in a western setting. A teleplay on *Schlitz Playhouse* featured Kelley as a cracker and a heckler against a young victim of small-town prejudice, played by Michael Landon. Then Kelley hit on something he rather enjoyed doing. In "Kill and Run" for the series *The Web,* he portrayed a scrupulous detective whose methodical process saved a young delinquent played by James Darren. With this type of role, he could show his urbane and grounded intellect while wearing the white hat of justice. However, all of these free-standing works were rushed, low-budget, one-time affairs. Screen Gems' *Playhouse 90* had a better reputation and drew a lot of quality crossover talent. In "The Edge of Innocence," DeForest played a small part but was surrounded by Joseph Cotten, Teresa Wright, Maureen O'Sullivan, and Lorne Greene among others. It was major league, but as actor Bill Campbell recalls, what any man in his right mind wanted in television was an episodic series, with his name at the top.[10]

5 Around MGM, Fox, and Paramount, Kelley made a most striking impression, and it was probably around MGM that Grace Lee Whitney became aware of him. She recalls being struck by his kindness, his handsome face, and, mostly, his eyes, which were the most beautiful shade of sky. Whitney was just starting out in Hollywood, making *Some Like It Hot* for Billy Wilder, with Tony Curtis, Jack Lemmon, and Marilyn Monroe, in 1958. The place to have lunch was the Formosa Café, centrally located among the studios of MGM, Screen Gems, and Ziv. As she remembers, Kelley was always around, visiting for a little while at the cafés and clubs that were favored by the actors and crew; then, of course, he went home. It seemed a naturally acknowledged fact that he was one of those rare married men who had a home he wanted to get back to.[11]

In the fall of 1958, work began on *Warlock* for 20th Century Fox. Again, Eddie Dmytryk had the director's chair; he also held the reins as producer for the project. Within the western, Dmytryk was able to interpret the dreams of the American frontier and shape them into a very weighty psychological drama. During the summer, casting had been set. Richard Widmark made an interesting choice for the bad-to-good antihero set against bad and good-to-bad antiheroes Henry Fonda and Anthony Quinn. For Dmytryk, this may have been an examination of all the shades of good and evil, boldness and cowardice, and the pressure cooker of the pack mentality—elements of the reality that he himself had lived through during the Red Scare's HUAC hearings. Set in the 1880s, the Oakley Hall story was about the damaged generation living with the consequences of the Civil War—a lost and scarred people who moved west for freedom, or forgetfulness, or escape from law and Reconstruction.

Kelley's old friend Tom Drake broke his career-deadening boy-next-door typecasting by playing the sadistic ranch boss Abe McQuown at

$1,000 a week with two weeks guaranteed. For years, Drake had bat-
tled drink and his demons, but he let them loose in the McQuown
role. Kelley was cast as Curley at $850 per week and five weeks guar-
anteed. Curley was a sweet outlaw and Widmark's friend; he was the
bandit next door. Curley was bad but not evil. His character was also,
indeed, the hero of the story, as Curley finds redemption for the sake
of Widmark's character. [12]

Aileen Pickering's riding lessons and the instruction he took later
on made DeForest a fine cowboy actor. As Carolyn recalls, "He looked
good on a horse."

However, there are some things a cowboy actor can't be ready for.
With self-effacing humor, Kelley told the story: "My gang . . . we ride
into town. There are about fifteen or twenty of us just hellbent for
leather, and we tie up at a tie rail and all swing off the horses one after
the other. And as I swung, I had spurs on. My foot hit the horse next
to me in the rump, and he kicked, and I went into the air." He used
his arms and hands to trace the arch and spin of his body in space. "I
did a loop. I knew I was turning over. I could feel myself in the air,
and the tie rail, you know, and I fell, and my head just missed that tie
rail. I uttered an obscenity while in the air and landed on the
ground . . . silence . . . I open my eyes, and I look up, and I see all
these horses. Here comes Eddie Dmytryk, big cigar, looked over. 'You
all right, De?' 'Yeah.' He said, 'God, I'm glad I hired real cowboys.' "[13]

A few days later, DeForest as Curley Burns was called for his big
saloon scene against Fonda's Clay Blaisdell, a man emotionally and
psychologically scarred by the Civil War. Curley, with bedroom eyes
and the old small trick of rolling a coin on the backs of his knuckles,
gave the impression that he was just an ol' country boy in the saloon
after a long day of dust and road apples, awaiting a test of his reflexes.
The squint, focus, and coldness of his delivery marked where the tem-
perament changed from good ol' boy to killer with just a taste of
goodness. Kelley would not examine his accomplishment in the role
but told a story on himself again: "Now, I had been working a great
number of weeks with a wonderful guy in Los Angeles, an Indian
[Rodd Redwing]. He was an expert gunman, and he was teaching me
a flyaway on a draw, and I was very worried about it. The director

came to me the day before, and he said, 'DeForest, I want you to be up in the scene with Henry Fonda, the showdown, because Princess Sophia of Greece is going to be here.' He was quite a joker, and I thought he was joking with me, really. The next day, though, it turned out not to be a joke. I was standing out in front of the stage and this entourage drove up, certainly enough the princess and all of her people with her, and they went into the saloon. And we were shooting on a stage in the saloon, and there was a big stairway in the back. So she and her entourage gathered on this stairway, and they were doing a closeup on me."

There was a stand-in for Fonda because he was attending the funeral of Tyrone Power that day, so all the attention was on Kelley. This was his flyaway draw scene, and he was sweating it. "I was afraid I was gonna drop the gun, not because she was there, but just worried, period. So, anyhow, we start to do this scene, and they're all up there, and I've just ridden into town to have a showdown with Henry Fonda. We hear he's a very fast draw, and I was a fast draw." Kelley got through his lines just fine. "And when Fonda draws, he draws so fast that I hardly have time to get to my holster." Curley dropped his gun, "and I give him something like a little 'woo-eee,' and I tip my hat to him in great respect. [Then Fonda says,] 'Now, pick up your gun, Curley, and you and your men get out of here.' So here comes the flyaway that I was sweating out." A difficult move—the gun on the floor was lightly picked up, spun around on the trigger finger palm down, and spun again with a change in degree of pitch—just enough to deliver the barrel smoothly into the holster by the time the gun hand reached the hip. "Now, I'd forgotten that Princess Sophia was here at this particular time, carried away with the scene. So I reach down to get the gun. It slipped right in the holster. I thought, oh, boy. So I started out with the rest of my men, going out these batwing doors, and I tripped over a chair and fell backwards, and I said, 'Oh shit!' I'm on my knees, and I thought, 'My God, the princess is here.' You could have heard a pin drop. Everything just stopped dead still. And I crawled out those batwing doors. Eddie Dmytryk had a very dry sense of humor and always smoked this big cigar, see, so, nothing. It just was quiet, and finally the batwing doors opened, and Eddie comes back where I'm still on my hands and knees, and the rest of my gang are stifling a laugh, and Eddie, with his cigar, bends over and says, 'De, I bet you sat up all night last night trying to think of what to say in front of the princess.'"

The next day, it got all over Fox that DeForest Kelley had said "Shit!" in front of the princess, "and I went into the commissary to have lunch, and I got a standing ovation." Although Fonda was not present for Kelley's epithet, he heard about it soon enough. During the weekend, Fonda attended a gala at the Beverly Hills Hotel that Princess Sophia also attended, and he mingled with her and her entourage: "He comes in Monday morning, and he says, 'De, come here.' I came over, and I said, 'Yeah?' He said, 'I heard about what happened Friday, and . . . I don't want you to worry about it. I danced with the princess, and she doesn't know what *shit* means.'"[14]

6 The Kelleys had a lot to be grateful for in 1958. They tended to the details of the home, even though they were renting as they always had. At Christmas, Carolyn and DeForest were enjoying their new baby bird, "Baby Kelley," and Carolyn remarked how the baby had won over the Reverend Mr. Kelley on a recent relatively peaceful visit, so much so that a little after his return to Georgia, he was moved to sign a card "Grandpa." Carolyn was filled with the Christmas spirit as never before in her life. De called her his ho-ho-ho girl, and she signed her cards, "De, Baby, and ho-ho." De had a copy of the Oakley Hall novel *Warlock* on his bookshelf, signed by the actors and crew of that fine film. He had a growing list of television work and a respectable credit list of satisfying movies. Carolyn noted in a letter to a friend: "Seems all westerns this year, this last week was not a western but he shot someone even in that one. I don't know how anyone so sweet could act so mean, he is just a good actor."[15]

Carolyn wasn't the only one who couldn't believe DeForest could be evil. Later, he would recall with remorse that Betty Daniels had never watched Kelley act the bad man and tried to tell him that she couldn't believe it. In the next breath, her De changed before her eyes. He grabbed her with a sharp, angular thrust and whispered some words that sounded like an epithet from the base of his throat. His deep, easy blue eyes went flat as a serpent's. He made her cry.[16]

Increasingly, Carolyn took the role of administrative secretary, accountant, and public relations officer for the Kelley enterprise. His progress was steady, and there were thoughts of buying a home, of Carolyn becoming their full-time manager, of a future beyond the scrape and struggle of the hungry, not-so-young actor. Carolyn was in her early forties, and he knew all she ever really wanted to do was stay home in a house of her own and tend to their own small world. That dream now seemed possible. His dream of being a working actor had come true. If the westerns kept doing well or if he could get a television series of his own, then the Kelleys would be in high cotton. A good, steady, working actor was what he was in Carolyn's estimation. She would never regard her De as a star at any time. In her mind, that was something George Reeves was.

Carolyn remembers clearly: "Then one day, we were out in Palm Springs at a coffee shop, I guess, and we came out to the sidewalk and saw the newspaper headline on the stand. That's how we knew George Reeves was dead."

On June 15, 1959, their dear friend became immortal for a postwar generation that devoured its heroes. More demeaning than celebrity, hero worship made his character performance greater than his personal character. In sad truth, he was not of larger spirit than the role he played. Reeves was diminished as a man by Superman and by drink, by vice and temptation, until it all destroyed him. Frustration and artistic suffocation weakened him in those mortal battles for a soul which DeForest later described as "joyous." Murder or suicide, Reeves's tragic entanglements and violent end did not change the fact that Hollywood had claimed another soul. The Kelleys never accepted the official report that he was a suicide, not from the first. Reeves's death was a lesson that was not lost on Kelley, and for the rest of his life, he had a visceral understanding of what celebrity and the pressure of being an icon for the public could do to a man's clarity and to his judgment. He would be ever patient with those who were confronting the many sides of hero worship.[17]

Back in 1945, DeForest and George had been drawn together by similarities in the gentleness of their characters, generosity, compassion, ambition, and drinking. Everything that could have been said about George also could have been said about DeForest, and perhaps they intuitively knew how vulnerable they really were in the cold light of Hollywood. What made all the difference for DeForest was his spiritual toughness, and Carolyn Kelley.

Chapter VIII
Playing the Heavy
1960–1964

"We may have to try that—resurrect that hombre."
—DEFOREST KELLEY, 1999

Occasionally, Carolyn's De emerged from the badlands and got cleaned up and dusted off for a role in *The Donna Reed Show,* a few of Barney Girard's *M-Squad* episodes, or *Richard Diamond, Private Detective,* starring David Janssen. Kelley worked in a wide range of shows with actors such as Richard Crenna, June Lockhart, and David Niven. He loved it all. But his forte was the bad hombre, and his genre was the western.[1]

For DeForest, it was all about acting, but to Aileen Pickering, it was his chance to release all the ills and anger within. The bad-guy skin was a safe place to express his rage and his hurt, to pistol-whip the world and kick it in the teeth. Everything he would not allow into himself in life he could funnel into his characters.

Ironically, for the sake of his art, he would become intimately aware of, and identified with, the very parts of humanity he found most alien. His dedication was there for the eye to behold; through the 1950s and into the 1960s, he sacrificed his looks and his charm to achieve a reputation as a bad hombre. As much as he enjoyed cloaking himself in the rottenness of his parts, it seemed many members of the viewing public inexplicably liked the son of a sidewinder. Viewers could find DeForest within his characters.

He saddled himself with a calendar filled with television work that ran dawn through dusk, week after week, and month after month. DeForest worked harder and faster than many of his colleagues. Carolyn had to work hard to keep up with his performances, payments, and royalties in her little black ledger.

Western shows on television kept him coming and going, out of the house and onto back lots, to local ranches, to Death Valley and Vasquez Rocks. *Boots and Saddles, Bat Masterson, Lawman, Rough Riders, Zane Grey Theater, Trackdown, Northwest Passage, Rawhide, Black Saddle*—the list just grew with the years.

According to union agreements, everyone had to assemble around sunup at a few agreed-upon spots and be driven to a variety of locations by union drivers. Each morning at the favored assembly area at the intersection of Ventura Boulevard and Sepulveda Boulevard in the San Fernando Valley, weary and hungover actors clutched their small bags of cigarettes, gum, aspirin, and other necessities for the long day outdoors. The stretch station wagons came around bearing the name of a particular show or movie, and they climbed in by the first light of day. There were dozens of features and television westerns in production at the same time, so during the workday there was competition for sites and sets, and sometimes scenes were disrupted by gunfire in the next ravine or a bar fight in the next street. There was a lot of camaraderie and horsing around. The fellows all got the same price, about $750 for a six-day week. There were some who found success, and they often left the cowboys behind as their heads and pockets grew bigger; others kept their manners. Some held on to their pride, and others would forget which end of the horse was the right one to kiss. In general, they were a congenial lot, a small brotherhood with the common bond of the western.[2]

Of course, everyone had to interview and read for his part and cajole the man in charge. Every now and then, some unsuspecting soul would question DeForest Kelley's ability to play the bad hombre, and, like Bette Daniels, he would suddenly be facing Kelley's alter ego. During one casting interview, Steve McQueen offhandedly dismissed Kelley as a candidate for a bad man in *Wanted: Dead or Alive*. In the next breath, DeForest turned on the man he was standing next to and unnerved the fellow so badly that McQueen changed his mind and gave him the role.[3]

Realism seemed to satisfy a need for bold experience, and *The Westerners* gave him a dose of dirt and blood he vividly remembered. The "Apache Trail" episode featured Peter Breck as the white hat, while Kelley played the despicable trading-post owner who cheated, stole, lied, and murdered Apaches. He went too far when he raped and kidnapped an Apache woman, and the Apache braves came for him. As part of the justice in the morality play, Kelley was to be tied to a post and whipped. As he realized what was about to happen to him, he tried to make a break for it, only to be brought down by one of the vengeance-seeking Apaches. The Apache whip man was well trained, but the heat, the sweat, and the lashes laid on his back made Kelley grit his teeth and whoop out loud. The lashes jerked his head, and he pulled back against the fencepost, but he endured the stinging rather than call the scene. He felt he had done a good day's work; once home, he was astonished to find his back full of oozing stripes that left bloody traces on the chair when he first sat down.[4]

He really enjoyed his days as a bad cowboy, with open-air shoots, sunshine, and Indians—"They were called Indians back then, you know," he liked to make the point. The gunplay began to affect his hearing, but he recovered marvelously from the falls and the beatings and worked without a stuntman. He delighted in being a sidewinder one moment, a gentleman the next.

At one point, he recalled a skirmish with some Indians. Kelley was to chase down a Navajo, and without Kelley's knowledge, the director pulled the Navajo actor aside. "Don't let him catch ya," the director told him. The Navajo took off with Kelley a moment after him, and to the Navajo's amazement, within a few strides, Kelley had him down in the dirt. Of course, Kelley was pleased with himself. The next day, the Navajo presented Kelley with a roadrunner pin. To dispel any uneasiness about the gift, the Native American actor said, tongue in cheek, "White man fleet of foot." Kelley was honored. He treasured the roadrunner all his life.[5]

2 By 1960, Kelley had made two western pilots for the production team of Bill Dozier and Bob Sparks, playing the heavy in each. As

Kelley recalled, both *Rawhide* and *Wanted: Dead or Alive* sold. In 1960, Dozier was thinking it was high time Kelley got a crack at a series for himself. Kelley met with Sparks, who referred him to the pilot's writer–producer in Westwood. "I walked up this little flight of stairs and in a tiny office with a desk, and here was this bear of a man sitting there. So we had a long talk about this particular show, and Gene [Roddenberry] told me, he said, 'We have no trouble with you. We'll take you to San Francisco and have you meet Jake Ehrlich, who you're going to portray, this famous criminal lawyer.' "

The series, to be titled *333 Montgomery,* was admittedly a bit ahead of its time, which made Kelley even more interested in the project. Based on the living and working defense attorney Jake Ehrlich of San Francisco, this was not to be a *Perry Mason* but something opposite, a defender of the innocent, the misunderstood, framed, or even guilty party.[6]

Just after Kelley's fortieth birthday, he traveled up to San Francisco and checked into the Sheraton Palace Hotel. He scrupulously collected his receipts and expense stubs for things like cabs, valet services, and dry cleaning. He tipped the bellboy fifty cents and got to work thinking through and creating his approach to his character and the notion of his own series. On January 29, a telegram arrived for him from 333 Montgomery. Ehrlich sent a cordial invitation to a February 5 cocktail party at the Mayfair suite at the St. Francis Hotel for all the cast and crew of the Screen Gems production—those who, Ehrlich wrote, "for some unknown reason . . . intend to immortalize me on celluloid television." Ehrlich was especially anxious to meet "the menacing heavy who is to portray me, DeForest Kelley."[7]

Kelley worked his charm on the Ehrlichs that evening and followed up with the delivery of a dozen red roses to the lawyer's wife. The *San Francisco Chronicle* echoed the sentiments of many locals regarding this Hollywood portrayal of the fabled barrister. The papers described Kelley as a young character actor who looked a little like Ehrlich, but "the face is familiar on TV. . . . Usually a sleek cunning murderer who keeps a sharp eye on the hero while paring his fingernails; because of this he is known to have the cleanest fingernails in Hollywood."[8]

Kelley received the script revisions from Roddenberry and worked hard on the final draft of "Never Plead Guilty." He did some simple editing of his dialogue and sketched some indication of body movements: the pointing finger, sweeping gesture, tilted head, lifted brow. He phonetically spelled out a few of the words he wanted to roll with a preacher's pace and timing. He sketched a combination of these things for a particular effect at certain moments in his portrayal. His handwriting in these pages was for his eyes only, and it lacked the arch and swing and sharpness of his penmanship for others. He turned his attention to Ehrlich's movements and distinctive dress.

The columnists in general made up a chorus of doubt. The barrister of San Francisco was to be played on television by a clergyman's son from Georgia, of all things, a gross miscasting. This fellow had made a career of playing heavies. Comments like these in the press might have stung, but Kelley kept the clippings and got to know that great bear of a man, Gene Roddenberry. His life was filled with direct experiences of war, danger, love, excess, and sex; Roddenberry's head was filled with wonderful things and brutal realities. Their personal styles were very different, but Kelley and Roddenberry were very much a team in a matter of days.

In DeForest, Gene found a soothing presence, and Roddenberry was the kind of human being Kelley was drawn to. Like Aileen Pickering, Bernard Girard, and Bill Daniels, Gene Roddenberry was a warrior with a lust for life, and Kelley found that endlessly interesting, exciting, liberating.[9]

One long evening at the Moulin Rouge Club, Roddenberry and Kelley were recuperating from a day's review and choice of actors for the jury, and they were discussing the next day's selection of a jury foreman. As Kelley recalled, the place was getting rowdy, and the dancing girl was on the floor writhing around, much to the delight of the onlookers, especially Roddenberry. Kelley selected a little advertisement from the club with a racy sketch on it and wrote:

> Dear Gene
>   Maybe the princess for the jury foreman?

After due consideration, the advertisement was pushed back to DeForest:

To hell with Kelley, how about a lady lawyer?

Roddenberry left his new friend a small note as they broke from work on Friday, February 13, 1960:

Have a good weekend, De. Stay away from tobacco, whiskey, and wild wild women—rest rest rest.

Seriously, all seems in good shape, got a feeling we'll knock em on their asses with this one

—Gene

Kelley collected his mementoes and expenses and the frequent cards from Carolyn and journeyed back home to await the airing of Screen Gems' *333 Montgomery*. What a fellow really wanted was his own series, and this could be Kelley's shot. He hitched his star to Roddenberry and awaited the will of the networks.

Carolyn and DeForest were on vacation at Rancho Mirage when Ehrlich's letter reached them. "My dear friend," Jake began, and described his negotiations with the Paul Wilkins Agency, MGM, and others. He wrote just a few lines about ongoing talks beyond the *333* series pilot. "I wish you every happiness. I saw you on *Stagecoach West*. I hope I will soon see you on *333 Montgomery*." Ehrlich's letter was evidence that Kelley could melt even a lawyer's tiny heart, as the tough old barrister wrote, "We think of you, talk of you, and love you. Please believe me."[10]

On June 13, 1960, the ALCOA Theater series presented Screen Gems' *333 Montgomery*, and *Daily Variety* reviewed the work as "a smooth and shining piece that might go . . . strongest argument for the package is DeForest Kelley, human, credible and strongly flamboyant when defending a client . . . central character makes the program." The *New York Journal-American* on June 14 reviewed Kelley as a combination of Lee Tracy and Lou Ayers in a role that was a cross between Perry Mason and Peter Gunn: "How can it miss? Not nearly as dreadful as most TV trash." But the much-appreciated nods could not save *333 Montgomery*. It was, after all, written and produced by Gene Roddenberry. "Like everything Gene did, it was a little ahead of its time. I was defending a guy who was guilty, and I got him off, and the networks didn't like it." Perhaps Kelley's shot at his own series was gone forever; nevertheless, he knew they were doing good work and "spent two wonderful weeks in San Francisco . . . we agreed it was one of the best times of our lives."[11]

3 Old Army buddy R. G. Armstrong came to visit Kelley and Girard. The Roswell boys had something of a reunion at DeForest's place. Armstrong had become a writer of plays, as he had dreamed. He had made the big move to Manhattan, where he accidentally wound up acting on the Broadway stage. Then came a screen test, and he was cast for the lead heavy in *From Hell to Texas* for 20th Century Fox in 1958; it was the beginning of a strong career as a character actor. "Here I come with a lead and looked up DeForest at [home,] and Barney was there, too. They were old-timers by then." R.G. recounted his slide into acting success, and DeForest laughed and laughed, "With that light in his eyes, delighted, as if he had fallen onto Broadway and then onto a lead role himself!" It was that quality that made R.G. declare his love for Kelley's soul.[12]

Western shows dominated the entertainment industry. "My God, they were everywhere," recalls Morgan Woodward, a veteran of the genre. Another veteran, L. Q. Jones, explains that the late 1950s and early 1960s were filled with half-hour, one-hour, and even ninety-minute cowboy shows that were expensive to make and required a lot more attention and logistical mastery than the usual modern show. *The Westerner* was the finest incarnation and the swan song of the gritty western series. The studio suits just couldn't handle creator-director Sam Peckinpah. Jones recalls, "The show got fantastic numbers and a million pieces of complaint." In December 1960, Kelley got word that *The Westerner* was to be canceled. Surely it had been the truest thing on television, something an actor or a viewer could really be interested in. He sat down to express his sympathy.

"Dear Mr. Peckinpah," Kelley wrote. "Having watched nearly all episodes of your superb series . . . I am compelled to write you a fan letter. . . . In my opinion, it is the best series that has ever been presented on television. . . . You, Brian, and your entire crew—and 'Dawg'—deserve highest praise."[13]

As long as the old westerns lasted, Kelley had work. Those *Bonanza* boys were among his favorite fellows to work with. Michael Landon and Kelley had known each other since Kelley appeared on an ill-fated Landon pilot a number of years earlier. Kelley loved Landon's laugh and his sense of humor. Kelley fit well into the David Dortort production company of warm-hearted men assembled to tell stories for family viewing. Kelley enjoyed Dan Blocker. Once they had some dialogue together, and Kelley remembered, "Hoss wore this great big hat, you remember the big tall hat. . . . He put a small transistor radio on top of his head in this big hat. You couldn't see it. And when we got under the microphone to start our dialogue, the sound man said, 'Cut, cut . . . there's an outside interference in here somewhere.' Dan would just step away from the microphone. 'Okay, roll it.' We get back under the microphone, and the little radio would start to play again. 'Cut! Cut! Noise!' That went on. Dan left that on about one hour."[14]

In "The Honor of Cochise," DeForest joined the Cartwrights again, this time as a Yankee soldier, Captain Johnson. DeForest's individual riding style was caught in the first moments of the story. As Kelley rode at full gallop away from an Apache threat, the camera picked up his narrow-chested and long-ribbed cavalry horse. Kelley rode rather far up on the English-style cavalry saddle, stirrups long and heels down and in. His shoulders moved only to the rock of the horse, his body tilted forward while his head and the horse's were close enough for the animal's ears to pivot back and forth in response to him and to the gunfire. Kelley's hands were light and easy on the reins shifted to the center and right of the animal's neck, the business portion of the reins in his left and the bitter ends in his right hand. He wheeled the animal just a bit around the camera as he flew past and comfortably kept the animal steady even while his character was in a panic. Arriving at his destination, Kelley fell into the arms of Hoss and Ben Cartwright. Dan Blocker's overwhelming strength guided Kelley weightlessly to the ground. Little Joe grabbed the horse, and the story began.

Captain Johnson was a tin soldier, despicable in his racism and his "just following orders" justification for his role in the genocide the federal authorities had conducted on the native population. Kelley's transformation into the captain was partially achieved by application of effective makeup. His long hair was greased to its deepest black. The sun had darkened his skin, and he wore eyeliner to accent the deepness of blue in his eyes. With the reflection of his cavalry uniform, those eyes became purple and black. With his high forehead and eyebrows shaped like heavy triangles, the well-lidded eyes became very prominent above the creases beneath. His aquiline profile recalled the beautiful face of his youth—well covered by dirt and his character's corruption. Almost invisible were the long, small nose and well-shaped mouth, seemingly too delicate for the broad cheekbones that suggested something of his own distant Cherokee heritage. The lower lip was as expressive in silence as the mouth was expressive in speech. DeForest was still a very good-looking man, and here the fluctuations from darkness to light, evil to angelic, were particularly noticeable.

Even on the Ponderosa, boys will be boys. "I never know when I'm going over the side with this kind of thing," DeForest cautioned. "Don't be mad at me. . . . 'The Honor of Cochise.' . . . Mike Landon and Dan Blocker were great pranksters and real funny guys and full of mischief, and I had a ride that was, God, I guess it was six or eight hundred yards that I was running from these Indians. I poisoned them with bad corn, and they were after me, and I'm just hell bent on this horse full out and ride into this gully where Mike Landon, Pernell Roberts, and Lorne [Greene] are there. And they don't know what I've done, so they're trying to protect me.

"So Lorne Greene walks out to talk to the Indians. There is a new director, I'll never forget it . . . the *Bonanza* boys were driving him crazy. So as Lorne is walking out to talk to this Indian chief, he was carrying a white handkerchief, and right in the middle of the scene, Michael Landon stuck his head up out of the gully, and he says, 'Hey, Lorne!' he says, 'those are redskins, not foreskins!'. . . You asked for it."[15]

In the end, Captain Johnson's cowardice and cruelty were revealed, and he was brought to federal justice, dragged to it by Hoss Cartwright and the good men of native and white races. So ended another *Bonanza* morality play about friendship, duty, and human decency.

Kelley's personal toughness was evoked in another *Bonanza* episode, "The Decision." The director and producer allowed him some creative depth, and he took the chance to experiment just a bit.

Kelley played a doctor accused of murder; indeed, he was guilty. He'd defended his wife's reputation and freedom to the death by killing a blackmailer who uncovered her past crime as an embezzler. Kelley made good use of the long dialogue that was part of *Bonanza's* family morality plays. In this one, the doctor was in prison awaiting his moment on the gallows, when Ben Cartwright came to beg treatment for Hoss, who had been shot. The doctor refused; he was preparing to die and no longer had any interest in healing. The doctor's story evoked sympathy from Cartwright, who took up the doomed man's cause. Kelley was entirely convincing as a man so devoted to his wife that his own life meant little in comparison. His portrait of a troubled man mirrored the actor's own moral spine and fighting spirit that lay just beneath the smooth, laidback surface of his personality.

4 Urban tales such as *Route 66, Slattery's People,* and *The Fugitive* followed a run of westerns. Grace Lee Whitney recalls that Kelley worked on *77 Sunset Strip* at Warner Brothers with her and that he was often at Warner Brothers while she was under contract: "We ran into each other everywhere. . . . When you're in that web . . . of episodic TV shows," everyone knew everyone.

DeForest worked very long hours for moderate pay; he enjoyed a great personal achievement when Carolyn was able to quit her pink-collar world and stay home. She turned full-time to the ledgers and books, the correspondence, and the public relations duties that came with a successful television career.[16]

DeForest's devotion to Carolyn had been heightened by her frailty, piqued by her strength and sacrifice. His priorities were set in stone for a lifetime, his gratitude was expressed in his behavior, and his loyalty transcended circumstances. Now he could reward all her faith and hard work with the lifestyle she had always wanted. She could come out on a location if she wanted, she could stay home and putter around the house, enjoy her animals, her friends, the days and weeks in the California sunshine. If she was ill, she could relax and tend to her body, or she could get ready for a party, or she could sleep until eleven A.M. if she wanted. Now it was time to find a home of their own.

By that time, of course, Aileen Pickering had come back into their small circle of friends, a steady, fiery presence that inspired confidence which the Kelleys sorely needed as they went through the home-buying process. By now, Aileen was a real estate agent, a very successful one, and she was able to fund her flying passions, support her family, and dabble in investments. Because she was still rather new in real estate, veteran broker Shelley Ames helped the Kelleys find their first home, and then Aileen stood by them while they went through the nerve-racking process. When they found their dream home not far from the corner of Ventura and Sepulveda, she was there to hold their hands.

It was a small, well-built home miles out of town among the citrus groves and ranches in the valley. "De and Carolyn were beside themselves, afraid [the owners] would take the offer. We were having drinks with Shelley Ames, and we waited for the word about the house. Carolyn was just undone—'Oh, now what are we going to do?' But De was a California vet, [and the deal was] about 3 percent . . . $28,000 for the house." At forty-six, Carolyn and her husband were about to buy their first real home. With Aileen at their side, it was going to happen, and they were petrified by the responsibility. They had that churning sickness at the thought of getting what they wished for—and losing it. All tied up in knots and coming undone at the same time.

By Aileen's reckoning, everything moved along smoothly, and some time after they had been settled in, she heard about a turtle a friend of a relative had found wandering around. What to do for this curious old thing? She called the Kelleys—"Oh, we like turtles! All right." Myrtle Kelley moved into the backyard of the house on Greenleaf. A number of Aileen's real estate signs were sacrificed for Myrtle's excavation and framing of an appropriate den.

The Kelleys would worry endlessly for Myrtle during the seasonal rains and the tremors that threatened earthquakes. DeForest would dig her out of the mud to check on her or rush around looking for her if she missed a meal. Carolyn and De enjoyed Myrtle's perambulations over the walkways and through the citrus, and soon she began developing a mode of communication with the Kelleys. They became attuned to a bump, a scrape, a turn of the head, the slowing and quickening that signaled hibernation and its end. Her human companions soon understood and appreciated her with sensitivity beyond time and mind. DeForest loved watching something slower and more methodical than even he was, something even deeper and more patient and perhaps wiser. He had to learn all about the care and feeding of the wonderful creature, and he spent long, profoundly quiet moments with the old tortoise. Myrtle was sweet, cute, and endlessly interesting. The new Kelley family member was a mythologically powerful living creature that could entrance and soothe and teach. She was a living symbol of their commitment to the earthly round of seasons and the simple days marked by the sun's journey from one end of the yard to the other. She seemed to know that the Kelleys were as dug in as she was, and once in, they would never leave; their home would be their heart. Myrtle the desert tortoise seemed to understand everything through those dancing prisms in her sunlit eyes.

Once the Kelleys had caught their breath, DeForest began to tend to the roses that were left behind by the previous owners. It seemed the house, the turtle, the rosebuds, and the sunshine all had a hypnotizing effect on the Kelleys, and they became ever more reluctant to leave their new world on Greenleaf.[17]

Then, with great anticipation, the little one came into their lives, the tiny puppy, part poodle, part schnauzer—a schnoodle! The little thing sat there on its first day in the new house while De and Carolyn tried to decide what to name the pup. Of course, drinks were called for to fuel the creative process. "Cheers!" They clinked glasses as the pup looked on. No results. "Cheers!" for another drink, and they clinked their glasses again and again. Eventually, they got the idea—Cheers Kelley it was.[18]

Of course, their old friends remained connected through the telephone and the mail. Grace Hartung was never far from Kelley's heart, and she got a phone call or a letter a few times a year. The old gang might lose track of one another but would reunite as the Kelleys passed by on a short vacation from Hollywood. At one point, De and

Carolyn made one of their runs to see Herman and Shorty Casey down in Long Beach, and they looked up Anne Jolly in North Long Beach. They visited for a few hours and then announced that they were going to see Bette. "We didn't know we were neighbors! Lost and found!" Anne declares. Anne and Bette could once again link up and support each other through thick and mostly thin. The cards and phone calls from the Kelleys continued after that memorable visit, but De's career swallowed him up again as far as the Long Beach gals were concerned. They followed him on television and delighted in his movies.[19]

5 Kelley received costar billing in a particularly terrible western called *Gunfight at Comanche Creek,* a vehicle for war hero Audie Murphy. Through June 1963, Audie and DeForest rode in a limo back and forth from the DeMille Gate to the Iverson Ranch to make the low-budget black-and-white that was so badly executed and edited that DeForest seemed to block it from his memory as soon as it was done. Sometimes a prominent bad role could be worse than no role at all, a nail in the career's coffin, and this was one of those.

In late 1963, DeForest worked with Eddie Dmytryk once again, this time in a melodrama based on a Harold Robbins novel, with Bette Davis, Rita Hayworth, and Mike Connors. Kelley, along with young Joey Heatherton, completed the cast of five primary players. Davis was a grand dame of cinema by then and commanded a special arrangement in lieu of a financial contract; the same agreements were made with Hayworth. Connors received $3,000 per week, while Kelley got $600 per week with a guarantee of ten days' work and $250 per day thereafter if needed. The Paul Wilkins Agency still represented Kelley and did the special negotiations for him. In this case, he arrived early to work one hour prior to his scheduled scenes for organized rehearsal time. This was his requirement of the studio and scheduling. He had never been in a film face-to-face with the likes of Davis, and he seemed to know that this was one of those opportunities that could be the beginning or the end of a lot of things in an acting career. He made damn sure that his character, Sam Corwin, was a living, breathing, and viable part of the production; he reached for levels of quality and elements of nuance that spoke well of his professionalism and his depth.

By the lights of Bette Creutze, Anne Jolly, and Carolyn, the character of Corwin, Hayworth's friend and art critic, was very much their gentleman DeForest in form and style. For them, he was more himself than he ever was as a heavy or a fall guy. This was his chance to break out of television and movie character types and move on to more demanding and pivotal roles. If he could hold his own with Bette Davis, he could prove himself with the industry. Kelley's part of *Where Love Has Gone* began on December 12, 1963, with Bette Davis.

Davis's reputation as difficult and extraordinary was well earned and well played as she made things enormously difficult for the crew. She was often hours late and sometimes simply did not arrive; at other times, she would work a bit and depart. Fortunately, though, she seemed on track for her major scene with Kelley; they were rehearsed one day and shot Scene 27 on the next, Friday the thirteenth. Davis was certainly the queen among her subjects, but DeForest handled himself well through the one-on-one scene with her.[20]

Kelley says that he enjoyed working with Rita Hayworth, and they seemed to revel in their very warm, well-timed flirtations on film. Kelley played an aging playboy, who kept his care and integrity well hidden under a jaded art critic's languid rottenness. It was generally a rather strange and sad movie. When it was reviewed in the fall of 1964, no one liked it, and it was panned throughout the industry. There also seemed to be an emotional gut rejection of the film because it was based on the sensational Stompanato murder case that involved Lana Turner and her daughter. To many, the book by Harold Robbins and Paramount's dramatization of the tragedy were in bad taste. Even as *Variety* reviewed the film as valueless and a waste of talent, it did comment that "DeForest Kelley impresses as an unscrupulous art critic."[21]

That small satisfaction did not change his career. DeForest, at forty-four, went back into the ranks of mediocre and all-purpose character actors. At his age and career plateau, there were some hard facts to be absorbed. With *Gunfight at Comanche Creek* and *Where Love Has Gone* panned everywhere, he was fortunate simply to make a modest living as a character actor. For nearly twenty years, he had done everything an honest and gentle talent could do to win at the game, and he could be rightly proud of his accomplishments. DeForest took rejection and despair and cultivated them into an ever-deepening understanding of the world and of himself. He focused on enjoying the people he worked with and the art of entertainment. Realistically, though, it was all downhill from there. In some circles, it was said that De and Carolyn were close to losing the house, their refuge and treasure, so even that small accomplishment might be taken away—just as they had feared when they bought it only a few short years before. Carolyn went back to work.

6 In 1964, the western began its long ride off into the sunset. A. C. Lyles was by then a producer for Paramount, and his studio sense made him very popular with the suits—he knew all about the bottom line. He would use slightly worn or faded actors, and he would have a good scene for each of them, and the audience could enjoy the casts he put together to tell fairly routine stories. Lyles made good use of his decades-long knowledge of Paramount's ways and means. His projects were on time, a feat in Hollywood, and Lyles could do it every time. The Lyles oaters were reliable B-movie fare, and they fed a lot of industry people and paid their mortgages besides. DeForest Kelley was glad to work for A.C. and Paramount.[22]

The Lyles westerns were intended for the audience who still appreciated a nostalgic cowboy tale or the mythic western. Those people who liked them were loyal to them, enjoyed them, and would miss them, but almost everyone in America knew the western genre. They had grown up with it and understood its symbolism, mythic memory, and clear morality. The western was a shared language among Americans, and it was dreamed of and powerful beyond the nation's shores. Yet, in 1964, the young American pioneer in fact and in fiction seemed to have nowhere to go and nothing to believe in. Indeed, there seemed to be no new frontier—at least, not for the common man and woman.

Screenwriter D. C. Fontana was a devotee of the classic westerns and had pitched a few of her own stories to Lyles at Paramount. She saw Kelley on the grounds and remembered him from *Gunfight at the O.K. Corral* and other movies.

Intuitively and intellectually, she, too, understood the western, and very soon she also understood that her new creative partner and employer, Gene Roddenberry, was on to something with a new series concept. She worked closely with Roddenberry from the earliest days of his western myth as applied to science fiction.

In the spring of 1964, Roddenberry approached Herb Solow, the new man in charge of television development for Desilu studio, with his new series idea, "Wagon Train to the Stars," to convey the essence of the show's dramatic momentum. Solow and others understood the concept and allowed Roddenberry to develop the pilot and assemble the crew.[23]

Roddenberry and Fontana and the accompanying executives reached into their cache of actors and actresses they wanted to have with them for the new series. Roddenberry wanted people he knew and could rely on. He called on the guys and gals who had worked well with him in his season-long show *The Lieutenant* from a few years before: Gary Lockwood, Nichelle Nichols, Leonard Nimoy, Grace Lee Whitney. And, of course, he included the star of his *333 Montgomery*, DeForest Kelley. Kelley remembered: "Gene called me and asked me to have lunch with him. He wanted to talk to me about something. So we had lunch, and he started to explain to me about this project he was embarking on. He described this character, this alien with the ears, and asked me how I felt about playing it, and I said, 'You mean this green eared . . . ?' He said yes. I said, 'No, Gene, really, I don't want to do it.' He had two properties at the time. . . . I said I would much rather wait—if he would consider me for *High Noon*. He said okay."[24]

By the time the real casting began for the *Star Trek* pilot, Roddenberry had decided that he wanted DeForest Kelley for the ship's doctor. Bob Butler, director of the pilot, was all in favor of John Hoyt, a veteran of stage and screen, and that, combined with the widely held industry opinion that Kelley could only play the heavy, was the end of Kelley as the ship's doctor. As he understood it, "I was up for *Star Trek,* but the network or someone turned me down." So he got back on his horse.[25]

In 1964 and 1965, Kelley was part of Lyles's stock company of middling has-beens such as Rory Calhoun, Lon Chaney, Jr., Dana Andrews, Richard Arlen, and Lyle Bettger, riding once more into a West that never existed. He enjoyed the light cowboy tales but no one could confuse these films with *Gunfight at the O.K. Corral, Warlock* or *Raintree County.*

Kelley worked on *Black Spurs,* filmed in the fall of 1964. Rory Calhoun made the respectable sum of $20,000 for a two-week hitch, the story and rights were purchased for $1,500, and Sheriff DeForest Kelley was shot dead on September 9 for $200.

Then *Town Tamer* was written by Andrew Craddock (pen name of A. C. Lyles) and produced for $225,000. Lyles, as the lead writer and producer, reworked the story to give Kelley a better part. He reveled in the role of Guy Tavenner, a cringing card sharp, an abusive gambler.

As Lyles liked to tell people: "I was in the commissary, and Michael Landon came over to me and said, 'A.C., you could do me a big favor . . . you've got a fight next Friday with DeForest Kelley and Dana Andrews. . . . I'd like to double DeForest Kelley in the fight.' . . . I said, 'Suppose you get hurt, break a leg. The series [*Bonanza*] would break down.'" Ace wanted assurances. "An hour later, I got a call from David Dortort. He said, 'It's okay for him to do it.' . . . Then NBC gave the okay, and they gave me a letter of release from responsibility." Everyone seemed very pleased with the idea, finally, and years later, Kelley liked to grumble about Ace Lyles, "That's the first time he ever got me doubled in a movie."

Kelley and Landon were of similar coloring and build at the time, and so the arrangement promised to be an effective fight scene. A stunt double named Bob Miles fought for Dana Andrews, and Michael Landon fought for DeForest Kelley, with casts and crews of both shows rallied around to enjoy the donnybrook Landon was wanting. The fight was set in a richly decorated lobby of a western town hotel. Kelley struck his wife, and Andrews came to her aid. It was Kelley as Tavenner who took the first punch and fell against a paneled wall and embroidered couch. Then it was Landon as Tavenner came back at Miles. Miles used a judo flip, a wallop, a stomach punch—he took a blow or two, and then Landon was hoisted and pitched over the hotel clerk's front desk. The fight was short and tight and performed on a few square feet of carpet.[26]

A few weeks later, at Universal, doing the *Virginian,* Kelley was asked if he would want a stunt double. He was unaccustomed to such niceties but thought he would ask for his favorite stuntman. He said, "Michael Landon," and they wouldn't believe him. "No, he doubled me in the last film I did." So he dared the fellow to call *Bonanza;* he did, and Landon told him to do something unprintable.

Kelley's mentor and Hollywood man, Bill Daniels, took the helm as producer and cinematographer for *Marriage on the Rocks,* a Warner Brothers vehicle for Frank Sinatra and Dean Martin. The small part of Mr. Turner belonged to Kelley, who went in on April 7, 1965, and did the work with Sinatra in three takes. The four hours of work, start to finish, brought him $1,500. Kelley had little to say about his few uncomfortable hours with the Rat Pack, though he did mention that at the time he was looking to get his "butt off a horse." But as long as the westerns paid the monthly bills, he kept swinging back into the saddle.[27]

In "Man of Violence," an episode of *The Virginian,* Kelley played a troubled alcoholic doctor caught up in a mess of regret and guilt. To Doug McClure, Kelley confessed that he believed he had killed a patient, played by Leonard Nimoy, through negligence. The doctor had been awaiting judgment in the desert sun, by exposure or Apache. Once more, within a few scenes, Kelley established a viable and sympathetic soul. His character was redeemed, as was Curly in *Warlock,* through the power of friendship.[28]

In July 1965, Kelley reported for duty with Paramount to make Lyles's *Apache Uprising.* The star of the film, Rory Calhoun, was famous for his brand of practical joking, and Kelley had had enough of it before long. "We were working outside, and it was very, very cold, and we had for our outside dressing rooms just canvas tents and electric heaters in them. . . . Rory was walking past me . . . I'm sitting in my chair, and here comes Rory with Chill Wills and a cup of coffee, and Rory comes by and he trips over me . . . and he drops the coffee on me . . . and he said, 'Excuse me, De, I'm so sorry. You know Chill Wills,' and I said, 'Yes, thank you.' . . . So I got up, brushed off the coffee, and I looked over to the side, and I saw a craft service man who takes care of the horses, and he had a big shovel . . . and so I called the craft service man over and told him I wanted him to do me a favor for a few extra shekels, and I told him I would like for him to shovel up a fresh shovel of manure and follow me. . . . So this guy shovels this fresh manure up, and I go into Rory's little tent, the dressing room, and I have him place this little beauty in his little closet and turn the electric heater on.

"He [Rory] was a very rugged guy. Fortunately, I got off at 3:30 that day and said good-bye to Rory. . . . So the next morning, I come in, and Rory is in a corral doing a fight scene with another guy, and he sees me as I walk on the soundstage, and he stops in the middle of the take. . . . I see him running, and I start to run. . . . He caught me and threw me down on the ground and said, 'You little son of a bitch! . . . Those clothes I had hanging in there, that sport coat and slacks. . . . I had to go on Art Linkletter's and do a live television show.' . . . Rory didn't play any more jokes on me after that. But I wanted to pass that little bit of nothing on to you."[29]

Another anecdote: "I was doing a scene, my death scene, where they tied me to a wagon wheel outside. This is true. They tied me to this wagon wheel . . . it was raining, and the Indians were shooting arrows at my body. They called for lunch and left me tied up. They had walked away and left me . . . but the first assistant came back real fast when I said I'm on golden [over] time." Lyles recalled the scene as well: "Now, the Indians had attacked the wagon train, and they captured De, and he was lashed to the wagon wheel, and we had a rain sequence, and the rain was going, and the Indians are shooting bows and arrows at him. The idea was to see how close they could come to him without actually nipping him. And it was around noontime. The cast and crew were hungry, so the director called lunch. . . . Halfway through lunch, someone said, 'What happened to De?' He was still tied to the wagon wheel. Oh jeeze!"[30]

"DeForest Kelley is good as the paranoid gunfighter who is shot down by the script long before a few Apaches nail him with an arrow," the reviewers agreed. In *Apache Uprising,* he created a major character in Toby Jack Saunders, a tormented soul reduced to the meanest kind of dog-killing, back-shooting, bad hombre. Each humiliation brought out of Toby a further gleeful act of menace, until Apache arrows released him from a life of cruelty. While DeForest recalled the role as one of his favorites, perhaps Toby Jack's whipped dog meanness was what haunted Kelley's private heart. This bad hombre was so malignant and tragic that the ghost of Toby Jack disturbed Kelley's sleep on and off for decades.[31]

7 DeForest was recalled by Gene Roddenberry and scheduled for another series opportunity in August 1965. That summer, working from their offices on the Desilu lot next to Paramount, Roddenberry and Fontana developed three properties: *The Long Hunt of April Savage,* the second pilot of *Star Trek,* and *Police Story.*[32]

Roddenberry still wanted Kelley as the ship's doctor on *Star Trek,* but he knew it would be a hard sell with the suits, and so he insisted that his bad hombre friend get a very expensive haircut, a modern haircut, Kelley remembered: "I had been wearing [my hair] long for westerns. . . . he wanted a brainy 'Kennedy' look." Kelley bucked a little but did as he was told. He went to Jay Sebring's and spent $35 for a cut.

Once more, something fizzled with Roddenberry's wish to have Kelley on *Star Trek*. The head of television at Desilu, Herb Solow, recalled that it was again the director, James Goldstone, who named the man for the part. This time, it was Paul Fix. Perhaps Roddenberry thought, as Kelley had always understood the case to be, that the bad hombre just wouldn't fly as a good guy on a starship, and he had to choose his battles at that time. But Kelley did perform in the thirty-minute pilot written by Roddenberry for *Police Story* for the 1966 season. Grace Lee Whitney was cast as a police sergeant, and Kelley was a lab tech working in the forensics department. In Whitney's case, she was done up to be an addle-brained and provocative counterpoint to Steve Ihnat, the very serious star of the show.[33]

During Kelley's short work week of only four scenes, Fontana could see that he and Roddenberry teamed well, and she thought Kelley's new look was quite an improvement. Robert Justman, Desilu's new all-around associate producer, was on scene during the making of *Police Story,* and he also made a mental note of Kelley. He quickly found himself liking Kelley very much as a man and as an actor. In only a few days, Justman saw that Kelley was wise and without guile, a very different sort for Hollywood. Both Kelley and Whitney were well received during previews of the pilot.[34]

On the heels of *Police Story* was another Lyles movie, *Waco,* starring Howard Keel, Rod Taylor, Wendell Corey, and Jane Russell, filmed in the fall of 1965. Kelley was Bill Rile, again a craven instigator of mean things. Without a stuntman, Kelley was hung over a barroom balcony to teach him a lesson or two. In *Waco*, Lyles and company tried for a harder edge, a sexier quality, but got very little in the end. The result was questionable for the kiddies and not enough story for the adults, and it was relegated to the dull oater bin by critics and the public.[35]

8 As the generation of writers, producers, and directors who had taken the country through World War II began to retire, a new wave of creators came through in Hollywood. These were war veterans with another program and another agenda. They entrenched themselves in positions of authority and creative power. Meanwhile, the next generation, their children, challenged the vets' certainty, bravado, and simple morality with their own vision, a reflection of their own experience. These children of World War II were students of nuclear annihilation, race riots, Vietnam, meaningless privilege, grinding poverty, experimental drugs, rock-and-roll. The youth of America put forth a shattering chorus of contradictions. As if on a cultural wave of crisis and angst, the mid-1960s pitted father against son, and they seemed bereft of a common understanding, of even a common language.

The mythic western didn't make any sense in this American landscape. L. Q. Jones remembers the fading away of the western in the mid-1960s simply: "People got tired of looking at 'em." Western veterans Woodward and Jones agree that there had been nearly one hundred westerns on the air over the years, but by the mid-1960s there were very few left. Stories had become repetitive, the really good television people had graduated in their careers to film work, and the pioneers of the western were retiring. While *Gunsmoke* and *Bonanza* endured on television and John Wayne dominated the western in movie houses and in the American psyche, the rest of the frontier died down under the weight of harsh social realities.

Then Sam Peckinpah exploded the western myth in favor of western realism. Peckinpah's reach for authenticity changed the western forever. Jones concludes: "No art to Peckinpah, he saw a chance and took it, whatever they say. . . . If they move, kill 'em . . . and Peckinpah was the master of it." There was blood and consequence, and Peckinpah showed it. When he cut loose, the violence and change were part of the culture, and he kept pushing the envelope with language and visuals. Jones remembers: "When he went a little further, reaching for authenticity—and he actually wanted to be more violent to sell more tickets—once he did, he was so successful . . . protests, ladies fainting and throwing up, and I guess it was Sam who pulled it off. [He] wanted attention and to make money, and he said he wanted to make it more truthful. Oh, BS, he wanted to make it and make money at it." By the time Jones appeared in *The Wild Bunch,* Kelley's kind of western was a thing of the past.

As the country began to tear itself apart, the schedule of the 1966 television season was finalized, and the *Police Story* pilot went unsold. With the western in its death throes, Kelley was looking at the end of the trail. At home, it was said, the Kelleys were talking retirement, at the very least a lowering of expectations.

In some ways, he was looking at the death of a large part of himself. An entire universe of self-expression and exploration was slipping through his fingers through no fault of his own. It seemed he'd been dealt his last hand.

With the loss of *Police Story,* he again managed to take disappointment graciously; he called Roddenberry to console him and thank him for "trying Kelley" once again. "Two shows that never sold. . . . He said, 'Wait, De. Don't hang up. The network has seen a screening of *Police Story* . . . and after looking at your work, they decided you would be right for the doctor.' "

Kelley remembered, "I did well on audience reaction indicators" as a good guy, a modern character in *Police Story.* Finally, with the haircut and the clean look, Kelley escaped the bad hombre typecasting. Roddenberry was unhappy with the ship's doctor in the second pilot,

Paul Fix. He wanted a new doctor, not an elder statesman, as Fontana remembers. The new doctor would be angled to be a bit older than the others but not much. Roddenberry had wanted Kelley from the first, and now, with *Police Story*'s audience reaction, he had the proof, at least for the suits, that Kelley was the right man for the job.[36]

In sum, Roddenberry wanted someone capable of more than medicine and counseling; he wanted someone who was confessor and physician and who could also ride shotgun on this "Wagon Train to the Stars." Kelley's signature role in the twentieth-century morality play would not be in a western disguised as a twisted heavy; rather, he would be a humane hero and a voice of human conscience. As a minister, healer, and gunman, no one could match the qualifications that DeForest Kelley brought to Roddenberry's enterprise. "So I came aboard and started with the series. . . . Doesn't that thrill you down to your little bitty toes?"

Chapter IX
Starlight
1966

*"I told Gene, this is going to be the biggest hit
or the biggest miss God ever made."*
—DeForest Kelley, 1991

On April 25, 1966, DeForest collected memos and notes and other information on *Star Trek* and his copy of "Your *Star Trek* Role" from Gene Roddenberry and D. C. Fontana. Later, he played down what it meant to him: "I had just done a movie before that and think I had . . . a two-part *Bonanza*. And I was hoppin' around doing one thing or another. . . . When this came up, I came in for seven out of thirteen [episodes of *Star Trek*]. Came home, told Carolyn about it, she said, 'What the hell. That's seven shows, you know, that's good, pay the mortgage, that's it.' I said, 'I just hope it goes seven.' " But Aileen Pickering recalls that two days later, DeForest and Carolyn came to her house with an NBC towel with a peacock on it, and they celebrated poolside. "There we go!" DeForest had the true light of joy on his face at Aileen's, hamming it up for the camera, doing his Tarzan's physique pose on the diving board with his Kennedy haircut curling in small waves around his head. It was undeniable—he was emblazoned with it: joy.[1]

What was so funny about it all was that Aileen and a friend had gone to a special screening of the first *Star Trek* pilot in the spring of 1966. She was so amazed by the whole thing that she called De and Carolyn and described it to them. Carolyn told her that De had been approached about the show. "Coincidence." Aileen reconsiders: in retrospect, it seemed a predestined course, and the future changed for DeForest as it changed for the world.[2]

The Kelley circle celebrated as the news spread, but Herman Casey, the big man who had meant so much to DeForest, did not live to see his nephew begin the new voyage. Shorty was still down on Long Beach, as were Anne Jolly and her son and two daughters and her mother, Billee, and Bette Creutze and her family.

Barney Girard had moved on to other projects. He had three fine sons and a future in feature films after a long and very successful career in writing and directing television. Though they had always loved each other, Barney and DeForest had less in common with each passing year. But in 1965 or so, Girard had a feature film script that he was jammed up on for a title. DeForest might have reached into his own feelings about his career when he gave Girard the title *Dead Heat on a Merry Go Round*. Irving Ravetch had long since sailed from sight, but his success as a screenwriter was certainly noted by his old radio friends. He had films such as *The Dark at the Top of the Stairs, Home from the Hill,* and the big achievement, *Hud,* in 1963. It seemed all three Long Beach boys were now primed for greater successes.[3]

In the Kelley circle was the center corps of friends. Joe Laden continued to wander the world but checked in with letters and phone conversations. John Walton had given up on acting and gone back to hairdressing, but he remained a close and constant friend. Olive LaFata and children had turned everything around; she was a very successful retailer of women's apparel. Bill and Betty Daniels continued to be mentors to their young friends. Bill's friendship with De was extraordinary for its ordinariness, something De did not have otherwise. There were A. C. and Martha Lyles and De's first fan, Grace Hartung; he refused to lose track of Grace as she moved from Long Beach back to her home in Muscatine, Iowa. He kept her posted on his victories, and this was certainly one. Of course, there was Aileen, who was always landing or taking off.

News spread to the folks back in Georgia and the Reverend Mr. Kelley. DeForest's uncle, Dr. Luther Kelley, had passed away a few years before in 1963 but was certainly present in DeForest's memory as he created a physician for the twenty-third century. The memory of the dignified and very capable surgeon was surely mixed with the abruptness that marred the healing nature of so many very good physicians, especially surgeons. Dr. Kelley's matter-of-fact declaration of his mother's terminal case must have been the abrasive sand De-Forest used as he created the demeanor of Dr. McCoy.

On May 23, 1966, *Star Trek* really began for DeForest Kelley. He drove his old Ford the usual route from his manicured and modest section of Sherman Oaks, down Ventura Boulevard, past the shops and cafés and Aileen's office along the way. Turning right at the end of Ventura, he moved along the descending artery that joined North Hollywood and Burbank to Hollywood proper. Farther east, Warner Brothers was snuggled up against the hills beside Griffith Park and Forest Lawn Cemetery, Hollywood Way and NBC. Beyond that were the horse ranches and bridle paths, where the *Bonanza* boys and wranglers had done their work and where Aileen had taught him to mount from the left almost fifteen years before. On his right were the sheer climbs and the homes burrowed into the Hollywood Hills, the old terra-cotta tile and palms and warrens of chic and shabby apartments, cottages, and hidden drives. Then the slide down Highland into old Hollywood, past Hollywood Boulevard, down by the Walk of Fame, the Chinese Theater, the Roosevelt Hotel, and all the old glamour haunts. Left onto Melrose, and Desilu studios appeared on the left just before the famous Paramount gates. Lucille Ball ran the big show at Desilu. Here was his new studio for seven of thirteen shows, at least—maybe more.

John D. F. Black, initially a story consultant and associate producer for the new show, recalled the very first glimpse of "De coming through the door to my office in his uniform fresh from wardrobe, the day before the first segment of *Star Trek* was to start shooting. 'How do you guys like me in my jammies?' His grin went from ear to ear."[4]

DeForest set to work with the team of Roddenberry as creator and executive producer, Justman as associate producer, and executive secretary Fontana. The crew they assembled over the course of two years of planning, fighting, sweating, and dreaming was drawn from Roddenberry's and Justman's professional pasts, especially Gene's *Police Story* and Bob's *Outer Limits*.

Dorothy C. Fontana, as executive secretary for the show, saw everything from seed to full bloom, from formats to rewrites and the beginnings of the *Star Trek* Bible. She recalls that DeForest was still uncertain about his appearance, with his swept bangs and waves. The $35 cut made his eyes appear bigger and warmer, and the smile when combined with the blue medic's tunic . . . wow! Fontana was very pleased with the combined effect.[5]

Kelley's apprehension about the show was summed up in his own unique style when he told Roddenberry, "This is going to be the biggest hit or the biggest miss God ever made." While Roddenberry found Eastern expressions of transcendence and mysticism more palatable, he respected the quiet man's old-fashioned ways. Creator and actor were men deeply concerned with spiritual and humanistic questions, however they were expressed.[6]

Roddenberry knew there were a few lines that could not be crossed with Kelley, and one small instance dramatized this. DeForest recalled: "I had great trouble when we started *Star Trek*. Roddenberry said no jewelry, and I had [my mother's ring] on, and he said no jewelry, and I said, no jewelry, no DeForest." That's all there was to it. Just like that, everyone knew he meant it. Clora's ring became part of Dr. Leonard McCoy.[7]

"Everything to do with McCoy we did with Kelley's input. We created McCoy with Kelley right there," Dorothy Fontana remembers. Roddenberry was the creator of *Star Trek*, but DeForest Kelley created Dr. McCoy.[8]

2 "The Corbomite Maneuver" was the first show shot and was the first exploration of the relationship between Captain James T. Kirk and his ship's doctor, as McCoy counseled Kirk in the turbo-lift. The dialogue about the young officer up on the bridge established that the doctor and Kirk were on a friendly, even brotherly, level. McCoy could rein in the captain for a little correction, whether or not the captain wanted to hear it.

The tone of the friendship was established in a few moments, as was McCoy's very human personality. In this first episode, the camera caught the self-deprecating humor and self-doubt in McCoy that sprang to life through Kelley's work with his voice, facial expressions, and body language. McCoy appeared very early on as a fully living man in front of the camera. No comic-book hero type, McCoy could be confounded, frustrated, flustered, and frightened, but always amused at his own quirks. The constants among all of his personal contradictions were his exemplary skill as a surgeon and his passionate commitment to his comrades. All this is evident in the very first show. McCoy knew he was in for a hell of a ride among bizarre creatures, superhuman heroes, and alien shipmates. The ship's doctor was the human being who had to live within Roddenberry's creation. Kelley established McCoy as a living, complex, and complete man within days of first breathing life into him.

Captain Kirk was played by William Shatner, a promising, classically trained Canadian actor of Jewish parentage. He was a peculiar mix of elements: power, stamina, looks, intellect, and complex weaknesses that made him a multidimensional actor, a man well suited to portray the Horatio Hornblower type Roddenberry had in mind. As Kirk, all his qualities and faults could be thrown at McCoy, could be shared with him and argued about or wept over.

Shatner's people at the Ashley Famous Agency worked out a deal that gave him $5,000 a week during the first year and twenty percent of his original salary on each of the subsequent five reruns plus bonuses. And there would be more income based on percentages of future considerations and $500 more per show should the series make good on its first year. Shatner had good business sense and made the best package he could under very experimental circumstances. Bob Justman was thrilled to get Shatner; he knew that Bill was a man on the rise, in great demand, and they were lucky to get him. His contract was kept close to the vest, as was everyone else's, but it was understood that Shatner was the marquee name and the man at the top of the show.[9]

Shatner later recalled: "I remember being in the office at *Star Trek* with De and Bob Justman that first day. I recognized him from *Raintree County,* and I was an admirer of his work. I had seen him in several things. I always loved the way he looked. I wanted to look like him, with his hair combed that way and his lean build and his unique way of talking."[10]

Kelley was the most recognizable face in the cast, but he fared little better than most of his fellow crewmen on the *Enterprise,* with a payment of $850 per show for the seven of thirteen. The total rerun share was not to exceed fifty percent of his initial payments. Everyone knew that reruns stopped paying altogether after five showings. That was the way things were done in 1966.

It wasn't all he'd expected, but it was a new lease on his career. He remembered his initial understanding of the arrangements. First he'd been offered the green, pointy-eared role in 1964 and had refused. Then Roddenberry had tried twice to get him for the doctor's role. Kelley said, "When the *Star Trek* pilot was shot, I was told that I would be the star of the show. Later, when the series went into production, I discovered that my billing would be as a supporting actor. Sure, I was disappointed, even though I've always felt that the only recognition an actor needs is appreciation from an audience for a job well done and the knowledge that he has given the best performance he could. But being a star is nice." Even in joy, there was a pang of disappointment—he always seemed to get less than first promised. Justman stepped in and made sure that Kelley's name was alone on one card at the end of the show. A separate billing for the veteran actor was the best Justman could do, and he thought Kelley deserved at least that.

After twenty-two years, this was the extent of his new riches, but to him riches it was. He stiffened his resolve, fought for a parking space, and let his joy creep into his work."

It took a while for older viewers to realize that this was Toby Jack and Captain Johnson, the multipurpose bad guy who had haunted television westerns throughout the last decade. But certainly they had never seen anything like the fellow who did wind up with the pointed ears, the second star of the show. A lesser-known actor, Leonard Nimoy had once played a scene with Kelley, but Kelley didn't recall it until Nimoy told him he'd left him to die in *The Virginian.* For years, Nimoy endured as Kelley had, living on determination. Now, he was so very important to Roddenberry's *Enterprise.* But the powers knew the actor was struggling and could force a minimal package on him. The deal was $1,250 per week and 10 percent above Screen Actor's Guild scale for the five reruns. This was acceptable to a hungry actor who then wisely began securing a house and a nest egg for his family on the new fortune.

Kelley remembered: "When we first started *Star Trek,* and I mean it was during the first episode, Leonard Nimoy and I went to lunch together, and Leonard had his ears on, which he at the time was not too keen about [and] was very worried about it, and he was telling me that he was concerned . . . and sometimes felt like a rabbit. We had a bunch of celery sticks and carrot sticks that were on the table, and so I picked up a couple of carrot sticks and handed them to Leonard. He said, 'De, don't ever do that to me again.' But those ears finally became a very important thing to him, didn't they?"[12] Kelley was always grateful to his instincts that he had turned down the Spock part. He acknowledged that no one else could have filled the role and transformed it into something as forceful as Leonard Nimoy had.

Kelley once said: "Roddenberry is a very talented man, and he has a great knack for casting. . . . I've seen how he works, and it's not easy to get principals together where a certain chemistry works. If you don't have that chemistry that's flowing between three people or four, it doesn't work, and you can't force it. It's one of the things that was a major factor with the three of us, me and Leonard and Bill. A lot of people thought there was a great deal of luck involved in it, but I think a great deal of it was shrewd casting."

James Doohan, a Canadian character actor and master of voice and dialect, came in as the rough-and-tumble Scotsman. As engineer Montgomery Scott, Doohan was engaged for five of thirteen, until everyone realized the problems with the chain-of-command issue, and Doohan's agreement was extended so that Scott could take the helm for the sake of story and believability. Grace Lee Whitney was called to portray Yeoman Janice Rand—a highly attractive aide to the captain, a potential romantic interest, and a visual invitation to male viewers. Whitney had built quite a career in television since her days at MGM. She was a recognized name and face in the public eye. Less well known was Majel Barrett, who crossed from one incarnation of *Star Trek,* as the executive officer in the first pilot, to the series, where she became Nurse Chapel, a romantic and somewhat fragile character.

Roddenberry's purpose was clear in his creation of a multinational, multiethnic crew. He was concerned with addressing many of the wrongs in American history by writing the American future. George Takei was the Asian swashbuckler as Lieutenant Sulu. He was the young, sharp helmsman destined for captaincy. When he was a small child, Takei and his family had been torn away from their American home and their Japanese-American world when they were sent to a detention camp after Pearl Harbor. A Northern-born black woman raised by a family who cherished their African-American heritage and their faith, Nichelle Nichols was a singer and entertainer, but as Lieutenant Uhura (the Swahili word means "freedom"), she would pioneer more new frontiers than any of her costars. "I really knew what [Gene] was talking about," Nichols recalls. "The amalgamation of life in America. But I never thought he could do it, I never thought it was going to happen. He never lost his determination that he was going to have a cast of men and women . . . with human frailties like anybody else . . . who in difficult situations would become heroes . . . beyond Earth."

There were three completely original episodes always in motion and others in some phase of development. There were six days to shoot an episode—that's all. There were the indoor sets to conceive, design, and manufacture.

At locations such as Lion Country USA, Roddenberry rewrote the script sitting under a tree as he saw the animals that he might use during the setup and shooting of "Shore Leave." Fontana rushed his rewrites back to the office for typing, then to mimeo, then back to Lion Country to distribute the new pages to the cast and crew.

Roddenberry often worked until three and four A.M. on his rewrites, and Fontana would be in early to type and mimeo and distribute before the set call. Then Roddenberry might get a little sleep on the couch in his office. The actors' usual schedule of up at five A.M. and to bed by ten P.M. seemed pastoral in comparison.

Star Trek had to create universes and aliens and a human society very nearly beyond imagination. Just getting the go-ahead for thirteen episodes essentially meant that they were immediately behind, because the scripts called for worlds and ships that had to be created from the vacuum of deep space. Then there were production problems. One of the earliest was how to get the actors to a planet surface for the story in the first place. That gave rise to original solutions such as the transporter, which then gave rise to story lines and dramatic devices based on the technologically fantastic. The problems and concepts were handled through Roddenberry and Justman. Apparently, it was Justman who came up with the idea of an orienting narration for each episode, to set up the drama and the players and give the audience entry to the story. This simple mechanism saved the writers wads of exposition. Most of *Star Trek* was told as something that had just occurred, often initiated with a captain's log.

Roddenberry's interfacing of his creative people with consultants, actors, studio heads, network execs, and science-fiction writers was as brilliant as his casting. An early alliance with writer Gene Coon promised the very lively characterizations and plots that he was known for. Roddenberry also had personal collaborations with real-life experts at NASA and with genius Isaac Asimov, who became his sounding board and confidant.

Gene wrote explanations and back story—a "Bible" for writers and crews. Consistency and believability demanded creation of societies, a cooperative union of planets and species, an enlightened military bearing, and a technical language that was both interesting and appropriate to humans in the twenty-third century as well as the mid-twentieth. Continuity of characters was essential but only part of Roddenberry's virtual galaxy. Only he decided what was appropriate to *Star Trek,* he called the shots about his universe, and he approved or disapproved of everything with the powers of Zeus.

Roddenberry was relentless in his search for kernels of the future in the cutting-edge present. His research trips to NASA and his correspondence with engineers and researchers resulted in the interactive computer, the tricorder, the sickbay equipment, and the other items that made *Star Trek* a surpassing glimpse into what was considered to be at least a century distant world of technology. Innovator Matt Jeffries perfected the ship. Justman brought *Outer Limits* veteran Wah Chang to Desilu. The perfected phaser and the tricorder were Wah Chang creations. Other innovators gave the *Star Trek* world its look and sound.[13]

Frankly, much like Dr. Lee DeForest, Gene Roddenberry had a tendency to take more credit than he perhaps deserved, but, as with so many creators he sowed the seed tended and grown by others on the

Star Trek endeavor. What more could a creator do? DeForest Kelley was always comfortable with innovators and gave them their due. He ascribed the credit for *Star Trek* to Roddenberry, without whom there would have been no *Enterprise* at all.

Through the initial weeks of production, the actors and their characters were evaluated. Of Kelley, it was said, "His contract should be renegotiated so that we may have him for more days per show at an agreed salary." Doohan, Nichols, and Takei were the foundation of recurring characters and performed well with contracts that were less stable and less lucrative than they had hoped. Whitney's role initially seemed to be the third or fourth major character in the show but soon was found to have uncertain value in the episodes, and she was dismissed before the actual premiere of the series.[14]

Truth be told, it was more likely that an assault on Whitney by an executive on the studio lot in the summer of 1966 had more to do with her marginal role and ultimate dismissal from the *Star Trek* crew than a budget crisis or character development. Anne Jolly's sad observation that Hollywood is a cruel and often dangerous place for a woman was borne out by Whitney's experiences. "When I got written out of *Star Trek,* De and Leonard were so supportive to me. I remember the way [De] used to say 'Grace'—he had a special way of saying it that just got me."[15]

3 "Man Trap" was the third show shot but the first one aired. Why? Because it was the first one that came together through editing and music and the works. That was Fontana's understanding of the situation. "Corbomite Maneuver" and other episodes were still hung up in postproduction. Others considered that the NBC suits chose it, while still others thought that it was most typical of what viewers would expect from a science-fiction series. Justman wanted "Naked Time" to be the first to go, because it was a character study. Who they were and why they were there were revealed in "Naked Time," and Justman thought that would be a good introduction of the *Enterprise* crew to the viewing public. He could have shipped a number of episodes to the network in time, but in the screenings with NBC, the executives settled on "Man Trap" over his objections. The show was ready on August 29, 1966.

On September 8, 1966, at seven-thirty P.M., the day after De and Carolyn's twenty-first anniversary, *Star Trek* appeared on television for the first time—with DeForest Kelley as the pivotal regular in the story. "And away we go to another planet for the sci-fi buffs to lick the dish clean," *Telepix Review* declared. There was a "lack of meaningful cast leads . . . with only violence to provide the excitement." Shatner, Nimoy, and guest stars Jeanne Bal and Alfred Ryder were reviewed as all right in the face of a flawed and plodding story. Kelley went unmentioned in this and most reviews. The *Los Angeles Times* and *Daily Variety* panned the first episodes.[16]

"Charlie X" was handily directed by Barney Girard's protégé Larry Dobkin and aired on September 15, 1966. Dobkin recalls little of the show, except that he wouldn't relive that part of his life, "not on toast." Life had a way of turning sour that year, and *Star Trek* was a blur to him, though he recalls the cast as very pleasant. But for D. C. Fontana, "Charlie X" was an achievement. It had been a "junked" story Roddenberry had been fooling with. Justman knew Fontana was a writer, that she was good, and that she would work on speculation. "Give it to Dorothy, and see what she can do with it," he advised Roddenberry. Fontana resuscitated the good that was in it. Justman recalls there was little in the way of physical action, but it was dramatic, and that was just as good: "Attention is what matters."

The highly regarded young method actor Robert Walker, Jr., became Charlie in one of the better-executed episodes of the series. Not long after, Fontana became Roddenberry's well-grounded creative shadow. Find a strong female character in *Star Trek,* and you'll find her somewhere in the mix.[17]

It was all a new frontier. Kelley recalled: "It was a fascinating time. . . . The first year was very hard work. It almost killed us all. We were working terribly long hours. We were pushing. . . . We all felt we needed so much more time than we were getting. . . . I began to see the possibilities for him [McCoy]. . . . Bill and Leonard and myself, we were all looking for ourselves that first year."[18]

A trio emerged as contract regulars were minimized and Kelley's role became stronger. As Fontana recalls, Roddenberry and the whole team saw the exquisite chemistry among Shatner, Nimoy, and Kelley, three men as different from one another as the characters they played. The actors truly enjoyed one another, and it showed in their performances.

The barbs, bristles, and brotherhood between Spock and McCoy began subtly. As Kelley explained, "It found its way into one of the early scripts. . . . There was simply a line of some sort. I really don't remember. I read it in a particular way for Leonard. He reacted to the way I read the line, and I reacted again to him." The doctor's jutting chin or squinted eye provoked the lifted brow and tilt of the Vulcan's head, and in reaction, the doctor's head pulled back in mock disgust or confoundedness, and so it went. The writers, especially Roddenberry's lead writer and line producer, Gene Coon, picked up on it. The two actors had a syncopated timing that lent itself to good use for comedic effect or dramatic clashing of wills. It was delicious all the way around.[19]

Kelley became the elder brother and straight man for the *Enterprise*. A few months into the first year, it became evident how some of that family related in a rather twenty-third-century way. Nichols recalled that early in their first season's voyage, she one day noticed Kelley staring at her—and Shatner and Nimoy were, too. Not because she was so beautiful—they were up to something, putting one another up to something. "So they decided that De, being the most gentlemanly and discreet of the three of them," would be the one to do it. He approached her and finally spit it out: "Who does your work?" She couldn't fathom what he was talking about. Her work? And the other fellows were moving in on her. She felt surrounded by Hollywood actors speaking a lingo she didn't get—then finally she realized. Teeth! "For God's sake, are those all yours?" Kelley exclaimed as Shatner and Nimoy closed in on her. The ship's doctor wanted a closer look, so Kelley examined her teeth.

Nichols always thought of him as her sassy gentleman friend. At times, he would tell her she had great gams, and he would tell folks everywhere, "She rings my bell." Their genuine relationship, between white Southern man and African-American woman, was something sweet and free of the scars of history, and that was really Roddenberry's message for every player, for every viewer.[20]

Nichols remembers Kelley: "I loved and adored him from day one. A kind person, but he was a strong person, and, like Bones, he was irascible, don't push his buttons . . . he would quietly put you in your place. . . . He had a sense of humor so wry and so dry—like persimmons, like lemons, so clever." He calmly went about the business of *Star Trek*. "His work, his craft, his art, was very private, very personal. So much so that you didn't notice it—you didn't see it. He didn't walk around [emoting, grumbling, talking to himself]—he just did it. He and Leonard were my self-adopted mentors." They "confirmed and encouraged who my character was for me." And, by example, she learned that rather than "being swept up in the heat and rhythm of someone else . . . you have to know your center and what you are going to do with it, and then allow yourself to respond—within character. Do not do something out of character." As good a maxim for acting as for life.

During the first season, a director insisted again and again that Nichols do something out of character. He pushed and yelled and bullied. She would not give in, though she was upset and shuddering. Kelley, always neutral, brushed by her, and, Nichols recalls "with that eternal cigarette hanging out of his mouth, [he said,] 'His problem is he doesn't understand the character, he doesn't know who you are. Just stick to your friggin' guns, Nichelle.' And I stood there gaping with tears in my eyes . . . because I knew that was what I was supposed to be doing." Finally, she was called to Roddenberry's office to answer the director's complaints. He settled the question. Indeed, she would do anything an actress was called upon to do, but the director was asking her to do something that Uhura would not do. Roddenberry confirmed that she was perfectly right. "It was De who knew I was in real trouble. It was the first season." She remembers it well. "Stick to your friggin' guns, Nichelle."[21]

Nichols had found living in the twentieth century a rather harsh reality. She had been made to feel like a third-class citizen outside of her *Enterprise* crew. Her crew could not shelter her from twentieth-century bigotry and sexism, and the twenty-third century was just too damn far away to make it all worthwhile. Finally, she had had enough of the studio, the suits, security, and the whole mess that pressed down upon her. She went to Roddenberry and told him she would be leaving the show. He told her, "If you leave, they win." Hold on, but why? She had her answer the next day, when she attended an NAACP fundraiser and met Martin Luther King, Jr. She happened to mention her intention of departing the show, and King said to her, with a preacher's certainty, "You cannot, you must not. Don't you realize how important your presence, your character, is? Don't you realize the gift this man [Roddenberry] has given the world? . . . Don't you see that you're not just a role model for little black children? You're more important for people who don't look like us. For the first time, the world sees us as we should be seen, as equals, as intelligent people . . . you are a role model for everyone. You are important there because of your color. This is what Gene Roddenberry has given us." A rejuvenated Nichols went back to Roddenberry and repeated the conversation. He was overwhelmed. She recalls that he said, "God bless that man. At least someone sees what I'm trying to achieve."

4 In October 1966, Anne Jolly received a letter from her dear friend Carolyn, written on a *Star Trek* memo pad with the Desilu Studios header. "*Star Trek* was picked up for an additional 10 shows, joyful news to all concerned. Glad you all watch and like it. . . . Tell your [young son] Curt that Dr. McCoy is getting new pictures made—the studio says they'll be ready soon and Curt will get the very first one." On November 28, the photo arrived, a shot of McCoy in the shining medical tunic. It was a glamour pose of the actor seated on a sickbay bed the way Dean Martin lounged on a piano. Kelley signed the photo and promised that they would soon meet in person.

The work was grueling—and Kelley looked rough. The makeup man had to spend special time to treat the ever-darkening swollen circles under his eyes. He drew a sketch of instructions concerning the layers of foundation and concealer and color. More "like a woman's makeup," the instruction revealed. Kelley kept the sketch. He was very self-conscious about the creases under his eyes, but there was nothing he could do—except hope that he could get through the next few months without his private life interfering with his work.

Truth be known, daily life was hell, for it was during those other-wise euphoric months that DeForest's father failed rapidly and dramatically. He was helpless in his heart and in his new role to do anything to ease his father's decline or to share the burden his brother was bearing for him. The stress and guilt wore on him, and the doctor's eyes always told on him. Sleepless and worried, he nevertheless betrayed nothing to his new comrades. Such was the way with Kelley that his suffering was absorbed into the very real presence of Leonard H. McCoy.[22]

DeForest wrote to his father and later talked about the letter: "I told my father that as I look back, remembering how he captivated all of us with his sermons, he was probably the real reason I became an actor. I didn't realize it, but I wanted to be an actor like him. A good preacher, like a good lawyer, is a good actor—and my father was a good preacher."

The preacher had endured nearly a decade without Clora and without his younger son; his had been a slow and tragic disintegration. Casey Kelley and his family had cared for the old man, tried to make him more comfortable, tried to put a little sunshine in his life, but to no avail. In November 1966, the old preacher died at the age of eighty-three. He never saw his son on the bridge of the *Enterprise*.

Yes, the old man was a fine preacher because he was a fine actor; DeForest's conclusion was not blasphemous. The expression of truth takes many forms, many actors. Devotion, integrity, and sacrifice were joyful return for a gift of great price; simply to know and explore that gift was well worth the cost. DeForest understood his own devotion as something just as serious and as all-encompassing as his father's calling.

In private prayer, DeForest conducted his own reconciliation. Melancholy, sadness, doubt, all of these things came and went and left their mark on him. "They're inescapable to someone in my profession. I never conquer them. I may delay an oncoming one for a while, but it springs whenever I least expect it. I ask myself, 'Why am I like this?' But there's never an answer. . . . One tactic that works, just temporarily, is for me to say a prayer for the day as I am getting up each morning." In asking God's help, he found solace. In his mid-forties, he declared, "I am still spiritually inclined. . . . I have been exposed to a great deal of temptation." His moral code remained steadfast and all the stronger for the testing. The gifts that Clora and Reverend Kelley had given him remained with him beyond their lifetimes, an affirmation of their prayers and an answer to their faith in him.[23]

Again, DeForest acted symbolically, for the only thing he kept to remember his father by was the Bible the Reverend Mr. Kelley carried during his years on the sawdust trail. Armed with Clora's ring on the one hand and his father's Bible in the other, he created a new type of American hero. Kelley's McCoy was a vital reinterpretation of the Southern white American.

5 Kelley was a very gentle man; Justman believed that Kelley had been gentled by rejection and compromise. He had innate authority just by being what he was. "Actors—is what we know of them who they really are? That's an age-old question."[24]

Justman recalls that in the first year of the series, Kelley was guaranteed featured-player billing, and Shatner and Nimoy were the stars of the show. "It became apparent to me as well as to Gene very early on that the character of McCoy was going to be a linchpin—a fulcrum upon which one side was balanced with the other. De was very effective in this role, and I was very aware of this." Justman was in charge of many things on *Star Trek,* including the nuts and bolts of the show, and "among my many duties was to generate all the title copy" beginning and ending the episodes. The shots that were used to promote the show were Justman's selections, and "I made sure that De got the best of it." When time came to negotiate the second season, Kelley's agent began working to get proper compensation and credit.

On December 1, 1966, Justman wrote to Roddenberry that he was way ahead of De's agent, Jimmy McHugh, Jr., because Justman himself had ensured that DeForest received better credit than he was actually contracted for. This, Justman wrote, was "because of the performance he gives us" and because Kelley was "one helluva nice guy. He has been more than the kindly ship's doctor to all of us." Justman and Roddenberry found a way to compensate Kelley before costar billing was possible. They quietly raised his salary to about $2,500 per show.[25]

The first season revealed the recognition of McCoy as a man for all seasons. He was an aging romantic in "The Man Trap," complete with salt monster and his own quick interpretation of a monster's possession of McCoy. In "Charlie X," he was the knowing but hesitant uncle to the foundling. In "The Naked Time," he was apparently the immune scientist searching for a cure while the rest of the ship lost its mind and the Vulcan went on a crying jag. In Roddenberry's "Mudd's Women," he ruminated like a cranky Navy ship's doctor, as he did in "The Corbomite Maneuver": "If I jumped every time a light came on around here, I'd end up talking to myself."

In "Shore Leave," he tangled with a white rabbit, a damsel in distress, and a jousting knight. In this episode, you had to wonder what they were doing with his makeup. This time, he looked more like DeForest Kelley than in many of the other episodes. His fans concluded that they had made him down rather than up to look less attractive and older than he actually was, in order to deflect romantic attention from him and onto Shatner and Nimoy. Fontana doesn't think so. One could observe the drastic changes in makeup and uniforms, boldness of color, and the emergence of a fluid but stabilized *Star Trek* look. "Shore Leave" was just a particularly good episode for McCoy.

They were free to travel during their breaks. Kelley went to see his brother, Casey, in Georgia. The Kelley boys went to Conyers looking for Emma Banks, the black woman who had meant so much to DeForest when he was a ten-year-old boy. They found the house but not Emma Banks. They asked to go in and were allowed to see the old home. It was just the same as he remembered. They went house to house in the poor section of Conyers but were told only that Emma Banks had been taken from the place in a "rolling chair" some years before. DeForest kept it in his heart to find her someday, or her children—to say thanks and to help if they needed anything.[26]

Carolyn and De made their way back to New York City to take in a little theater. One day, they decided to catch a matinee performance of a musical. In the lobby, Carolyn went off to the powder room. DeForest waited for her. "There was a vacant candy stand, and I was leaning against it, and a couple of women saw me, and they came over and handed me their programs to sign, and I signed them, and after about ten minutes there was a whole mob. I looked up, looking for Carolyn, and I couldn't see her. I was in the middle of a seething, actually a seething mob. And finally, I saw Carolyn coming up, just her head, coming up the steps. . . . I literally was surrounded, and I couldn't get away, and I started to make the move, and I couldn't get away, and Carolyn waved . . . They finally had to call the ushers. . . . The women were getting up out of their seats, mind you, in the theater, and coming into the aisle to get me . . . and they were all standing up in the balconies and yelling '*Star Trek*' and 'McCoy.' "

The show was held up, and finally De and Carolyn were shown to their seats in the middle of a row of nuns. The Kelleys were protected by habits on both sides. People still passed their items for him to autograph down the line of nuns. He told the nun next to him that he had never been mobbed. She said to him, "You must remember something: With every little blessing, there comes a penalty."

He was truly shaken—not even in his earliest movie-star fantasies had he yearned to be surrounded and smothered by celebrity. He was unprepared for the feelings of anxiety, the pressure of panic. At the end of the musical, he and Carolyn had planned to visit backstage with the star, Joel Grey, but "the ushers came and got me, surrounded me, got me to the side of the theater, and put me in a cab like a mechanical doll or something. That was the first time I was ever mobbed, and it was completely shocking."[27]

The one sure way to unnerve DeForest Kelley was to need him too much for the wrong reasons. Need scattered his calm and disturbed his equilibrium. Being mobbed was the nightmarish accumulation of false desire and discord. Thereafter, the Kelleys seemed to burrow further into their Greenleaf home, their sanctuary. Carolyn also was deeply affected by the event and other milder occurrences over the months. She became ever more reluctant to venture out, lest they be thrust into the limelight. She kept her husband close to her side, glued to the hip—and that was all right with De.

Chapter X
Dammit, Jim
1967

"You know what they're sayin' on the set?
You'd have T'Pay T'Pau T'Prong T'Pring."
—DeForest Kelley, 1967

Gene Roddenberry had an ace up his sleeve in the shape of Gene Coon, who came aboard recognizing the importance of Roddenberry's mission. It was Coon who injected humor and humanity into the script rewrites; that was his forte. He was the spark of life and love on the *Enterprise*.

Coon's very good friend Bill Campbell had long ago crossed the line to television, though he was best known as a young, handsome sidewinder in westerns and had become a steady player in John Wayne pictures. Campbell picked up a little work with the *Star Trek* crew, the first time as the imperious Trelane in "The Squire of Gothos." Coon wrote the episode and the character specifically for Campbell, as Bob Justman recalls. What was delightful in Trelane is what is so delightful in Campbell.

Campbell remembers: "In my lifetime, I met maybe five people I found it impossible to dislike, and strangely enough two of those were on *Star Trek*: DeForest and Gene Coon. And if they liked you, you knew you had a compatriot." Kelley told Campbell that he had had to think long and hard about *Star Trek,* but since it was for Roddenberry, he decided to risk it. And Roddenberry told Campbell that

Kelley was one of the best actors he had ever worked with. Campbell joined the mutual admiration society.

As he recalls, Kelley had an authoritative presence; he likened it to Clint Eastwood's. His authority came from magnetism and self-knowledge, not from force and airs and entourages. While McCoy might have been described as an H. L. Mencken type, Campbell saw that Kelley recognized the deeper mechanisms in the character and in the body of the material as written.

Campbell knew that Roddenberry and the supervisory suits were "cold-ass businessmen," but they knew for their own purposes how clearly Kelley stood out. Even without lines, he compelled notice just standing there on the bridge of the *Enterprise*. From the earliest inception, Kelley created a rare and genuine continuity within his character. Although Campbell felt that Kelley did not consider himself a star, he surely worked like one.

Campbell emphasizes McCoy's place by saying, "You've gotta remember that he was really the only one people related to, he was the humanity. Sure, you had Scotty . . . a caricature—the others were defined" as bits and pieces of real people. The one whole human being was McCoy. Kelley didn't care a damn about science fiction, but when Campbell thought about it, *Star Trek* was really a western. He pointed out to Kelley what he was wearing, the boots and the phaser. Guest stars like himself and Morgan Woodward added to the impression of "Wagon Train to the Stars."

During the twelve-month shakedown cruise, there was a shaking out of personnel, and two distinct groups developed, divided primarily by age. Among the actors, only James Doohan, playing the ship's engineer, was as old as Kelley was. Roddenberry, Bob Justman, and Coon were veterans, men who had been in uniform during World War II. A Canadian, Doohan was a veteran of hot combat who was wounded several times on the beaches of Normandy. Upon recovery, he became a pilot, considering it safer than infantry. In the Canadian Air Force, he was known for his skill and fearlessness. Coon was a veteran of World War II and a radio correspondent on the front lines of Korea. Justman had been a radioman for the U.S. Navy, and now he was the executive officer for Roddenberry's enterprise. Campbell had been on PT boats in action and took pictures of the Japanese wasteland after the atomic bombing. Roddenberry had been a B-17 crew-man and pilot. Only Kelley had been spared even the slightest abra-sions of war.

Kelley didn't quite fit in the veterans' camp, but that was a famil-iar situation for him, and he didn't mind being odd man out when it came to combat stories and high-stakes poker. He was always invited to the card games that Roddenberry held for the guys, but he rarely attended. The regulars were Doohan, Coon, and Campbell. Rodden-berry's sailing, partying, and carousing were done without Kelley be-cause he, like Justman, would rather be home with his wife. Roddenberry's appetites, drives, and habits were not for Kelley to judge—he had long ago given that up—but Kelley lived by the maxim that discretion was the better part of valor.

The second group included most of the actors. Shatner and Nimoy were born within days of each other in 1931. Earth and fire, willful and ambitious, they had been teenagers during World War II as had most of the cast. They were the next generation. Kelley, eleven years their senior, took his place beside them as an elder brother. He did not fit in with these younger people, either.

Harve Bennett looks back and sees the very clear dividing line be-tween the generations and how singular Kelley was in the *Star Trek* cast. "He was a *professional* film actor. Uniquely, he had come through the Hollywood system as we came to know it in the '30s and '40s, in the great days of the Hollywood studios. He was a studio contract player, part of a permanent company of players. He had learned the protocol of how people worked together in a necessarily cooperative profession." And he never presumed to be above his fellow actors. "This is interesting, because all the others—and this does not deni-grate them—all the others came up at a different time and with a dif-ferent orientation toward acting. They came on during the transition to television, with no studio system, no long-term contracts; and those actors, then and now, are free-lance animals, strangers to the be-havioral system of the old studios."[1]

Kelley was one who understood the need to keep pulling together for the good of the company and for the future of the cooperative ven-ture. This was what he was taught in his first days with the Long Beach Community Players, and it was essentially the anthem of the

First Motion Picture Unit. Kelley being Kelley himself was a large part of the difference; as his friend Leonard Nimoy recalls, "He was always older and wiser than the rest of us."[2]

Kelley found the human dance all very fascinating. There were Friday wrap parties, birthday parties, or cocktails at the local bar after hours. There were occasional gatherings at the Nimoy home. Kelley would drink his vodka with a little water and a twist, a drink known as the "DeForest Kelley," and observe all these human passions and dynamics to his heart's content, then head home to Greenleaf and Carolyn, Myrtle, and Cheers. He was always like that, so honestly interested and so completely disconnected. He was, as Campbell so well describes, "the man in the mist." He didn't really belong, but they needed him, and he needed them.

He looked forward to the stories. He never knew what he'd be called upon to do week to week, and that was a challenge and a delight for him. Often, McCoy was held to griping and protesting command and Vulcan decisions, as in "Tomorrow Is Yesterday," the first occasion of time travel for the *Enterprise*. McCoy was a first-class worrier if left behind on the ship while Kirk and Spock were off on an adventure without him. He often got the memorable lines, such as the one he said to an old flame of Kirk's in "Court Martial": "All my old friends look like doctors; all his look like you." He performed with a variety of actors. In "Space Seed," he demonstrated McCoy's courage without the humorous protests as the superhuman warrior Khan held a knife to his throat. Of all the actors, he said, "I enjoyed working with Ricardo Montalban best, because Ricardo was part of motion pictures. I was at Paramount . . . Ricardo was at MGM, and we had a chance to exchange a lot of lunches together, and I was privileged; he is a marvelous actor." Montalban's Khan became a favorite among *Star Trek* villains.[3]

Endearingly, the actor revealed McCoy as a man with weaknesses, regrets, self-doubt, and the plague of real people everywhere: fatigue. There was a tendency toward daydreaming. McCoy would lapse into a Southern drawl, when "however" came out as "hawyevah" and "can't" as "caynt." McCoy's well-concealed capacity for violence was revealed in "This Side of Paradise," on a planet with vegetation that spewed love spores. The Vulcan kindled a spark with a lovely earth woman played by Jill Ireland and proceeded to hang from a tree. Meanwhile, McCoy made himself a drink. After a little idle time with a mint julep under a tree, some little tin soldier came along to disturb the doctor's reverie. McCoy inquired, "You wanna see how fast I can put you in a hospital?" Just a glimpse of Toby Jack was all Kelley needed to make McCoy a threatening individual.

"The City on the Edge of Forever" began shooting on February 3, 1967. A year from pen and paper to airing, the long-awaited and painfully delivered Harlan Ellison masterpiece became the classic episode of the series. It was Kelley's favorite, because to him it demonstrated what the cast could do when it pulled together cooperatively in an ensemble work. Of course, it didn't hurt that in the final script, McCoy was what all the trouble was about.

Crazed by a drug overdose, McCoy had fled into the early twentieth century through a time portal. On the other side, he encountered a tramp. His rather funny examination of the humanoid was followed by poignant emotional and physical breakdown. "I'd give a lot to see a hospital right now," was the most coherent line he uttered. And then McCoy's recollection of twentieth-century hospital realities brought him to tears.

Kelley was so impressed with the drama under production that he sent the daily call sheets and the script to Aileen Pickering, a gift of what he felt *Star Trek* could be. "I thought it was the best ensemble piece of work and that it captured a certain flavor and mood. . . . I thought it was one of the most dramatic endings that I'd ever seen on a television show." The other scripts he stored away and eventually gave to an order of nuns to raise money for their charity work.[4]

2 On February 15, 1967, Kelley was rather suddenly back under Paramount's arches, when Charles Bluhdorn, head of Gulf and Western Industries and owner of Paramount, acquired Desilu Studios. The corporate mind of Paramount understood *Star Trek* far less than even the rather bewildered Desilu. Roddenberry's relations with the new regime were combative, and his ongoing relations with NBC were increasingly adversarial. Goodwill and patience seemed to be stretched on all sides, and Justman, Solow, and others were caught in the middle.[5]

Paramount executive Rolf Larsen recalls that when Desilu was absorbed by the studio, *Star Trek* came over with the rest of the productions and operations. "Paramount never knew what *Star Trek* was or what it meant to people. Norway [Roddenberry's corporation] and Desilu was *Star Trek*'s home. Paramount was kept at arm's length by Gene Roddenberry, really."[6] Bob Justman adds that Herb Solow also wanted to keep Paramount out of the *Star Trek* family as much as possible. Everyone seemed to know the new regime could be trouble.

The second season had gone into production after an already hair-raising round of negotiations and hard-ball games with the network, the studio, science-fiction writers, and a new force: *Star Trek* fans, led by Bjo Trimble and Roddenberry. It was all very involved, and Kelley kept very much out of the fray, although he appreciated the efforts of the fans. In general, he responded to circumstances with an encouraging word or a shoulder to cry on, but for the most part, he stayed clear. He focused on his home, friends, and Carolyn. Of course, he was delighted to get back to the *Enterprise* and McCoy for another season.

As Fontana describes it, the totality of McCoy was clear evidence of an actor doing a damn good job. His was the warmth and the humor, and Fontana and the entire company knew they could rely on Kelley/McCoy no matter what. As the days and weeks passed, the directors and actors were watched carefully to note and cultivate any gems that might emerge. Everything learned was put to good advantage in future stories.[7]

McCoy was given catch phrases. Eleven times, it was "I'm a doctor, not a [blank]." Then there was "Dammit, Jim!" and "Blast it, Jim," and "What in blazes," or simply "Spock!" Most grinding on the actor's nerves was "He's dead, Jim," uttered a total of twenty times. His fulminations against cold logic, military expedience, and surrender to technology were reflections of the times, a real mirror of modern anxieties.[8]

By that time, Nimoy's Spock was sweeping the fan world, and Nimoy was quickly becoming the dramatic focus of the show. His salary was raised to $2,500 a program, with accompanying escalations of percentages and privileges, which made his income considerably greater than Kelley's but still only a fraction of Shatner's. Personal appearances and publicity commitments were to be first-rate and well paid. "Spockamania" was everywhere, and the fan mail was wild. There was no use in anyone denying that the exotic and erotic Vulcan had captured the audience's imagination. Shatner and the whole company could do as they would, but nothing was going to change the fact that what was good for the Vulcan was good for the *Enterprise*.[9]

All the hard bashing between Nimoy and his representatives, Roddenberry and Justman, NBC and the studio, left one sad casualty on the battlefield. Sadly, the good relations between Nimoy and Roddenberry were gone.[10]

As Nimoy's new contract was being resolved in the spring of 1967, Justman began his campaign to have Kelley billed as the third star for this second season. This was a much happier and more peaceful process. In his memo to Roddenberry, Justman explained that there were no complications from any office on the initiative and that "NBC welcomes the idea, as they think very highly of DeForest Kelley and the character he has helped create."[11]

Sure, there were ongoing difficulties with Kelley. As Solow and Justman wrote, there were some things that came by way of Georgia, whether they liked it or not. For instance, "nuclear" was "nookeler" in Dr. McCoy's mouth. Some diseases and techno-babble got twisted on his tongue, leaving Kelley helpless with laughter and frustration as he blew scene after scene. To this day, it tickles Justman: "nookeler, and everybody would crash" laughing.[12]

It was Coon who had developed one of the most beloved concepts of the series, the Prime Directive, and he was the driving force behind the expansion of the characters. He used the actors' own interests, such as Shatner's karate and physicality, to enliven roles and scripts, and Shatner became the hot human heart of the *Enterprise*. Coon welcomed Nimoy's creation of the FVNP—the Famous Vulcan Neck Pinch—and the Vulcan salute, a sacred sign used by Orthodox Jewish priests. A hand gesture that signified that here was holy spirit, that God was present, this recognition was the essence of the salute. "Live long and prosper" was at its root also the prayer of benefaction: "May the Lord bless you and keep you. May the Lord turn his face upon you, and give you peace." Exotic and esoteric, Nimoy had a rather irresistible effect on viewers.[13]

And Kelley was let loose as the human conscience of the ship. His was the humane courage of an extraordinary but altogether human soul. He explored his character as the weakest link in the chain, the one afraid, the one who was vulnerable. The strength of character that grew from the wisdom gained in human weakness made McCoy Kirk's confidant and Spock's worthy counterpoint. His vulnerability was taken advantage of in a number of stories that suggested the future uses of the Vulcan mind-meld.

Nimoy wrote that the mind-meld was a Roddenberry concept. Spock was a hypnotic character, his people capable of mind-touch, communing, and joining. The first human Spock probed was a psychotic fellow played by Morgan Woodward. "A far more dramatic way to extract information than a lot of questions," Nimoy wrote. Leonard also liked the exploration of the Vulcan way and the element of touch in the drama.[14]

Writers caught the mind-meld concept and made Dr. McCoy the preferred human subject. McCoy's rescue by the mind-meld when he was overcome by mind control in "Return of the Archons" or "Spectre of the Gun," was a rather surgical approach on Spock's part. On the other hand, in "Mirror, Mirror," the mind-meld was something more, as Spock forces McCoy to reveal what he needs to know of an alternate universe. Spock's hypnotic effect caught McCoy in an instant, the Vulcan fingers wrapped around the thin wrist, and McCoy was his. It is a vampire's motif with undercurrents of mystery, danger, and eroticism. That the mind-meld was seduction and could be forced and could be a weapon was all seeded in this one episode.

The monetary recognition received by Nimoy and Kelley seemed to be of no consequence to Shatner. The chemistry among the three in various combinations pleased him as much as anyone. But the idea of Spock overtaking Kirk's central role in the show set battles in motion on the set that spilled over into every branch of the production.

Cast members were angered and frustrated, and some were cut to the quick by Shatner's increasing need to disrupt, redirect, or negate the roles and lines other actors were attempting to work with. Takei,

Doohan, Nichols, and Walter Koenig, a young man brought in for the role of a Russian helmsman, were all shocked by Shatner's behavior. He was a classically trained actor whose attitude had been shaped to focus on his role and on the production as a whole—and minor players had better keep out of the way.

Shatner rode roughshod over everyone except Nimoy, who would not allow it and as a star didn't have to, and Kelley, who would not engage Shatner at that level. To a degree, Nimoy assumed a leadership role in the cast as a star and a gentleman. He had his own stardom and acting future to be concerned with, but he was a good man to lean on just a little. The crew trusted him. Kelley was Switzerland—established, neutral, and sweetly refusing to get involved in the fracas and gossip—unless it had a direct impact on Kelley or McCoy, or unless it was funny.[15]

Kelley always insisted that *Star Trek* could not live without Shatner, nor could it live without Nimoy. He never hinted that he thought it couldn't live without him. Solow spoke about his years with *Star Trek* and actors. He said of Kelley: "De is a sweet, decent man . . . the most professional actor we had in terms of experience. . . . He never got involved in any politics, he never bitched . . . a producer's dream. Because De created no problems on the set, there are no stories about him. There are Shatner stories, Nimoy stories, stories about Walter . . . Nichelle. . . . But lovable, hardworking, on-time De is just De."[16]

Kelley was not a doormat, he was a serious actor, but he was quiet in his correction and in his venting. He could stew, smoke, or cuss just a little, but no one recalls him being disruptive, and he surely never threw a fit. He never misdirected his anger or ridiculed anyone. Nimoy recalls that if Kelley had a problem, he brought it to your attention quietly and reasonably, and when he was done, he was done.[17]

The show rested on the shoulders of Captain Kirk, Bill Shatner. Kelley appreciated the situation Shatner was in. The whole series would go if everything worked out well, but if Shatner faltered, the show itself would falter with him. Shatner was a driven personality, overwhelming for some, but Kelley had known fellows like this all of his career. And Shatner had that little extra something that no one else had. As Kelley recalled, "Of course, Shatner loved to do it to people. . . . He was an artist in it, certainly with me. You know, we all had our differences here and there, but we had this thing going, and no matter what we thought of the other one, he could look at me in a certain way or do something and crack me up completely." Bill had the power of mirth, and DeForest was helpless against it. It was a kind of medicine Kelley sorely needed for his melancholy. He loved to laugh, and Shatner was a laugh riot. His comedic spell over De made Bill Shatner unique and irreplaceable in DeForest's life.[18]

DeForest kept out of the line of fire, but the conflicts just kept going between Roddenberry and the actors, Roddenberry and the studio and NBC, between writers and directors, directors and actors, as Nimoy and Shatner vied for their places on the show. People ran to Gene with complaints small and large. Through it all DeForest steered clear and resisted the impulse to come to Gene's defense, or Nichelle's or Bill's. It was hard work to be detached, but by God, someone had to do it.

Finally beyond wit's end, Gene wrote a letter to his three leads and brusquely shamed them. He included Kelley because he knew Kelley wanted to be acknowledged as an equal in the life of the show. Justman recalls that the letter was purposely sent to De so Shatner would not feel isolated and picked on. Gene wrote the riot act for Bill and for Leonard, but all he could do to De was warn him that with a little effort he, too, could become a pain in the ass. DeForest chose not to put forth the effort.[19]

Nimoy recalls that Kelley was a great help to them throughout the series. "He played the older brother . . . to Bill Shatner and me. . . . It was not always easy." Kelley was a natural peacekeeper. Looking back with humor and affection, Nimoy recalls: "I'm thinking [of] one particular time when Gene had finally understood that he was totally incapable of dealing with Bill Shatner and me—ha! He sent a very tough and nasty letter addressed essentially to Bill and myself, but he also included some comments to De about—maybe lurking in him was also the kind of treachery and infidelity and matters of hostility that Bill and I were expressing! . . . De might rise to the occasion . . . and attack Gene the way we did! That is what it was all about. De was one of a kind . . . a great guy."[20]

What was the key to Kelley? Nimoy admits, "I wish I could tell you. . . . I was always fascinated by the simplicity of his life. He seemed to be the kind of guy who could sit on the back porch with his wife and watch the grass grow. On the other hand, when he was at work he was totally professional, always there, worked as hard as if not harder than anybody else . . . always very precise in what he did. The work was clear, never cluttered . . . it was always without ego.

"He always had wisdom and stability. He could be upset as anybody about not getting his just desserts, by the way, but he was always a gentleman. . . . He had a longer and, I think, more successful relationship with Gene than the rest of us . . . because of his sense of stability . . . and his wisdom. He was able to keep it alive.

"He wanted work, he wanted to be involved in interesting projects. I think he pursued his relationship with Gene very successfully in that respect because Gene was a working producer. Also he pursued his relationship with A. C. Lyles. . . . He kept those relationships alive, I don't mean to demean him in any way, but I am sure there was an interest in his profession, interest in his career, that was being served to some extent in keeping those relationships alive."[21]

Assuredly, Kelley was a sophisticated Hollywood veteran and knew whom he wanted to work with. Since *333 Montgomery*, from the first day and the first meeting in that tiny office, there was a cooperative energy between Roddenberry and Kelley. Now, finally, they would journey together through the creative process of creator and actor, at least for a while.

Roddenberry had found science-fiction writing the best vehicle for his spirited human inquiry—hence *Star Trek*. On the other hand, Kelley's qualities of traditional expression and faith set him apart. Carolyn's experience as a little girl in Catholic boarding schools and convents scarred her about all things religious or spiritual. Kelley's way of being was the expression of his faith. Grace Hartung confirms: "He was a lot more religious than he ever let on." Through acting, he could reach out and connect with the world and perhaps touch some small higher truth every now and then. His copy of the "Actor's Prayer" that he kept in his billfold was by now worn to transparency and had become integral to his life and the very private but spirited human expression of his work.

3 Now a star, Kelley had a stand-in and stunt doubles. While the days of crashing fights and falls and flying dismounts were over, there were still plenty of opportunities to get hurt. In "The Apple," he recalled "there was a big explosion, a mine explosion that blew up in front of us [Shatner, Nimoy, and Kelley] and the special effects man had placed TNT into it. . . . That's what it sounded like. It was a terrible explosion, and the three of us absolutely went deaf with it. [We had to go] to Hollywood to a doctor's office, and it was a pretty big shock when the three of us walked in. . . . They thought 'they landed.' . . . But until this day, I have a constant reminder of that show, a continually ringing ear." The tinnitus that Kelley and Nimoy suffered seemed manageable over the years, but Shatner was driven nearly mad with it—a deeply embedded and constant shrill noise became his background music for life.[22]

What saved them all was their ability to laugh. Kelley had been driving an old '57 Ford, and in 1967, he bought the famous Kelley wheels, the '67 Thunderbird, and Carolyn got a Cougar. Nimoy had just bought a Buick Riviera. They were beside themselves with the pleasures of state-of-the-art sound systems and good upholstery. Kelley remembered that they parked side by side on the Paramount lot every morning, with a third space for Shatner's Corvette, motorcycle, GTO, or something: "But anyhow, I got off early one day, and I went out. . . . I had left the wheels turned when I had parked in the morning . . . Leonard was just coming around the corner of the soundstage. I didn't really see him until a moment later. . . . I started the car, and the wheels were turned, and I went right into his new Buick." Nimoy almost fell off his bicycle. "It would have been a great shot," with Kelley as Kelley and Nimoy as Spock, exchanging insurance information.[23]

To Kelley, the production crew on the show were the greatest pranksters of all. "They were the ones that hung Leonard's bicycle to the ceiling," and he couldn't find it for days. A lot of silly things went on. "Everybody was hiding stuff, and Leonard became very paranoid about his bicycle. He had to lock it up every time he'd park it . . . and the grips got out there and unlocked it, and he thought it was stolen. And I think we were working in the medical lab most of the day, and they laced it up above. His bicycle was over his head all day long. . . . Just kids at heart." And Kelley had that new car. "I was very proud of it, and I started to drive it off the lot one day" and discovered a hellish racket made by nuts and bolts rattling in one hubcap. "That was their idea of fun."[24]

Kelley could surprise a gal with his silliness, as Fontana once found out. During the filming of "Amok Time," she was in the main office on the first floor, doing phone work with the windows facing the street. It was high summer, and she had the windows open. In costume, Kelley sauntered by, then leaned in through the window and said to her: "You know what they're sayin' on the set? You'd have T'Pay T'Pau T'Prong T'Pring." And he followed it up with a big grin. Fontana just sat there, tickled, aghast, charmed. Kelley lived for moments liked that.

When Bette Creutze of Long Beach caught up with *Star Trek,* she was very impressed by her gentleman friend. She says, "He was close to Dr. McCoy, and they both had a funny sense of humor." The sneaky kind.[25]

The folks down in Long Beach certainly had not forgotten their Community Playhouse friend, and in June 1967, George Eres wrote a nice article for the *Independent Press-Telegram.* Once again, Kelley told his story: the son of a Baptist minister in Georgia come west to find freedom in Long Beach. He recounted his friendship with Barney Girard, his time in the Army, and his Hollywood hopes for Anne Jolly. "I though she could have a career in films, but she wasn't interested."

Movie and television credits were listed, and three photographs were used: Jim Breck of *Tension at Table Rock,* Sam Corwin of *Where Love Has Gone,* and an image of Dr. McCoy identical to the one sent to Anne's young son Curt. Kelley admitted to a film life as an outlaw and killer, but the article summed up: "At 45, he finds that the Dr. McCoy character has proved very satisfying. 'It's changed my image.'" At nearly forty-eight, Kelley was receiving a level of attention he had not known since his brief shining moment twenty years before with *Fear in the Night.*

Back then, he admitted, he thought he had the world by the tail. Now he knew better than to give in to the expectation of success. He reserved his joy for the simple things—such as Myrtle's emergence from hibernation or a really good line for the Vulcan—but it was hard not to hope, hard not to believe, hard to breathe. This time, though, he just knew better. He would always be the odd man out.[26]

Clearly, Kelley sometimes could not get a break, especially in areas of publicity and glamour appearances. As an example, Justman and Solow recalled that Roddenberry handled a request from Barbara Walters and the *Today* show for interview time with Shatner and Nimoy. This was big doings, especially since it was scheduled for airing during the crucial premiere week in the fall of '67. Roddenberry pushed for his third man to be included on the Walters show. Finally, in June, Justman was informed that in spite of Roddenberry's efforts, the answer from NBC's *Today* show was no to DeForest Kelley. Kelley was hurt by the exclusion, and the hurt would continue as omissions multiplied. He did not begrudge Shatner and Nimoy their limelight— they surely could keep "Spockamania"—he simply wanted to step into the public eye with them, as naturally as McCoy stepped in as a third of the trio on some strange new world.[27]

In the fall of '67 the *Enterprise* began taking some serious hits. One of the worst occurred on September 5, when Coon, who had created Klingons and established many of the traditions within the series, departed the *Star Trek* family under the weight of personal issues and sheer exhaustion.

David Gerrold's comedy "The Trouble with Tribbles" brought guest star Bill Campbell back as the first Klingon, Captain Koloff. Campbell remembers that for a brief time, they were discussing bringing his Klingon character to the show to work regularly, but Roddenberry was unsure of it. He didn't want to go the way of costumes and lizard heads. He was concerned that multitudes of aliens would make it too easy to cover holes in characterization and story. Now, with Coon's departure, the need for good original stories was even more desperate, but Roddenberry still resisted the temptation of developing aliens as creative crutches—"a real sad situation," Campbell recalls. With Coon gone, something of the heart of *Star Trek* departed, not to return for a generation after his early death, but was still held in the hearts of the characters he gave so much life to.

LONG BEACH—DE AND BILLEE

INNOCENCE—DE AND ANNE

CAROLYN

CLORA'S SALUTE

PARAMOUNT MAN

DE AND PHIL

BILLEE, ANNE,
BETTIE, AND
CAROLYN

SHERMAN OAKS:
DE AND CAROLYN

THE COWBOY

EVERYONE'S DOCTOR,
FROM *STAR TREK IV:*
THE VOYAGE HOME

Courtesy of the
Kelley Home Archive

FRIENDS: LEONARD, BILL, AND DE,
FROM *STAR TREK V:*
THE FINAL FRONTIER

Courtesy of the Kelley
Home Archive

DE AND PHIL AGAIN

LONG BEACH: DE AND CAROLYN

THE CONVENTION TRAIL

FIFTY-FIVE YEARS

4 Complicating every part of *Star Trek* was the fact that Roddenberry's own health was declining. His professional, creative, and personal burdens became ever more crushing, which meant that Justman
would have to roll the stone up the hill more and more on his own. He
got some help from a highly capable and energetic young apprentice
director named Charles Washburn. His first full-fledged show was
"Catspaw," and it was a very complex episode to set up and shoot.[28]

Washburn was taken with Justman's genius. Justman knew production, logistics, strategy, and the way consequences rippled from
the smallest change until they reverberated through the entire project. On time and on budget with the details nailed was Justman;
Washburn looked on in awe. Justman could sift through papers,
charts, and story boards, mumbling and gesturing to himself until it
all settled in his mind as a working and workable plan. He was a
master of this flowing four-dimensional chess game that was a television series. The seventh day of an episode was the first day of a new
six-day shoot. The crew communicated with hand signals, looks, ges-
tures, and all of it meant something and went through the communi-
cations officer liaison, otherwise known as the assistant director.

One of the first African-Americans in this role, Washburn was a
young trainee with a whole future ahead in a white-dominated industry. He was determined that nothing would or could get by his vigi-
lance. A small part of his duty routine was to check in Shatner, Nimoy,
and Nichols, who arrived for a six-thirty to seven A.M. makeup call.
Then Kelley came in at seven-fifteen with Takei. A smile and a wave
were always Kelley's greeting to Washburn on his way to the dressing
room. Nichols had eyes and makeup, Nimoy had the ears, and Shatner
had the wig. Kelley went through the usual, depending on the creases
under his eyes and the nature of McCoy's day. He sat for his makeup
or sometimes went ahead with it himself. When the customary round
of orders for breakfast was taken, he might have a half grapefruit and
nothing much more for the rest of the day. He seemed able to live well
on liquids and cigarette smoke.[29]

Kelley remembered: "When I was doing the series, I was quite a bit
huskier . . . and Shatner was always with the barbells, and he'd come
in [flexing and posing], and every day when I got off, I'd go and take

the makeup off, and you strip to the waist and get all this stuff off. I'd come back through. He'd be sitting up in his little chair, you know. . . . I'd flex, and I'd walk by him every day. One day, he says 'Look, cracker-ass, why don't you knock that off?' . . . I called him bubble-butt."[30]

Washburn recalls fondly that the production crew was a caring bunch. As a trainee, his talents were to be honed on the job. While the veterans taught and encouraged the new fellows like him, the guys who were fading were protected by all. Washburn was in charge of the turbo-lift doors: "I loved to see it all done just right. I manned the button for the doors to swoosh open. No matter how [Shatner] pivoted, hesitated, or charged, I would key the man on the doors just right." But the man on the doors was wedged into a tiny, hot space, he was a real old-timer, and sometimes he just got sleepy as they went through shots and setups and retakes. "I didn't know this, but the guys did." Washburn recalls how Shatner would bounce off the doors and someone in the crew would yell, "Check the light!" It must be the light, the only signal triggered by Washburn's button—the light told the old fellow in the dark space to pull open the turbo-lift doors—or someone was going to go into those doors face-first. Washburn agreed: the light was usually the problem. Sure enough, the next time he hit the button for Shatner's exit, the system worked fine. Once initiated, Washburn understood that no one ever needed to know the truth the crew kept to themselves. The truth was that Al the doorman was past his game and worn out. Washburn remembers that "Check the light!" was crew lingo for "Wake Up Al!"[31]

Roddenberry and the writers of *Star Trek* presented treatments of the political and social issues of the day to the viewing public in varying degrees of disguise. The lessons of these morality plays were already second nature to Kelley. He had no egocentric need to expiate the sins of his grandfathers. He did not rail against the abhorrent customs of the American South or publicly condemn the behavior of some other white Southerners in the late 1960s; his protest was his way of being and his interpretation of McCoy.

Kelley told "Tribbles" writer David Gerrold during his interview, "I always wanted the show to do a script that featured Nichelle and myself. Something where the two of us were thrown onto a planet where there was a great racial problem, only reversed. The fact that I am a Southerner and she is black and that we're trapped on this planet together could have been a very good story." Gerrold commented that, in fact, such a storyline had been worked on but never brought to fruition.[32]

Herb Solow passed the word around that *Star Trek* was good for another twenty-three-episode season on October 18. In the same month, Roddenberry wrote an exclamation to all: *Star Trek* had surpassed the *Monkees* in fan mail. *Trek* was number one in the country! In a mood of celebration, Roddenberry made a gift of the year's blooper reel for the Christmas party of 1967. "We worked terribly long hours, and *Star Trek* was a very difficult show to do at that time, and I don't know, we just more or less exploded in one way or another." Kelley was embarrassed. Roddenberry was not only aware of Kelley and Majel Barrett's rather earthy outtakes, but Roddenberry was by then Barrett's lover, and Kelley was a little crimson when those takes were in the blooper reel. "We could all have been blackmailed," he recalled, but he was guilty of little more than cracking up and being the frequent target of Shatner's habit of kissing men on the mouth.[33]

Chapter XI
Rising Star
1968

"I have achieved personal contentment to a degree. I consider myself a mature actor. My ambition is peace and perfection."
—DEFOREST KELLEY, 1968

While the *Star Trek* cast and crew knew full well the anchor that De-Forest Kelley was, Gene Roddenberry's fan mail reflected some confusion among viewers regarding what McCoy was about. Often, there was the sentiment that the doctor should be nicer to Spock. There was some curiosity about this sometimes humorous, sometimes cranky surgeon. One fan simply stated, "I still haven't figured Mr. Kelley out."

If the viewers didn't know McCoy and it bothered them, then all the better. The combination of fan mail, Kelley himself, and the need for more good storytelling seemed logically to suggest a more equal triumvirate in the scheme of scripts, more storylines for exploring the character of Leonard McCoy.

Toward the end of the second season shooting in early 1968, D. C. Fontana surveyed the actors to get their observations about their characters. She queried Kelley about a son for McCoy. He thought about it a moment. No, he decided, a daughter. And so Joanna McCoy was born. In fact Kelley had always preferred the company of women. For Fontana a whole new direction for stories was created in that moment. She began to think of the story she would write about McCoy, Joanna, and Kirk.

Meanwhile, Kelley let Roddenberry know he wanted tours of some facilities where he could see and touch the latest in medical science. So Roddenberry included Kelley on some of the creative crew's fact-finding missions to Edwards Air Force Base and other centers of innovation.[1]

Kelley read every medical article he could find in papers and magazines. He was hungry to understand what McCoy was doing, especially because of his fans. Again and again, he received letters from young people declaring their intentions to go to medical school or into medical research or to pursue other healing arts because of Dr. McCoy. Carolyn and DeForest were very much impressed with the intelligence, hope, and personal quality of the fans as reflected in their mail. McCoy was having an impact on the youth of a troubled country. They wrote that McCoy and *Star Trek* gave them hope, dreams, aspirations. Kelley meant to be the best doctor McCoy could be for them, though he and Carolyn did not really expect these fans actually to become nurses, doctors, or researchers.[2]

The last episode of the second season wrapped on January 10, 1968. Herb Solow had departed, Roddenberry's endurance was waning, and it looked as if Bob Justman was the last man standing, with Fontana and Charles Washburn hanging on. *Star Trek* was increasingly under fire from NBC and Paramount because of its cost and low ratings. *Star Trek* fans and science-fiction writers were vocal boosters of the show, but the Neilson ratings continued to decline. With Solow gone, NBC and Paramount no longer heard balanced and businesslike arguments in favor of the floundering and very expensive *Enterprise*.

As if seeking a calm place in all the fantastic mess, fans, scriptwriters, and journalists turned toward the one steady, very human fellow in the impossible world of *Star Trek*. In February 1968, *TV Star Parade* featured a hefty article on DeForest Kelley. In "Never Out on a Limb," he was able to speak his mind. "I've been told that I always act like a gentleman. . . . I try to be one as much as I can be. I have deep feelings for the welfare and comfort of others. . . . I refuse to be crude and selfish in any way. . . . I have achieved personal contentment to a degree. I consider myself a mature actor. My ambition is peace and perfection."

"DeForest Kelley's Hidden Youth" was a final version of the type-script "DeForest Kelley's Strong Right Arm" by Brenda Marshall, which Kelley kept among his personal papers. In these articles and over the years, again and again, DeForest cited Carolyn as the reason for his success and his strength. Now the public began to know the love story they were living.

He admitted his melancholy: "I get depressed, and she always helps." Again, his star was rising, but as a cast member on an endangered show, sorrow and uncertainty tempered his joy. The saving grace for DeForest was that as much as he loved the work, the *Enterprise,* and Hollywood, he loved Carolyn and Greenleaf more. That, sadly, was rare among men of the turbulent late '60s, and the contrast brought recognition and respect to the Kelleys. They seemed to be such a special island in the sea of stress and ego that was Hollywood and television.

Renewal of the show was announced after the airing of "Omega Glory," guest-starring Morgan Woodward, on March 1, 1968. By the end of the week, NBC had received some 70,000 letters of thanks from viewers. *Star Trek* was tentatively set for Mondays at seven-thirty, but by the end of the month, the show had been relegated to the outer quadrants of television viewing, with a tentative berth late in the week and late in the evening. Defiantly, Roddenberry wrote to the cast, "This marks the third year of *Star Trek,* and I have every hope that you and I will be together to celebrate its bar mitzvah." With this memo, he also announced his move to the position of executive producer—all the better to steer the *Enterprise,* or so it seemed at the time.[3]

With the third season approaching, Gene Roddenberry and Majel Barrett went on a road trip to Palm Springs, armed with scripts to work on. There, he received the call from NBC. The decision had been made—*Star Trek*'s new time slot for the season was final: Fridays at ten P.M. "Majel remembers that something went out of him that moment, and they returned to Los Angeles almost immediately, knowing the show was doomed."[4]

Justman remembers that with a late Friday night slot, they had lost too much of the viewing public. "Gene gave up." He was executive producer, but he moved off the lot. He looked at final cuts and final scripts but no rewrites. Justman sadly recalls: "[if it had been] eight or eight-thirty, we would have been home free."[5]

Roddenberry kept the crew and cast informed with "all hands" notices and reviews. For the third season, he noted that Captain Kirk would be better served if he were allowed to be a tough son of a bitch with brief asides of insight, doubt, or humor only in the presence of McCoy or Spock. He called for Spock to be a multidimensional exploration of an alien world and psyche while never detracting from Kirk's supremacy as commander and focus of the show. Then he asserted that fans of all ages were demanding more Spock-McCoy duels: "how much the fans loved the bickering between our Arrowsmith and our Alien." An ongoing tension between characters was appreciated by viewers. Let them have at it, but keep them loyal in their hearts. Surely it was a lot more fun than most relationships on television. "They want our men to have the guts to differ without necessarily in the last act falling tearfully into one another's arms and apologizing for earlier harshly speaking to each other." Roddenberry knew it, fans knew it, and so did the men portraying Arrowsmith and the Alien.[6]

Kelley continued giving interviews, often explaining his unattached and simple approach to the tumult of Hollywood. A small, revealing article was published in *TV Picture Life* in spring of 1968, "I'll Never Forgive Nimoy and Shatner." Kelley had no proof, but he believed that his two costars had been behind his costar billing. Nimoy and Shatner got credit for a selfless act of fairness. When they would not fess up, he figured they must have done it. He continued his "Aw, shucks" denial of his own ambitions: "About this star business . . . I didn't ask for it. Sure, I'm glad it happened, but even if it hadn't, I'd have been happy just to be on the show playing Dr. McCoy. . . . When I was much younger and just starting out, I thought that I had to have success. It meant glamour and stardom. But I soon learned that I was a success almost from the very beginning. For one thing, I had Carolyn, my wife. We've been married twenty-two years, you know. For another, I was doing just what I wanted to do—act. Sure, sometimes the jobs were few and far between. But when I got a role—big or small—I had a chance to create a living, believable human being out of a one-dimensional character who had previously only existed in a few lines in a script. I believe I've created a real person in McCoy."

The first two seasons had focused on the power of the larger-than-life Captain Kirk and the alluring otherness of Spock, bringing glamour and mobs of adoring fans for Shatner and Nimoy. Kelley understood that McCoy was to be the human presence between the two extreme personas, neither of whom would ever be mistaken for a real person. Only McCoy was real. "McCoy is merely human. At times he feels fear. At times he can perform really dangerous acts. But he's always just a man who feels and who thinks and who searches. And who makes mistakes." Kelley was as loyal to his costars as his character was to theirs. "We need one another."

Life away from the set was, at least for Kelley, an opportunity for rest. "After each day's shooting, we're tired. We just want to get home, have dinner, and relax before going to bed. We're usually asleep by nine o'clock, because we have to be in makeup at the crack of dawn. Lenny has a trick he sometimes pulls. He calls Bill and me at about eight-thirty and reminds us to go beddy-bye." Kelley devoted weekends to Carolyn and rest and the next script.

He didn't socialize or hobnob. He didn't need to. Justman was won over by Kelley's talent and professional courtesies—and his devotion to Carolyn. The quality of that marriage, Justman remembers, "set them off, made Kelley different." At last, with *Star Trek*, Carolyn was once again free to stay home and manage the domestic affairs. Mrs. Kelley became the supervisor, the agent, the accountant, the public relations man, and all of the fan mail went through her, too. Carolyn and DeForest did their very best to answer the growing fan mail, and at the very least, they read the letters with attention.

A man who worked on the set once told reporters, "He's really great, there's talk of him being nominated for an Emmy next time around. He's just finished a segment where he ages to a ninety-year-old man. When he walked off the set, a burst of applause from the other actors and crew broke out. He didn't go to the screening room later, but I did, and the audience there also applauded his work. If you ask me, it's about time Hollywood took notice of DeForest Kelley and made him a star."[7]

Kelley shrugged off such a forward compliment of his talent: "The really big kick I got out of doing that show ["Deadly Years"] was the effect my makeup had on my wife, Carolyn. When she saw me as a ninety-year-old man, she almost fainted!"

While Nimoy was nominated for an Emmy twice, neither Shatner nor Kelley was given such recognition. Like Kelley, *Star Trek* was always more popular with the people than with the industry and the critics.

2 Over the course of the show, Tony LaFata often spoke with Kelley, discussing episodes and the world of *Star Trek*, and he really enjoyed the time-travel stories. Kelley talked about a recent day in the life of Dr. McCoy: "Aw, Tony, this show—a whole day shooting with Nimoy . . . a fine actor, but those damned ears! I don't care what I do, it's like working with a dog—those ears. . . . You could kill yourself, but those ears will take the scene."

In "Bread and Circuses," the pull of comedy, drama, and a head-on collision between the two characters made an otherwise flimsy story a memorable chapter in the lives of McCoy and Spock. On beaming down, McCoy was in an expansive mood, wishing just once to beam down and tell the people, "Behold, I am the Archangel Gabriel." When Spock protested the scenario, McCoy countered with a suggestion that a pitchfork might work for Spock. Once captured and forced to fight gladiators in the arena, McCoy was quickly down, and the powerful Vulcan inquired if he needed help. "That's the most illogical question I ever heard in my life!" Back in the cell, McCoy's earnest thanks were rebuffed, and he turned on Spock. Within inches of each other, McCoy gave him hell, saying, "You are more afraid of living than dying," because, alive, the Vulcan's true nature, his human nature, might get the better of him. McCoy's insight seemed to wound Spock. Fans took umbrage at Bones's insensitivity.

3 Kelley kept his professional and personal balance, resisting envy and the temptation of celebrity by enjoying the simple things grandly and the grand things simply. There were roses to deadhead and the car to wash. Carolyn had trash to be taken to the curb. On working days, De rose at five. His wife could sleep all she wanted now. He showered, dressed, and whistled softly through a silent house. Before departing for the fifteen-hour day, he almost always left a love note and a drawing for Carolyn.

The daily rounds of the house and Carolyn's presence created a small land of tasteful simplicity. She remained the center of his life. She was the very Earth to him.

Now, as a grown man himself, Tony LaFata came to know the Kelleys as elder friends. Carolyn was very shy, though quick with repartee. She was devoted almost exclusively to her husband's success. Tony realized his godmother was shy to the point of anxiety, and it took real courage for her to go out and do what was asked of an actor's wife.

At fifty-two, Carolyn had a very famous husband who had to do public appearances. As hard as it was for her, she took the initiative at social functions. She would put herself into the mix first to protect him from the mob, from the sly joker or the gold digger. She was a quick study of any individual or gathering; she knew what was what. That people didn't seem to notice her anxiety and her fervent desire to be back home was a testament to her self-control and acting skills. She was still a hell of an actress, just as her Community Playhouse reviews had declared.

As Tony explored the world as a musician and a creative mind, Kelley became more understandable to him. He was intense, just plainly, overwhelmingly intense—no self-aggrandizement, no begging for accolades, but altogether wrapped up in his head, in creation, interpretation, and performance. He strove for the perfect performance, all the while knowing full well that it wasn't the perfection of performance but the pleasure of work that feeds the actor. The pleasure he got from the process as an artist was separate from the finished product. He understood deeply what he was doing and what it meant in his life.

Tony thought that Kelley as an actor was a lot more flexible than he was given credit for. If you contrasted Toby Jack with Vince Grayson with Sam Corwin with Leonard McCoy, Kelley's talent was evident. If one really knew Kelley, and then saw his work, one would have no doubt just how good an actor he really was. Thoroughly quiet, modestly present, lean and leaning, he had his body language at his command, as well as his voice, his face, his bedroom eyes, and his reptilian stare. The one-dimensional bad guy was nothing. Whether a suicidal drunk or a flamboyant defense attorney, Kelley could do it all. Take another look at his work.

In the early summer of 1968 Carolyn and DeForest did get out of the house and travel a little. De could not recall how it all came to pass, but he had been invited to Washington State to be an honored guest at one small town's fair and parade. He christened himself the "Wenatchee Apple Queen," and he and Carolyn rode in a convertible along the parade route. "I met a little girl . . . who was running along-side the car with a sign—'We love you, De' or something like that—a young sixteen-year-old or twelve-year-old, whatever she was. . . . It turned out to be a wonderful day for her. And so when I got back to Hollywood, I received a letter from her. It was really not a letter, it was an article about her going to Washington in order to see me. And so, in reading it, I was so impressed with it that I sent it to a movie magazine, and they published it."[8]

Kristine Smith recalls the event, the Wenatchee Apple Queen, and the television show that changed lives. From her memoir:

On the second day of May in 1968, I was thrilled to learn that DeForest Kelley—my beloved "Bones"—was going to be appearing in the Wenatchee Apple Blossom Festival on May 4. I raced to Mom and Dad, imploring them to drive me there from Cle Elum (two hours' distance) to see him. They told me that was impossible, as they had to plant the field. "But if you want to go, you have your driver's license now, and you can take the car." [Kris and her friend Corean decided to hit the road together.]

When we got to Wenatchee, a full two hours ahead of the scheduled parade kickoff, I found the first parking lot available, parked the car, and released a huge sigh of relief. I had no idea where the parade route would be, but at least we wouldn't get killed driving there. [They found the route and waited.]

I finally said, "You know, if we play our cards right, we *might* get a chance to actually *meet* DeForest, not just watch him go by!" I told her, "Here's Mom's movie camera. I'm going back to the car for the autograph books. If anything happens while I'm gone, be sure and film it!"

I raced back to the car, grabbed the placards and the autograph books, and raced back. Luckily, I hadn't missed anything. We "loitered" shamelessly, pretending occasionally to "window shop." Suddenly, I heard Corean gasp, and then she said, "Oh, my gosh, there he is!" I followed her gaze and just about fell over.

Confession time: I had never (until this moment) been overly impressed with DeForest's looks. Not that I thought he was *un*attractive; I just had never really considered him "drool material," and neither had Corky. We were both unutterably stunned to see how extraordinarily handsome he was in the flesh. And he was smiling, even grinning! This was not what we had expected to notice in "our" Dr. McCoy! I said, "Geez, Cork, he's adorable!" She asked, "What do they do on *Star Trek* to make him look so . . . plain?" I shrugged my shoulders and said, "I don't know . . . but they should stop it! He's *gorgeous!*"

[Parade watchers and *Star Trek* fans gathered around the Kelleys' car.] He was genuinely appreciative of their attention, and he spoke easily with each of them, thanking them for their interest in and support of *Star Trek*.

Butterflies inhabited my innards. I wanted to go to the car and greet him, but I was afraid I'd make a fool of myself if I attempted it. I held back and hemmed and hawed so long that finally Corean elbowed me and said, "Go on over and get his autograph. I'll film it." I took a big breath and said, "Ho-kay. If I survive it, it'll be a miracle!"

I stepped up to the car. Mrs. Kelley spotted me first—I was closest to her—looked up at me and said "Hi!" with a big grin. I muttered, "Hello . . ." and took a step back to recover. "De," Carolyn said, "over here." DeForest looked over at me, grinned, and said, "Well, hello there!" "H-hi," I managed to stutter. "May I have your autograph?" "Certainly," he responded. "Thank you," I said. "You're very welcome."

That night, I capitalized on the day's events by using it as the week's creative writing assignment. I wrote an essay entitled "The REAL McCoy." [Her teacher prompted her to send DeForest Kelley what she wrote. She finally did send it off.] School let out shortly thereafter for the summer, and I promptly forgot all about the letter and essay to DeForest, what with the assassinations of Martin Luther King and Robert Kennedy holding center stage that summer. One day in August, an envelope arrived from Paramount. Oh, my gosh. . . . My heart climbed into my throat as I opened it. Inside was a brief letter—one that would change my self-image and my life forever. It read:

Dear Kristine,

I was so impressed with your letter and story that I turned it over to Teresa Victor, Leonard Nimoy's Girl Friday, with a suggestion that it might make a good magazine piece. She in turn contacted Pat Langdon of TV Star Parade *who is interested in using it for a holiday story.*

Seems you are in for more fame.

Live long and prosper,

DeForest Kelley

Needless to say, my parents and sisters had to peel me off the ceiling several times a week for the next several months as I waited for the "debut" of my first-ever published article, *about* my favorite actor, *submitted* by my favorite actor!

Shortly before the article appeared in the Holiday/January '69 issue of *TV Star Parade*, I again wrote to DeForest, thanking him for the "boost" in launching my writing career. He wrote back,

Maybe this will be the beginning of something interesting for your future . . . we hope . . . and we shall be looking forward to its publication. That should really make you a celebrity in your own right in Cle Elum! Stay happy as you are now—and live long and prosper . . .

Sincerely,

DeForest Kelley

I wrote one more letter to Mr. Kelley, letting him know the outcome of my "adventure in celebrity." I was going to write still another, but both of my parents derailed the plan. Mom explained: "Kris, the man has been very kind to you. *Don't* drive him crazy with your incessant letters. Leave the poor fellow alone, now." So I stopped. Cold turkey. Just like that. For seventeen years![9]

4 Roddenberry made it clear that he was the administrative head for the third-season effort. As the shooting commenced on May 21, 1968, he made it very clear to Isaac Asimov how it was going to fly: "This year, I am pulling back from actual line production . . . and will try to operate . . . administration and policy." He explained to Asimov, as he had to NBC, that with a chance in a good time slot, he would have continued as producer and creative head of the show. In the late-evening Friday slot, he simply would not. Losing Roddenberry at the helm meant the death of the show. Now all he could do was hope the new lineup of production people could pull off a miracle. "We might get a mid-season shift to a good time slot." Such was Roddenberry's hope and everyone's prayer. With the ax poised over their heads, the crew of the *Enterprise* went to work without their captain and creator.[10]

Fred Freiberger came in as producer, and associate producer Bob Justman became coproducer. As much as that slight hurt Justman, he kept going. Roddenberry was sorely missed as the Great Bird of the Galaxy. He had had one contribution that no one could argue about: he was a great rewrite man, and the widely acknowledged "Roddenberry touch" was painfully absent from the scripts.

No matter what went wrong, all corners called for Justman, and he kept answering. Freiberger became the scapegoat for the third season, then and now. He looked back: "My ordeal in a German prison camp lasted two years." His ordeal with *Star Trek* apparently has no end.[11]

On August 24, 1968, *TV Guide* presented "Where's the Welcome Mat?" Kelley admitted to some hurt pride, and he finally showed just a little exasperation. "When I see the trade papers, after a whole season, still list only Bill Shatner and Leonard Nimoy as costars, I

burn a little inside. . . . I've had a rough road in this business, and
billing can be an actor's life's blood. What I want as a costar is simply
to be counted fully. I've had to fight for everything I've gotten at *Star
Trek*, from a parking space at the studio to an unshared dressing
room, and sometimes the patience wears raw. I know that my role is
more passive, I know that Bill and Leonard have the easier parts to
write for. But I've been through episodes where I'm standing there,
without a word, for twelve pages of dialogue. Once I got left out of an
episode entirely. I went to the writer—he also has producer status on
the show—and he said very apologetically, 'De, I'm sorry, but it was
an oversight.' An oversight! If a producer-writer on my own show for-
gets me, then I've got problems."[12]

Though a little rougher in this interview than in others, Kelley
generally charmed writers. He made them feel kind and generous for
their interest in him. He listened intently to interviewers, thought
about the answer before giving it, and made them feel welcomed and
respected. He told them personal details of his life and drew them,
and therefore the readers, closer to him, through the fourth wall and
the great barrier that seemed to keep him apart from everyone else.
But in those moments, he controlled the details—about dogs, roses,
and the special meal of black-eyed peas he made every New Year's
Day. He was in command during interviews and heavier on interpretation than biography, but he always meant what he said. Where is the
welcome mat? He really wanted to know.

A few weeks later, September 20, 1968, the third season began
airing at ten on Friday evenings. Older viewers did not tune in, college kids were out partying, and the littlest ones were in bed.
"Spock's Brain" was the sad premiere, one of the worst programs ever.
But it gave Kelley a good quip for use concerning Nimoy for years to
come: "I should never have reconnected his mouth."[13]

Kelley revisited the O.K. Corral for the third time in "Spectre of the
Gun," aired October 25, 1968. About this episode, he related that his
medical research sometimes included quizzing his own doctors. "They
were going to have me go into this dentist's office to get something. . . .
They were going to have me go in and assist him [Doc Holliday] by
pressing a certain nerve or something and then have the guy pull the
tooth—with no pain." Kelley's own dentist showed him how that

really could work, and he showed him some of the techniques for blocking pain using pressure points. Kelley was very disappointed that the particular scene was cut from the script.

Finally, Kelley carried a romantic episode, "For the World Is Hollow and I Have Touched the Sky." It really needed but didn't get the Roddenberry rewrite, but Kelley swayed the girls in the audience anyway. Again, as decades before, it was his vulnerability—in this case, it was McCoy's illness and loneliness—that made him appealing. Even beyond his vulnerability, he appealed to women with plain, old-fashioned sex appeal.

While Roddenberry had expected Kelley to be a draw for the older women in the viewing audience, he now found that "suddenly, after all these years, De Kelley's a teenage sex symbol." Kelley thought it funny, endearing, a little out of his orbit. At one point, a young lady sent him a revealing photo of herself with a marijuana joint. Her note read something like, "You've turned me on so many times, now it's my turn." For all of Kelley's urbanity, he was a little shocked, but he kept the items as souvenirs. When he felt feisty, he might admit that this was his favorite little piece of fan mail.

Kelley lampooned publicity and his colleagues' attempts to capitalize on their popularity. One publicity release declared that "unlike Nimoy and Shatner, Kelley has not cut a record." The fellows were doing all they could to promote Star Trek and themselves, but Kelley wasn't going to be part of it. He thought about making records. "If he [McCoy] did, I'm sure the kids would buy it just to have something from one of the three of us. The other day, I kidded Nimoy on the set by telling him that I was going to make a record. I was going to call it 'Sounds from Sickbay,' and it would consist of grunts and groans."[14]

Significantly, he admitted that through Star Trek, "I have renewed faith in myself." In another interview, he made it very plain to whom he credited this new lease on life: "Roddenberry went out on a limb for me, pulled me out of a big rut. I feel very lucky." Nothing would ever change his devotion to Roddenberry.[15]

5 Kelley's new good fortune meant that the house was repaired and refurbished. The cars had been replaced—"the greatest luxury I've allowed myself is an electric garage door opener; that gives me the greatest kick." While he had the same deeply buried desire to spend his money freely as many other Depression-era Americans did, Carolyn was firmly on the other side of that fence. She squirreled away as much as she could. She accounted for every thin dime; she watched sales, shopped around, and looked for bargains. She held the purse strings, she wrote the checks, and her boy's toys were held to a minimum. DeForest seemed to know it was for the best; he had a weakness for the good things, always had. They had been poor for so long he was thoroughly delighted with the new cars, the garage door opener, and the other trappings most middle-class families began to expect as their due in America. He was a man with expensive tastes who was held to a minimum of acquisition. The result was a sparse collection of the very best in furnishing, clothing, and collections, all kept in a pristine condition. The sum was genuine elegance.[16]

The kids in the neighborhood were pretty good about letting Dr. McCoy live in peace. His routine of driving away before sunrise and arriving after dark kept him gone during most of the kids' waking hours. There was a Catholic school nearby. The folks next door had a station wagon full of little ones, but to these kids, the Kelleys were neighbors and had already lived there forever. DeForest was nothing special, part of the scenery. Some of the schoolkids came around and knocked at the door. Carolyn was a bit weary of that, but she assumed the role of door answerer for the duration.

Shatner and Nimoy were having to deal with security issues, mob control, and invasion of privacy. DeForest and Carolyn also thought they might have to move, not because of mobs or unbalanced fans but because of schoolchildren. Overall, though, they managed to keep their home safe and secure with nothing more than rose bushes in front of the house to protect them. They stayed on Greenleaf.

DeForest told anyone who would listen that a happy marriage was based in friendship and sharing fully whatever is happening in the other's life. "Whatever Carolyn had done during the day, the week, is just as important to her as my work is to me. . . . Whenever I find

myself wrapped up in my work, I ask her what her life has been like."
Sure, there were quarrels, some doozies, "but make up, try not to go to
bed mad, and if you wake up mad, that's when you're in real trouble."

This kind of gentle consideration was extended to the cast and
crew of *Star Trek*. With Carolyn's help, he remembered birthdays,
sent get-well cards, and had flowers delivered to crew members and
their families on certain occasions. The polite habits that were instilled
during the glamour years at Paramount were still very much alive in
Kelley twenty years later. "De really cares about people," Nimoy
said at the time. Shatner observed of his style: "There is a simple, unassuming niceness about the man that's rare in any business."[17]

The Kelleys were surrounded by a nation thoroughly wounded
and spent by the events of the decade. DeForest sympathized with the
young people wandering the country and bleeding in Vietnam. That
generation was searching for meaning, for something to believe in.
They joined cults and exotic religions and experimented with their
bodies, with drugs, with life itself. Kelley empathized with their
desire for liberation. "If there is any kind of religion left in me now
[in 1968,] it's directed toward the Science of the Mind faith. And even
there, it's kind of withered. . . . Whenever I think of religion, I still
feel ridden with guilt." He had come to his own individual spirituality, through investigation, thought, experience, and reflection on the
teachings of his childhood.[18]

On November 21, 1968, NBC released a feature typescript for promotional purposes about *Star Trek* and DeForest Kelley. The public
might want to know that the Apollo 7 astronauts were sharing a cold
in outer space and that the *U.S.S. Enterprise*'s physician was called for
consultation. "I do not make house calls, but under the circumstances
would be pleased to beam aboard and take care of the common
cold.—Bones."[19]

A strange juxtaposition of fact and fantasy and how frequently
they happened. The mixture was important in the lives of children—
but to astronauts and scientists, physicians and engineers? As the
Star Trek lingo crept into everyday language, as the characters
became more popular than the show, as symbols began to be plucked
out of the *Star Trek* universe and used in 1968, it was fascinating.

As the decade drew to a close, the *Enterprise* also approached its end. The superhuman conveyance in which Roddenberry invited a generation to explore its own final frontiers would soon sail no more. Yet one more dimension remained to be explored, one that would give the viewers one more fable, one more tale of a hero of a different kind, one more reason to hope. This small passion play by Joyce Muscat declared that transcendent healing could be achieved through human love. Fittingly, the instrument of healing was McCoy.

"The Empath" aired on December 6, 1968, and dramatized the supremacy of mercy and the transforming power of compassionate courage. It called for a shift in mind-set, from alliances forged on survival and loyalty to a deathless, selfless brotherly love. The sacrifices offered by the Empath were great and finally won the survival of her world. But McCoy's offerings were greater, because he took conscious action twice to offer his life. More, he then sacrificed himself for his friends and for a world not his own. Then he further refused the healing that would have saved him because it would have harmed others and violated his physician's oath.

Helpless, the other two heroes dealt with the doctor's suffering in ways true to their characters. Kirk railed against the circumstances and made impassioned pleas, while Spock held McCoy to comfort his dying friend. In this moment, there is a dramatic change in the triumvirate. While the human emotions in Kirk continued to battle away, looking for a moment of chance and struggle, a wordless understanding was reached between the stoic Spock and the emotional McCoy, as compassion and comfort were given through the alien's hands.

The captain's defiance and passion owned him, and he was excluded from that understanding. Of course, the captain saved the day—the human voyage still belonged to Kirk.

This, more than any other episode, revealed the core essence of humanity's hope: the supremacy of mercy. "The Empath" was the doorway to a nascent mythology of the future.

6 By January 1969, everyone realized that they were at the end of the trail. Roddenberry encouraged one more fan-based campaign to save *Star Trek*, even "if all it accomplishes is annoying the hell out of NBC." Kelley had fan clubs once again, in San Francisco, Chicago, and the Midwest. "*Star Trek* has been my best break. I sometimes wish it happened ten years earlier," he told reporters. Nimoy recalls that "he was not without ambition; although he appeared to be, he was not without ambition." Kelley's rising star and his growing popularity were tied to a show that had already been written off.[20]

Finally, after years of impending doom, the last show went into production. A pall descended on the cast and crew. Shatner would have none of it. There were visitors on the set, and for them, for the crew, and for himself, he put on a performance of nonstop jokes and clowning meant to distract one and all from the end of the show.

A free-lance writer and fan, Joan Winston, was a visitor on the set during the last of it. Kelley took a liking to her. He talked, as he was inclined to, about Cheers and Carolyn and home. He took her to lunch at the Paramount commissary. She commented on Shatner's visible physical distress. Kelley explained: "Bill, being the star of the series, feels a certain responsibility for the well-being of the cast and crew. . . . The tension comes from burying his own problems, so he can joke and keep things light on the set. This takes a great deal out of him, and his performances take the rest. He is not a man to do things by half measures."[21]

On the last day, Winston witnessed Nimoy's last transition from Vulcan to Terran. There was complete silence as the ear tips came off for the last time. "Then everyone dived for them." Kelley told her that Shatner had collapsed that morning. She wrote, "De had been in the makeup room, and in the mirror he had seen Bill crossing the set with his Doberman, Morgan. He saw Bill suddenly go white and sit down on the floor. De ran over to see what was wrong. He helped Bill into a chair and asked what was the matter. He had hold of Bill's arm and could feel great heat radiating from him." The Asian flu of 1969 took Shatner down. Kelley called the medical office, and a nurse came. She gave him medication so he could finish the last day. Winston wrote: "I don't know what his temperature was, but they had to apply new makeup after every scene because it was melting right off his face." Nevertheless, Shatner's clowning continued to the bitter end. Finally, with the last scene, he let himself be carried off by the crew on a sofa used in the last shot—waved on his way by Winston. "With your shield or on it," she whispered.[22]

Winston recalled a half-hearted attempt at a farewell, but it was too sad, and no one stayed. The props and goods were boxed or hauled away, and only a bare soundstage was left by the time the last fellow closed the door. By then, even Bob Justman had walked away.

To soothe the transition from Starfleet to the unknown future of 1969, DeForest and Carolyn hit the road, doing a little publicity, hoping for a little miracle. On March 27, Anne Jolly received a letter from DeForest and Carolyn, who were on their way to Philadelphia to do *The Mike Douglas Show,* then to New York, where they planned to see four Broadway shows. As Carolyn, put it *"Star Trek* has folded . . . we're hoping something new and exciting will happen." It didn't.[23]

The show had been officially canceled in February 1969, and its last episode, "Turnabout Intruder," aired June 3. Justman wrote that television producer Harve Bennett's *Mod Squad* pummeled the last episode in the ratings for the last night. Many years later, a little fellow asked Kelley what was the worst thing that happened to him with the series. He replied, "When they canceled it."[24]

Aileen Pickering recalls: "I was just livid" when they canceled *Star Trek*. It hurt because it devastated DeForest. Around that time, as Aileen remembers, she handled some properties in Sherman Oaks, Studio City, and the hills that lay beyond the little town centers. She was closing on a new home for William Shatner. As she had admired the grounds of his place, she was particularly taken with a Saint Francis statue that watched over the birds and critters in the backyard. She knew Shatner was Jewish, so she asked about the saint and if her friend DeForest could have it. Sure, he didn't care—that was the answer from Shatner, as she recalls. Soon after, there were Aileen and DeForest at Shatner's new home, muscling the three-foot concrete icon to her car. "St. Francis is a sissy," Aileen liked to declare. But he had weight and presence riding in the back of her car, and they were exhausted by the time they got Saint Francis to Greenleaf, where Carolyn watched them stumble through the gate to the rear yard. De and

Aileen let the icon roll down the decline to the shady back wall. There they stood him up to keep watch over Myrtle and the birds and squirrels. There he remains. It never occurred to Aileen that DeForest was a Baptist and had little company with saints, and neither did it seem to occur to DeForest—it was simply taken for granted that Saint Francis had come home to Greenleaf. One can't look out into the richly flowering yard of roses and citrus without Saint Francis looking right back.[25]

Chapter XII
DeForest Lawn Revisited
1969–1974

"One day chicken, next day feathers."
—CAROLYN KELLEY, 2001

DeForest Kelley had been an elder brother to his fellow actors through three seasons of *Star Trek*. He had been a dream to work with—and in some ways, to him it was a dream. "I divorced myself from the problems because I'd been in the business long enough to know not to upset my stomach over a TV show. I'm a much happier person for having walked away. Fame, I got enough of that—not as much as Bill or Leonard, but enough. It's funny with actors—you work your ass off to get people to pay attention to you, and when they do, you go nuts. I always had the attitude, 'This thing's gonna fold, and then I'll go back to working in movies.'"[1]

Would he have fought harder for his star if he had known that there would be no going back? During the series, R. G. Armstrong recalls Carolyn often saying to him and to DeForest, that while R. G. was out there making movies, DeForest was hooked in with *Star Trek*. But R.G.'s imagination rushed between historical fact and future fantasy, and he saw clearly the surge of creation and invention that took DeForest from the radio tower in Roswell, New Mexico, to the *Starship Enterprise*. But the show was dead, and DeForest had to recover quickly to position himself for life after the *Enterprise*.[2]

Carolyn knew that, as strong as he was, someone as decent and pure as her DeForest could be bloodied and broken in the outer world, and she became more protective of him. Aileen Pickering knew De's heart, saw the center of his soul, and she was furious with "them" for pulling him toward stardom, toward thrilling highs and lows, only to shut down the *Enterprise* and DeForest with it. Nimoy had gone over to *Mission: Impossible*, Shatner had to fight off film and television offers with a stick, and Kelley went nowhere. His friends and loved ones held their breath.

Then it got worse. In June 1970, Betty Daniels phoned and said Bill was dying. DeForest and Carolyn rushed to the hospital. Carolyn recalls: "We went to them, we arrived, and there was Bill in the elevator, with a look of disbelief that we had come for him, but that is what friends do. We were with him and Betty." Bill died, and Betty became their sister in grief. For years, she was a constant companion, staying with them for weeks if she felt like it. The Kelleys tried to do for her what the Danielses had done for them: care, give strength, and love her unconditionally. DeForest lost his mentor and confidant; without him, he was all the more alone in the world.[3]

As if sent from out of the ether to brighten their uncertain middle age, the real Captain Kirk materialized on their doorstep—literally. Tony Kirk had gone to school around the corner from Greenleaf, then to Notre Dame High School, and then to the Navy and heavy combat in Vietnam for four years. He was looking for a little peace, a little meaningful niche in the America of the late 1960s, when he signed on with the U.S. Postal Service, and by 1970, he was working in Sherman Oaks. "To me, the movies were like church, actors, the screen," he explains with hushed reverence. He had delivered Joan Blondell's mail, Kenneth Posey's mail, Boston Blacky's mail, but his heart belonged to the Kelleys. "I knew he lived here—'Hi, Mr. Kelley.' Finally, one day, he called me aside, and he said 'Call me De. Carolyn and I are just regular folks.' OK. We just hit it off."[4]

He remembers: "If he never made movie one and he came to the door, it would have been the same because of the kindness. He treated me like a human being." Carolyn was a laugh riot. Sometimes she'd holler at De from deep inside the house, "Are you going to answer the goddamn door?" And Tony and De could only grin and shake their heads. Often, Carolyn would answer the goddamn door herself and smoke with Tony, and they'd get down and dirty and laugh like hell.

Tony recalls: "We—Carolyn and I—didn't like science fiction, but we all loved the westerns. I didn't start *Star Trek* until I met De. Westerns . . . the movies—were a sacred thing, John Wayne was better than president of the United States . . . but I loved the bad guys." And Tony Kirk knew those westerns, and he knew Hollywood, and "Lou Costello was my mother's brother. I literally grew up on the Universal lots." He remembered being on the lots to see the Keystone Kops, he was on the set for *The Mummy,* and *Jack and the Bean Stalk,* and it was a wild, wonderful universe. "Shyness is a terrible thing, because that is where I belong [in the movies]. De thought so, too. [He'd say,] 'Yeah, you got it—I can see you running out of the liquor store with hostages . . .' and DeForest would laugh a belly laugh.

"De and I played quiz games. [He'd say,] 'I think I saw your uncle in this and that.'" With Tony, he could weave his stories standing at the door, mail in hand. He told how Richard Widmark would sit in his room with his phonograph, his private passion, and how well he and Widmark got along together. Tony knew De's movies. "We talked . . . about westerns, where his heart was." He loved it that Tony knew little of *Star Trek* and everything of westerns. DeForest told him that when he was spitting chaw in the movies, it was licorice in his mouth. He told him about a lot of things. Tony liked to ask questions: In *The Law and Jake Wade*, how did they get the arrows in De's chest? De told him they shot them down a cable, and it hurt like hell all three times. "He knew my uncle was Lou Costello," and that joined them in a certain understanding of hardworking people, celebrity and art and the price of fame.

DeForest Kelley kept McCoy just under the surface, alive and well, ready for just the right moment. Most hot days, DeForest and Carolyn had a cold drink waiting for Tony Kirk, but one day, the heat got to him before he got to Greenleaf. He had a huge bag of mail. He was dehydrated and dizzy, and he had never done anything like this before, but as he wound his way up the path through the roses to the Kelleys' door, he began to pass out. The mailbag on his back took him over the side and into the roses. DeForest rushed to see what the thrashing around was about and came to find Tony lying helpless on his back like Myrtle, among thorns and buds, scratched and bloody, just barely with it. As Tony came around, shaking off his heat exhaustion, it was McCoy's ticked-off voice that he heard: "What in the hell are you doing to my beautiful roses?"

On another occasion, DeForest was in the front yard looking at something on the lawn. Tony came over to see. A hummingbird. "He's dead, Jim," De as McCoy said, and collapsed in gales of laughter. For years, this went on, to the delight of postman and patron.

2 The Kelleys' lives may have seemed unbearably quiet to Aileen Pickering, but most things did to a flier and a natural pioneer. DeForest and Carolyn entertained frequently, often attending or giving ten dinners a month. The usual guests were Betty Daniels, Aileen and friends, artist and Army buddy Roy Knott and his lady, John Walton and friends, A. C. and Martha Lyles, and Barney and Mary Girard.

The Girard sons had small glimpses of their father's friends. The most lively impression they had of DeForest and Carolyn was the great amounts of liquor both of them could take in and still operate. This impression was shared by Olive and Tony LaFata. Olive was concerned, worried. Yes, they were a partying generation, smoking and drinking was normal daily life, but there were long-term consequences, and guys and gals had to be careful. The money just wasn't there, and being unemployed could lead one to sickness and despair. Olive made it clear that the Kelleys could count on her just as they always could, *Star Trek* or not.

The series had its five reruns soon enough, and only Kelley's movie residuals were reliable income. Old friend Tom Drake was a featured salesman at a city car lot and had moved out of their lives. He was drinking and chain-smoking himself to death.

In January and February 1971, DeForest teamed up with Ace Lyles and Rory Calhoun for *Night of the Lepus,* which they called "Rabbits." Kelley's Elgin Clark showed the signs of the inner battles Kelley was fighting during those years. Worry shaped his face. He began wearing the neckerchief that became his trademark to distract the eye from signs of age at his throat. A good-looking middle-aged man, he was kind of worn at the seams but stylish and romantic and nearly gone to seed.

Lyles recalled that at one point, he and Kelley went to a country store for refreshments, and in no time the place was mobbed. The cashier had called his friends to tell them that Dr. McCoy was buying milk.

Of *Night of the Lepus,* Kelley said, "God help us." When it started going bad, there was nothing an actor could do. Then they created the effects of huge, rabid rabbits, always more huge rabbits. Kelley could only shake his head and say he enjoyed making the picture and then move on.

The first few roles Kelley was offered after *Star Trek* were cameos as various physicians. They wanted a guest appearance by McCoy, not DeForest Kelley the character actor. He wanted challenge, wanted to springboard from *Star Trek*'s McCoy to something even deeper, more satisfying. McCoy and the adventures of the *Enterprise* had made him a better actor; now he wanted to challenge this new level of accomplishment. He got less than nothing. Once he was offered what he understood to be a large role in *The Bold Ones,* a highly regarded series. He didn't much want it, so he asked for a hell of a lot of money. They gave it to him. He worked hard, but things went haywire. He watched it and saw that they had chopped it up so badly that it was worse than nothing—it was just pitiful. He was embarrassed by it.

The Cowboys was one hopeful sign in 1972. John Wayne and a bunch of kids had made a resounding case for the revival of the western with a beloved tale of youth and age, truth and grit, mostly about fathers and sons. Written for the screen by Irving Ravetch, the story was adapted for television, and the pilot featured DeForest Kelley, a refreshed and hopeful scruffy cowboy. He looked every bit the western actor and made a great impression with those fans who caught the one and only episode. When even this did not take with the networks, Kelley seemed to throw his hands up in despair.

Sadly, he confessed: "After the series, I decided that if I wasn't going to get anything that was stimulating for me, that would lift my spirits as an actor, then I didn't care to do anything. . . . The longer I got away from it, the less I cared. I'm not very proud of it." How deeply all this hurt him, only a few knew.[5]

Don Smith and his wife were a couple somewhat older than the Kelleys, and they were just getting settled in the house next door in

1972 when "my wife told me there was a somebody actor next door named Forest. I thought Forrest Tucker? Well, I had long been a [fan], all those years having been a science-fiction addict since eighteen or nineteen. I thought the [most of] John Campbell and *Astounding Stories,* then *Analog.* He told us all, *Star Trek* was it. He gave it a triple A. *Lost in Space, Buck Rogers*—but Roddenberry produced literature, so I always thought about [literature] watching *Star Trek.* I was so happy Kelley had star billing the second season. Obviously [he was] the glue that held the series together.

"Then I had DeForest Kelley next door. I said to Marge, 'Oh my God.' But when I went next door to introduce myself, you know, Carolyn came to the door. I said, 'I am your new neighbor, my name is Don'—and right behind her was De. He came forward and said, 'Hi, I'm De Kelley.' I mean, like he'd known me for years, and I thought, this can't be. I been a good boy! I saw him as a friend from the beginning, and through all the years he always has been a good friend. And I'm a good friend to him."

By 1973, "the roses were in and established. My house had been run down, and we did so much to bring it up. De really appreciated it."[6]

The two men met nearly every morning at the wall they shared in their backyards. One square block was missing from the top course of the wall, which allowed the fellows to just see each other and exchange things over it. Don left a section of the paper that De and Carolyn liked, and Don received the crossword puzzle from the otherwise much-maligned *Los Angeles Times.* Other hours of the day, DeForest might be out having a drink or watching Myrtle, and De would saunter over to discuss the news or sports with his neighbor. "I saw him a couple of times at the wall . . . and Carolyn would want him inside." She would call from inside the house, and De would tell her, "I'll be there" again and again, until finally there was just a change of tone—just slightly, a sternness in it—and DeForest would continue his visit with Don.

That is how it was. When all was said and done, Kelley had the last word in his home and was ultimately in control—if he cared enough to stand his ground. And through all the years, Don recalls DeForest was hopelessly romantic, and helplessly in love with Carolyn. Now and then, when the magnolia trees were in flower, DeForest would get his long pruning pole and cut a few perfect blooms for Carolyn. He would place them floating in a large bowl of water and put them by her bedside to find upon waking. This he did after twenty-eight years of marriage and for the rest of their lives.

Aside from visits at the wall, Don had another role in the Kelleys' lives. It was a plain fact that neither De nor Carolyn was very handy when it came to electronics or plumbing or machinery. "The know-how and skills—De knew he could call me over the wall, he'd tell me his problem in the house, I could come fix it, or I could tell him what was what. Mostly I just fixed it."

DeForest spent large amounts of time outside. He loved the garden, he tended the roses himself, and he would be out there two or three days a week, pruning and tilling, fertilizing. He surveyed every detail of the perimeter, often with Myrtle. "De and Carolyn had a soft spot in their heart for that hard shell," Don recalls. She was a hard-shell Baptist. "And of course, you know, the first Christmas cards, De and Carolyn and Cheers (well, of course it's Cheers)—oh, it's the dog's name!" The squirrels would leave rinds of oranges hollowed out for De. Wild ones found their way into the Kelley yard. Don declares that Carolyn has some kind of rapport with wild ones; a cat (Maggie) and a squirrel (Cutie) were feral. Cutie and others would feed out of Carolyn's hand. And DeForest and the blue jays—he kept a bowl of peanuts near the door. He would step out the door and raise his peanut over his head. The jay would swoop down and get it, eating out of his hand.

3 Occasionally, the Kelleys exchanged dinners or drinks with Majel and Gene Roddenberry. Majel recalled that they were "the only ones that Gene and I saw outside of work. We would go out to dinner, as much as they would allow their private life to be looked in on." Gene's will would not let *Star Trek* die, and everything else paled in comparison. *Star Trek* was not only his bread and butter, but only *Star Trek* preserved him. The thing was still alive in syndication in 1972. Stations carrying the show were multiplying like Tribbles. There were rumblings from the creator, studio, and network. The core of fanatics was spreading, converting people with the show's quality and with repetition in favorable time slots on local channels.[7]

Odd, but it really was happening, and the crew of the *Enterprise* had better get used to it. Strange threads often run through people's lives to interweave their experiences. *Star Trek* became one of those threads running through a growing multitude of people, a common ground in American culture. For those who dared, it also made the world seem a universe of potential exploration, because its stories were based not in the past or in fiction of the present but in the wide-open possibilities of the future. The best was yet to be. To all the world, it seemed that this single canceled television show could fill the mythological void left by the disappearance of the entire western genre. Even beyond that, it seemed that *Star Trek*—a syndicated ghost ship—had a sacred mission: to spread the contagion of hope.

Even as the show and its fans were ridiculed, the messages of the *Enterprise* grew stronger. Children growing up during the Vietnam era were given little to dream on. The nuclear family was often a dysfunctional, abusive, or neglected one. Nuclear war seemed imminent. The environment was ruined. The hippie culture had devolved to bitter burnout. Drugs and peer harassment made education difficult; cynical teachers and the lack of mentors made the adult world a bleak place. Then Watergate further shattered trust in government. This generation rediscovered *Star Trek* quite by accident, during their dinner hour or before bedtime, and they clung to the *Enterprise* as to a lifeboat in a storming sea.

In 1973, Bjo Trimble, a leader in Roddenberry's earlier "Save *Star Trek*" campaign and veteran of collectors' and genre gatherings, held her Equicon, a *Star Trek* fan convention. A young man, Richard Arnold, had followed his mother into *Star Trek* fandom and recalls that DeForest Kelley attended Equicon on a Saturday. It was his first appearance at a convention, although they had been going on for a few years. Economically and professionally, DeForest and Carolyn had to investigate this avenue of celebrity. Kelley's costars had found these love-ins exciting as well as lucrative.

Arnold remembers the "happening" atmosphere, the near hippie-commune togetherness that everyone shared. The joy was *Star Trek* and sharing the love of it. The actors themselves were showered with applause, howling, hugs, lovely gifts, and heart-rending descriptions of how *Star Trek* had made its fans better human beings, had inspired them, had eased their realities.[8]

There was something alive and sweetly innocent in the expectant faces. It was also very unnerving to have all that attention thrown at you. Arnold recalls: "To say that he was a bit nervous would be an understatement. . . . Bjo sat De behind Lois Newman's dealer table, and my mom and I babysat Carolyn while De signed autographs." The crowd focused on him, pressing toward the table, and "De . . . kept being pushed . . . so the security people started yelling, making De even more nervous. At one point, De looked over at Carolyn, who gave him a supportive smile, and then he turned back to the crowd and continued signing."[9]

Onstage, Kelley wooed his audience and was in turn overwhelmed. His face just slightly turned from the audience—he was regularly brought to tears by the "Trekkies," as Roddenberry had named his many progeny. Fans were taken aback when they first noticed the effect they were having on their doctor, but it seemed right enough, and he didn't seem to mind shedding a dignified tear or two before them.[10]

He was master onstage, but being in the pit, signing autographs at tables or walking through a hotel, could bust a man's nerves. Kelley was rattled while James Doohan reveled. Jimmy was an accomplished entertainer in public, and many a fan turned around in a lobby to find Scotty breathing down their necks or hunkered down talking with children. He sought out such joyful interactions. That was something Kelley had a hard time with. Worse, some fans didn't get the autographs they had waited hours for, and some feelings were hurt. That was something Kelley just couldn't abide.

De and Carolyn began to work on a style of fan management that pleased many and hurt the feelings of no one. They quickly found their roles as everyone's well-respected aunt and uncle—just a little aloof, just a little controlled—completely present and caring for the moment they could give you. Then they would disappear to their hotel room or some other place. On the job, Carolyn swallowed her shyness and anxiety, opened her arms to the bright, shiny faces, and slyly observed the few who might have been up to no good. She stayed out in front, with DeForest just behind her. He was then free to sign or talk or smile with yet another Trekkie.

With such momentum, Roddenberry wasn't about to give up. When an idea came across to make an animated version of *Star Trek*, Roddenberry approved it, hoping that this would boost the *Enterprise* closer to a new series of adventures. Herb Solow recalled that if Roddenberry "hadn't that kind of ego, *Star Trek* would have died." There would have been nothing new that could be called *Star Trek*, because Roddenberry was *Star Trek*.[11]

Leonard Nimoy used his star power to secure work for his costar friends and insisted that the animated version of *Star Trek* include all of the original voices. Nichelle Nichols wrote, "It was only Leonard's deep sense of fairness that kept the classic crew together for that show. In June 1973, we reunited." Kelley quipped, "Here we all are, a bunch of cartoon characters." But it was welcomed work, and some of the twenty-two scripts were really very good—especially with D. C. Fontana producing and in the writing mix. Having been birthed in radio, reading dialogue for animation was child's play for Kelley. He really enjoyed himself, but it didn't feed the need for art that still harried him.[12]

Through Filmation, DeForest and Carolyn were notified that a young boy with a terminal illness had a special request. When his parents asked what the boy would most like to do in his short time left, the boy had asked for a visit from Dr. McCoy. Kelley recalled with hushed humility, "There was a little boy in Denver, Colorado, who had a bone marrow disease and was doomed. He was in the university hospital there, and they were doing all kinds of experimental work to try to save him. He knew of his fate—he was very adult, a little man, not a little boy—and his parents asked what he would like most to do, and he said, 'I'd like to meet Dr. McCoy.' So they put a phone call in to Filmation, where we were doing the animated series, and asked if I'd be willing to go to Colorado to see him." Carolyn recalls, "Of course he went; I helped him pack." She was also at his side throughout the encounter.

DeForest stayed with the boy. "The doctor said that it was amazing how the boy seemed to come to life—his whole system seemed to just regenerate with the joy of what was happening. I found it a very emotional experience. When I came back, I kept in touch with him by phone. [Then] his father called me . . . to tell me the boy had passed away. . . . He said that he would never forget what it meant to his son at that time of his life."[13]

Through his grief, that father reached out to thank DeForest for granting them all a wish. He was thanking him for a television series and for upholding the principles so beautifully described therein. De-Forest's life was changed by that one little boy in Colorado, who in just a few days taught him what Dr. McCoy was really for.[14]

Chapter XIII
Beginner's Luck
1974–1978

> *"I'm the star of a ghost."*
> —DeForest Kelley, 1976

The endless reruns were like magnets to young viewers. Many seemed drawn to Kelley as if they were comforted by something they saw in McCoy. What they sensed was Kelley himself. What they liked so much in the doctor was the actor. *Star Trek* fan J. G. Hertzler thoughtfully recalls that the thing about Kelley was that one looked at him and always expected the truth. He tapped into viewers' deep need to trust someone, somewhere, and McCoy/Kelley never let us down.

Hertzler considers that the program gave viewers some distance, some wisdom, some breadth of perspective. The father confessor, the respected country doctor, was the seat of the real soul of the *Enterprise* during that mission back in the 1960s, and it would always be so.

Fans like Dan Madsen also felt that the man playing the role was larger than the role itself. For him, as for many fans, that was an intriguing part of Kelley's growing mystique, because players are so rarely equal to their roles. In this case, Kelley surpassed the character he portrayed.[1]

Fan Larry Nemecek recalls a quintessential McCoy moment. In the "Doomsday Machine" episode, the *Enterprise*'s encounter with a planet-eating ice cream cone was memorable especially for Kelley's glare at William Windom, "the best go-to-hell look" Nemecek had

ever seen. Kelley did certainly have command and could correct someone with a glance and discipline them with a glare.

Richard Arnold became closely associated with the *Star Trek*
world. He knew that Kelley was a most gentle man, that people were
naturally careful around him. Arnold knew he never wanted to see
disapproval, and certainly not disappointment, in Kelley's eyes.

For young men, here was a dramatic image to learn from. To be a
sane, strong, and wise man in a crazy reality was going to be a challenge,
whether in the last half of the twentieth century or in the twenty-
third. Kelley's Dr. McCoy was virtually alone in depicting and defining the qualities of a gentleman. McCoy taught many young women
how to recognize a gentleman—if they ever actually came across one.[2]

All of this evolved without Kelley's active participation. It was a
fan creation, something phenomenal and out of his hands. With repetition, *Star Trek* breached the bounds of television and evolved from
folktale to folklore.

Kelley's own life had been changed in the almost five years since
he had actually worked on the series. He had lost his mentor and his
profession, and he had gone through a transforming experience with
a little boy. He was sorely in need of a personal fresh start. There was
always talk of a new *Star Trek* series, of a movie, of something, but it
did him no good as an actor, an artist, or a provider. In the summer of
1974, the Kelleys packed it up to try their luck on a new frontier.

2 Kelley's agent booked him to perform in *Beginner's Luck* at the
Hayloft Theater in Lubbock, Texas. On July 9, 1974, Cheers super-
vised while the family packed, then rode shotgun as De and Carolyn
drove to Texas. Kelley explained his purposes: "I wanted to get way
out of town, and boy did I get out of town. I went out there. I wanted
to get out of Hollywood. I hadn't been on a stage [in more than twenty
years], so nobody would see me [deep in the heart of Texas]."[3]

In Lubbock, the director of the show greeted them and began to
work with DeForest. The director was Phil Weyland, and he describes
himself then as "a twenty-six-year-old New England Yankee who
lived in Lubbock and had studied theater at Texas Tech . . . and had

appeared in or directed about a dozen shows at the Hayloft. Some of the actors I worked with at the Hayloft were Andy Devine, Nancy Kulp, Peter Breck, Dwayne Hickman, and Linda Kaye Henning. Dinner theater was a burgeoning business at that time for a wide spectrum of actors. . . . There were quite a few star names that were appearing at that time at the larger dinner theaters in the U.S., like Mickey Rooney and Van Johnson."[4]

Weyland writes that the Hayloft was an Equity (union) theater. "The name actors appeared in Lubbock for various reasons: trying out new plays, checking out the experience to see if it was to their liking (like De), gauging how interested audiences were in a particular actor (like Kulp). Theater owners from all over would call each other and find out how 'so-and-so' was as an attendance draw. They liked Nancy. . . . She and I later toured in several cities. The audiences loved her. Linda Carter . . . appeared there. . . . The managers wanted her to get some experience before they launched her acting career in Hollywood."

Kelley had come to Lubbock prepared, Weyland recalls. He had memorized his part in the script before arriving and was anxious to begin work. Once rehearsals were under way and he began to feel more comfortable with the role, his creativity and inventiveness increased at each rehearsal. If he thought up a funny piece of business that hadn't been rehearsed previously, Weyland would be sure to tell him to "keep it in" during note sessions after rehearsals and performances. Notes are given to casts after a rehearsal or production in most theatrical productions. Sometimes they are given individually or in a group. Weyland says Kelley was fun to collaborate with: "If either of us thought that something wasn't working . . . then we changed it. I can remember discussing and altering concepts . . . but never arguing about them."

A few name actors who appeared in Lubbock at the Hayloft had an attitude, Weyland says, "or felt that they had been exiled to Siberia to make a buck. Not DeForest. That was one of the reasons we got along so well. He wanted to do a good job . . . I wanted to do a good job. Everybody wanted to do a good job. Egos or pretentiousness never got in the way. After twenty-five years, I barely remember the plot of *Beginner's Luck*. It was about a man and a woman who had married and split up. The comedy centered around the interactions between the woman, the woman's new boyfriend, and DeForest as the ex-husband."

On a Tuesday, July 16, rehearsals began. Weyland recalls: "The cast contributed greatly to De's enjoyment of the experience and the success of the production. Michael Griswold had been flown in from Los Angeles. It was common to hire at least one main supporting actor from L.A. Michael was terrific and worked easily with De. Jane Ann [Weyland's wife] was perhaps a bit younger than the role called for. I felt that her talent easily overcame any question about the age difference between the characters. I think I was correct in that judgment. I was slightly concerned about it, but the concerns faded as the rehearsals progressed and the performances began."

It had been a long time for Kelley since the Kenley Players and the Long Beach Community Playhouse. Weyland found the openness and camaraderie that Kelley so easily extended was also a touching indication that he needed someone he could lean on just a little as he approached opening night. Weyland recalls having a final dress rehearsal without an audience at the Hayloft. Kelley had various quick costume changes between scenes. Since this was not an ordinary theater with wings, the changes had to be made outside the four aisle exits. The house went dark, and the music played between scenes. Weyland was waiting in the lobby with the actor who helped with the costume changes each night during the run. At the end of the music, the costume change was to have been completed. "But there was no De in the lobby to change. The other actor and I looked at each other, wondering where he was. The music finished. It was quiet and still dark. I then heard DeForest in a whisper saying, 'Phil? Phil? Where are you? Where am I supposed to go?'" Looking back on it, the moment had a new meaning. Weyland hadn't really thought that Kelley needed him, but perhaps he did.

After rehearsals were well under way on *Beginner's Luck,* Weyland mentioned to Kelley that he would be busy with a high school theater workshop during the days and evenings immediately after the play opened. "Since I lived in Lubbock and would be in town for much of the run of the show, I wanted him to know there was a good reason I wasn't going to be in the audience for most of the performances. My wife was in the play, I had come to enjoy DeForest's and Carolyn's friendship, and I wanted to make sure he knew my absence wouldn't be because I lacked interest." Kelley was not aware that a dinner theater director was paid only until the show opened and then immediately moved on to another show or project. "He was taken aback by this news. His facial expression changed, and he twisted his mouth as he was wont to do when he was deep in thought. As we talked, despite my explanation, I knew he was a bit piqued, very unhappy, and, I sensed, a bit angry, too. My impression was that he felt I was deserting him and leaving him alone without any guidance. The play hadn't opened yet, and he was still insecure about his performance." Everything had gone quite smoothly since Kelley's arrival and Weyland felt that their relationship as director and actor had been productive and enjoyable and that they were becoming friends in the process. "His mild anger dissipated over the course of the next few hours, but his disappointment remained, and he reminded me of it often."

Opening night arrived. As Weyland expected, Kelley was extremely nervous. "Nothing unusual about that for a performer, but De had been away from the theater for quite a long time, and that fact fueled his apprehension." Weyland watched the stage actor come to life. "You related to him, and you were interested in him, and he was the star on that stage." But offstage and while preparing to be onstage, he was terribly nervous, conflicted and funny.

It was July 23, the show opened, and it worked. The director recalls, "The first performance went very well, with only a few small technical glitches. DeForest was superb. The audience reaction was better than even I had anticipated, and DeForest had successfully initiated his five-week run at the Hayloft. When the play opened, and then he heard sound of the audience's appreciative laughter, I knew he realized he would not need constant supervision from me. His stage confidence had returned."

By the way, Weyland recalls, "De was a sharp dresser. Whatever he wore, he looked good in it. I am reminded of this because of the pink pants he wore in the show. There aren't many guys who can wear pink pants and look good in them. He could and did. (Those were the pants that he cut out a swatch from the inside of the cuff, signed, and sent to me after the show closed and he was back in L.A.)

He was an impeccable dresser. All the clothes he wore in the show were his . . . and they added to the character he portrayed."

Kelley rather reluctantly agreed to talk to Weyland's two-week theater workshop for high school students at Texas Tech. "I thought it was revealing that he wasn't too keen on discussing 'the biz' . . . even with high school students." Weyland recalls vividly his first revelation about Kelley—"One of the students asked De whether he should pursue an acting career. DeForest became quiet and serious. His tone and manner changed. It was an unusual tone I never heard from him before and never heard again." The answer was no, but Kelley knew young people had to try. A weary, sad, but certain *no* was the advice he gave every young thespian all the rest of his days. "His demeanor when he answered the question gave me one of the most eye-opening insights into who he was. It was the first time I really began to understand his disenchantment with the then-current Hollywood system."

Weyland learned about Kelley's bitter disappointments in Hollywood and especially about the most recent dismissals by the industry. The problems in Kelley's career after *Star Trek* had been a real personal blow. Television and film had changed in a few brief years, and the actor's life was too harsh for a gentle studio veteran. He had left town with no intention of throwing himself back into the fray once he got home. DeForest Kelley was done with being a Hollywood actor.

Weyland remembers: "*Star Trek* meant little to me at the time. . . . I think he enjoyed my naiveté concerning the whole phenomenon that was reawakening at that time in the mid-'70s. It was a fun subject to discuss and for him to explain to me."

The local theater critic had his fun with the *Star Trek* tie-in for *Beginner's Luck,* but the Hayloft asked for it, since they used a still of Dr. McCoy for the front of the playbill. "And God, they started flying in from everywhere," Kelley exclaimed. Trekkies flew in from the coasts and from Europe.[5]

Sometimes a woman with an infectious laugh would make the entire evening. Sometimes a sour audience deadened the air, and there was nothing to be done. "The weekends were typically sold out with about 400 people," Weyland remembers. "The attendance would rise as the week progressed. Tuesday and Wednesday would often be around 100 or so. There were poor attendance days, but almost always limited to early in the week. For 90 percent of the plays presented there, it was not unusual to have a few really miserable attendance days. I alerted De to this so he wouldn't be discouraged. I also told him that on those low attendance nights, it would be important to speed things up a bit and not wait too long for laughs that may or may not come or wouldn't be as extended."

Jane Ann Dixon, Weyland's wife recalls: "I had never heard of De-Forest Kelley before being cast opposite him in the play . . . and had never even watched *Star Trek*. So, I was in shock at the number of people who came to the show solely on his reputation in *Star Trek*." She finally told Kelley that, and he took it in stride. "It seems I remember that as the play ran its course, he would ad-lib now and then to play the audience. But he was always the gentleman and never the 'star.' "[6]

Of course, now Phil and Jane Ann watched the *Star Trek* reruns when they could, and Phil remembers that they saw Kelley's personality coming through McCoy—"we could see him." Weyland recalls: "My directing job was much easier and a complete joy, because he was talented, funny . . . fall-out-of-your-chair funny! . . . How screamingly funny he was. . . . I'd really like the fans to know that the humor that they saw in *Star Trek* was easily extendable and could and did carry an entire evening's performance to the delight of audiences during that run of *Beginner's Luck*."

Weyland remembers that *Star Trek* would not leave Kelley: "I can see him. . . . Rehearsal was interrupted one morning when De was called to the phone . . . frustrated. I later found out he was on the phone talking to a poor fellow who was insisting that De explain the finer points of the phaser! All calls were screened after that." Another instance comes to mind, "the time when the fan just pulled up a chair and joined the four of us when we were eating at a restaurant in Lubbock." But Kelley was as gracious and patient as a man could be in both situations.

Kelley accepted Weyland's coming and going. At the end of the play, Phil and Jane Ann were leaving Lubbock and moving to Dallas. During the first part of the run of *Beginner's Luck,* Weyland would be in Dallas, looking for an apartment, checking with agents and theaters for work. He told Kelley that Jane Ann would let him know how things were going through letters and phone calls.

After each show, any actor who appeared at the Hayloft was required to hang out in the lobby for a bit and sign autographs. Weyland remembers that Kelley was quite charming at these sessions: "He stood in the lobby and just chitchatted with the people who had attended the performance. I don't think that it was really something that he was eager to do . . . but he did enjoy the after-the-show sessions to some degree. There were 'Trekkies' who came, of course . . . but the audience and after-the-show chitchatters consisted primarily of adults who came to the show for an evening of entertainment. The audience enjoyed meeting an accomplished actor from Hollywood who also happened to have been in a well-known TV series. Many discussed with him his work other than *Star Trek*—and I think he enjoyed that part."

Kelley liked to tell a story about the chitchat part of the evening: "Well, I was down there, and I was signing autographs in the lobby, and I looked down and saw these pairs of cowboy boots in front of me, and I looked up, and there was a beautiful cowgirl and a cowboy standing next to her. They said, 'We came down here to see you not because of *Star Trek* but because of all those cowboy pictures you've been in. We own a cowboy store here in Lubbock.' He said, 'You come down Monday morning. We'd like you to pick out a pair of boots.' " He did as he was told and went to their place on Monday. "I picked out a less expensive pair. They said, 'No, you don't want that . . . you want this.' So that's where I got these boots." They were made of Gila monster skin with black uppers and angled heels. He loved them. Over time, he adapted his movie-star details and accessories to denim and Gila boots—and so created his unique style for public appearances.[7]

Jane Ann kept Phil informed about the show while he was in Dallas. She described the goings-on at the theater; that De broke up, or once De skipped a page in Act One, or some audiences laughed at things no other audience laughed at any other night. Kelley told Jane Ann that Carolyn had rescued a turtle from the highway, stopped traffic and all. Kelley was upset about that part, but they seemed pleased to have a turtle in their bathtub. The Kelleys recreated their homey routines in the Alhambra Hotel in Lubbock.

Based on the strength of his performance, Jane Ann and Phil Weyland tried to talk Kelley into extending his role and getting on the road with the show. He mulled it over, talked to Carolyn, gnawed on it further, and just couldn't give an answer. Weyland realized that six weeks in a city on a circuit would not work for Kelley, because he wanted to be on Greenleaf with Myrtle at what Weyland dubbed "TurtleHalla." He could have done well if he wanted to, and while he seemed to enjoy this show, he couldn't resolve the pull between performing and being a homebody.

But Weyland saw how the old stage actor recovered his mastery of his craft: "De started to loosen up as the show progressed. I remember seeing one of the performances and being surprised at how readily and quickly he had re-adapted to the stage. He was home. Yup. He didn't have to catch a short acting pass from Bill or Leonard. He, in those few weeks onstage, could grab that proverbial ball and run the entire length of the acting field. That's what made his not continuing with the theater so disappointing. He had the talent, class, and style. And I wanted to be associated with those qualities professionally."

But Kelley's nerves were a wreck. Characteristically, he told this story on himself again and again: "Had a horrible experience in that play. I [in character] was trying to make up with my wife. We were separated, and she had agreed to see me again and talk to me about certain things. So I go over to her house, and I feign an injury, turning my ankle. She let me stay overnight and sleep on the sofa. . . . While she went up to get some bedding, I am quickly undressing and stripping down. I was trying to get undressed real quick before this girl comes downstairs, and I had a gold chain and medal around my neck that Carolyn had given me for our fifteenth anniversary, and it was a center-stage situation, and in getting undressed, I ripped open this cowboy shirt. My finger got caught in the gold chain, and the chain flew into the front row, and I saw it, and it rather disturbed me. . . . I proceeded not only to take my pants off but my underwear. Oh, boy, I mooned the whole line . . . I mooned the whole west side. . . . I'll tell you, it sure loosened that audience up! Thank God it was a unique stage—I'd never seen a stage like that. It was like a square center theater, and it would rise after each act and go up to the second floor, and thank God they had lifted the stage straight up, and I just went right up and got off . . . went to bed."[8]

Actually, he kept on going and finished the evening in fine form, as Jane Ann Dixon confirms: "He joked about it with them during his curtain speech. He was so embarrassed!" He did get the necklace back, but the incident stayed with him, both as a funny story and as a reminder of how stressful theater had become for him. During the six-week course of the show, he lost twenty-five pounds and had to get all of his clothing tailored again. He was sustained only by the play, smoking, and cocktails. In his heart, he wanted to go home to Greenleaf; the actor's life was eating him alive.

On August 11, Kelley wrote his own letter to Phil Weyland. He considered the idea of playing a circuit with *Beginner's Luck* but continued to be unsure. "Should it happen, I will certainly ask for you—you know my feelings in that area." He wrote glowingly of Jane's performances and wished her to continue the role if he continued his—"if the age difference doesn't bother you. . . . Cheers sends a 'flea bite.' . . . We have acquired a turtle Carolyn found."

As the show's run came to an end, Weyland checked in with the Kelleys. "I remember Carolyn saying that she and De wanted us to have something to keep our future happy memories in." The Kelleys presented their gift to the Weylands. "It was a large, dark green scrapbook with the names *Jane Ann* and *Phil* embossed on the cover in gold lettering. A card written by DeForest was enclosed that read: 'For Jane Ann and Phil—May this book reflect many Happy Memories—DeForest and Carolyn.' They were most sincere, and we were very pleased by the thought and gesture. It wasn't a gift about doing the show . . . it was a gift from friends to friends."

Weyland adds: "I think that De and Carolyn saw much of their early selves in the relationship that Jane Ann and I had during that time period." And he recalls, "During an evening at home during the latter part of the rehearsals, Jane Ann and I had just finished watching a *Star Trek* rerun. When it was over, Jane Ann said she thought that Carolyn and De were what we would be like twenty-five years in the future. I remember agreeing. If the fates had allowed Jane Ann and me to stay together and live in L.A., I have no doubt that we would have seen quite a bit of De and Carolyn over the years. Somehow I miss those events that never took place."[9]

3 The Kelleys returned to Greenleaf and life on the convention trail. *Star Trek* was spreading, and now the actors were being paid to do personal appearances around the country for certain store chains and promotional tours. Kelley and George Takei wound up in Virginia at one point at a Toys "R" Us store. Kelley saw and remembered a young girl from the summer in Pennsylvania with the Kenley players. One of her sons recalls, "I dig DeForest Kelley—my mom going up and hugging Bones!" That was something a boy would never forget. The Incredible Hulk was there, too, that day.

On July 11, 1975, the *Los Angeles Herald Examiner* discussed a recent *Star Trek* convention attended by Kelley and James Doohan. The paper acknowledged the emerging mainstream power of *Star Trek*. Reporters were still trying to define terms used by the fringe fanatics, such as "phasers on stun" and "Beam me up, Scotty," and time and again, they underestimated the web of connections created by endless reruns and fan-driven events, magazines, and clubs. *Time* magazine on September 8, 1975, allowed the "Trekkie fad" out of the closet and into its Modern Living section. The first time the entire cast reassembled, in Chicago, *Time* reported that the crew had been "adrift for six years in interstellar limbo." Nationwide and earthbound, from "Abu Dhabi to Zambia," the crew was stuck in a never-ending time-warp of syndication. Sixteen thousand Trekkies attended the Chicago gathering. Hucksters sold collectibles, books, and blueprints of the *Enterprise,* and the economic possibilities were clearly endless. The *Enterprise* was gaining speed and power, and there was very nearly a public mandate that the heroes return.

All of this profited Kelley exactly nothing. Appearances at conventions paid the bills; though he went to fewer of these than most of his costars, he recognized their importance, economically, emotionally, and professionally. He made frequent visits to the unemployment office, and when he saw Grace Lee Whitney in the line at the Ventura office, he told her that the fans had been asking for her. She was amazed. What was a convention? Who had been asking for her? With Kelley's kind referral, she began her journey back to the *Enterprise* and the people who appreciated her own personal trek: the fans.

Kelley recalled: "I was afraid we were going to talk about making a movie the rest of our lives." Part of the original crew was assembled to talk some more for Tom Snyder's *Tomorrow* show in early 1976. It was a very popular late-night talk show hosted by a man known for his intellect and edgy interview style.

Kelley had gone ahead and adopted a McCoy look. The hair was the same, with sideburns only a tad blunted. The face was the same, and he looked and sounded every inch his alter ego. He was indeed in something of a McCoy mood. Quite simply, McCoy harbored the toughness in Kelley, the argumentative spice. Snyder encouraged that in his guests. Kelley, Doohan, Walter Koenig, and Harlan Ellison were up to the game of Snyder's show.

Doohan was the natural leader and the expert on *Star Trek* as a business and as a phenomenon. He had an almost military certainty and directness that night. Except for writer Ellison, fandom was the thing that fed them, and the phenomenon exacted a professional and personal price. "Cult" was the word that sprang to Kelley's lips in the first moments of the show. While *Star Trek*'s fandom gave them means to earn a living, adulation, and recognition, some of the individuals in that universe were trying—some made unreasonable demands. Even the environment of their celebrity status was itself small and manufactured. Koenig was most forward in his admission of feeling unreal; he said his life was science fiction because of fandom. Koenig the man and Koenig the actor were invisible in his chosen profession but adored in the alternative universe of the convention world. Something was counterfeit about the whole thing.

Tellingly, Kelley explained to Snyder that *Star Trek* was the most popular television show in the world, with 155 stations broadcasting around the clock. Yet they were not still doing the show, and Doohan pointed out that they had not received a dime in five years. Of all the money the *Enterprise* was making around the world, none of it came to them. Kelley engaged in a quick bit of repartee with Snyder, and then a few powerful words came out of his mouth with Snyder's prompting: "I'm the star of a ghost." And for all the world, he looked the part of a haunted man. Doohan, on the other hand, was powerful and confident, describing the show and many of its consequences as "beautiful." Ellison thought that perhaps he would have insulin shock from all the "sweetness and light" being cast onto the dark set of the *Tomorrow* show. Doohan said with a bit of warning that they could supply a bit of the sour if need be. Doohan and Kelley both squinted through their curls of cigarette smoke as if monitoring the horizon for any verbal threat to their *Enterprise*. One had the distinct impression that both men were ready to defend her.

Kelley related a story about a mentally retarded girl who was completely uncommunicative until she encountered *Star Trek* on television. She made sounds for the first time. Intrigued, her father took her to the set. She began to speak. Kelley believed it earnestly, speaking with gravity. *Star Trek* had profoundly touched lives, and he had met that girl, and he knew. To him, the incident was the mustard seed, all the proof a person needed to know the value of the show. There was a "real magic" intrinsic to the show. He asserted that inquiring people were encouraged to explore philosophy, science, and cultures with the show's inspiration. He declared that the real effect of the show was now "reflected throughout the universities."

Doohan, too, had encountered some of the most serious examples of *Star Trek*'s healing and lifesaving touch. He was also grateful that the fans insisted on the original cast for the return of *Star Trek* and predicted that there would be sequels as long as fans wanted them.

Where Kelley was empathetic, Doohan was down-to-earth. They had known the show's effect and affect personally and did not take lightly the unforeseen and rather phenomenal consequences of their work. It did seem that Kelley was getting a little hot under the navy turtleneck and light blue jacket, the smoke rising with the temperature. Yes, they were all a little tired of conventions and the cult fringe, the same questions, the same longings and wishes they did not have the power to fulfill.

Professionally, everyone agreed that a motion picture rather than a television treatment was a real risk. Kelley was concerned that the whole franchise was dependent on one throw of the dice. The drive to have a real epic dazzler to fill the big screen could destroy the human adventure, the very strength of *Star Trek*. Doohan wisely reminded everyone of the gratitude they should have, for while they were living, they could know that they had been part of a classic—a real classic that would carry on beyond their lifetimes.

Once Ellison warmed to the subject, he was so funny in his descriptions of execs and Gene Roddenberry and the bedeviled agony of the Hollywood pathology that the panel was lost in laughter. The tendency of the suits—the execs—was to demand a big show, bigger than anything televised, bigger than anything imagined ever in the history of the world. Ellison's treatment of a sad reality had them all in stitches. Then, through the side of his mouth, Kelley suggested a plot for the biggest *Star Trek* story of all: the crew would go out in search of Christ and find he's Lucifer. That stopped things cold. "I don't know we're quite ready for that, DeForest." Snyder bounced back and moved on hurriedly.

4 Overall, Kelley's frustration was not with Trekkie trivia or needy fans or clinging typecasting. It was the lack of *Star Trek* that bothered him, this eternal holding pattern they were in. He would not, could not, dismiss the importance of the *Enterprise* spirit.

As far as Kelley could glean from his personal contacts in the Hollywood studios, it was common opinion that Paramount was out of its mind for dragging its feet on the new *Star Trek* incarnation. He recalled a friend's exasperation: "If this was Fox, they'd be on their third *Star Trek*." Kelley hoped they would finally settle on a ninety-minute movie of the week or something—anything.[10]

Then, suddenly, *Star Trek* had an impact that not even Roddenberry could have predicted. The nation had been shaken by the constitutional crisis of the Nixon impeachment, and 1976 had to be a year of promise and renewal. President Gerald Ford was petitioned by *Star Trek* fans, led by Bjo Trimble, to make a statement of transcendent American optimism. Ford agreed and allowed scientific reality and science-fiction fantasy to come together for a moment for all the world to see.

One day, one event, and the crew of the *Enterprise* crossed the chasm between entertainment phenomenon and cultural icon. On September 17, 1976, Kelley, Roddenberry, Nichols, Takei, Koenig, and Nimoy assembled at Edwards Air Force Base to witness the debut of the maiden space shuttle *Enterprise,* named not in honor of past warships but in honor of the future exploration vessel. The U.S. Air Force struck up the old television series theme. The American promise would be alive and well and an integral part of a future reality. Never before had there been anything like it in the world. Here was NASA's first leap toward a new frontier for the common man, and it bore the name of *Enterprise*. The actors and the creator were overwhelmed by the homage. They were shaken to their boots, chilled with emotion, DeForest Kelley in tears."

After this experience, Kelley went back to Greenleaf and picked up his routine as if it were just another week, another month. The cycle and balance of things brought him peace and patience. He made time for fan mail. He made time to write to his friends. He wrote to Phil Weyland just before Christmas, 1976: "We were surprised to hear about your divorce . . . so much better to find these things out now while you are young—oh, to be that young again. . . . We have not done the film yet. Should start this spring for Christmas of '77 release. My career has consisted of *Star Trek* convention appearances—these have been lucrative, but it's not film. It seems Shatner is the only one not afflicted with Space Identification. Otherwise, we have no complaints, and I'm sure what's to be is to be in this business. . . . A play floats through my mind occasionally but floats out when I think of the trauma!" He added that Carolyn had taken up calligraphy. He disclosed the death of Cheers shortly after their return from Lubbock but also the joy of the new Lhasa apso puppy, Fancy. Friends say that it was Kelley's insistence that he didn't need a fancy dog—a mutt would do, no fancy dog—that gave that fancy dog her name.

With the season's change, Kelley wrote again to Weyland on old *Star Trek* letterhead on March 12, 1977: "I am sorry to hear things are not working for you in Dallas—I wish I could lay the proper advice out for you, Phil." He confessed that he was out of the game and would be of little help to Weyland if he came out to Los Angeles to try his luck. "*Star Trek* is supposed to go in September. None of the cast have seen a script or made a deal yet. They have enormous script problems. . . . I'm sure you know that I feel you are a very talented man, and I'm positive you will find your way into your proper slot in this business. If I get a thought that might be helpful to you, I will let you know. . . . Myrtle the turtle is still asleep—she should be coming out soon."

Through 1977, Kelley enjoyed a renewal of energy and hope. He began to allow fans to see more of the man who was DeForest Kelley. He wanted to do something different for the fans, something they would like, from him to them. The Kelleys appreciated poetry and read often from their favorite authors. Most favored was Don Blanding, the premier poet of Hawaii.

Kelley loved Blanding's collected works and long poems. He often reached for those well-worn volumes on his shelf to read a little something. Perhaps he would give this poetry thing a try and read to the Trekkies. The result was a caricature, a humorous but honest account of the real adventures of the *Star Trek* family: "The Big Bird's Dream." Once he was satisfied with his longhand version, he handed it over to Carolyn for her rendering with calligraphy pen. Together they produced a gift for their audiences. He copyrighted the work and enjoyed reading it to people all around the country. They loved it, and they loved him for taking the time to write for them.

5 No science fiction could replace *Star Trek*, but an ancient myth of father and son could finally make *Star Trek*'s return not only a matter of public mandate but also a matter of huge profits. *Star Wars* debuted in 1977, and over at Paramount, dreams of avarice danced in their heads. The success of George Lucas demanded an answer from Paramount and Roddenberry.

The old *Star Trek* had been a large factor in the gathering momentum for science fiction in television and film: *2001: A Space Odyssey, Space: 1999,* Harve Bennett's *The Six Million Dollar Man* and *The Bionic Woman,* Roddenberry's brief *Questor Tapes* and *Genesis II.* Nothing filled the demand created by *Star Trek*. The Trekkies kept on, and women were the foundation and survival of *Star Trek*. It was they who organized *Star Trek* conventions. Joan Winston and a league of ladies made the commune happening happen. As Jackie Edwards, a lifelong fan, says now, "Techie boys don't bond" but Trekkie girls do, and often it was for life. Among these were Bjo Trimble, Carolyn Poppovich, Kathe Walker, and newcomer Sue Keenan. Official fan clubs that were sanctioned or supported by the actors themselves grew, as did others that gathered based on fantasy and role-playing.

There were fanzines of fiction and erotica and poetry; fans created original art and music and a worldwide network of pen pals. Young men attended the conventions, read the fiction, and began their participation in the flowing mosaic of the *Star Trek* phenomenon. *Star Trek* fans willed to create their alternative world if no one else would answer the call. Winston and others long ago registered that this was a woman's world, and it would accordingly endure.

Of course, no one who was in a position to make money from these well-intentioned people hesitated to do so. Cottage industries sprang up, people made Tribbles, and seamstresses created uniforms. Larger concerns became interested in the Trekkie potential as a market with its own well-known wants and desires. Television stations had a treasury of seventy-nine episodes that were often edited to the very bone of coherence to make room for more commercials. Some stations ran episodes by air date or by theme, and some had festivals and played all the episodes back to back, hour after hour.

Carolyn and DeForest were at home on Greenleaf when a local station presented a *Star Trek* marathon. They tuned in out of mild curiosity, and then—"Well, they weren't sure if they'd been paid for the episodes," Tony Kirk recalls. He by then had become the Kelleys' expert on the series. "I was in my mailroom, and Carolyn had the number"; she had a log of the payments for each episode. Kirk told her to "read 'em off and I'd tell her or check up on it." The marathon ran every episode, and Kirk could list most of them from memory anyway. From examination of the marathon, the logbook, and Kirk's brain, a few interesting conclusions were drawn. Some episodes were indeed missing from the Kelley logbook. Not only DeForest but the entire cast "all got paid for a few episodes that had been preempted the first time, and no pay after," Kirk recalls.

After all that, Kirk came around on his route, and "De was going to hug me. Carolyn was cracking up, and De said, 'How many times have I told you not to watch those things!'" Ever since Carolyn called him about the marathon, their relationship deepened. "'Who is this lovely mailman?'" She would swoon and laugh. "I loved her, friendship with De aside, truly." Even with Kirk, Kelley was in control of what he revealed to the world around him. "I only knew what he wanted to show," Kirk is certain.

Meanwhile, Weyland had come out to Los Angeles and was struggling through the labyrinth of the entertainment industry. Kelley had warned him. Weyland would take any job anywhere in the industry, never mind what he knew, never mind the education or that he had been a director. Kelley had been in the business longer than Weyland had been alive. Weyland couldn't blame him for getting out of the game. He had come to town with a thousand dollars that lasted only a very short time. He worked as a security guard, did odd jobs, scraped by, talked to DeForest and Carolyn on the phone. Kelley always remembered his friends, and he had real affection for Weyland. Finally, Weyland's phone rang: "Ya know . . . " Kelley called on Weyland to be his stand-in for *Star Trek: The Motion Picture*.

Back in those days of the late 1970s, an actor could still designate a position like that. Of course, Kelley felt compelled to make sure his stand-in from the original series wouldn't want the job; with a decade gone by, the fellow had indeed moved on. Weyland was brought on board the *Enterprise*. How was that for beginner's luck?

Part Four

The Starshine

Chapter XIV
I Must Be McCoy

"I'm contemplating writing a book, and I'm thinking
of calling it I Must Be McCoy.*"*
—DEFOREST KELLEY, 1978

In February 1978, Kelley received his "flight manual" for the motion picture. And that was the extent of the action. Months came and went, and the *Enterprise* remained stuck in space dock. Journalists and fans alike assumed that the actors were the experts on the studio's inner workings, Roddenberry, and all things *Star Trek*. The constant barrage of well-meaning but unanswerable questions and queries drove the actors nuts. Their own frustrations increased because they weren't getting any answers, either.

A few years before, *Star Trek*'s man of letters, Leonard Nimoy, had rather stunned all the degrees of fandom with *I Am Not Spock*. In 1978, Kelley was asked his reaction to the book. In true Kelley style, he evaded giving his opinion as he told the truth in the same breath. He told the reporter, "I'm contemplating writing a book, and I'm thinking of calling it *I Must Be McCoy*."[1]

In late August 1978, the crew finally did assemble at Paramount for *Star Trek: The Motion Picture*. Phil Weyland was thirty years old when he walked through the studio gates to begin his new assignment as Kelley's stand-in. He found a maze of alleys, nondescript buildings, and soundstages, scurrying activity everywhere. Where does a guy go? He wandered around and finally found the soundstage for *Star Trek*. Kelley emerged from the shadows to greet him.

Earlier that morning, DeForest and Carolyn had been discussing his first day on the Paramount lot back in 1946. They were trying to guess what Weyland must have felt as he wandered the hallowed ground of the grand old studio for the first time. That was very sweet of them. But the world Weyland entered was quite different from the one Kelley had known. Kelley had been brought in as an actor with a contract upon discharge from the army. He had a movie to do and a future as a star. Weyland never got that kind of welcome.

What he got was a bad Starfleet haircut from an octogenarian barber. And he did get an introduction to Paramount's ambassador to the world, A. C. Lyles. Weyland could tell that Kelley thought the world of this impeccably dressed showman, but he never could figure out what Lyles actually did at the studio. Kelley told him that Lyles was the man to know. Weyland felt a little disoriented by this strange new world.

However, the job itself was clear enough: take Kelley's place while the cameras and lighting were prepared. When the director was satisfied, Weyland stepped out. Finally, Kelley stepped in as Dr. McCoy—for the first time in a decade. He was nearly sixty years old.

Weyland vividly remembers the hush that swept through the entire soundstage when Nimoy made his appearance in makeup and black costume—a simultaneous inhalation of disbelief, joy, welcome home. The Vulcan was in the building. It was a marvel. Even his costars were affected by the virtual beam-in of the first officer. Weyland was not a Trekkie, was not invested in the franchise, but it hit him in the chest, too—*Spock*.[2]

The story had the crew assembling aboard the *Enterprise* to save Earth from a probe calling itself V-Ger. Kelley had longed for these first days of reunion, but the script brought everyone up short. Kelley admitted, "I was worried when I saw the script, because the characterizations were not there, the relationships were not there." He was so concerned that he joined up with Shatner and Nimoy to fight for the characterizations that might be worked into the shooting script. They had professional and personal responsibilities toward Kirk, Spock, and McCoy and a duty toward their fans. In this regard, they were indeed the experts, but their expertise was ignored.[3]

For all of his worry, Kelley kept his empathy. He was well aware that as the new guy on the block, Stephen Collins was going to have a hard time of it as the new captain of the *Enterprise,* Captain Decker. The former Captain Kirk was now Admiral Kirk. The real problem was that even though Collins knew nothing of the *Star Trek* universe, he was still caught in the orbits of arguments among the cast, the crew, Roddenberry, and Nimoy and Shatner.

Kelley explained to Collins what warp drive was and what phasers were. He told him what was where on the bridge and who all these very driven people were. He taught him that the brotherly combat, the push and pull, was the way of things and would always be; this was the *Star Trek* family. The scrapping would go on around him, with him or without him, and how much it upset Collins was really up to Collins.

Collins remembers: "I had never seen an episode of *Star Trek.* . . . I had no sense of him as an actor, no preconception of him. I knew nothing about 'Bones.' De was the one who took me aside and basically translated the ballgame . . . Bill, Leonard, and all that. De was an ambassador who explained to me the manners of the court . . . so generous." Collins's dressing room was next to Kelley's, and he spent more time with him than anyone. "I had the immediate sense that this was a wise man. . . . There was something very un-actorish—even [then] I kind of knew. . . . Very few actors are as well rounded as he was. . . . He had his feet on the ground—in a kind of quiet, settled, serene way. I then knew and now I see truly how rare it is. . . . He didn't seem preoccupied with himself, he knew who he was—very few actors do." To Collins, Kelley communicated his surprise and delight with all the incredible success of *Star Trek.* "He was tickled the whole thing was happening, but it didn't own him. He was able to enjoy it." Collins paraphrases a line in an ancient text: "'Act but do not be attached to the fruits of the action.' . . . De seemed to know that [and that he was on] an incredible ride. [McCoy] was absolutely De, very ironic, detached, but warm. Warmth together with the detached irony made him incredibly lovable."[4]

So the days of the motion picture began. Weyland's work was hard and thankless, but it was a job and an education. He thought highly of Collins: "It's like he was on an IV of peace and propriety." Weyland's earlier relationship with Kelley was a quiet pleasure and a little-known fact. Few people knew that Weyland had been Kelley's director or that he was Kelley's friend. Their quiet camaraderie grew under the new circumstances. While Kelley was waiting for a scene or a shot, Weyland was in his place; when Kelley was at work, Weyland was in the background. But there were hours of restless boredom, and they hung out in Kelley's dressing room shooting the breeze. Weyland recalls: "He would usually slip into it in the context of a question asked by me," and suddenly Rhett Butler might say, " 'Well, Scarlett . . .' "De would very much look like Gable when he twisted his mouth, and . . . he exaggerated the impression to be funnier."[5]

Then one day, Kelley got mad. Nimoy wrote: "We recreated the transporter effect entirely from scratch. . . . A camera unit and special effects crew spent countless days and hours shooting tests in the transporter room—as though it had never done before." It sounds obnoxious, but it really was exhausting and dangerous for Weyland and the other man standing on the lighted grid platforms of the new transporter. Weyland's footwear melted; his partner's booties had burned through the soles.[6]

When Kelley found out that Weyland and another stand-in had stood over that hot transporter-room floor grill for hours without a break, he made short work of the situation.[7]

The environment on the soundstage tested everyone's resources. "Gene was very much on the outskirts of the movie," Collins believes. "He was present, but he was not really in the inner circle . . . diplomatically difficult for everybody." Yet just below Collins's perception was a rancor between creator and actors so thorny that Nimoy still recalls it vividly: "De was in a complicated spot with Gene because he was with us on the stage and was one of us when Gene hated all of us, wanted to see us all die . . . ha! So he could replace us with an inanimate ship! Which wouldn't give him any trouble or complain or upstage him!" Wisely, Kelley reserved his greatest allegiance for the collective, the sum of its parts, the art called *Star Trek*.[8]

Nimoy reflects: "Bill Shatner and I were trying very desperately to make a movie out of it . . . trying to dramatize events within the movie" about a probe and a ship. "I think Collins must be very angry at us, by the way . . . you know he was in a very troubled *Star Trek* movie." The battling and stubbornness that Collins witnessed was largely the result of their attempts to save the character-based love affair with the fans. Shatner and Nimoy were fighting for "internal drama," but "he must have thought we were trying to pirate the film from him." When he learned of Collins's experience with Kelley and his overall impression of the man, it was no surprise to Nimoy: "Clearly, that would be De's role, the peacemaker."

Collins recalls the peacemaker. "It is truly rare in any human being—that ability to hang on to himself when everything else was going crazy. I never saw him get upset to the point that he was lost to it." Kelley comprehended the situation and simply dealt with it as things developed. "De pretty much stayed out of it . . . a lot of negotiations, between Bill and Leonard—and between Bill and Leonard together and everybody else. My sense was that they increasingly took the reins creatively and said, 'look this is what *Star Trek* is' from moment to moment." They basically had to do that, Collins thinks, because director Bob Wise, by his own admission, didn't really know. And nobody else did, because they were trying so hard to call it *Star Trek*, but the demand for a blockbuster compelled them to make it into something else. "And Bill and Leonard were insisting, day to day, on what *Star Trek* was really about moment to moment."

Kelley hung back; he knew very well what was good for him and good for the *Enterprise*. Collins's impression was that "De just knew, 'Well, when the dust settles . . . I'll be there as much as I'm gonna be there. Somebody's got to play my part, and it's going to be me.' I think he understood that the movie needed him in a very simple, essential way—and it did. He was so direct and so without guile."[9]

Kelley longed for the cooperation that made the series a joy to him. When the series had been in production, the actors, writers, Roddenberry, and others would gather around a table and discuss the episode or a scene. Kelley pined for that atmosphere, and there was none in 1978. He was very aware that the strain showed. "We didn't have much getting used to each other to do. It all fell back in to place. But we were all kind of going our own way, as opposed to the series, where we were always working together, interrelating constantly. The movie didn't seem like that to me." As McCoy was reduced to a two-dimensional figure, Kelley had trouble working with what he was given. "I had to do nearly fourteen takes on what was left" of a scene with Shatner. "I just couldn't play it." It was a reunion of men and women, but a difficult one. Kelley's heart ached for a high-quality story, a "City on the Edge of Forever," with minimal special effects, something "terribly exciting in its unique simplicity." He cooperated with his colleagues in dreaming up alternatives to the blue-screen emptiness that now had hold of the crew of the *Enterprise*. He was denied at every turn. Shatner and Nimoy took the rough road and kept battling through the weeks, to save what they felt were their creative lives.[10]

Kelley was without illusions. He was wise to the realities of Hollywood and where the leading stars stood within the industry. Weyland recalls that finally in late November, they were coming to the end of the endless film. They were working on the huge finale, and the three heroes were running away from the probe. "De turns to me and says, 'Ya know, Phil, ya know why we're doing this sequence last? I tell ya why . . . because if any of us get hurt, it's at the end of the movie, and they don't care.'" Or perhaps they thought the stars would just keep running.

From August through November 1978, the filming never ceased. Roddenberry rallied morale by having a photographer go around making shots of everyone. He made gifts of them, framed and signed by the Big Bird of the Galaxy. Weyland's was of Kelley in costume, with the eternal cigarette in his slender hand pointing the way to young Phil—a sweet and meaningful image.[11] Roddenberry chose a picture of Kelley wearing the beard and looking rather formidable, and he signed it lovingly to his old friend. Kelley took it home and hung it on his wall. It was time to wrap it up and hope for the best at the other end of postproduction.[12]

A young, well-educated computer consultant came on the job after the fact to try to help sort it all out. Ralph Winter faced a huge task. Miles and miles of film welcomed him to the *Star Trek* family, but he determined to get the job done and made a reputation for himself as a young fellow who could untangle the Gordian knot of the motion picture. In 1978, no one within the studio walls really knew anything about computers, how to use them or what they were capable of.

Winter's training, work ethic, and mental agility were recognized, and a career in film, not computer technology, was begun.[13]

2 The motion picture proved once and for all that it was the character-driven play and those specific characters themselves in the play that made all the difference in *Star Trek*. Whether anyone in power would realize the fact that an authentic *Star Trek* movie had not yet been made was something else again. Stephen Collins remembers the thread of the old *Star Trek* that ran through this first effort: "It's actually the interplay between De and either Leonard or Bill that provides the movie with the familiar ring that it does have . . . to the extent it does. Take De out of the movie, and there is almost none of it there. Bill captures a little of it, but it's really De's presence, in the early going and all the way through, that reminds audiences that it's okay for them to laugh."[14] Indeed, it was Kelley's presence that reminded the audience that this was the same crew that everyone had known a decade ago.

Kelley eventually penned his despair humorously: "When this picture's released, we'll all be dead!" The crew reassembled for the premier of the movie in Washington, D.C. Carolyn mustered all of her courage and accompanied her husband on a promotional junket that took them to Australia, New Zealand, and Hawaii for Christmas.[15]

The entire experience left DeForest with that dull ache again. The fans would determine what happened afterward, but still he worried that the studio would recast the crew, or maybe they just wouldn't want him anymore. He told *Starlog* that he was relieved that the movie had finally been made, but obviously he was still hungry for the work. Then he told the story that had affected the rest of his life, the one about the little fellow in Colorado. "So, you see, *Star Trek* has had an amazing influence on all our lives."[16]

Over the years, Collins has come to the very same conclusions Kelley had reached decades ago. In Collins's words, "Entertainment is a kind of ministry. I wish I could talk to him about that now, because as I get older, that seems to be the only point of it. I use the word broadly, something that ministers to people, it doesn't have to be the

teachings of Christ. But when you minister to people, you are provid-
ing something that they need. I have come to see entertainment at its
finest to be healing to any given individual. I have so much evidence
of this that increasingly it is the only thing that keeps me interested
in acting." Art also engages the actor after the fact. Collins receives
"life-changing mail—life-changing for me. I sense that De felt somewhat the same way. You never know who is out there, you never know
what they're going through. My guess is that De had a sense of that,
a big sense of that."

Collins remembers that Kelley told him " 'This *Star Trek* thing will
follow you around for the rest of your life, and mostly it will be a good
thing.' Because, again, I had no sense of it at all. He said, 'You'll see
now that you're a part of this, and there is this incredibly loyal group
of people out there who will never forget that you were part of this
crew.' " And that has been borne out over the years.

Walter Koenig was very right—this fiction of *Star Trek* had invested the actors with great powers and gifts granted by the fans and
the phenomenon itself. Kelley knew very well that in Hollywood, he
could not get on the Paramount lot without a pass, he could not help
his talented friends get work, and he became a ghost the moment the
machine ceased to need him. He stated again and again that he had no
power over the industry or over *Star Trek* as part of that industry.
What he thought meant nothing. There was something forlorn in his
admissions, but his sense of helplessness was not resignation. Wisely,
he placed the ultimate power in the hands of the *Star Trek* fans.

He was philosophical about what fans came to call "the Motionless
Picture." He refused to blame anyone for the debacle. It was time to
settle in once again on Greenleaf. He could not predict what would
come next. But in the meantime, he declared, "I'm just going to live
until I die."[17]

3 Well, not quite—there were things to do, such as recapturing the
sense of his long and curious road over the last forty years of living
and acting in Southern California by retracing his path. Forty years
had come and gone since he had stepped off the bus in Long Beach, a

young man fresh to life and ready to become an actor, to go to hell in the process if he had to. Then he had found Anne and Billee, Grace Hartung, Joe Laden, and Barney Girard, all of whom were still in his life through letters and phone calls.

It had been a very long time since he had been to Long Beach, and when the Long Beach Community Playhouse put on a gala in February 1979, he was their guest of honor.

The place was full of the most la-de-da people in their finery. De and Carolyn were seated when Carolyn became aware of a warm bosom just behind her neck. "Don't drop those puppies on me!" Carolyn growled happily as Anne Jolly leaned over her shoulder for a hello smooch. Anne was filled with delight. There had been so many years and so many miles between them, and now it seemed right that they were all back together—De, Carolyn, Anne, Bette, and, of course, the unsinkable Billee, Anne's mother.

Anne had been through a lot but had finally found a man who equaled DeForest in loving devotion and honest steadiness. She had raised three good people and was looking forward to grandchildren. So her life also had come around full circle as she settled into a beautiful home and a beautiful life on the white sands of Alamitos Bay. Once again DeForest and Anne were anchored solidly together for the coming voyage of the rest of their lives.

Anne recalls that the recovery of this thread of their lives was sweet for everyone involved. De's soft, dry sense of humor and Carolyn's throaty laughter had been missed. When DeForest made his entrance to Anne's new abode, Billee greeted him with love and an offer to go down the street and get him some of the Tava drink she used to take care of her boys with. De was very thin, thirty pounds less than when she knew him before the war—any mother would want to fatten him up. They talked and laughed for hours, God they could talk for days.[18]

Aileen Pickering returned to Greenleaf and the Kelley circle after a banner year of flying. In 1980, she had been flying over Europe with very little operational gear, the radio was gone, all the equipment was fried, and there was fuel on board. The ultimate crisis came while circling over a French airport near Cannes. Aileen could not get the landing gear down. She believed they had run out of luck. Her copilot was even more petite than she, but they both knew they were going to die if they didn't get the wheels down. With the strength of desperation, her copilot hand-cranked the landing gear down in increments, bit by arduous bit. The wheels came down over the course of what seemed to be hours. Finally, with the wheels mostly deployed, Aileen was forced to crash the plane—and walk away. Her racing association declared her Flier of the Year for her courage and skill under pressure. Her life was the antithesis of her friends' back in Sherman Oaks, but it seemed she could not go for very long without checking in with them and Myrtle.[19]

Tony LaFata had been away, making a life and raising a family. He and DeForest had kept in touch, and now DeForest seemed more himself than he had been for years. The typecasting and burden of McCoy through the decade of the '70s had stifled him. He told Tony about the conventions: "I used to hate these things . . . dragged by a team of mules," Then the fans seemed to work magic over him, and he admitted, "I just love these people; they respond." He fed on their love. He was a stage actor, truth be known, and here was the ideal audience ready-made for his one-man show if he wanted to work it that way.

Kelley was rather unpredictable about the depth and quality of his interactions. He seemed to have an intuitive timing about when to act, how, and with whom. Detached encouragement of young people continued, whether or not he was at a convention, but very sporadically and individually. Young Dan Madsen had a dream of launching his own club and newsletter. He had written to all of the actors to ask for their support, or at least their permission. That's what polite Trekkies do. The polite and engaged Trekkies began calling themselves Trekkers, suggesting a certain capability and adventurousness in their own lives while keeping their identities as progeny of *Star Trek*. Madsen was one of these. He received one answer—from Kelley. For Madsen, DeForest and Carolyn became long-distance supporters of his interests and aspirations. Their presence in his life made him feel particularly happy and important. He met up with them at conventions, and DeForest sat down for interviews and to talk about Madsen's life.

Madsen's club exceeded all expectations, and within a very short time, it became "*Star Trek*: The Official Fan Club," and his newsletter became an official magazine recognized by the *Star Trek* people and

Paramount. He ascribes a lot of the credit to the faith Kelley had in him and the simple, soft expectation that he would do well. He recalls that over the years of writing about films, celebrities, and fandom, DeForest and Carolyn were the first, the best, and the most beloved of all.[20]

As the years progressed, De and Carolyn's time was increasingly occupied by doctors, dentists, and recovering from their ministrations. Social life declined, but they still would have the Long Beach gang up to see a play, or they would go down to Long Beach in the Thunderbird to visit for a few nights. He made it a point to visit Shorty, Herman Casey's widow. He was contemplating the meaning of age, the twilight on life's horizon. He had no real fear, rather a wish to understand, meditate, and experience the progress of life with smooth awareness. His brief letters to Georgia kin reflect nostalgia that, coming from his pen, suggests long hours of reflection on a life he was grateful to have had. He was rather young to be so preoccupied, but he was an old soul with plenty of time on his hands.[21]

There were, of course, many things yet on that horizon before the twilight. And vanity did have an upside. DeForest realized that the "DeForest Kelley" vodka drinks were having an impact on his appearance—the doctor's eyes always told on him. In the early '80s, Aileen Pickering observed that he drank less, and, sure enough, the old boy was looking like himself when he turned sixty-two onboard the *Enterprise*.[22]

Chapter XV

"Someone suggested they get Harve Bennett, *Rich Man Poor Man*— fix it in a minute."

—DeForest Kelley, 1984

Paramount was in deep fiscal trouble. A second *Star Trek* movie was a gamble for everyone. The studio as an institution was risking the farm on Gene Roddenberry's old television series. But they were not going to risk it with Roddenberry at the helm. Harve Bennett recalls that he had been at Paramount only two weeks, with the assignment of creating and producing new television programming, when his life got turned around. He was made producer of *Star Trek* in a rather stunning rush of decisions.

Bennett recalls: "Briefly, *Star Trek* the movie had come out in 1979. I always thought of it as a tone poem, an Ode to *Star Trek*, in which nothing much happened. The studio considered the *Star Trek* franchise to be a beached whale. My friend Barry Diller called me to a surprise meeting. There was Charles Bluhdorn, the head of Gulf & Western and an avid *Star Trek* fan. 'What did you think of *Star Trek: The Motion Picture*?' he snapped. I looked around the room. Staring at me were Diller, Michael Eisner, and the young Jeffrey Katzenberg. I recalled that during *Star Trek* [the movie] my kids, normally glued to the screen, had to go to the bathroom five times, not to mention pop-corn and candy trips. I remembered wanting to join them. For just a moment, my life passed before my eyes, but, I decided, truth was the only answer. 'Well, sir—frankly—it was boring.' Bluhdorn whirled on Eisner and said, 'You see? By you, bald is sexy!' Eisner flushed, and I figured my relationship with him was over. Bluhdorn turned to me and asked if I could make a better movie. 'Oh, yeah,' I said."[1]

Then Bluhdorn popped the question: " 'Can you make it for less than forty-five-fucking-million dollars?' I said, 'Well, where I come from, I can make five movies for that."

Bennett now realized the challenge he faced. "My God. I did *Mod Squad,* which beat *Star Trek* in the ratings. I knew nothing of *Star Trek* and had never seen it." He entered a three-month Trekkie im-mersion. He screened every episode at least once. He concluded that one-third of the episodes were brilliant and that, usually, the brilliance rested on the power of a well-written focus on the trio of Kirk, Spock, and McCoy, whom Bennett characterized as Decision, Wisdom, and Passion. "I was drenched in *Star Trek*. And, to the point, the clear emergence of DeForest Kelley. DeForest was the most consistent member of the cast. He handled the most interesting situations with the subtleties of a well-trained actor. He was never over the top, he was almost perfect, which was not true of some. I said, 'God, this guy is steady, and, something else, he's funny.'

"I came away from these *Trek* learning courses knowing I had iso-lated the extraordinary energy core of the show. *Star Trek* was really about a triangle of characters passionately trying to solve human problems from three different behavioral perspectives. In this corner we have Spock, the endearingly cold intellectual, in another corner we have Bones, overpassionate, cynical, sometimes mocking. And at the top of the triangle, 'in command,' we have a dashing boy-man, quick to take action (not always the 'wisest' action), just as quick to own and correct his mistakes. These three personalities, triumphing through disagreement, somehow reflected the hope that mankind would progress in the centuries to come. And I came to believe that when this 'Trinity' was cooking, the shows had drive and energy—without it, the shows were often dull.

"I also had to be educated about *Star Trek* fandom. I realized it was a series of circles with a cult in the center and concentric circles of lessening extremism. But those in the center were kind of fanatics, and it was scary, because I got some hate mail—how dare you—and mind you there was a perception, perhaps, that I was replacing Gene. Not true. Gene was a consultant on everything we did. Sometimes that was difficult for me because Gene was not a collaborative kind of guy, and the studio of course left me to handle him. The ordeal for me was trying to deal with someone who didn't want to be dealt with. And, his vision of *Star Trek* had become highly utopian, whereas, I was drawn to the writing and the vision of Gene Coon and what he and the actors had hit upon in the best of the series." For this insight, Kelley always praised Bennett.[2]

Beyond all that, Bennett had to go where no other producer had gone before. "He had to take on *Star Trek* without ever having had anything to do with it or being aware of its enormous cult following," Kelley recalled. "He had to screen all those episodes, read the fan mail, the fanzines. He even went as far as to correspond with some fans. But as he did all this, he began to soak up *Star Trek* and speak the language." And that was the key, because Bennett was a creative writer-producer; he and screenwriter Jack B. Sowards were somehow going to write the *Enterprise* back into her rightful place in the hearts and minds of the fans.[3]

Kelley's loyalty to Roddenberry had always been above question, but his true allegiance was to the whole *Enterprise*. Kelley was an independent man, and he moved forward with the changes for many reasons, professional and personal. In a rare movement for him, he took the initiative. Bennett continues: "In that regard, then, the first phone call was from DeForest Kelley. I don't think I ever had the chance to tell him how much it meant to me, especially considering what we now know I got out of those screenings. The person I respected most on the screen was the first to support me. He said, 'Hey, let me know if I can help with anything.' I presume he saw in me the same kind of professionalism I saw in him."

Kelley had been shell-shocked by the *Star Trek: The Motion Picture* script. Now he did not like what he saw in the initial screenplay for the second movie. "I strongly disliked the first script handed to me, so I had a big conversation with Harve Bennett. . . . I said I would rather not be in it, because the role was not meaningful, and the script was not a good *Star Trek* script." Bennett and Kelley discussed the issues, and Bennett listened. Kelley recommended a veteran *Star Trek* writer to help transform the work into a *Star Trek* script: Harlan Ellison.[4]

One difficulty to overcome was the placement of Spock's death. Bennett had convinced Nimoy to be in the film by promising him a glorious death scene. He suggested using Hitchcock's trick in *Psycho,* the killing of a major star in the first third of the movie. Nimoy signed on. But in the ensuing months, word was leaked of Spock's death, and a huge letter-writing campaign of protest resulted. With the element of surprise lost, Bennett and Nimoy were convinced that Spock's early demise would be a disaster for the film. Therefore, they decided to use Spock's death as the climax of the story. Kelley, knowing the high sensitivity of the audience, found the changes very satisfying.

Star Trek veterans Samuel Peeples of "Where No Man Has Gone Before," and Judy Burns of "The Tholian Web" were the writers called in to make notes and comments on the developing screenplay and to advise on the overall world of *Star Trek.*

Then Bennett secured the services of screenwriter and author Nicholas Meyer. The young man took everyone's contributions and was allotted twelve days to make a script. He performed without a deal and without official credit. His thoughts were, "Forget about my writing credit, because if nobody else does this, there's not gonna be any movie." He commented later that he was young and dumb at the time, but also he felt a pivotal career challenge here. He was convinced that *Star Trek* had never hit its pitch, and he could take a big swing in the present circumstances; maybe he could knock one out of the park. Further, he would have the director's chair. He let the rules of business take a back seat.[5]

Meyer had been a student of film and human behavior all of his life. The son of a gifted and successful psychiatrist, he grew up in New York and was educated at the University of Iowa. He worked for Paramount in New York as a publicist and wrote *The Love Story Story* and then moved on to screenplays and novels, including *The Seven-Per-Cent Solution.* He was nominated for an Academy Award for the screenplay adaptation of his work. Then there were novels, *The West End Horror* and *Black Orchid,* and screenplays such as *The Night That*

Panicked America and the well-received *Time after Time*, which he also directed.[6]

Meyer saw the literary themes, the classic seafaring parallels, and the dramatic potentials of Bennett's decision to bring back Khan, a Captain Ahab in his prowess and his obsession. He could thus reestablish the heroes as the heroes of the television series. He saw the dramatic science-fiction role of the Genesis Project. Bennett was committed to a character-driven work, the budget guaranteed an elegant use of special effects, but the proof would be in the drama and adventure of the story. Of *Star Trek* itself, Meyer had an essential understanding but no fawning love. Thus, he was able to do the hard jobs required by dramatic expedience. He rewrote all that Bennett gave him.

The twelve days of creation worked. Kelley commented: "I feel that Meyer brought it to life and really made it a kind of *Star Trek* script. . . . When he sent me that draft, I said, 'That's more like it.'" Kelley was firmly on board.[7]

The story has the *Enterprise* crew becoming mentors and trainers for a corps of cadets. The *Enterprise* went on a training cruise while Chekhov and his commanding officer found Khan, the genetically superior emperor of the twentieth century whom Kirk stranded on a remote planet. Pursuit, danger, and revenge move through a story based on the *Star Trek* characters and their actions, their history within the adventure.

Then there was the consultation and correspondence with Roddenberry. Bennett's diplomacy was hard-pressed when Meyer and Roddenberry had two different visions of the *Enterprise*'s future and different impressions of what Starfleet was and who these characters were. Though Roddenberry had likened Kirk to Horatio Hornblower in the original series, now, all these years later, Roddenberry could not abide Meyer's Horatio Hornblower naval texture or his Ahab interpretation of Khan. Roddenberry protested the many human weaknesses and foibles Meyer injected into the story as a whole. Meyer commented: "Its themes are entirely earthbound—death, aging, friendship." He created a style that was virile, emotional, and nautical. Meyer soon found that his interpretation of the *Enterprise* "flew in the face of a lot of Roddenberry's dicta."[8]

Meyer pointed out that Roddenberry believed in the progress and perfectibility of man, but he himself did not. It was clear in the correspondence between Roddenberry and those creating the second film that in many ways, the creator had already moved on to dreams beyond the *Trek* of 1966. This was his *Enterprise,* many fans, friends, and coworkers would protest. No, it was not, declared many others. It was a painful situation all the way around, except perhaps for Meyer, who seemed focused on the momentum of the project and content to let the others wrestle in the passageways.[9]

Writer-director Nicholas Meyer's reputation pulled Ricardo Montalban back into the guise of Khan. Although Meyer was new to directing, Phil Weyland recalls that he was regarded as something of a genius on a number of levels and was the only man Weyland never second-guessed about direction. As Weyland went through his days as Kelley's stand-in and as an observer in real time on the soundstages, he heard and saw everything. He knew that there was one thing everyone agreed on: they all had great respect for Nicholas Meyer.[10]

Constantly in flux but with the crew at last on board, the youngest fellow among them, Meyer, took the helm, and the second motion picture went into production in the fall of 1981. Then, as Bennett recalls, "I think it was DeForest who said on the set of *Star Trek II,* 'Ba the way, ah don't think Chekhov ever met Khan.'" Uh-oh. Bennett asked, "Can we squeeze it through? 'Yeah, he was probably down in the toilet on D Deck the whole episode.'"

A key element in the character story within the screenplay was the realization of what the fans had appreciated all along: the aging of the *Star Trek* characters. Bennett elaborates: "The medium of film has given the modern audience an experience unique in the history of man: They have been able to watch their favorite actors age over a period of decades. DeForest and I agreed that there was an attempt to hide the aging process in *Star Trek I.* So I told him, 'We have to play the reality that all of the characters have grown older,' and he helped me a great deal with some of the supporting players who wanted to be face-lifted" by tricks of the camera. Shatner was persuaded to accept the spectacles and the shadows of midlife through Bennett's diplomacy and his very lucky insertion into the discussion with Shatner of Spencer Tracy as an example of a great leading man who aged gracefully while we watched. At the time, Bennett did not remember that *Judgment at Nuremberg,* which starred Tracy, was Shatner's first film and that Tracy was an idol of his. Shatner's performance as an aging hero had depth and nuance and promised a future wisdom for James T. Kirk.

Bennett recalls that another problem to be solved was that each member of the *Star Trek* crew wanted his or her moment in the sun, and they kept lobbying for scenes featuring themselves. He was aware of the rancor: "Fair to say, every cast member gave me notes, and some of them were so egocentric that it taxed every one of my diplomatic skills. The problem was that each of the characters had had 'star turns' in the various seventy-nine episodes of the TV series, or a total of seventy-nine hours of screen time to be divided. A feature picture is two hours long and cannot provide solo material for all of the supporting players, since the emphasis must be on the principal triangle of Kirk, Spock, and McCoy. I know this was very difficult for some of the actors, but I tried to give each one their moments, more than moments." Ralph Winter confirms that it was a difficult transition for the cast, but it was required by the demands of film.[11]

Of course, the family that was the *Star Trek* crew had their agendas, and confining themselves to the demands of the film was not only difficult, it was hurtful. Winter remembers the opposing camps inside the production and that Kelley was the only one who crossed seamlessly from one camp to another.

Bennett continues: "There was additional historic tension between Shatner and the supporting cast based on conflicts during the original series and Bill's alleged demeaning of the cast members other than Nimoy and Kelley. It is true that Bill could be sometimes aloof from the others because his earliest training was in the Shakespearean star system at the Toronto festival. His idol was, and still is, Christopher Plummer, whom he treats like a star.

"Leonard whose background was a mix of community theater, writing and directing was truly well cast as the intellectual. He could have done many things with his life. To me, he was the least actor-ish and most well rounded, a Renaissance man. Of the three stars, it was DeForest who assumed the role of team captain on behalf of all of us. For example he was never late, he never quibbled. I heard him many times say, 'Oh let's get on with it.' He was always invaluable onstage."

Meyer believes that Kelley saw life in relatively simple terms, but that by no means diminished his impact. "Eye-to-eye he met you—he saw you," Meyer asserts. De was unblinking in his approach, as gentle and laidback as it was. Meyer felt Kelley believed that others who didn't have this insight and directness were not to be judged. Their illusions and desires were to be handled with humor while De went on his way. To Nicholas, DeForest always seemed a little surprised to have been allowed to pass in the profession though he lacked the howling ego. Nicholas maintains, though, that De must have been ambitious to have lasted so long.[12]

DeForest did indeed have the star persona. Kelley was Kelley no matter what the role, but Nicholas suspected that his range was slightly broader than he ever had the opportunity to show. Nicholas was reminded of Bogart in that regard. Bogie was Bogie until *African Queen,* and then we saw the actor he was. Perhaps the same could have been said of DeForest if life had gone another way and the studio system had endured long enough for his star to rise.

Bennett comments: "In my mind, I always thought of him in the same breath as Joseph Cotten. In *Citizen Kane,* especially, as [Cotten's character] aged, he had so, so much Bones in him." Meyer and Bennett detected a sadness in DeForest Kelley. Somehow in his compassionate, unblinking way, Kelley understood too much of life's reality.

Mixing his kind wisdom with a great sense of humor, DeForest was a favorite of extras, actors, executives, and John Belushi. He recalled that John had offices on the lot and visited the *Star Trek* set. At one time, he was talking to Shatner about the *Saturday Night Live* lampoon of *Star Trek.* Kelley piped up that he hadn't seen the skit. Belushi took him right over to his office and played a tape for Kelley. Upon seeing Belushi's Kirk, Kelley confessed, "I became hysterical. I had to go [immediately] and do a scene with Bill. I just started cracking up with every move. Bill said, 'What the hell is wrong with you?' I said I'd just left John Belushi's office. He said 'For God's sake, De, forget that stuff. We've gotta go to work now.'" Kelley was well known for his helplessness once the laughter started rolling. Shatner had to round him up and get him settled down before the scene could continue, but Kelley never forgot Belushi's Kirk. Just the very thought cracked him up. Belushi gave him a copy of the tape and signed it, "Live Long and Prosper." After Belushi's death a short time later, Kelley quietly sent the tape to Long Beach for Anne Jolly and her family. He could not keep such a painful reminder of a life wasted, and yet he could not do away completely with that reminder.[13]

For everyone on the mission of *Star Trek II*, Kelley affected a balanced and comforting attitude that Bennett dramatized as "Ahh, I've seen it all, and this is a crock of shit, but I'll do my job." Kelley was a veteran who had enough confidence to say that he'd been in too many bad movies to get tied up in knots. Meyer observed that Kelley could really smoke and smolder, but overall he kept the brew from boiling over and smoothed the way for the real work to get done.[14]

The real work was leading steadily to the end of McCoy's comrade, nemesis, and brother. These last scenes were actually filmed late in the production calendar, because the loss of Spock was unreal for everyone. As the time approached, Nimoy began confronting the dramatic consequence of his very logical professional decision to end his tenure with *Star Trek*. Everyone seemed a little seasick. Everyone except Nicholas Meyer, whose detachment made the final writing and execution of the film an interesting and well-made package. Now Meyer had no reason to do anything any differently. Nimoy himself was a little shaky and marveled at Meyer's surgical focus.

Nimoy and Kelley had worked out their scene including the neck pinch that would disable the doctor and make Spock's sacrifice possible. Nimoy wrote that Bennett approached him and queried, "Leonard, I was wondering whether we could add something to this scene . . . a thread." Nimoy wrote that at that point, he was overwhelmed by the sequence leading to his character's death, and Meyer was trying to get a good scene, but Bennett was thinking of the franchise. "Could you do a mind-meld on McCoy?" Then Bennett asked Nimoy what Spock would say to Bones. The answer was "Remember." Nimoy was in such a frame of mind that he did not consider the ramifications of the scene. It was just as well. In that moment of the mind-meld, no one knew what the future was—so it was all the more powerful. Kelley had not been clued in on the adjustments Bennett and Nimoy had made. When Nimoy touched his face and whispered "Remember," he figured something was up. Kelley's profile was just right, and at the moment of joining, the camera recalled the remark-able beauty of his youth.[15]

Kirk's run through the passageways was an emotionally wrenching progress toward a scene no one wanted to take place. Shatner carried the moments, and suddenly Kirk was twenty years younger as he slid down the ladder into engineering. In the face of death, Kirk was age-less. Kirk's run remains a powerful sequence of the human will rush-ing toward death, desperate and defiant but inevitably defeated.

Kelley just refused to say the "dead" phrase that would, he thought, crack up the audience and make a mockery of what they were doing—instead, the line was given to Scotty: "He's dead al-ready." Kelley later said that he was glad of it, and the scene played well.

The agony of heart for Nimoy and Shatner was palpable as the men struggled through their lines, including Bennett's: "I have been, and always shall be, your friend." And Meyer's: "The needs of the many outweigh the needs of the few—or the one."[16]

2 Kelley was very unhappy with the final minutes of the screenplay. He believed that it was important to allow McCoy and Kirk to com-miserate privately over their friend's death. A drink in the admiral's quarters was called for. It was dramatically appropriate on the one hand and a kindness to the audience on the other. Let McCoy reassure and heal the grieving even as he himself was grieving, but such a scene had been written out in favor of a father-and-son scene between David and James Kirk.[17]

Roddenberry couldn't understand the trailing out of the end of the picture. He, too, believed that no one could pay attention after Spock's death. Nothing else was going to register through the Trekkie shock.[18]

The first preview audiences agreed: the shock and grief were too much. Bennett set about to modify the ending. Meyer objected but did not stand in the way of the new material. The rewrite included an end scene on the bridge ("There are always possibilities"), a sequence shot by ILM in Golden Gate Park, San Francisco, revealing Spock's torpedo casket intact on the planet, and the use of Nimoy's voice in the closing *Star Trek* credo ("Space, the final frontier").

When this version was screened for a new preview audience, the screening ended with a tearful standing ovation or, as *New York Times* film critic Janet Maslin was to write in her review, "Now that's more like it!" Bennett says, "I'd like that quote on my tombstone."

Variety chimed in with praise for *The Wrath of Khan* and delighted in the recovery of the *Star Trek* magic. True Trekkies and uncounted hundreds of thousands of casual Trekkers shared that relief. The *Star Trek* boys were back, and, of course, upon examination, the ending did indeed promise more to come. There were cheers all around in spite of the shock. In short, Bennett was feeling pretty well.

Though many *Star Trek* fans could not see through their tears at the funeral ceremony, they recovered enough to register the rest of the film. They heard Kirk utter Bennett's line: "Of all the souls I have encountered in my travels, his was the most human." The end was wrapped with a farewell and a few more memorable lines that reassured viewers that anything was possible with the *Enterprise*. "He's not really dead, as long as we remember him," McCoy soothed the audience.

While Roddenberry was very reluctant to acknowledge the second movie as *Star Trek*, he finally said, "I'm grateful it did what it did." It gave him life after the first motion picture and new frontiers for his creation. While he maintained his distaste for the naval and literary adaptations made by Meyer, the men and women who had worked on his creation since 1966 were of one accord. Shatner spoke for them all: "*Star Trek*, really for the first time since the second season of our prime-time run, was back on track. We'd finally found the creative footing that had previously proven so elusive, and additionally, the chemistry and camaraderie between our characters were back in abundance."[19]

Paramount was euphoric. Michael Eisner and the rest moved quickly to keep the *Enterprise* powered up for another movie. Unheard of, but it was going to happen. Meyer declined a return, citing creative differences; he didn't like the sunny planet shots that were tacked onto the end without him. Dead was dead in Meyer's book. He didn't like the machinations.[20]

A day after *Star Trek II* opened, Eisner called Bennett and gave him the go-ahead to write *Star Trek III*. Bennett remembers: "I said, 'This is great, I'm part of the *Star Trek* family,' and I determined it was time to go to my first convention." The next one scheduled was mammoth: Houston in the summer of 1982. "Think of it, the Astrodome, 50,000 people, Shatner, the cast. Perfect.

"I get to Houston on a Friday expecting a reception that night and a Saturday appearance, expecting to be picked up on a sedan chair and be taken to the convention, you know? I walked into the lobby to find bedlam, and out of the bedlam comes Bones McCoy. Now he's not DeForest Kelley to me, he's Bones McCoy, because I'm in a new world and he's gonna take me through it, right? Bones McCoy, who has weathered every crisis imaginable on *Star Trek,* is now ashen white and coming at me with a look of sheer terror in his eyes. 'Harve! Thank God you're here.'

" 'Bones,' I said reflexively, 'what's wrong?' 'Everything!' he says. 'I think the promoter is a thief and there are a thousand people in front of the Shamrock Hotel and they can't get in and they're chanting and the newsreels, the photographers! It's going to destroy us!' " Kelley's eyes were as big as saucers.

"I said, 'Okay, I got it.' I called the Paramount publicist at the Shamrock. He was even more panic-stricken than Deforest." Bennett set up a conference room as a command center—at the very least, it was a quiet place to think about what to do. Bennett's background as a producer in live television had long ago prepared him to address the chaos he now faced. He called all the local television stations and arranged a press conference for that night to feature Kelley, Takei, and Nichols. They formed the vanguard for the rescue mission.

They went to the Shamrock Hotel manager and asked for the Grand Ballroom. They learned that the guy at the head of the event had absconded with the money, and no reservations had been made for the hundreds of people who expected the normal convention process. The *Star Trek* actors and Bennett would have to come through for the fans to make amends and give them the best makeshift convention they possibly could.

"We set up the Grand Ballroom," Bennett recalls, "and the cast circulated with bullhorns—'We're gonna have our own convention!'

And they gave the details. Shatner was not due in until the next day, so DeForest was out in front and took the role of MC. At eight P.M., the place was packed. All the cast members worked it for about five hours. We did what there was to do. And when they left, they'd had their convention." By Saturday, the "Con of Wrath" was history.

Bennett reflects: "De was the one person who could have handled the situation because of the essential dignity he brought to the screen and into the room."[21]

Chapter XVI

That Green-Blooded Son of a Bitch

1983–1985

"Something made Harve pick up the phone and call me," Nimoy wrote with gratitude. Bennett asked Nimoy to direct *Star Trek III*. "Who would have thought this early defector—would eventually return to be our director?" Kelley rhymed later. Nothing could have suited Kelley more. He knew Nimoy was thoroughly capable of anything he set his mind to—and, of course, he knew the interior life of *Star Trek* better than anyone.[1]

Bennett would have to write the *Enterprise* crew out of the grief he and Meyer had left them in. He would also have to grapple with some of the more metaphysical and spiritual issues of *Star Trek*'s reality; because once *Star Trek II* really sank in and became part of *Star Trek* lore, some weather change occurred. Nimoy registered the change. He wrote, "Out of death comes a new vision of life. . . . And out of the fearless decision to explore Spock's death came this enormous new energy, which would extend to a third *Star Trek* film . . . and beyond."[2]

The new energy created an archetypal gravity now invested in the three heroes and their story. The *Star Trek* crew had crossed from static icon to active mythology through the passion play, once introduced in 1968 with "The Empath." The first stage was the self-sacrifice of Spock for his comrades. In this peculiar situation, the sacrifice was of a character people had known for nearly twenty years. Something inexplicable was occurring between fact and fiction, among creator, actor, and audience. While the role may have died, Spock had not. The Vulcan belonged to the many and existed in some archetypal stasis. Fans at many different levels of interest perceived a symbiotic relationship among reality, creativity, and myth. Perhaps for the first time ever, creators, actors, and audiences participated in the conscious creation of a cooperative mythology.

Kelley admitted many times that he was reluctant to really examine what it all meant, that it was mind-boggling, and that he was dazed when he thought too long about it. Longtime fans shared his reaction and yet disclaimed their own perceptions with "It's only a TV show." Of course it was. But it was also more. As Bennett had pointed out, these characters and these actors were growing old before our eyes. They had become part of the living memory of literally millions of human beings. An alchemy of dreams, needs, perception, and identification came with this mythology of the future.

Nimoy recalled: "The major theme in this film is about friendship. What should a person do to help a friend? How deeply should a friendship commitment go?. . . . And what sacrifices, what obstacles, will these people endure? That's the emotion line of the film. For me, that's its reason for existence."[3]

Bennett's realization of how he could carry on the story after Spock's death is an example of the cooperative living mythology. He honestly credited the source: "Somewhere along the line, I read a fan poem in one of the hundreds of fan magazines about *Star Trek*." There, from a fan's fantasy, was Kirk's recognition that he should not have left his friend, his noble self, behind, and he must return to the Genesis planet. Of course, Kirk and the crew had to go back. This was Bennett's solo exploration into the world of the characters of *Star Trek*. He wrote with a deep understanding of the crew, especially McCoy.[4]

2 In the spring of 1983, while Bennett and Nimoy put a film to-
gether, Kelley welcomed the quiet round of weeks and months at
Greenleaf. Then Carolyn Kelley did the unthinkable: she quit smok-
ing. Done, gone, cold turkey. DeForest and friends marveled, but De-
Forest was worried that perhaps he was expected to follow suit.
Otherwise, life went on as it always had on Greenleaf.

From mid-August through the end of October 1983, *The Search for
Spock* was the focus for fandom. How would Spock return, or was that
just wishful Trekkie thinking? Bennett wrote of the story's development: "Admiral Kirk finds Dr. McCoy behaving strangely. The reason
was the mind-meld just prior to Spock's death. This mind-meld was so
powerful that the doctor actually carried the Vulcan's living spirit
(which we later called his Katra). If Spock's body could be retrieved—
well, there are always possibilities. The Klingons, already established
as villains, would clearly seize upon Genesis as a weapon of mass destruction and form the dramatic conflict for the story. In this context,
McCoy becomes the most important factor in restoring the Vulcan."

Bennett explains the Katra concept: "I went to the world's greatest
living expert on Vulcan, Leonard Nimoy. We discussed the possibilities of saving Spock's eternal soul. He referred me to an episode of the
original series entitled 'Amok Time,' which was educational. It suggested to me a high order of spiritual transference among Vulcans, and
that stimulated further thought. But it was Leonard who led me to the
Katra, and it was Leonard who named it. After all, it was Leonard,
without doubt, who supplied the spiritual and historical background
for most of the Spock behavioral matrix."

This tale of friendship and unconditional loyalty was not without
its backlot stories of Hollywood struggle and *Star Trek* family dys-
function. After all, film production was an odd kind of human reality.
There was occasional friction between veteran producer Harve Bennett and freshman director Leonard Nimoy. Nimoy wrote: "When
Gene Roddenberry was first informed that I'd been hired to direct this
picture, his reaction was to say, 'Well, you've hired a director that you
can't fire.' That wasn't very supportive, but I realized it was absolutely
valid, and in a way, I took that to heart, and it empowered me to stand
up for myself a bit more than I probably would have in a situation

with less leverage." He gritted his teeth under the necessary and sometimes unnecessary management and intercession. Members of the cast still battled and protested the silliness or simple lack of their moments on screen. Bennett recalls that Kelley had to step in on the production's behalf just to convince Takei to do the "Don't call me Tiny" scene. Takei never liked it, but he did it, and he continued to dislike it; however, it did prove to be what Kelley promised: a memorable and defining scene for the swashbuckling Sulu. People loved it, because they could see themselves pitching the tin soldier over their shoulder as they made good the doctor's escape.[5]

As the film proceeded, Tony Kirk saw Kelley get a little hot under the collar. There had been some difficulty with Starfleet secrecy on the second picture. The beginning scenes were a play on the harm done by a leak about Spock's death to the fans. This time, there were rumblings about the death of the *Enterprise* herself. Precautions were taken to make people accountable for their scripts, and the set was secured. This didn't sit well with Kelley. One day, Tony Kirk was on his route, and Kelley came wingin' by in the old Thunderbird and pulled up alongside. He said he wanted Tony to come on to the set. Tony knew it was supposed to be a closed set, "but they don't want anyone, in case they give away the story?" Kelley sounded like McCoy when he was steamed. " 'Story? Here's the goddamn script!' " He threw it on the dashboard. "'And it's on James Doohan's coffee table, so what the hell should they care!' " Tony did get on the set.

Phil Weyland agrees that Starfleet secrecy was a pain in the ass. Kelley didn't like it; no one did. But there weren't many choices, considering the size of the franchise and the fan hunger that swooned and swayed with every rumor, often causing yet another wave of protest, inquiry, infiltration.[6]

Weyland had taken the opportunity to jump ship—to Shatner, to work not only as his stand-in but as his dialogue coach for *TJ Hooker* and the *Star Trek* films. Weyland did not want Kelley to feel abandoned, but Kelley told him to go where the money was. Kelley signed a glamour shot of himself from back in the '40s to Phil, with a little line about being jilted for Bill.

Despite all the precautions, security was breached, and fan and media attention strayed from the return of Spock when it was understood that the *Enterprise* herself would be sacrificed for the return of the Vulcan. For Roddenberry, this blunt manipulation and destruction of the vessel he had created was something of a betrayal. Many attributed the leak and the following acrimony to Roddenberry himself.

The starship's crew, Nimoy and Shatner particularly, agreed that the end of the *Enterprise* was dramatically logical and called for and that it was done with proper respect. Kelley seemed uncertain. Weyland remembers that when he was upset, when he was conflicted about something that was going on with his work on *Star Trek*, Kelley always resorted to calling Roddenberry to get square on the issues. For Kelley, Roddenberry was where the buck stopped, and he needed to check in with the Big Bird of the Galaxy to restore his equilibrium on the issues flying around the soundstage. After the call, it seemed Kelley smoothed out and came to some kind of peace with what had rattled him. In this case, he was asked later by fans how he felt about the death of the *Enterprise*. "I felt more or less like you did," he answered. "We were all in rather a state of shock. It's a very emotional moment. Quite frankly, I was rather surprised that it finalized as it did."[7]

Kelley had the lion's share of the memorable scenes. He had his work cut out for him as the living vessel of a Vulcan's essence. He recalled what it was like to work for his old on-screen nemesis. Tongue in cheek, he described the dynamics between Kelley the actor and Nimoy the director: "That was the worst three months of my life, and the man is intolerable. He's Vulcan. I was a basket case when I worked with him." Kelley remembered the Vulcan director: "In a scene where I am supposed to be grieving . . . I went in and raised hell about the scene." McCoy watched over the empty body of Spock, and the camera closed in. "This is a true story so help me. . . . He has his eyes closed, can't see anything 'cause he's dead. He doesn't know what I'm doing. I swear in the middle of the take, the right eye opened. The eyebrow went up—to see what I was doing!"

Leonard Horatio McCoy had to step forward and proclaim that he was the keeper of Spock's Katra. "McCoy, Leonard H., son of David." He told fans, "Son of David. They wrote it son of Leonard. I wanted son of David. They thought I was using it because I was fishing it out of the Bible. It was my father's name." Indeed, in some ways, Kelley was reclaiming his father's legacy, and through McCoy he made a very public and permanent reclamation.[8]

Bennett and Nimoy had reversed Meyer's maxim and contemplated that the needs of the one outweighed the needs of the many, and Dr. McCoy was a perfect vessel for this contemplation in action. Bennett gave the one, Kelley, the best of his attention. Each crewman had a role to play on behalf of the one, assumed to be Spock but arguably McCoy. Nimoy and Bennett began a tradition of ensemble work within the *Star Trek* films.[9]

Nimoy's stunning rebirth as a creator of *Star Trek* revitalized the entire franchise, and Kelley had surely become the carrier of the essence of the *Enterprise*. He later declared that he had no doubts about Nimoy's ability to lead them back to all the strengths of *Star Trek*, no doubts from the first day on the soundstage.

Their quiet partnership mirrored their scene after Spock's rejoining. There was a dramatic exchange between Kirk and the reborn Vulcan. With Kirk's prompting, Spock remembered his name and recognized the crew. Then he looked deeply into McCoy's eyes, and for a number of reasons, the scene was without dialogue, mostly to spare any jealousies that might have erupted by following Shatner's scene with a better scene. Kelley improvised McCoy's grin and the *tap-tap* on his temple as if to say, "This is where you were," and, of course, the raised brow of the Vulcan assured everyone that the Spock–McCoy relationship had also survived the adventure. Theirs was a quiet alliance of respect and improvisation, the steady foundation of the enterprise.

"An emotionally satisfying science-fiction adventure," *Variety* declared.[10] Bennett's script was tight and hit the bull's-eye, while Nimoy's maiden attempt at direction was even tighter. He had proven himself. He kept the focus on the characters, and the fans returned in droves. Like *Wrath of Khan, The Search for Spock* made more than $80 million at the box office. Here, finally, Kelley as McCoy carried half of the dynamic with Shatner as Kirk. At sixty-four, Kelley saw his stock with fans soar ever higher. Kirk's devotion to his friends endeared Shatner to fans for a while.

As the film approached its major release date, Kelley did have some security concerns at the obligatory Hollywood to-dos. He sometimes took John Walton and others to screenings, premieres, and events. He most often took Tony Kirk along, because he loved him and because Tony could protect him in any situation. The night of the press showing of *Star Trek III* in Westwood, he asked Tony to come with him to the men's room because of the crowds; sometimes the fans could get out of hand. "He loved making me the Mafia guy. And he's at the urinal. Me in the black suit [as he guarded the door, some fans tried to get in, and Tony squared off]. 'Boys, do yourselves a favor. Turn around and walk out that door. And you'll live to see another day.' They scrammed and Kelley laughed so hard his shoulders were shaking, and he couldn't pee."

3 Public appearances, television interviews, and the promotional circuit of conventions followed the release of *Star Trek III*. Now, it was not all sweetness and light at these conventions. On one occasion, the Kelleys brought Bette and her man and Anne Jolly and hers to a Southern California convention. Anne remembers vividly one of their dinners together. A young female fan would not let De alone, fawning over him and then becoming very suggestive—with Carolyn sitting right there. The guests held their breath. The woman was trying to force her hotel room key on him—into his hand, into his pocket. Carolyn was on slow burn, as was De, as he tried to redirect the situation graciously—and he did so with resolve and patience until the vixen finally gave up. Even DeForest and Carolyn sometimes encountered the dark side of fandom.

DeForest Kelley and *Star Trek* fans both knew that some individuals among them were not fans at all, but rather opportunistic celebrity chasers and gold diggers; they knew and cared nothing for *Star Trek* or DeForest Kelley. Nevertheless, it was often hard for Carolyn to let him go into that environment of temptation and false interests. It got harder for her as the years marched on, and he became ever more popular while she entered her late sixties and waited for things to return to the normalcy and quiet rhythm of Greenleaf.

Fans multiplied after the release of the third movie. They were swept up in the energy of the mythology and its players. Fandom was ever more convinced these three men had a relationship that mirrored the fidelity and devotion of their characters. Certainly, after this film, anything less seemed incomprehensible. Kelley had made the point back in 1976 that many of the fans wanted to have some communication with the actors, to ask them questions and know them as human beings. Many fans came to know that while the stories were classic and the creators' visions were intriguing, the men and women who created the show were as much part of the phenomena as of the creation.

Kelley often tried to explain to the convention-going fans that the crew of the *Enterprise* did not socialize and rarely spoke, unless or until *Star Trek* brought them back to Paramount or to a convention. Even then, there was not a lot of personal or intimate exchanges. They really were a family but could not be all the things fans wished that family to be. Still, the *Star Trek* family was also something more than Kelley could really explain.

Fans everywhere appreciated the fact that Kelley had carried *The Search for Spock,* much as McCoy had carried Spock's soul. They recognized the passage of time and the preciousness of what they had in Kelley. To make sure he knew how they felt, the convention known as SpaceTrek presented him with an honorary Academy Award—by unanimous decision, of course. During a standing ovation, he was presented a trophy by Kathe Walker and her committee. The fans' love was returned without reservation. Their love for him was not a fiction, and his response was genuine. He belonged to them as much as he could belong to anything. Through all the decades of struggle in Hollywood, a victim of circumstance and timing, from star to character actor to typecast television star and a ghost, the industry had never given him so much as a nod. These people appreciated what he had done. They listened to him, and they remembered. They saw what he was trying to do with the role they had made last nearly twenty years. He held their golden statuette, and when he could speak, he strongly said, to them and to the entertainment industry as a whole, "I'd rather have it from you."[11]

4 Later in 1985, Carolyn's mother, Rhea, passed away, and so did their beloved Betty Daniels. Twilight was approaching Greenleaf. They were the elders now. DeForest enjoyed the surge in his career. It was a spectrum of joy spread out ahead of him. He intended to savor it; as a wise and mortal man, he knew it could not last. He remembered the cornerstone of his life. It was Carolyn and De's fortieth year together, and he proudly told anyone who would hear, "I make the living, and she makes the living worthwhile."

All around him, he saw evidence and validation for his life's work and his way of life. For him, in his traditional way of thinking, the reason for McCoy's existence was the good that was done by *Star Trek*. There were more accomplished, self-actualized, and humane people in the world because of his work on *Star Trek*. This was reality, and he was humbled by it. In many ways, the fans were his children, because they were his participation in a future beyond his own lifetime. In large part, it was for them that he was determined to finish the course, no matter how long it lasted.

At sixty-five, Kelley said of *Star Trek*, "I'm not tired of it. The thing I do not like about it is the long wait between films. . . . If the script is good, they are a joy to do. But when the script is bad, man, I was ready to fade out after that number one." For him, the answer was always more *Star Trek,* not less. As he got older, he told the fans that he wondered if Paramount would keep calling him back, or if he'd be well enough to answer when he was called again. With nearly the next breath, he would declare his rock-solid devotion to *Star Trek*: "I'll be coming on in a wheelchair." He meant it. Then, very often, he would finish his talk with the fans in a deeper, quieter manner and say something directly to them. Once, after a long pause, he said, "I was just going to tell you how much I love you all." He meant that, too.[12]

Chapter XVII
Any Problems,
Just Call Me
1986–1987

DeForest Kelley had found it amazing that Leonard Nimoy could step into the director's role with such ease and mastery. Nimoy had found Harve Bennett's watchful and uncompromising oversight a difficult but effective training. Now, with *Star Trek IV*, Nimoy was going to direct and act throughout the picture, on his own and at full power. Kelley was beside himself with admiration and confidence. He had the pleasure of waiting on his comrades while they labored in the salt mines of creativity and business. He enjoyed doing the daily shopping and helping Carolyn with the cooking. Sometimes he made the meals.

For the holidays, he turned the day over to a slow-cooked traditional Southern recipe. Anne Jolly kindly shares the New Year's meal by DeForest, with attention to De's way of describing things:

> DE'S PEAS (DeForest Kelley)—4 goodly servings
> 1 pkg. black-eyed peas
> 1 large onion
> 4 hot Italian sausages

Rinse and cull peas. Remove thin skin from sausage. Mince onion.

In heavy pot (Dutch oven type) crumble and brown sausage. Add onion and sauté until limp and golden. Add peas and enough water to cover, plus approx. 1 inch. Bring to boil, turn to simmer, place lid on a bit askew so just a trickle of steam can escape. Cook 3 or 4 hours, until they are the way you like them. Stir them every once in a while during cooking, and add water if necessary. If, when tasting, you'd like a bit more spice, add a dash of cayenne pepper.

Sprinkle with a little salt and pepper.

In February 1986, when his own physician handed him an issue of the *American Medical Association News,* Kelley was astounded to find a featured article on Leonard McCoy. It was a first for the august AMA, and it was a large article at that. He was appropriately impressed. It became his most cherished printed item about his work. Kelley's McCoy had certainly infiltrated the mainstream of the medical profession.[1]

Meanwhile, the writing of the next *Star Trek* script was once again a cooperative effort. The studio gave *Star Trek* the green light following Nimoy's promise to Paramount—the promise to lighten up. Bennett and Nimoy decided on time travel, and Nimoy insisted that this time, "circumstances would be the problem. Lack of awareness, lack of concern. Ignorance would be the problem, not a person." The story and the scripts bounced from one pen to the next, one meeting to another. "If they're coming back to the twentieth century, what are they coming back for? There's a problem in the twenty-third century, which can only be solved by something that's now gone extinct." Nimoy and Bennett went for the challenge of a major film with a significant message. Whales were the logical Holy Grail of *Star Trek IV*. Steve Meerson and Peter Krikes were writers who were signed on in the early going. They established the hospital scenes, the plexiglass scenes, but circumstances and uncertainties dissolved the coalition. Then, suddenly, it was late in the day, in Hollywood terms, to be without a script.

With their backs to the wall, Bennett called on Nicholas Meyer. Meyer didn't read the working scripts; he trusted his instincts and knowledge of the characters. Saying, " 'Under the Gun' is my middle name! I'm the twelve-day wonder!" Meyer dove in.

In the story, the *Enterprise* crew must travel back to Earth to answer for their disobedience during their last adventure. They find Earth under attack, and, upon recognizing the avenging probe's signals as a form of whale song and knowing that these whales are extinct in their century, the crew must go back in time to pick up some whales and return with them to placate the probe.

Bennett and Meyer took the bookend approach: Bennett did the beginning and the end, and Meyer did the material concerning San Francisco, the whales, and fish out of water. "His irreverence is what really makes the film fun," Bennett recalls. Mayer says, "I can even tell you exactly where I started and where I stop. First line of mine in the movie is, 'Judging by the pollution content of the atmosphere, we've reached the late twentieth century,' and I go out right before the line about D. H. Lawrence and the whales. That was Harve's." They rewrote small percentages of each other's work. Then Mayer punched up the humor.

"I stayed away from *III* because I didn't want to resurrect Spock." He thought it cheapened the impact and truth of the comrade's loss. But by *IV*, the Vulcan was back, and the enterprise needed Meyer. "I thought, 'Be useful. These people were awfully good to you, awful good. You be good back.'" He was. By the spring of 1986, Kelley was due at Paramount to bring McCoy to life once again. From March through May, it was one of the best filmmaking experiences of his life.[2]

2 *Star Trek IV* was a cooperative struggle that created something beyond themselves and greater than themselves. With a cooperative mythology, it is hard to know where what began, but in fandom there had been some questions arising from *The Search for Spock*. Some fans were concerned about the perceived minimization of women by *Star Trek*. In *Star Trek III*, Dr. Carol Marcus and Amanda might have had legitimate roles and were missing; Uhura was given a small scene and then disappeared until the very end; Lieutenant Saavik was suspected by fans to be bearing Spock's child, essentially relegating her to the homestead. Usually unacknowledged in this argument was the very feminine role of the physician as healer and vessel of eternal life. The *Enterprise* herself was a mother goddess. The mother's sacrifice for the sake of the children is one of the oldest and highest myths of ancient humanity. The *Enterprise* destroyed herself so that the crew might live on, a holy event in the spiral of life.

On almost every point, fan concerns were answered with *Star Trek IV*. Earth herself was rescued by the return of her lost children (the whales), through a woman's devotion and expertise (Gillian as played by Catherine Hicks), and the *Enterprise* was reborn in return. It was very galactic, and the film was so funny people laughed over lines and howled through moments containing nothing more than looks between actors.

"He's not exactly working on all thrusters!" McCoy declared as the renewed but untried Vulcan reported aboard the Klingon Bird of Prey. Kelley improvised his "I don't doubt it" response to Spock's monitoring of distress calls. McCoy had the laughter rolling as he protested his captain's decision to save the world by time travel. There were so many good lines for McCoy that he seemed to be playing straight man to himself. The timing was just right with Bennett's first act. The rush toward adventure was all the more exciting for the audience's wish to slow it down to get more of the interplay between McCoy and his rather demented chain of command. Once Meyer took over, the Earth-bound twentieth-century adventure rocked through a carefully structured course of rollicking laughter, like a ride at Coney Island.

The ensemble missions consisted of Kirk and Spock to the whales, Chekhov and Uhura to the USS *Enterprise,* and Sulu to the helicopter. Fans enjoyed having the crew on camera in one combination or another throughout the story, and that was a key element to the success of the entire film. "Then, of course, we always have the magical strength of Bones McCoy, for whom life has become, through three pictures and seventy-nine episodes, an increasingly interesting burden," Bennett told Dan Madsen. "Oh, joy," was McCoy's weary response to Kirk's inspired list of missions. Bennett continued, "As he grows older, he becomes more lovable. And he can set up more fun with just a look. Of course, Jimmy Doohan is like an old vaudeville comic. . . . So, putting those two together really worked well."[3] McCoy and Scott were dispatched to procure, and perhaps incidentally invent, transparent aluminum. McCoy warned Scott, "Don't bury yourself in the part," but Doohan was alight with his romp, and Kelley went along to make it Scotty's well-earned moment.

Nimoy's Spock and Shatner's Kirk carried the comedic tempo. "You are not exactly seeing us at our best," Kirk admitted to Gillian, the expert on whales. "That much is certain," Spock agreed. They gave people fits when Bennett and Meyer's down-to-earth lines came through those very unique characters. From colorful metaphors, to LDS, to an exchange about Italian restaurants, to "Just one damned minute, Admiral," the movie was a reward for Trekker loyalty and a treat for whomever they might drag with them to the theater.

Through Nimoy's sense of fairness, Phil Weyland and other coworkers got some screen time as they created the crowd that surrounded Nimoy, Shatner, and Hicks at the Cetacean Institute. Weyland was the tall fellow in shades with cameras strapped across his chest following Kirk around.

Kelley freely shared his joy in the making of *Star Trek IV* with friend Dan Madsen, who visited the sets of the films and by the mid-1980s had become a dominant publisher in the *Star Trek* world. Of course, for Kelley, the highlight was the filming at a California hospital. "That was a great kick! My greatest kick was when I came down the hall, and that little woman is lying on the table, and I ask her, 'What's your problem?' And then when she comes down the hall, saying, 'I grew a kidney! I grew a kidney!' That was hilarious! It was so funny to me when we were doing it. That little woman was so marvelous."

"If you have any problems, just call me." McCoy patted her cheek and then wove his way along the corridor. Bennett recalls that he wrote that particular moment to honor his assistant, Sylvia Rubinstein, who had waited a long time for a kidney transplant. If only Bones could have been there for her. Just call him. Such sentiments were echoed in every audience watching the film. Nearly every heart paused for a loved one. If only they could have called Leonard McCoy.

Bennett remembers the fun of the hospital, "a sheer star turn. I didn't write it, but it is all Bones as leader. Even Shatner kind of had to back off, because he had to be the fish out of water in the hospital.

My assistant, may she rest in peace, died before the movie was released. The hospital segment is dedicated to her."

Bennett also recalls that much of what McCoy criticized about modern medicine was very much Kelley's opinion as well. He also understood everything he said in those lines—he was an actor who did his homework.[4]

Kelley continued his account with Madsen: "We were in those surgeons' gowns, and we were working on the second and third floor of the hospital." The actors often had to go to other parts of the hospital. "I got on the elevator in this surgical gown and a mask around my neck, and you should've seen the looks on their faces when they saw me!" Delighted by the whole thing, he rose to the occasion and stole the show.

Hicks performed the difficult role of the one character outside the *Enterprise* crew throughout the story. Her role had been three different ones until late in the rewriting process, when the elements were combined and created Gillian, the down-to-earth yet high-strung woman who proved herself a courageous equal to the twenty-third-century heroes. The entire affair could have been daunting for any actor, but she found a warm and welcoming band headed by Leonard Nimoy and complemented by the charms of DeForest Kelley. She recalls: "My first impression of DeForest was of a gentle man . . . so kind. He made me feel . . . he was like a kind father. He reminded me of my father, who was a gentleman. So welcoming, in a way that younger men aren't anymore. You knew he respected women, and he treated you like a lady. He made you feel like a lady. I found him very attractive, I suppose. He was very sexy. You knew he was a wonderful lover, you knew he appreciated women. He was very masculine and yet very refined. I really found him . . . really sexy. I remember thinking that the whole time, that physique that men had in the '40s and '50s, a very slim man. I didn't feel he was frail but very skinny, the slouchy way men were in the early movies."

Nimoy understands the allure that Kelley had for both men and women. In Hicks's case, it was a romantic appeal; for Stephen Collins, it was wisdom. To Nimoy, the elements that are perceived so differently by men and women are exactly the same. Kelley was without threat or challenge, a model of detachment, excellence, and warmth.

The man in the mist worked his magic over men and women alike, and very few were immune to his magnetism.

Hicks says, "We enjoyed each other. He got me, and I got him . . . a twinkle in his eye, I think, when we were together. He probably thought I was a nice young woman. They all appreciated that I wasn't an egomaniac, because it was their movie, and I had a fairly large part. They could have been resentful, but I also could have been icky, and I think De appreciated that I was a lady. I felt he was a good actor, he was great, he knew when a line was up, he knew how to make something funny."

Of Carolyn and DeForest, she remembers: "I did get the impression—he reminded me of romance, of being married, of my parents being married and being cozy together. [Marriage] made them very happy, still in love, and they'd have their cocktails at five o'clock . . . their very '40s romance." They were reclusive but had "no odor of oddness. I felt they were content. They were very gracious." Conversing, the martini, the old-fashioned way of being social—Hicks enjoyed her experience of the Kelleys through the filming and subsequent work promoting the movie. For her, it was a glimpse of home.[5]

Meyer protested the decision to allow Gillian to return with the crew to the twenty-third century. "In my version of the script, originally, when they all leave to go back, she didn't leave. She said if anyone's going to make sure this kind of disaster doesn't happen, somebody's going to have to stay behind. The end in the movie detracts from the importance of people in the present taking responsibility for the ecology and preventing problems of the future by doing something about them today, rather than catering to the fantasy desires of being able to be transported ahead in time to a near-utopian future society of the *Star Trek* era."[6]

3 Tony Kirk joined Kelley for a few golden days at Paramount during *Star Trek IV*. He recalls that George Takei offered him Saurian brandy and walked him all over the studios. He saw the rig that rattled the set of the bridge of the Bird of Prey during time warp. The thing was strung to a crane and bounced like hell. Kelley had commented that that scene rattled his nerves as much as McCoy's, with all their lives suspended on a few wires. The whole operation was revealed to Tony; he was in seventh heaven.

The parking lot at Paramount became the focus of some of the most arduous filming in studio memory. For the first time in decades, the low-lying lot was transformed into a pool, and the large blank wall of a building beyond the lot was painted for background. What was once DeMille's Red Sea became San Francisco Bay for the Bird of Prey's crash and deliverance of the humpback whales. "For a while we were thinking of actually filming that in San Francisco Bay, but it turned out that the tides and currents were too swift and dangerous, and we didn't want to subject our actors and crew to that," Ralph Winter told Madsen. So they created the bay in the studio parking lot, heated millions of gallons of chlorinated water, and it was all hugely difficult, with the wet Vulcan popping in and out of the director's role.[7]

"Leonard walked in with a great deal more confidence. I have never said this to anyone," Kelley told Madsen, "but I felt a new spirit about Leonard with this show. One that I had not witnessed with him before. . . . I'm sure it was a great relief to Leonard to have had *Star Trek III* be received as well as it was. I think in the meantime he gained a certain confidence that was shining about him on this show. He walked around many times as if he had a real surprise for everybody. It was like he was carrying something around in his head that said this was going to be a winner. There was a little smile on Leonard's face all the way through this, and there was some kind of lifting spirit about him. . . . He enjoyed the scenes between me and him, there was laughter and a new and kind of wonderful feeling on the set." Obviously, Kelley was very proud of his friend.[8]

Tony remembers that on the set Nimoy was always the welcoming kind. He was eating ice cream sandwiches all the time because he had given up smoking. He had a huge project on his shoulders, but he made time for Kelley's guest and seemed to accept the regard that Kelley had for Tony. Whether postman or surrogate son, Tony Kirk felt that Nimoy accepted him simply as someone Kelley cherished.

Tony had some time with Kelley in the small trailer that was his dressing room and private area. "He had enough munchies in his trailer . . . he had, I bet you, fifty cartons of cigarettes." Kelley explained why like a Southern hound: "See, if ah eveh get in a fight with Cahylyn, I could hold out heah foah weeks!" Carolyn called De all the time at the trailer. Tony remembers, "As long as they were married, he would always say 'I love you' . . . always." Then, of course, he would look up with an Irish smile in his eyes and say into the phone, " 'got your boyfriend here.' "

Harve Bennett and Leonard Nimoy were at a crossroads in their relationship during *Star Trek IV*. As often happens, the personal heartache was invisible in the final product, an unfortunate price paid for the sake of cooperative creation, but their relationship soon resumed on a new and even better level. Nicholas Meyer, on the other hand, had enjoyed the writing and sped on to his next project.[9]

The proximal and distant orbits of fandom woke up and noted *Star Trek IV*. It was the great crossover story and drew many thousands of people who had not considered themselves Trekkies or even Trekkers. Many were brought to tears in the very first seconds of the film, with its dedication.

The nation had suffered a terrible loss with the explosion of space shuttle *Challenger* on January 28, 1986. Bennett was petitioned for and fully supported the fans' wish for a dedication of the film to the *Challenger* crew. The studio felt that it might seem pretentious for a fictional franchise to enter the world of space reality. Bennett told Madsen, "My argument: There is nothing pretentious about the only television series turned movies which has a direct relationship with NASA and a definitive historical role making such a dedication. The *Enterprise* is in the Smithsonian Air and Space Museum, for God's sake."[10]

Nichelle Nichols and James Doohan had worked for NASA; the maiden vessel was, of course, the *Enterprise* back in 1976. Nichols herself had helped recruit three of the lost pioneers: Ellison Onizuka, Judith Reznik, and Ronald E. McNair.

At test screenings, the dedication brought standing ovations; across the country, there were tears. Once again, the strange juxtaposition of fact and fantasy, myth and future realities, came to a crossroads and met in the heart of *Star Trek*.

There were a lot of conventions to do before the *Star Trek IV* premiere for the holiday season of 1986. Just before the push of publicity began, DeForest and Carolyn received a small note and some photographs from the little red-headed girl they had met when De was the Wenatchee Apple Queen some seventeen years before. DeForest learned Kris Smith had gone on writing, had become an animal advocate and foster mother to a serval, a spotted animal with Vulcan ears, a small cat if one compared it to a lion. Kris would be at the twentieth-anniversary convention in Spokane and wanted to give him a hug for launching her writing career. He wrote her a quick note of congratulations.

When De and Carolyn arrived in Spokane, they found nothing from Kris indicating where she was or how they would find her. His official/unofficial fan club president, Sue Keenan, and the Kelley members were set up as usual to raise money for his official charity, the North Shore Animal League. The show went on with enthusiastic crowds and the usual *Star Trek* ambience.

During his last question-and-answer period for the convention, the minutes wore down to a farewell and applause, but he took one last question. "Yes, you." Kris managed to say in front of thousands of eyes, "I just wanted to thank you for launching my writing career." Found her. "Well, I've been lookin' all over for you!" He told the story and had her stand up. The crowd applauded her good fortune and his mentoring. Then she asked for a hug. She got it in front of everyone, many wishing they had her luck. "We're proud of you. Keep up the good work," he told her, and she promised she would. She found them again at the rear of the convention room. They visited a moment and shook hands. "Stay in touch," he told her. Later, she found him again dining with fellow costars and Gene Roddenberry—she had Kelley radar, apparently. After that, she saw De with Carolyn as they were walking out for their ride to the airport. He spied Kris trying to be small in the crowd and called her over, bringing Carolyn in Kris's direction. Carolyn wanted to read the animal advocacy articles, wanted to know about Kris's life. "We mean it. Stay in touch!" Carolyn said, and with some stealth she gave Kris their home address. Later, Kris wrote that the Kelleys again had changed her life: "I took charge and reinvented myself."[11]

A short time later, Fancy was boarded with friends, and the Kelleys joined Roddenberry's right-hand man, Richard Arnold, for a journey back to Richard's native England. De and Carolyn delighted in the English countryside and sent their favorite pictures around to their friends and fans, especially the one of them in front of a butterfly sanctuary. Arnold recalls that Kelley's public appearances had a significantly different flavor. The English were so low-key and polite that De and Carolyn felt comfortable reaching out and mingling with fans. Smooth and balanced, the English allowed more freedom of movement and sense of expansiveness than De and Carolyn had known for many years, or ever would again.[12]

The holiday release of *Star Trek IV* at the end of 1986 brought a resounding affirmation for this humorous and humane type of trek, evidenced by a total domestic return of $110 million. Among convention-going fans, there was an increase in the service aspect of the phenomena. Fundraising and charity support by the various clubs and associations within fandom reflected a continued responsiveness to the mythology.

Star Trek IV brought in a whole new level of fame and fortune for the cast. Somehow, Kelley continued to feel safe on Greenleaf, though the address was widely known in fandom. Sammye K. Beron, his neighbor across the street, observed the limos coming and going, picking him up and dropping him off. The Kelleys had always kept to themselves, but they were still good neighbors. They had watched Sammye's children grow up from the small front windows of their house. They had frequented the children's lemonade stands over the years. Carolyn had taught Sammye's daughter some calligraphy, but really, they were an island unto themselves. Still, the neighborhood kept its protective ring around them, especially as *Star Trek* entered its golden years.[13]

After *Star Trek IV*, Kelley was recognized everywhere, and the Kelleys' small routines were restricted even more, but De and Carolyn took no more precautions than they ever had. They had added some lighting in the backyard and kept drapes lowered, but that was wise for any aging couple. He continued to do the regular shopping, usually a daily trip, and he enjoyed the recognition from some of the other patrons. The cashiers, deli staff, and grocers were very familiar with Mr. Kelley and his daily rounds, as were gas station attendants, drugstore clerks and managers of a few favored clothing stores.

The galloping success of *Star Trek* in the 1980s did not change Kelley one whit. Anne Jolly recalls that once she was visiting Carolyn at the Kelley home during filming. The limo drove up to the curb, and De got out. He came in the door, gave kisses on cheeks, disappeared into the bedroom, returned in his work clothes, and proceeded to wash the windows.

The world outside Greenleaf consisted of doctors' offices, a few restaurants on Ventura, and the drive in the '68 Thunderbird straight down 405 to Long Beach and into Anne's or Bette's driveway. Behind the frontage of roses and surrounded by walls, De and Carolyn had always been perfectly all right and continued to be. It was, however, rather lonesome.

A goodly portion of the Greenleaf interior was turned over to fan mail and the cottage industry of requests for autographs and other items. The Kelleys knew a lot about their real fans. Boxes of mail came from Paramount, large envelopes full came via Sue Keenan, handfuls came directly, and Tony Kirk carried all of it. Kelley was getting mail from men and women who as young people had written to him about their intentions of going into medicine because of Dr. McCoy. Nearly twenty years later, they were nurses, counselors, researchers, animal and environmental advocates, veterinarians, and physicians. These were his *Star Trek* people. No matter how often he got such a letter, from an old fan or a new one, it warmed him to the reaches of his soul, and he collected them one by one.

He told Madsen that his greatest joy was receiving the two or three letters a month from people in the medical field who attributed their life choices to Dr. McCoy. There was a marked increase in these letters after the release of *Star Trek IV*. If his youth had been different, he might have been a doctor himself, but, as Kris Smith later wrote, he could have only been one healer—no one knew how many he had helped create with Dr. McCoy. Perhaps Bones in the modern hospital setting of *Star Trek IV* reminded the medical community of their inspiration. The letters were pouring in. Kelley declared: "You can win awards and that sort of thing, but to influence the youth of this country . . . is an award that is not handed out by the industry."

4 Costars and friends often observed how the world might change, but DeForest never did. Morgan Woodward comments that people never seemed to realize, or if they did they did not appreciate, how old Kelley really was. While Woodward and the other cowboys long ago rode off into the sunset and were enjoying their ranch, villa, or condo, Kelley was on the *Enterprise* chasing Klingons, Vulcans, and whales.

Tony Kirk remembers with glee that shortly after *Star Trek IV*, he came by on his rounds and found Kelley up on the roof. He must have been checking for leaks or something, but he was just stranded up there. He glowered down at Tony, and that throaty rasp came at him, "Why the hell did you let me come up here? What the hell is the matter with you?" Tony recalls Kelley got a small lesson in caution: "I left him up there."

Kelley did the very occasional personal appearance for public events. Julius Erving, Dr. J, was retiring from the New York Knicks at a game at Madison Square Garden on May 6. Kelley was a Lakers fan and greatly admired Dr. J, so he made the trip to New York. For the occasion of Erving's retirement, famous fictional and actual physicians were in attendance for the halftime ceremony. Kelley awaited his turn as they called out the names of these doctors, including Ruth Westheimer. Kelley became increasingly nervous, there was a lag between the sound of his name, his rush forward onto the court, and—he was suddenly convinced no one would recognize his name or they didn't care. This was, after all, not a *Star Trek* convention.

Then, like an earthquake below and a tornado above, the thousands of basketball fans realized who the tall, thin fellow kind of half running and half sauntering out of the shadows was. The howl and thrumming of the crowd was overwhelming: it shook the camera and seemed to lift Kelley off the parquet floor and pass through him from all directions. He was stunned, more surprised than anyone. He could only raise his hand in Vulcan salute, and the crowd hurrahed its recognition and affection. Amid the thunder, he spun and made his way toward Dr. J in the center of the court, who was as impressed as the crowd, so excited he hardly knew what to do. Kelley remembered, "And so when I got close to him, he stuck out his hand like that . . .

and did a Vulcan salute high five." The crowd went wild. The crowd was on its feet for Dr. McCoy for well over eight minutes. Everyone at Madison Square Garden except Doctor Ruth knew damn well who he was.[14]

Heady stuff for the son of a preacher. As with so many other outstanding events in Kelley's life, he answered all of that attention and energy with the balancing therapy of chores at home and evenings among the roses.

The Kelleys kept on the move with conventions. Julia Woodson Jackson recalls her time with DeForest and Carolyn at a convention in Columbus, Georgia. "The Kelleys made us feel at ease as soon as they walked off the plane. They were so warm and friendly that I felt a great relief. As people approached Mr. Kelley, he was always very friendly and genuinely interested in them." It was quite a drive from Atlanta to Columbus, about ninety minutes or so. She and her friend Eric hoped that they would be able to pass the time well. Eric was driving at about 75 mph, and Kelley asked wryly from the back seat if Eric could go any faster. He did, and was promptly pulled over. Luckily, Eric was a police officer from Macon and the patrolman recognized Kelley sitting in the back of the car.

Before they reached the hotel, Kelley asked to stop at a store to pick up a few things. He insisted on doing the shopping himself without bodyguards. Once settled in at the hotel, he let folks know he was expecting an older couple he and Carolyn had become friendly with after the death of their son, a young man who was a devoted *Star Trek* fan. How many fans and families De and Carolyn tended to in sickness and grief was something they kept to themselves, but indications are that there were quite a few.

Julia accompanied Carolyn on her rounds and into the ballroom when DeForest was speaking. "Mr. Kelley had a close call signing autographs at one point as fans pinned him to the wall. Eric and I buffered the fans and made sure no further rushes could occur." Julia observed De's manner; he never went through a door or got onto an elevator before a woman. "They stopped to admire every animal they came across, even in the airport." He knew Julia's perfume as compared to his wife's. Julia thought how lovely it would be to have a husband like that. Eric and Julia spent several hours just talking with

the Kelleys about life, with no mention of DeForest's celebrity or profession. Upon departing, he kissed Julia on the cheek. "Three days
later, I received a package from them containing a mug that said 'Remember Us,' signed by De and Carolyn." Julia had just finished a
cross-stitch about Southerners and Southern ways. She sent it to
them, and DeForest hung it on his wall, and there it remains.[15]

5 A few months later, Kelley was pleased that with the great success
of the *Star Trek* films, Roddenberry's vision of a more evolved and
egalitarian Starfleet was given the go-ahead for development as a TV
series by Paramount. Could Roddenberry do it again, and, if so,
would the fans follow him again? Roddenberry recalled David Gerrold, Bob Justman, and D. C. Fontana for the refit and modernization
of *Star Trek* for television.

Kelley told the story: "I was at the studio one day, and I was walking down the hall, and I ran into Dorothy Fontana. So I went into her
office to talk with her for a while, and she handed me this script and
said, 'Would you do me a favor? Would you read this scene?' So I sat
down and read the scene, and I said, 'Dorothy, I just don't know
whether or not I can do this. I have a feeling that this show should be
their show entirely, and I don't know whether an intrusion by me
would be appreciated or not.' But I did tell her that I thought it was
a beautiful moment and that I liked it very much. But I've always liked
what Dorothy did. She's very talented. She can do more in a moment
than a lot of people can do in a long scene. So then Gene called me,
and we had lunch together, and he expressed his desire for me to do
it, too. And then I began to think about how much Gene has meant to
me, and he's had such an influence on my career since 1960. I thought
it would be a nice thing to do, and I thought it would be, in some
manner of speaking, a way for me to say thanks for all that he had
done for me over the years." He did it for love, and he did it for scale,
the minimum an actor could accept according to union rules.[16]

Fontana remembers: "I picked De." He was the heart and soul of
Star Trek, and she wanted him; therefore, she made McCoy the tran-
sitioning element from one generation to the next. He read her three

pages, but as she recalls, he was unsure if they would want to see him in the pilot. "I do," she said.

Bob Justman remembers that the scene was inserted at the last moments before production. It was a secret. Even the call sheets didn't give Kelley's name. Roddenberry signed a script over to him: "It may be fun, but it will never be the same." Kelley worked on "Encounter at Far Point"on Stage 9 for three days in May 1987. He wanted to be silver, rakish, and angelic, he wanted for McCoy the old age he wished for himself. But in final appearance, he resembled "The Deadly Years" McCoy. His makeup call was for eight-fifteen, and hours later he drank his lunch through a straw. At last, his patience worn to a frazzle, he told Roddenberry's assistant to call for the limo—he was going home. Justman remembers that day: "Things weren't going well." Folks scrambled, and Justman recalls, "He was in the right mood—feisty. One take. Beautiful."[17]

When Harve Bennett saw the scene, he was tickled with the Southern slide of the old McCoy's voice, and Kelley told him why it was there: "Well, I got to thinking about it and thought that perhaps he [McCoy] might go back to the ways he had known when he was younger . . . some more time in the South and just through his natural aging process, he could've fallen back into it somewhat. But Harve was quite fascinated with that!" McCoy was 137 years old, a cantankerous and endearing projection of Bones. His encounter with the new generation's other—the android called Data—was sweet, funny, poignant: "I don't see no pointy ears on you, boy."

McCoy's last line made Trekkers catch their breath. Fontana recalls, with a break in her voice: "My finest hour, when I wrote for him, 'You treat her like a lady, she'll always get you home.'"

The baton was passed, and *Star Trek: The Next Generation* was launched. Indeed, Fontana did more in that moment than she could have realized. When it was all over, Kelley had a new collection of humorous anecdotes to tell fans about. His fan club president, Sue Keenan, and company gave him a beautiful belt buckle for his 137th birthday, people stopped him on the street to tell him how much younger he looked in person, and he gleefully declared that he could not be killed off. Fontana had made him rather immortal in the pantheon of *Star Trek*. There were always possibilities.

During the 1980s, Ronald Reagan, Kelley's old C.O. and public relations officer with the First Motion Picture Unit, was enjoying a long U.S. presidency. Ace Lyles had an office within the White House, a kind of liaison between Hollywood and Washington, D.C. More than once, DeForest and Carolyn were invited to the White House, and they courteously refused each time. Lyles spent twelve years in all with an open door to the Republican presidents, and De never took him up on the chance of a lifetime. Lyles could be as frustrated as anyone with the Kelley laidback style and the decades-long resistance to playing the industry game in any meaningful way. Lyles felt that Kelley had never reached his rightful place in Hollywood. But when he called on Kelley for Paramount, Kelley was front and center, always a Paramount man at heart.

Lyles was well aware that the seventy-fifth anniversary of his beloved studio was approaching. He had in mind to do something historic, something truly great in public relations. He traveled to visit with Olivia de Havilland, knowing that if this grande dame agreed, then everyone would follow her to a great commemorative event at Paramount. Yes, she would come to Lyles's party. He called a galaxy of stars to appear on July 12, 1987, at the lovely gates on Melrose.[18]

Kelley arrived in his usual best, tweed jacket, padded shoulders, silk ascot at the neck, looking sturdy and every bit the movie star. Friends recall his story: He was searching out his place when he turned around to look into the lovely violet eyes of Elizabeth Taylor. A little star-struck, he recounted quickly that though they had no scenes together, they had both been in *Raintree County,* and he began to introduce himself. She offered her hand and said, "Oh, but Mr. Kelley, I know who you are." Mr. Kelley was flummoxed the rest of the evening. Lyles's picture of the Paramount stars was a magnificent portrait of past and present stardom. Kelley was both postwar studio player and current star. Nimoy and Shatner were in the crowd, but in the middle, right in the heart of things, was Kelley.[19]

On September 7, 1987, the Kelleys quietly celebrated forty-two years of marriage. A New York convention in October gave De and Carolyn a wonderful opportunity to do something especially for Carolyn's delight. On her seventy-first birthday, they went out on Long Island to visit her beloved North Shore Animal League. Mike Arms was the chief of operations at the time and had been the liaison between the Kelleys and the League since they began their support of the premier no-kill shelter a few years before. Much to Arm's disappointment, he had to be out of town when the Kelleys arrived, but Marge Stein and the NSAL staff were there to greet their benefactors. For Marge, it was her first celebrity visit. She recalls that everyone decided to roll out the red carpet, and they made a big to-do and rented a limo to get the Kelleys out of the city to Port Washington. Marge recalls that the staff waited with hearts aflutter, and then the limo rolled up, DeForest got out and said something like, "Carolyn will never be able to get me to take out the garbage again," after getting the royal treatment.

They donned the vivid blue NSAL shirts and had a huge amount of fun with the puppies and kittens, the visiting children, and the staff. At the League, they saw just how a nonprofit organization could succeed in the most humane of efforts. The League was so successful that they trained other humane shelter staffs and thereby created other no-kill adoption facilities. The NSAL effectively found homes for thousands of little ones and had never destroyed an animal. They even arranged adoption care in the event that an owner became ill or passed away. Vet bills were eased for the poor and elderly. Animals and people were trained to take care of each other. No aged or ill animal was left to die. Each one was treated as a precious patient. De and Carolyn were in animal nirvana.[20]

Marge Stein and staff were most taken with the palpable bond of love between Carolyn and DeForest. He "spoke his heart into everything, he was a noncelebrity, he was a star," with the down-to-earth simplicity of a Gary Cooper, Marge recalls. The Kelleys had been very generous for years with annual checks and rallying support for the NSAL among Trekkers and through their fan club run by Sue Keenan.

Eventually, Keenan and friend Sandy Zier made their own trip to Port Washington and spent the weekend as volunteer staff, even going out on rescues. The ladies redoubled their efforts, having seen for themselves where and how the contributions were spent. Arms observes that there is a common theme among all of DeForest Kelley's fans: they are all animal lovers. It is their common denominator, their goal, and that is very interesting to Mike, who has dealt with celebri-

ties and fans for many years. Kelley attracted many of his most devoted fans because of a gentle soul that was perceptible through his
performances and obvious in person. Regardless of their situation or
station in life, these fans were devoted friends to the animals before,
during, and after their involvement with *Star Trek* and DeForest
Kelley. These fans and Kelley reflected well on each other, because
they had a common purpose beyond a television show and an actor's
career. There really was a connection, and with a crew like that, De-
Forest and Carolyn knew they had a fan base unlike most celebrities.
Overall, the Kelley fans were gentle, courageously vulnerable women
and men, and to a head they acted on their compassionate beliefs.

Kelley always treated the North Shore Animal League as if the staff
and their mission were a gift to him. He and Carolyn sent lovely notes
of thanks with their checks and encouragement, but "we are very in-
debted to him," Marge Stein concludes.[21]

In truth, it really was a gift to him, and to Carolyn. As Arms recalls, Kelley's eyes changed when he held or consulted with an animal,
even when he talked about them. The staff was so impressed, they
told Arms that Kelley wanted to know who each animal was, how
long it had been at the League, what the story was. In these moments,
people saw the real Kelley. Arms remembers, "I came back and the
managers were out in space, not because of who he was but what he
was. He was genuine . . . he was very pleasant and extremely [con-
cerned] about the animals." Unguarded, innocent, empathetic, Kelley
let all the walls come down. Kelley's lonesome small world deep inside
was not unreachable, but one would have to have fur and paws to get
there.[22]

Kelley often explained to Trekkers why they should support the
North Shore Animal League and other humane efforts. He told them
that those animals, wild and domestic, were our other life forms, intelligent, sensitive, loyal, and in trouble through no fault of their
own. This was our challenge. How could we be fit to explore the
cosmos and engage other alien intelligence if we could not be humane
among our own Earthbound sentient beings?[23]

6 Kris Smith, like everyone else, respected the Kelleys with a great reverence that was at best tongue tying and at worst plain crushing. She just couldn't stand the formality of such a relationship; it didn't seem natural. She wrote a few tart funnies to DeForest, a lampoon, a poke in the eye, and much to her relief and joy, he shot it right back at her. Carolyn enjoyed it just as much or more than De did, as Kris discovered Mrs. Kelley's famous wit. From her home base in the Northwest, Kris wrote and encouraged other fans to have a little fun. Very often, the whole clan met up at the *Star Trek* conventions. Sue Keenan had ground rules that all the fans miraculously managed to follow. They were deferential and kind; they were genuine and treated the Kelleys like their most honored elders. DeForest and Carolyn enjoyed that, but they also enjoyed the infusion of silliness that allowed them to be more themselves with the fans they chose to play with.

At home on Greenleaf, Tony Kirk delivered things from Kris Smith, sometimes daily. She and her friends sent the most sidesplitting letters and bizarre artifacts that often left De and Carolyn helpless with giggles. De and Carolyn launched a barrage of witty rejoinders and repartee. Carolyn took the lead in writing letters, making phone calls, conspiring with the fan or with the actor, depending on the deliciousness of the plot. It was a whole lot like being foster parents to elves. The timing could not have been better.

The household was trying to live fully, as infirmities became difficult to overlook. Only Myrtle trekked along as she always had. Fancy was getting old. Carolyn's very bones were betraying her. The typist's fingers, which had earned their living for so long, ached with twisting arthritis that began to spread through the hips, the toes, and the back. Kelley was determined to take the best care of her he could, but he himself felt like hell a good part of the time, although his doctors could not tell DeForest what was eating at him.

But there were rumblings about *Star Trek V*. It was Bill Shatner's turn in the director's chair. He and Bennett were on the story, on the script. Since the great reception of *Star Trek IV* and the announcement of Shatner's directorial debut, Kelley had counseled patience with and sympathy for Shatner. *The Voyage Home* broke all the *Trek*

282 TERRY LEE RIOUX

records, and it was the great crossover film for general audiences. How Shatner could follow it was beyond Kelley's comprehension. He spoke up to try to preempt the doubt, the blows, and the criticism that were sure to come from every corner of the quadrant. To Madsen, he said, "People will no doubt try to compare *Star Trek IV* to *Star Trek V*. You know, I've been in this business longer than Bill or Leonard or anyone in the cast, and I don't ever recall . . . a film that has so universally been received as *Star Trek IV*. . . . It's very difficult to find another film that has been received so positively. You have to go back years to find one."[24] It was going to be a hard row to hoe for Shatner. Kelley tried to soothe matters even before the beginning of production.

Chapter XVIII
Don't Say I Didn't Warn Ya
1988–1990

Gene Roddenberry's new enterprise, *Star Trek: The Next Generation*, was proving that he could assemble a team that could do it again, and he was regaining some of the power and prestige he had lost with the *Star Trek* film. Kelley proclaimed his pleasure at Roddenberry's success, and he would always speak fondly of the new television show's personnel, but over the years, he liked to comment, "I've only seen one episode, guess which one." To him, as to a number of the original crew, there was an unpleasant déjà-vu when they looked at the program, but they seemed to accept the new generation of actors warmly when they met on the lot or at a convention. Roddenberry, then, was still the father of *Star Trek,* and with *The Next Generation* his authority was reestablished over his domain. Professionals and unnumbered fans credited Harve Bennett with the Willie Mays save of the *Star Trek* franchise. But for the next generation, Roddenberry ruled once again.

Though Roddenberry's authority over *Star Trek* rose, young Rick Berman did the actual work on the new *Trek* offspring. Berman and Kelley met while working on the *Next Generation* pilot. Berman found a professional home with the *Star Trek* franchise, but in Los Angeles, it was nearly impossible to find a suitable house in a suitable neighborhood. In those days, it was a seller's market, and people competed for good homes. Kelley loved his little piece of Sherman Oaks, and when a home went up for sale across the street, Berman and two others quickly bid the same amount for it. Kelley did a little peddling, put in a good word, and the Bermans became part of the quiet refuge hidden just off Ventura Boulevard.[1]

Kelley liked to joke that if he fell on hard times, he could ask Berman for a job. Berman thought De and Carolyn were the most excellent neighbors. "Central Casting" could not have done better, he said. Kelley insisted on taking Berman's trashcans in every Wednesday and dragging them forty yards back to the garage. Berman remembers: "De was the kind of neighbor that everybody dreams about . . . the kind of neighbor that people talk about having thirty, forty, fifty years ago. They don't really exist now. He would bring over little pots of jam or little plants that he would dig up out of his garden, always stop and talk to me and to all three of my kids. As charming and lovely a neighbor as you could ever want."

Through the spring and into summer 1988, Shatner was the driving force behind story and script. Nick Meyer was unavailable, so hammering the story into a dramatic *Star Trek* installment fell to David Loughery. While Paramount okayed Shatner's story premise of God and Satan, Bennett and others were sure it was unworkable and would repel many Trekkers for many different reasons. Some Trekkers were notoriously independent thinkers on religious issues, and others were profoundly religious; some were both. Vulcan spirituality and mysticism was one thing in the *Star Trek* universe, Jehovah was another. Bennett's shorthand for the premise was a "Shaggy God Story."

The story for *V* has a messianic Vulcan kidnap some delegates. The *Enterprise* was dispatched. Sybok, a half-brother of Spock, was determined to find the God he believes has called to him from the center of creation. His ability to tap into and relieve the woundedness of individuals through a variation of the Vulcan mind-meld gave Sybok a following of believers. The *Enterprise* became Sybok's transportation to the godhead. Only Kirk defied Sybok; the crew abandoned their captain.

Bennett and Shatner came to a kind of middle ground with Shatner's determination to have Kirk face God/Lucifer alone. Loughery tried to bend the story more toward interplay between the characters. Then Nimoy and Kelley were consulted.

Star Trek V was giving Nimoy and Kelley fits. Nimoy led the way, making his objections to the theme, drama, and character integrity of the entire story as it was. Shatner's insistence that his beloved comrades should betray Kirk was a fantasy Kelley and Nimoy could not accept.

Actually, one rather interesting aspect of Shatner's original concept was the story line that once God turns on the three heroes, their loyalties return, and Spock and Kirk descend into Hades itself to retrieve McCoy, who had already been carried over the river Styx by the Furies.[2] Kelley may have been reminded of his own Christ/Lucifer premise he had suggested on Tom Snyder's show back in 1976.

Bennett was reluctant to involve himself in the *Star Trek* world for a fourth time. Overall, it was rather miraculous that the family of *Star Trek* was still intact, but Bennett felt the strain. Without him, there would have been no continuing voyages, and yet Roddenberry continually refused to recognize Bennett's place in the *Star Trek* family. Bennett felt like an orphan at his own party. Still, Shatner had convinced him to give it another go and promised that he could walk away with his head up if the project became a misery to him. After six years, Bennett, Nimoy, Shatner, and the peaceable Ralph Winter reassembled to co-create, in spite of growing pains, creative differences, and the occasional lapse into Hollywood paranoia.

As always, Kelley kept his distance by spending his days on Greenleaf awaiting his friends' declaration of unanimity, and he allowed Nimoy to battle for his interests within the film and the interests of *Star Trek* as a whole. However, while Nimoy kept the pressure on to change the story and address the integrity of the characters, Kelley's weeks were not the calm passage of days they once had been.[3]

Rick Berman and Kris Smith independently recall the struggle with the suits as *Star Trek V* took shape. Kelley insisted on something akin to a modern actor's rightful pay. He wanted $750,000 and thought he had it. Somehow, the number was reduced to $500,000, and he dug in, flatly refusing to sign on. Bennett remembers that "the situation greatly worried the creative team, because we knew De was irreplaceable, and we made our feelings known to Paramount management." The studio suits had the audacity to suggest that Dennis Weaver or Hal Holbrook could be had for such a reasonable price. Berman remembers, "To actually come on and play De's character . . . I don't know whether they really thought they could get Hal Holbrook to play Bones or whether they were doing that as a negotiating tactic, but De-Forest held tight, he dug his heels in, didn't budge, and at the last minute they paid him what he was asking for. He felt very, very good that he had stuck to his guns." Berman also soon recognized Kelley's priorities, for Carolyn was ill most of the time that the Bermans lived across the street. "The fact that he was more than happy to dedicate his life to taking care of her was something that was very strong and unwavering." And perhaps for Carolyn and their security as elderly people, Kelley dug in and insisted on a fair salary. It was not pride or a feeling of entitlement, it was what a man does to provide. "It was a big gamble," Berman concludes. The good guy won.

For Kelley, the deep ache of the artist had become a physical ache that just would not go away. Anne Jolly remembers his attempts at doctoring himself, year after year. He ate slower than Myrtle and saw a lot of physicians with no real results. For years, diverticulitis was the label that didn't really fit. He had a growing love of chocolate, calorie-packed and soothing; and the vodka was a daily treat. The combination seemed like a good idea at the time.

Don Smith recalls that conversations over the wall took a turn for the worrisome. Finally, Kelley told Smith a few things about his physical state that made Smith take an assertive tone. He made Kelley recognize the seriousness of his symptoms. "Physician, heal thyself" was a command this actor couldn't fulfill. Smith was a force to be reckoned with when his mind was made up, and Kelley did as he was told. The doctor he consulted quickly admitted him to the hospital with a collapsed colon.

On September 1, 1988, it was Dr. McCoy's turn to be a patient, and the surgery was rather more extensive than anyone wanted to think about. As with so many things, De and Carolyn were very low-key about the facts and tended to keep mum about their fears. They had long been a world unto themselves, and the habit had become so strong that anything else was barely imaginable. At the hospital, he deflected his worries with Hollywood élan. "I saw him and Carolyn often in hospital, before *Star Trek V,* for the colon work in his private room." Tony Kirk recalls the smoking jacket and those rose-tinted glasses on the librarian's chain of beads he always wore. "He's signing pictures and smoking incessantly. He looked like Mr. Movie Star." He gave the nurse a hard time with his smoking. The nurse would bustle around: "I smell smoke." And Kelley was all star: "Well, of course, mah deah, I am smokin . . . a class A filter cigarette, a Mahlbura."

Once before, as Tony Kirk recalls, he and Kelley were visiting Carolyn, who "I think dislocated her hip. De was up there, we visited, and De said, 'I'll walk with you and smoke.'" Tony recalls that in the corridor was a little boy on a gurney. "He looks up at De, De says, 'Don't worry. If anything goes wrong, I'll be right here.'" The little boy and his orderly were mighty impressed, and the boy was very pleased that he had Dr. McCoy on his surgical team.

Kelley sought to control information before it leaked out to the media and fans. He informed Richard Arnold as the *Star Trek* liaison and A. C. Lyles as the Paramount liaison. He told them his understanding of the facts and how he wanted to play it, which was invisibly and privately. He had to let them know that there was something happening in his life, in case leaks became misinformation, some awful Hollywood gossip out of their control. De and Carolyn had been in Hollywood a lifetime, and they knew that cheap, morbid media attention was the very last thing they wanted or had the nerves to tolerate.

His fans, through Sue Keenan, were well trained and very deferential to his wishes. His fan club quietly absorbed the news and made his hospital stay quite enjoyable with gifts and funnies and cards. While it was beyond his notion of seemliness and privacy to have his fans to the hospital, Carolyn took pictures of him with all the goodies in the bed and around him on the trays and walls of his room. His face was shining with a wide grin of delight meant to thank and reassure the fans. A few of the ladies kept in touch by phone with Carolyn, as concerned about her as they were for him; his ill health was a disconcerting role reversal for everyone, including himself.

Carolyn spent most of her time with De, but one day Tony Kirk came along on his daily rounds. "I went to their door, and Carolyn answered. I asked how he was. As sick as he was, he sprang into the hallway—'Tahdah!'" De presented himself for inspection. He had recovered from surgery and came home in a matter of days. "Oh, man! A big hug. He said, 'They took everything out, like a turtle, everything goes right through me.'" Tony was pleased and greatly relieved. De felt much better for the surgery, and his spirits were good.

2 On September 26, DeForest was in wardrobe ready to begin *Star Trek V*. He had been cleared by doctors to go ahead and work. He was determined but barely 120 pounds. He really felt so much better, finally rid of the queasiness and gnawing that had shadowed his daily life for years. He actually referred to it as the ten-year tummyache. He was buoyant. Ralph Winter knew that some concessions were made for Kelley, as thin and fragile as he was. The uniforms he wore were padded to give him some appearance of sturdiness. Phil Weyland claimed the honor of donning Dr. McCoy's costume for running at Yosemite, where the filming first began on October 9.[4]

Fans knew there could be trouble with this story in the opening moments of the film, as Kirk freehand-climbed a cliff wall. "If I'm not careful, I'll end up talking to myself," McCoy mumbled to himself as he watched Kirk climb. Spock's arrival in rocket boots for a little exchange with the captain pulled the audience in, but the first "Goddamn" in *Star Trek* history was uttered by McCoy, and there were audible gasps in the theaters.

Hope returned with the master shot, the campfire scene. "I felt the idea of having Kirk, Spock, and McCoy sitting down and being with each other with no adventure involved and nothing to deal with was wonderful. It put the whole *Star Trek* experience on a very human scale and, in a very positive way, recognized the validity of the relationship these three have had over the years," Nimoy said later in an interview. In those moments, there was intimacy, howling humor, the love among the actors, their acknowledgment of their lives passing before our eyes.[5]

The Vulcan harp had to be relearned. The lines were funny, with marshmellons and snorts of bourbon and "God, I liked him better before he died." Kelley's singing voice had long ago gone the way of Sunday school, but it was his own idea to put attention on his lack of talent—because it was funny. As Bennett recalls, his singing off key at the beginning was Kelley's idea, and he wanted "Row, Row, Row Your Boat." Bennett remembers, "I said 'Fine. Let's do "Row, Row, Row Your Boat." Then he sang it, and I said, 'But you can't carry a tune!' De said, 'Exactly.'" They went for it.[6]

Bennett recalls, "One of my long-term joys was watching Bill, with DeForest's help, grow closer to the other cast members, until he finally won their hearts when he directed them in *Star Trek V*." Unanimously, the cast and crew were well pleased with their director. In some ways, Shatner's honest and respectful direction was evidence that he had been innocent of consciously wounding actors' egos and careers. Phil Weyland swears that that is so, and he had spent more time with Shatner than just about anyone during that decade of *Star Trek* films and *T. J. Hooker*. Shatner meant no harm. Perhaps it is important to note that although harsh and mean things were said about Shatner over the years, he did not pick up a verbal weapon to slash back at his detractors; in fact, he began to use the weapon of sharp humor upon himself. If he lampooned, mimicked, or clowned, it was almost always at his own expense. This director, the soft-spoken funny man, was also the genuine Shatner. He worked with patience, focus, and a rather innocent mercurial momentum that propelled him through a daily schedule that would have killed a man half his age.

Many scenes were cut, and sadly the one and only scene between Kelley and Weyland was edited out. Weyland was one of the wounded to be treated by Dr. McCoy on the planet surface. As McCoy treated his patient, Kelley whispered his real happiness that they were finally acting together after all these years. Weyland's special makeup was gory and impressive, but in the final analysis and for technical reasons, the moment just didn't work. Much to the disappointment of both men, the scene was lost, and so was the clip that would have been among Weyland's most cherished keepsakes. Some of the rough and tumble that took place on the Planet of Intergalactic Peace was determined to be a bit too dangerous, and Kelley was doubled on horseback.

Nimoy remembered: "Bill's such a physical guy to begin with and immediately found that was going to spill over into this film. There was much more running and jumping than I normally like to do. I was constantly going up the elevator, down the stairs, across the cliff, down the rocks. We shot in the heat of the day and the cold of the night. It was a fun film to do, but it was also a very difficult one."[7] Somehow Kelley kept up, with sheer grit, an old cowboy actor's pride, and a sense of humor. Kelley later boasted about "my friend Spock" leading the way down shale rocks that were slippery and sharp. "He was slipping and falling . . . and having had experience in cowboy movies, I was pretty sure-footed and I was trying to pick him up on the way down, and he has since referred to me as an old rugged mountain goat."[8]

The film work was uncomfortable for Kelley, but not because of the physical challenges he faced. Bennett remembers, "One of the most intense times we had, DeForest and I, was on *V*, my least favorite picture. Bill had story approval, and he was obsessed about the search for God. And I had been unsuccessful in redirecting the obsession. De was against it, I was against it, though we tried to keep our enthusiasm up as well as we could, believing that if the journey to find God was fascinating enough, the inevitable disappointment at rainbow's end could be tolerated."

In spite of the looming dread about the story and the production, Kelley maintained his role as the warm and welcoming interpreter of the *Star Trek* world. Laurence Luckinbill was brought aboard to play Spock's brother Sybok. A veteran of the stage and the Hollywood scene, Luckinbill knew he was entering a world of actors and egos, of decades-old competition and controversy. Luckinbill agrees with the sentiments of so many: Kelley was delightful. He was first and foremost a part of this team, a member of this rare fraternity, and "he was not well." In spite of illness and a "thousand-yard stare," Luckinbill goes further, "he was the most warm and welcoming—*ever*." Luckinbill recognized the code of the Southern gentleman and the generosity of the old-fashioned Hollywood star.[9]

As the husband of Lucie Arnez, Larry knew a lot about the golden age of television, about the Hollywood families and alliances that were no more. He could hardly be dazzled by the *Trek* universe or its personnel, and he had little to do with the other *Star Trek* people. Kelley was exceptional. He pointed out that as a young man of the Depression, he saw Hollywood as a way out, as a way to better yourself. Actors and artists of the '30s and '40s often hoped to be the first in their families to become ladies and gentlemen. That was the point and the goal of young DeForest Kelley. He hadn't changed. In *Star Trek*'s world and in modern Hollywood, he was "odd man out," and Luckinbill will always be grateful for the experience.

Luckinbill found himself drawn to Kelley and found him available, natural, and just private enough that he did not want to break though that veil of courtly privacy. He enjoyed everything Kelley had to give and could ask no more than that.

For Kelley, *Star Trek V* was very difficult. The theme was uncomfortable, and he was asked to perform the most controversial scene in *Star Trek* history with Sybok and David McCoy. Shatner constructed a euthanasia scene, haunted by the slow death of his own father, but McCoy had to live it out. The scene challenged every sensibility he had, and it questioned the very essence of McCoy.

He had to get some things resolved before he would go ahead with this pivotal event in McCoy's life. He took matters up with Shatner and Bennett. While Bennett appreciated his gentleness and his minimal acting style, he also recognized that Kelley was not, therefore, necessarily a passive or meek man. He had some very strong views about his character and about *Star Trek*. Over the years, Bennett found him to be "so naturally suited to film acting, the performance style in which less is more. That is not to say, however, that he didn't have an actor's ego. But that ego was not De's, it was McCoy's. In defending the truth about McCoy as he saw it, De could be a tiger."

When Kelley had to speak up, he did, and with a quiet determination that in this case was compounded his De's knowledge that the fans would be surprised by the character revelations courtesy of Sybok. Like the fans, he had always believed that Bones took to wandering the galaxy after his wife broke his heart. He was a Southern romantic, a good father of an unseen daughter, a wounded healer in matters of love. What Shatner wanted was a revision of *Star Trek* history—patricide was the deeply hidden core of McCoy's purgatory of remorse. McCoy calls the passionate Vulcan's form of mind-melding "brainwashing." Sybok compassionately asks McCoy, "Your pain is deepest—I can feel it. Can't you?"

"My God, don't do this to me." McCoy found terror where others found hypnotic stupor.

Kelley knew that the doctor was being asked to handle a no-win situation, and he wanted that to be stated somehow. He knew he was in for controversy—hardly his favorite situation. He did not want those who knew and loved McCoy to lose faith in the good doctor. He had to find a scenario that might be understandable to himself and McCoy and the fans.

Luckinbill worked the scenes with Kelley, brought him along, and their performance was all the better for it. Kelley found a way through the scenes, and as McCoy, Luckinbill remembers, "he just was that character." They later sat together through the first cut, and Kelley gave Luckinbill the lion's share of the credit for the power of their performance.

So why did he remove his father from life support? Kelley's answer was "to preserve his dignity," and McCoy visibly sank under the burden of such a cross. He sacrificed his sense of self and his peace for the rest of his life to end his father's suffering. That was the cost. McCoy knew it and was willing to pay it. As McCoy released his father, Clora's ring gleamed on film, a reminder of the man behind the act.

The terrible irony of a cure discovered not long after the act of mercy killing brought the argument back to center. It was not right; it was not wrong. That was the hideous consequence of violating a lifelong oath. Right or wrong, it poisoned McCoy's soul. With these elements established, Kelley went ahead and tapped into the deep and decades-long empathy for the wounded healer.[10]

Bennett recalls the performance as a "wonderful achievement. The internal flashbacks, McCoy with his father, I would never have dared to do so wrenching a scene with a lesser actor. That may be my highest testament to his abilities as an actor, that he could pull it off. He could make us weep and cry and forever see Bones in a slightly different way, understand why he becomes what he becomes. For me, still, that sequence is remarkable. And those two scenes [the campfire and the flashback] are the things that I remember most about him as an actor. It really was improv; it was not so much scripted as it was him."

McCoy's humor and anguish arose from Kelley's irony and innocence. The scenes dramatized the essence and attractiveness of McCoy and the actor who played the role. As a wounded healer, vulnerability was his strength. As an actor and as a man, it was the source of his magnetism. Luckinbill remembers that on film the eye was drawn to him, even as he was still, and off camera he had the same magnetism. Luckinbill is startled by his own conclusions so many years later: "I loved him."

3 With the conclusion of *Star Trek V,* Bennett walked. Kelley understood and later rhymed, "Harve Bennett left in a huff, simply saying he'd had enough. Give him credit, he stood his ground, I miss knowing he's around." The crew was uncertain about their future without Bennett, and "after we did *V,* Paramount's faith took a dive."[11]

Bennett explains: "I had a completed script and a production go-ahead on *Star Trek: The Academy Years,* the story of Kirk, Spock, and McCoy as cadets at Starfleet Academy. The story was told in flashback by Bill, Leonard, and De, so they opened and closed the film. At the last minute, the green light was withdrawn, and I was asked to come up with something new and shoot it within nine months for the *Star Trek* 25th anniversary. I could not conceive of doing a quality picture in one-third of the usual time. My contract coincidentally was up, so I left. I was not in a 'huff,' but I had had enough." With Bennett's departure, the cycle of future mythology had come to an end.

4 *Star Trek V* got a lukewarm reception from the critics and fans. Much of the blame for the film was placed on Shatner's shoulders. Kelley didn't skirt the issue; he was a stalwart friend to Shatner and simply explained that this excellent directorial debut was plagued by a faltering script and budget woes from Paramount. Shatner admitted that he had been trying to create an epic, "delving into man's universal desire to believe. . . . I was sure it had marked the end of the *Star Trek* films once and for all." It seems that Shatner thought he had failed where others had succeeded valiantly; the years of the "cosmic clown" were upon him. He was most harsh with his own image. He lampooned everything he was and did. His lampoon of *Trek* and

Trekkers was a mild joust that fans would not forgive him for, but
they seemed neither to know nor care that he was hardest on himself.
Fortunately, Kelley did know, and he did care. Shatner-bashing could
go only so far in Kelley's company, and then a small growl or a look
would put an end to it. At conventions, he often ended his light-
hearted razzing of Shatner with a statement of his love.[12]

Kelley's background as a preacher's son was generally known; the
extent of his personal faith was not. Only later, as he spoke about it at
conventions, did one get the idea of how very uncomfortable he was
with this kind of storytelling, and the fans soberly agreed. Of course,
he knew he'd have to discuss the patricide scene with Trekkers from
now till Kingdom Come. The inspirer of physicians had euthanized his
own father. But first Kelley would have to bear a most painful dismissal of his work. After illness, surgery, and jeopardizing his health
to get on with the show, the sixty-eight-year-old actor was slapped
with mean reviews, and it hurt. At *Star Trek* conventions, he was
healed and strengthened by the fans' appreciation of his efforts and
artistry.[13]

During the holidays, the Kelleys customarily received lovely gifts
in the mail from fans and friends. One veteran fan, a young woman
who had impressed Roddenberry with her letters so much back in the
'60s that he kept them in his files, was Peggy Latimer. This year, she
decided to send her Southern actor homemade jellied crabapple and
wild muscadine. He wrote a thank-you note. Her health rapidly de-
generated thereafter, but she was buoyed by the flow of letters from
DeForest and Carolyn. "Suddenly I was special. I was awestruck by
the fact that here was someone very special, very much in the limelight, very much didn't have to give me the time of day, much less
handwrite notes of encouragement [to] boost the very flagging spirits
of someone unknown." Carolyn sent a magazine subscription to help
Peggy pass the time in hospitals and recovery rooms. When Peggy
could, she made things to express her appreciation. She believes that
their support, especially Carolyn's, helped save her life. For their
forty-fourth wedding anniversary, Peggy sent them a traditional
cross-stitch commemorating the event. De hung it on his wall, and
there it remains.[14]

Carolyn did the lion's share of the correspondence and followed through on so many acts of kindness that there is no recalling them all. She waves them away as something anyone would do, nothing much. "A nice gal," or "I like that boy," is how simply she explains the reasons for her efforts.

She had her desk stocked with supplies and calligraphy pens, accessories, and stencils for homemade gifts. She loved order and neatness and a routine of good works. Their social activities declined in 1989, as doctors and diagnostics, hospitals and rehab became the routine for Carolyn. The correspondence was something Carolyn looked forward to and could do well in her tiny office or out in the sunny living room.

Of course, Kris Smith was a most fervent pen pal, and Carolyn often responded with news articles and things she thought Kris would be interested in. Kris sent things back. Their devotion to animals gave them common territory. Kris's serval, Deaken, became a talisman of their devotion to animals and each other. The Kelleys sent gifts for the cat. Carolyn and Kris signed off to each other lovingly. Kris came to regard the Kelleys as her California mom and pop, and she began to dream of a better life away down there in the dry heat and light. She wanted to have a go at Hollywood as a writer or creative person inside the studios. The Kelleys sent her information on Los Angeles. She made her research trips and went on job interviews. The Kelleys sent travel luggage for the serval.

Sue Keenan stepped up to put a roof over her head while Kris got settled. Tippi Hedren's Shambala preserve would do the same for the aging serval, Deaken. In May 1990, Sue, Kris, Carolyn, and De drove up to Hedren's to have a look-see at the famous cat. As they entered the big cat sanctuary, De realized that this beautiful land was the location they had used for "Shore Leave," where Roddenberry wrote away under a tree and Kelley played a doctor vexed by a white rabbit, the chivalrous defender of the fair maiden.

Kris knew that the Kelleys appreciated the wild things, and though Deaken had been hand-raised, he was all cat and had to be respected as such. Carolyn did not need protection as she walked fearlessly into Deaken's cage and Deaken accepted her magical ways. DeForest hung back a little, not wanting to challenge the male cat's territory and claim to his ladies. While Tippi explained her life's mission of rescuing these beautiful animals and offering temporary shelter to those like Deaken, Kris and the cat were able to spend some time together. They took pictures and enjoyed their day trip. But it was clear to De and Carolyn that Kris and Deaken pined for each other.

Soon after, the Kelleys resolved to do something rather extraordinary for Kris and Deaken. Over the weeks and months, Carolyn scanned the real estate listings. The Kelleys dropped their reclusive ways and searched the San Fernando Valley, often driving miles through the neighborhoods in the T-bird looking for an appropriate lair for the Vulcan-eared cat and the red-headed girl.

Chapter XIX

The Last Best Hope in the Universe for Peace

1990–1994

The Trekkies and Trekkers grew up to write, direct, produce, act, and add artistically to the *Star Trek* universe. Others put their economic skills to work as conventions became huge, dealers' rooms were packed, discretionary income flew from one palm to another, and everyone made a buck or a hundred thousand. This did not disturb Kelley's sensibilities. He felt that *Star Trek* was underutilized as a commercial force, that *Star Wars*, *E.T.*, and other efforts were pushing the limit of commercialization but that *Star Trek* had never hit its potential.

Certainly, the actors had not reaped the huge rewards that the franchise and Paramount did. Kelley fully supported Shatner five years before, when he kicked until he was paid $1 million for *Star Trek IV*. For V Kelley himself dug in and insisted on some recognition of his value. What a minuscule percentage that was, considering the benefits his labors returned. For *Star Trek VI*, Kelley gleefully rhymed, "For I never thought that I'd see the day—When Spock would control my movie pay—Even so, I'll never get rich—Because of that green-blooded son of a bitch!"[1] Really, with Nimoy as executive producer on *Star Trek VI,* it was agreed in 1990 that Kelley was to be paid $1 million, a stunning amount of money for two elderly folks on Greenleaf. Under Nimoy's reign, Kelley was assured of a comfortable old age come hell or high water.

The Kelley trips to Long Beach were becoming far too adventurous in the 1968 Thunderbird. Friends remember that Carolyn mourned the loss of the old friend. But they had been stranded on the thoroughfare between Long Beach and Los Angeles in that old classic car, still mint from bumper to bumper but with a failing metal heart. "I'm a doctor, not a mechanic!" never failed to get help from motorists, but it was hardly a reliable or safe way to go. So, with a good deal of regret, they went out and bought a Lexus, with a car phone and every other accoutrement. The story goes that months later and with ten thousand miles on it, the doctor of the *Enterprise* returned the Lexus to the dealer. What could be wrong? the staff inquired anxiously. He said sheepishly, "We'd just like to know how to get the windows down."

These were good times, savored as the last taste of the wine at the bottom of the glass. There was so much joy, and so many good things were happening. There was so much to look back on, so many people to thank.

The Kelleys made no big show about their donations, but there was a steady outflow to charities and personal assistance. Some fans found checks in the mail for such things as funeral services for loved ones. Sometimes the Kelleys made small loans here and there and later refused to accept repayment. The North Shore Animal League and other humane and medical associations benefited, and, just as one would think, De and Carolyn never, ever forgot a friend. "He must have figured I'd had a hard life. They sent me a check for a round-the-world trip," Anne Jolly recalls. "But you know, I don't know how it will be for them, if they'll ever need it." Rather than spend it, Anne has tended to it. It'll be there, just in case, for the Kelleys as long as they live.

Long Beach was something of a time warp, and Kelley hadn't changed much over the years—not at all, really. He'd fold into the couch, at loose right angles, arms spread along the back, so thin and handsome. He settled in comfortably and enjoyed hours of quiet conversation and good-natured laughter. Anne and DeForest smoked while the others abstained. If folks got a little rowdy, they dared one another to slide down the pole that served as a fire escape to the beach below. When it was time to decide what to have for lunch or supper, De proved that it was still hard for him to express an opinion. Most queries were answered by a slow, warm "I'll call Paramount." It was his answer for everything: call them, they'd know.

From outside and below, there came the sounds of the water, bathers, dogs barking. Then sunset and quiet. Time for bed, and everyone went to the back of the beach house. The Kelley room was filled with books and simple furniture and a deep, welcoming feeling. De could slide the window open and hear a little traffic, but the breeze brought in the salt air to sleep by. If Carolyn was restless, De might get up and go to the tiny bed in the office. There he might contemplate the painting of feline yellow eyes on black background with a tiny mouse looking up from the bottom of the frame. He entitled it "Oh Shit." On another wall, he could admire his own painting of Emma and her home in Conyers that he had done decades before. His feet hung over the end of that little bed, and he slept there in the salt air surrounded by the whisper of the waves. In the morning, there would be a simple breakfast. Anne's man Don Crews observed De's routine: eat ever so slowly, rise from the table, go to the sink, wash the dishes and utensils, put them in the rack, dry them with a towel, put away the dishes, and tidy up. "Damn that De!" Don declares, and Anne laughs with him; De has spoiled a man's kitchen customs forever.

Bette Creutze always hosted the St. Patrick's parties, which were a roaring good time. She was happily married to a man named Ireland, so where else could the Kelleys celebrate St. Patrick's Day? In winter, they were at Anne's overlooking the bay for the Christmas boat parades. On one of these occasions, Anne recalls, her daughter's dog, Maggie, took advantage of the boat parade. While everyone was out on the balcony watching, the retriever ate all the snacks. When they came in, Maggie ran for it. Right away, De was working like hell in the kitchen trying to whip up more snacks so Maggie wouldn't be in so much trouble.

2 For months, Kelley had gone door-to-door looking for houses for rent. He inquired if the landlord would allow a big cat. Imagine the stunned and stammering responses. A big cat? How big? What planet? Dr. McCoy? It was frustrating for the Kelleys and for Kris. He persisted, for the sake of the cat, Kris, and Carolyn, who could be brought to tears by the very idea of a distressed animal. Finally, a house was secured not far from the Kelleys. The day before De's seventy-first birthday, he and Carolyn went to Encino to welcome Deaken to the Valley.

Not many weeks later, the Kelleys decided to bring their beloved Fancy to the vet for her release into the next world. Tony Kirk in person and Kris Smith in correspondence were comforting in the process toward this decision and in the bereavement. De wrote to Kris and thanked her for her support and her kind offer to step in if they needed someone to do it for them or with them. He wrote that he knew it was the right thing and, echoing that whispered line of McCoy's, he had done it "to preserve her dignity." Only Myrtle remained on the homestead, and she, they were sure, would outlive them both. De and Carolyn took solace in that and did not open their home again to the joy or the grief of another pet.[2]

Kris and the gals of the Kelley fan club had a grand sense of timing for their hi-jinks and it was high time for another round. The Kelleys had been notified nearly two years before that Paramount had nominated DeForest for a star on the Hollywood Walk of Fame. Most dear to De's heart was the added recognition that much of his career had been in films, some very good films. His star would be emblazoned with a film camera, while his fellow *Star Trek* crew members were issued ones with television sets. But months became seasons, became years. He dryly commented that he might not receive his star during his lifetime. Kris found the quip distressing; something had to be done. DeForest unwrapped yet another package from his Kelley girls, to find a picture of . . . his Hollywood star? His name, the motion picture camera, the granite and brass. And there was a note with one small question: "We were there, where were you?"

Then he laughed like hell. The girls had gone to a tourist trap and bought one of the little mockups and had his name put on it, and they had one made for Carolyn, too—God knew she deserved one.

The Kelleys cherished things like this and set them up in their den. Their garage had been outfitted with pristine white cupboards and closets that were filled with mementos, from the poignant to the risqué. They kept fan mail, photographs, T-shirts, and all kinds of things. People made them gifts, needlework, afghans, stuffed animals, and many, many turtles. In the house there were cherished items, such as the belt buckle Sue Keenan gave him for his "137th birthday," a neckerchief worn by Clarke Gable, a brick from the Atlanta theater that premiered *Gone With the Wind,* the photograph for Paramount's 75th anniversary, the *Star Trek I* picture signed by Gene Roddenberry, and sketches of De by Army buddy Roy Knott. The house was accented with these items, the refrigerator top covered with cute critters, turtles posed on tabletops and by the fireplace. The props and bits of costume that De had squirreled away over the years were routinely sorted through and sent out to Sue Keenan or someone else raising money for the North Shore Animal League or another good cause. De held on to very little of himself and collected the things of others.

When word got out that there were a lot of fake autographs circulating and that some actors hired assistants to sign or had their signatures copied, he promised fans that anything having to do with DeForest Kelley was from DeForest Kelley. He told fans that he could not account for the actions of others, but he promised them that they could trust him. He gave them his word—and the crowd roared their appreciation for his high regard of them. If you got something from DeForest Kelley it came from the house. Tony Kirk carried it away in his mail pouch. That was their cottage industry, and it took a lot of time. The Kelley's continued to read as many letters as possible. Carolyn wrote, and DeForest signed. Now and again, he'd write his own brief letters of gentle reassurance.

3 With the 25th Anniversary of *Star Trek,* Paramount believed it could do well with another film in spite of the disappointing returns for *Star Trek V.* The general consensus was that this was the final voyage of the original crew. *Star Trek VI* would be a departure from the esoteric themes of the last four movies. As with many episodes in the original series, this story by Leonard Nimoy not only examined a current state of affairs but also predicted future events in our own world. In this case, it was not technology, environment, or other macrocosmic affairs; rather, it was very specifically an unraveling of the cold war, which in this dimension was just a few years away. Once again, *Star Trek* was a wonder of fact and fantasy, mythology and reality. In the story, the Klingon Empire had scuttled itself on its warlike imperialism and disregard for environmental and social concerns. The Empire and its people were devastated by a cataclysmic event and facing extinction. Ambassador Sarek and his son Spock saw the tragedy as an opportunity to end the generations-old antagonisms and warfare between Klingon and Federation forces. Ambassador Gorkon of the Empire was to spearhead the Klingon diplomacy but was murdered by extremist cold warriors. Nimoy was given carte blanche, and while he dreamed up the Chernobyl-themed Klingon crisis, he enlisted Nick Meyer to do the screenplay and the directing. While the creators worked the screenplay, Nimoy recalled, Gorbachev had been kidnapped and the USSR began its final descent.[3]

Ralph Winter was brought back as executive producer with young Steven Charles-Jaffe. The creative minds at work chose to create a story that was rooted in the original *Star Trek* tradition of social and political commentary. "I would not like to create a movie that ends with a bang or pulls too much on their heartstrings. I just want to tell a good story that seems to relate to today," Meyer said at the time. "What I wanted to do was to widen the world of *Star Trek* before closing out the series 'Where's the rest of this vessel?' 'Where's the rest of the world in which it functions—the Federation president's office and the chancellor of the Klingon High Council?' "

Meyer prepared for this next and last go-around. Roddenberry's health was failing, but he still had a lot of authority because of *The Next Generation* and the promise of *Trek* far into the future. Meyer had tangled with Roddenberry before, but now the sleeves were rolled up, and Roddenberry didn't like what Meyer was proposing. Treachery on the *Enterprise* and within Starfleet just didn't sit well with him. At the time, the villainy was coming from Saavik, the strong female originated in *Star Trek II* by Kirstie Alley. Meyer commented, "I created the character of Saavik in *Star Trek II*. She was not Gene's. If he doesn't like what I plan on doing with her, maybe he should give back the money he's made off my films. Maybe then I'll care what he has to say."[4]

The *Enterprise* crew was recalled and ushered into a chamber of powerful Starfleet leaders to learn why they were needed one last time. The situation was explained, and Kirk said, "Let them die." When African-American officer Cartwright contended that the refugee population of Klingons would be so much alien trash, the camera cut away to the pained reaction of McCoy.

Meyer describes Kelley's style, saying he was a consummate "Reactor," at his best reacting and listening to others. While Nimoy played with passion and tension, Kelley held the emotional presence among them. He had an intuitive mastery of camera work. He was very much aware of what he brought to the party, as far as Meyer is concerned.

Meyer remembers that Kelley's range was slightly wider than he had first believed. He was reminded of Henry Fonda, that same deep inner complexity. Kelley was self-effacing to a fault and so laidback— you had to come to him, he made you come to him like the whisper that had to be focused on to be heard. That was his modus operandi, the soft magnetism.

Meyer recalls that in his righteous indignation as Bones, he was an Adlai Stevenson and had to summon the spirit to confront the scene. McCoy was naturally placed where he could support everyone else, and Meyer had the most trouble directing Kelley when he had to be out there leading the scene. Particularly demanding scenes did make Kelley anxious. In the case of trying to save Chancellor Gorkon's life, Kelley pulled Meyer in to help him. "I knew it was a difficult scene to do. I had asked Nick Meyer to go to the set with me. I wanted to see the set, where this was going to take place. I visualized the scene as being so difficult that it couldn't be fun, and I was right. I wanted to get it over with so I could enjoy the rest of the movie. People had to believe McCoy was doing everything in his power to save this man, or it wouldn't ring true . . . then McCoy is crushed that he lost him."

During the shooting, a large lamp above exploded and came crashing down in pieces on McCoy and Gorkon. "One piece hit me on the shoulder. A long, flat piece hit the table, just missed hitting David's head. It would have killed him." Kelley accomplished the scene with an added timbre of remembered fear. "Sweet Jesus," McCoy whispered. Meyer's knack for vivid realism in a fantastic setting made McCoy's efforts visceral. In spite of the padded uniform, he was now an undeniably elderly doctor whose devotion made him climb up onto the table and pound at the Klingon's chest. His failure to save Chancellor Gorkon exhausted him, crushed him, and the arrest was a frightening surprise for an old man too defeated to resist. With Meyer's help, Kelley performed a particularly difficult scene; to achieve it, he allowed his frailty to be evident. Kelley allowed his vulnerability, now emotional and physical at the age of seventy-one, to pull the audience in with him over to his side of the fourth wall, into the moment with him.[5]

"A singular wit, doctor," his prosecutor acknowledged as McCoy stood trial and managed to make a joke. But the doctor's regret and pain over the loss of Gorkon were clear. "He was the last best hope in the universe for peace," McCoy declared, honest and desperate. Meyer appreciated the passage of time for DeForest Kelley and Dr. McCoy. Meyer let Chang—Christopher Plummer—have at the old doctor during the Klingon trial. "Age combined with drink" and an accusation of incompetence wounded McCoy; again, Meyer caught Kelley's reactions. It worked remarkably well.

The most arduous part of the filming involved Kirk and McCoy as prisoners convicted of murder and conspiracy. There were evening sessions devoted to Kirk and McCoy and the ice planet. "The first five weeks of this show, Bill Shatner and I spent together, only the two of us, and it was a real rough shoot, a real tough shoot. First six or eight nights, we shot all night long, and then by the time we were just beginning to learn how to sleep, they turn you back on the set, and you can't sleep for the next five or six days. But we had a lotta fun doing it."[6] During these nights Shatner and Kelley got to know each other better than they ever had. "What is it with you, anyway?" McCoy inquired of Kirk. It seems, however, that Shatner found out what it was with Kelley during those long nights and days of shooting. From then on, there was an undeniable devotion in Shatner's already high regard for his older brother.

At one point, someone snapped a shot of Meyer and Kelley smoking cigars on the set of the ice planet's mining operation. There was a good bit of happiness on both faces. All was well for a time; if you could have frozen the days and weeks to last for years, it would have been all right with Kelley.

Kris Smith and the Kelley gals got to watch some of the filming as De's guests. Kris remembers that he was in his glory as fuzzy McCoy. Unshaven, with furs wrapped around his neck and shoulders, he was a sturdy and confident image to behold. Kris chided him about wearing furs—he might have some explaining to do with Deaken later on. De begged his innocence—he just worked there. Toward the end of their visit he was called to the set, and in a mystical moment, DeForest Kelley disappeared from her eyes, and Leonard McCoy became present. It registered in her heart and mind that she had never met McCoy in person before! If only time could have stopped then and there. Kelley felt good, and he knew he hadn't looked so good since *Star Trek II* and perhaps for the last twenty years or so. The "fuzzy" McCoy of *Star Trek VI* was DeForest Kelley just as he wanted to be.

He had long known critics and the public had had a field day with the aging *Star Trek* crew, from the fond and funny *Saturday Night Live* to rude commentary, he had heard and read it all. He celebrated his aging in his poetry: "They've critiqued our bellies, wrinkles, and hair—We just keep going, we don't care."[7]

Phil Weyland had open-heart surgery just as the film began and had missed Kelley's close encounter with falling lamps and Klingon blood. Once reunited, the two could exchange aches and pains while smoking outside the *Star Trek* soundstage. Now that smoking was banned almost everywhere, they found themselves out in the alleys, and Kelley enjoyed visiting with folks passing by. A. C. Lyles was never very far away, and, like Kelley, he had not changed much over the years. Lyles was impeccable, dashing, a Hollywood treasure in Italian shoes and starched collar. Lyles and Kelley were two of the last of their kind.

Tony Kirk and his wife picked up passes at the gate on a day when they were filming the trial. Tony encountered eight-foot Klingons between takes at a big table of food, "I'm eating the chocolate cookies, and this Klingon lifts my wife by the belt." He illustrates by lifting his fist up over his head. "De just fell out, he was laughing so hard."[8] The Kirks met Christopher Plummer; he and Kelley seemed to get along well. Kelley said of Plummer, "He's the greatest Klingon you've ever

seen." Kelley enjoyed all the elements of the movie, a strong drama
with pathos, comedy, and thrills. He was a very happy actor.

The food table also figured in one of Kelley's favorite convention
stories: "Oh, the muffin story. . . . Bill Shatner had done a convention
someplace and related a story. Christopher Plummer walked by me
one day, and he had this muffin in his hand, a toasted muffin. And,
gee, the fragrance was so good, and I said, 'Gee, what is that?'" Plummer told him and pointed out the toaster before he moved on. "So I
popped two of them in the toaster, and Bill was standing at the table.
It was a big long table with this food on it. The makeup man said, 'De,
would you turn around? I wanna check your makeup.' So I talked to
him awhile while the thing was toasting. I heard the thing pop up,
and I looked around and went over, and there was no muffin. You
know who, Mr. Big Guy, was standing over there with a mouthful of
muffin, trying to eat 'em before I . . . boy, he can put that stuff away.
I looked at him, and he looked like he was choking. And I said, 'Can
I do something for you?' And he said, 'Yeah. You can call nine eleven.'
Now he goes there to the convention, and he comes back on the set
and says, 'De, I told about the muffin, and they just loved it. . . . Boy
what a time we had with that.'" De knew he was lampooned in Shatner's version of the story and promised comeuppance. He bided his
time; he was a patient man.

At home, Tony Kirk was asked his opinion about the *Star Trek VI*
artwork. The promotional posters were in Kelley's living room. Tony
didn't have any trouble deciding on one. "It's the only one you're in,
dammit!" Kelley just laughed. "I like that one, too."

On the *Star Trek* sets, the party was nearing its end. They all managed to enjoy themselves, and there was a heightened sense of being
in a special place. The production was slow, because people were reluctant, like Nimoy eight years before, to allow the last day to come.
"The making of *Star Trek VI* was by and large a real pleasure, and
everybody, for whatever reason, seemed to be having a really good
time. The only day that I remember being really curious was our last
day of shooting. Suddenly, everybody slowed down, nobody could
say their lines. . . . These guys don't want to say good-bye."[9] Meyer
accepted their reluctance and kept them going through their paces,
acknowledging the end of twenty-five years. Ralph Winter recalled:

"We finished on July 2. We ended up filming the last scene of the movie on the last day . . . a little more somber than anyone expected."

The job was done, but they were family, and Kelley was their elder brother, father, a steady and patient soul. He was just waiting for the right moment for little brother Bill's comeuppance. A huge convention in Los Angeles took place, with nearly seven thousand in attendance. The big three assembled backstage—Kelley went first, then Shatner, then Nimoy. The time was ripe. De told his version of the muffin story, and the crowd howled. When he was done, he introduced Bill, De recalled: "He was so mad—he tried to smile. Leonard says, 'Geez, De, he is fuming.'" Bill vented to the audience that De had stolen his opening story, and it was open season on DeForest Kelley. "He starts to nail me to the cross. He really is working me over something awful." Bill kept it up, dissing De royally. Leonard commiserated: "He's really upset." De said, "'I wish to God I had a hook.' And the stage manager of the Shrine auditorium said, 'I've got one.' I said, 'You're kidding!' So he came out with this about fifteen- or twenty-foot pole with a spear on it, and I said, 'C'mon, Leonard, let's go.' Leonard laughed and refused to budge. 'Well, I'm damn well going to.' I went out with this big pole, and his back is to me. I had this long pole as I came out; the crowd went up in a big scream. I was about to pull the thing, and he turned around and he saw me, and I jumped back and ran off. As I went offstage, he said, 'Look at him. He's so old he forgot what he came out here for!'"[10] The place thundered with laughter. Brothers indeed they were.

Finally, a screening was arranged for Gene Roddenberry's consultation. Of course, the sharp military and nautical themes Meyer insisted on were going to send him to the moon. Roddenberry arrived in a wheelchair. A slow death was taking place. "He had fought for his vision of *Star Trek* literally to the end, passing away less than forty-eight hours after screening the film," Shatner recalled. Kelley had been grieving over Roddenberry's health and suffering for months and had told Trekkers he had wished to have just one bit of McCoy's arsenal in his own hands for Roddenberry's sake.

On October 24, 1991, the Great Bird of the Galaxy lay down on his shield. He left an entire generation he'd mentored with an image of the American future that was inclusive, inquisitive, and filled with adventures toward a common good, toward human wisdom. He was salty, a carouser, a combatant, a father, and he was truly a visionary, the likes of which had never been seen before. He was a man created for his time, the creator of a future vessel for everything and everyone to be poured into. People would just have to accept that even the most visionary, gifted geniuses were simply human—frail, faulty, and beautifully human. It was what Roddenberry had been saying all along, and that did not diminish his gifts or the gifts he gave. Roddenberry the paradox was for others to grapple with.

4 A short time after this, Nicholas Meyer wrote an essay trying to define *Star Trek* and his relationship with it. Even as a man who came to it as a professional and an artist, he was swept into a rather odd state of mind, very similar to the one that independent Trekkers experience.

When he was asked about *Star Trek,* it always put him in mind of Arthur Conan Doyle and Sherlock Holmes: "Doyle has been called willfully obtuse where the appeal of his creation was concerned. Sir Arthur's strained relations with his Great Detective certainly sounds a familiar echo when I try to sort out my feelings for *Star Trek.* 'Holmes takes my mind from better things,' Doyle remarked, referring to his underrated historical novels. He might have added, 'I can do it. But I don't get it.' I know the feeling."

Meyer confessed that he could not see the fruition of Roddenberry's utopia, that "at its absolute worst *Star Trek* is a plaid-pants, golf-course Republican version of the future where white men and American values always predominate (despite blatant tokenism), and gunboat diplomacy carries the day." Still, Meyer has found that there was something compelling, attractive, and effective: "*Star Trek* can grab hold and not let go."

Star Trek is a mirror showing many facets of our present and past. It is not a future, but it is an alternative mythology. It is a huge canvas for any number of artists to paint upon. Meyer and Bennett have referred to *Star Trek* as the universal pop culture allegory. Meyer wrote:"Many kinds of wine can be poured into the *Star Trek* bottle—

which may help to explain its longevity—but its humanism remains a buoyant constant. Religion without theology. The show's karma routinely runs over its dogma." Of the characters, Meyer wrote: "They are pleasant and familiar archetypes of what we see piecemeal in ourselves or observe in others. Not profound, certainly; lacking in detail, surely—but vivid. Unforgettable."

Finally, he wrote, "no personal response to *Star Trek* on my part would be complete without mention of the actors who embody these now mythic roles. What the crew of the starship *Enterprise* possesses in abundance is that most extraterrestrial quality known as charm. . . . Age cannot wither nor custom stale their infinite variety. Now when I see them on the television I always feel as though I am watching parts of my extended family—for so indeed they have become. . . . With *Star Trek* it is always the actors who bridge the final gap between my head and my heart. They batter down my rational resistance to Roddenberry's world with their very selves."

Meyer "gets" *Star Trek* just fine, for what he apprehends, as a professional and an intellectual is what has apprehended all of us for a lifetime. "I acknowledge that there's more things in heaven and earth than can be satisfactorily explained. Human nature with its perverse conundrums is one; *Star Trek* is surely another."[11] It was Nick who pulled the final farewell from our shared dreaming past "the second star to the right and straight on till morning." The collective adventure as we knew it was at a close. We were on our own.[12]

The very weekend of Roddenberry's passing, DeForest and Carolyn were to attend a convention. Sandy Zier from Baltimore was traveling to meet them, and they confirmed that they were coming. Zier remembers clearly that she waited for them rather hidden away on a stage alcove as the Kelleys arrived. "Is Sandy here?" Carolyn was asking someone as she made her way up the stairs. Finally, they all met for a big hug, and Carolyn was crying—and that was not her style. De admitted they were all having a tough weekend. "I had to be here," he said, for Roddenberry and for the fans.

On November 1, the crews of *Star Trek*'s first and second generations assembled at the Hall of Liberty at Forest Lawn to honor Gene Roddenberry. The Kelleys did not do funerals; that was a historical fact. But DeForest was there.

Then he hit the convention trail, to cities such as St. Petersburg, Baltimore, and Los Angeles. For the fans, he talked about everything under the stars, about his life, about the small bit of the future that he could predict with certainty. In Florida, at Joe Motes's Vulkon, he told everyone, "I want to make two announcements. On December 5, the entire cast of *Star Trek* is going to be inaugurated into Mann's Chinese Theater. On December 18th, I'm going to get a star on Hollywood Boulevard." The crowd broke into cheers. "And I want to see every one of you there!" The crowd broke up in laughter and applause.[13]

5 Back in 1938, Kelley had wandered those streets, lost, underfed, confused about the decisions that were making him. He had stopped by the famous Chinese Theater, and bought a postcard; in crude pencil, he wrote to his brother, Casey: "some place."

On December 5, 1991, the crew of the *Enterprise* gathered for their enshrining in the monument to Hollywood immortality. Kelley looked for the Kelley gals in the crowd. He spotted Kris Smith and mouthed thanks for the sweater she had given him to wear. The crew was blinded by flashbulbs, and a din arose—questions and laughter. The air was filled with high emotion, the crew alive with nervous twitches. Nimoy was a little misty, others were hyped almost out of their skins, and Kelley kept ducking his head—the sure sign that he was close to tears. The ring was on his hand now, on December 5, 1991. It was Clora's birthday.[14]

It had been a long, hard career for Kelley. No one really knew the whole story, or ever really would. No one knew about the postcard written by a poor boy of eighteen, uncertain of his fate and even of his soul. The men and women standing around him were family. His emotions ran so high he could hardly contain himself. He was first to sign his name in concrete. Shatner, as always, was giving him some kind of hell; they were laughing.

As peacekeeper of the extended *Star Trek* family, Kelley was careful and diplomatic. He drew the line where and when he needed to. Mostly, he drew the line on Shatner. The burdens of Captain Kirk were impossible to measure. Over twenty-five years, Shatner was constantly measured by the impossible yardstick of a superhero from Iowa. He turned himself into a "cosmic clown." He blew fortunes and worked around the clock, De and Carolyn worried for him. At its very base, DeForest's sympathy, love, and patience for Shatner were well grounded by the tragic lessons of another actor who had portrayed a superhero from Iowa. The cost was ruin by celebrity, death by hero-worship. Kelley's beloved friend George Reeves had lasted only a few years; Shatner had survived twenty-five. Reeves's short life was the root of Kelley's compassionate loyalty to Shatner.

Flashbulbs blinded De, and as he stretched out his hand to sign his name, reporters yelled at him to lift his head and smile, and he left out the *S* in *DeForest*—more laughter.

The *Star Trek* crew made the rounds of public appearances and conventions marking the twenty-fifth year, and Kelley continued toward the long-awaited day of his star ceremony by doing publicity for *Star Trek VI.* He was far more comfortable with fans than he was with reporters or television interviews. Often, he managed to work Myrtle the turtle into the conversations, and he told the *Daily News* that after the month of life on the road, "I'm going to crawl in that hole with her and just turn it off."[15]

While all this was going on in fantasyland, Aileen Pickering was flying around the world in an antique 1950 Bonanza—literally around the world. It was arduous, magnificent, and death-defying. She landed in Jordan and met King Hussein; she landed in India and met Mother Teresa. Aileen still can't find the words to describe that encounter. She made it safely home for Kelley's victory day on Hollywood Boulevard.

On December 18, 1991, the honorary mayor of Hollywood, Johnny Grant, kicked off the event. Harve Bennett recalls DeForest's entrance to the ceremony as something akin to Zeus descending from Mount Olympus. He rode the escalator slowly down the front of the new Galaxy entertainment complex. Later, he told Kris Smith it was one of the longest few moments of his life. The *Star Trek* theme played loudly. It took forever to get down that escalator. He had run out of things to do a moment into the descent. The crowd whooped and applauded; the traffic rumbled by. Eventually, he arrived among the people. A. C. Lyles began the accolades and promptly mentioned Carolyn and De's fans and the presence of his designated star polishers. Leonard Nimoy declared, "He is the rock upon which much of *Star Trek* stands. De, may you live very, very long and prosper." Grace Lee Whitney thanked De and Carolyn for their support over the years. George Takei, Walter Koenig, *Star Trek VI* co-producer Steven Charles-Jaffe all had a moment. Bennett gave a very quick account of the Con of Wrath. Nichelle Nichols wrapped it up. Then the declaration was read: "Be it resolved that the mayor and the city council of the city of Los Angeles, by adopting this resolution, honor and congratulate DeForest Kelley on his star on the Hollywood Walk of Fame and for his contribution to the motion-picture industry." Grant made it all official.

Then it was Kelley's turn up on the podium. His nerves were shot; he wiped away the tears of joy. He focused and bore down, sounding a good deal like Leonard McCoy: "I would like to thank all of you wonderful people for coming out here to help me celebrate this special, special day. I'm particularly proud that Paramount Pictures happens to be sponsoring my star, made so because in 1946 . . . as a young man I started my career at Paramount, and there are so many people to thank, from Bill Meiklejohn all the way through Gene Roddenberry." He especially thanked Eddie Dmytryk, who stood by quietly in the crowd. He thanked the gang who put the day together for him. "I'm particularly proud that all of my 'roommates' are still here, and I'm proud that I can look at Leonard and I don't have to say 'He's dead, Jim!' We're all so happy." What a year it had been. "I celebrated my forty-sixth wedding anniversary with this lady sitting here, who, speaking of support, I can assure you I would never be here without her." He strongly declared, "I have often said—and I say again—that I make the living [and his voice broke], but she makes the living worthwhile. Thank you."

Photographs were taken of the *Star Trek* crew, the participants, and the unveiling. In the crowd, unbeknownst to their Hollywood friends, were De and Carolyn's beloved allies—Bette Creutze, John Walton, Don Smith—and sitting at Carolyn's side was Aileen Pickering.

Tony Kirk couldn't get away from work; he was fit to be tied. Anne Jolly had her most la-de-da gown picked out for the occasion and the day before came down with something even gargling with kerosene could not have cured. She was beside herself.

Kris Smith, Sue Keenan, and Sandy Zier made up the entourage of fans. They followed the motorcade to the reception in beat-up commuter cars, feeling a little small, a little out of place. The Kelleys were in a limousine, of course, and DeForest, ever the thoughtful one, kept waving, encouraging the girls.

At the reception, he made the rounds and visited the fans' table to let them swoon happily. He introduced a friend of his to Sandy Zier and referred to her not as a fan or an acquaintance but as a friend, and Zier felt like gold. He conferred with Kris Smith quietly a moment, admitting that he had forgotten to read the little poem she had written for him for the occasion. She was mortified; then she caught the glee in his eye. He was pulling her leg. The poem she'd written for him: "How very lucky I are, to have my very own fucking star."

Kelley truly was the rock upon which much of *Star Trek* stands, and life was good. He was free of *Star Trek,* but he had not particularly wanted to be free of it. His life did not change otherwise. He and Carolyn celebrated Kris Smith's steady assignment at Warner Brothers in administrative support. Myrtle went through her round of days and began the slowing down toward fall and sleep. De and Carolyn were free to wear a path to doctors and dentists and therapists, the cycle of weeks for a rather frail couple. A convention every few months renewed his connection to a world that loved him, and Carolyn went along when she felt well enough.

6 In late 1992, Sandy Zier enjoyed the return of DeForest and Carolyn to Baltimore. Sandy had been in touch with Mike Arms at the North Shore Animal League and mentioned that the Kelleys were coming. Arms took advantage and asked to be allowed to present DeForest with a plaque of recognition and gratitude from the League.

Kelley was in fine fettle that weekend. He wore his Black Bart outfit, the very good bad guy in black striped shirt and reptile boots. Arms introduced him to the crowd and read the inscription on the award he had come to present to Kelley for "saving orphaned animals." Kelley held the plaque over his head proudly and told the crowd that there should be two more names on the plaque: Sue

Keenan and Sandy Zier. He told them Sue was the finest president he could imagine, a woman who "could keep a fan club alive for a lazy actor and a turtle." He educated the crowd about the services of the League. He enjoyed himself completely, razzing the Kelley girls from the stage, toying with the sound system, cowboy Kelley in full swing. He read odd bits from the local paper. He told them, "When I was in school every morning in chapel we had to sing 'Maryland My Maryland.'" He tried to get the Baltimore audience to sing it. They giggled with nervous laughter. He looked around. "Hi, Kris," he said casually to the red-headed girl. "Put that damned camera down," he said to the Kelley girls. "Howdy, hello." Then he warned the audience, "Don't get them started."

A fellow asked what it meant to be a cultural icon, with awards and ceremonies. Kelley quickly said, "Well, it makes ya feel like you're already dead." He tried not to think, he said, about being a cultural icon, "because if I did, I'd probably go nuts." He continued, "We are very grateful to all of you. I stand here to salute you for your support and friendship." When asked what he would remember most when he looked back over the years, he said, "This. You. The fact that so many were inspired" toward medicine and kindness. He called it all "a very fulfilling thing to go down with."

Mortality was very much on his mind that weekend at Sandy's convention. He wanted to say more than his plain words could express. "I'm happy in the Valley, with the very same wife," he declared. It was all of his choosing, he was in control, and the simple life was its own reward. Yet he knew the end of *Star Trek* was a passage for them all. "I always thought *Star Trek* was something constant, such as the sea," he read from his poem of *Star Trek*'s farewell. For two days, he gave out hugs and laughter. They knew he loved them; they could feel it. Then the Kelleys went home.

7 Tony Kirk began the process of buying his own home in 1993. The anxiety and waiting, the uncertainty and commitment, wore on him and his wife. She was a mess; so was he. Kelley counseled understanding; wives were like that, and it was good for them to cry. He smoothed Tony's nerves, even as the "real Captain Kirk" was convinced that another tour in Vietnam might be preferable to first-time home buying. The highly emotional process was worth it, Kelley assured him. Owning your own home was the best medicine in the world, as far as he was concerned. Then, the next day, Tony found a check for $1,000 in the mailbox, and there were others as time went by. Tony thought about how edifices and public areas are named for great benefactors in the community, so he decided to do the same. He says, "I have the DeForest Kelley garage door opener, the DeForest Kelley patio furniture," and other things named for Kelley in his humble abode. When Tony told Kelley what he'd bought with his most recent gift, De would say, "Good," and was visibly pleased.

When Tony called to wish the Kelleys a Happy Thanksgiving, he was told that when De had gone to get their usual honey-baked ham, he discovered a tire was flat on the Lexus. "He was madder than hell—he was disgusted. 'I didn't know what to do, Tony, it's a Lexus.'" Tony offered to help, and De accepted with the stipulation, "No off-the-wall bullshit tire—get a Goodyeah."

Just as neighbor Sammye Beron knew the Kelleys had watched her children grow up from the vantage of their home's windows, so Beron watched the Kelleys grow old from hers. For years, De had been thin and hunched over, and Carolyn was never well. They were not hearty people. But no one intruded, and they faced their later years on their own terms, just as they wished. Don Smith knew the Kelleys better than anyone on the street. He was as reclusive as they were, those neighbors over the garden wall. She recalls the mail truck parked on the corner.

Nearly every day, Tony had something for the Kelleys—a special parcel, a gift box, or, fairly often, a piece of registered mail De had to sign for—often, it was a sneaky way of getting his autograph. One day Tony had such a letter, on January 9, 1994, and De came out to sign for it. Tony told De he had quit smoking—"and he flung me" to the side saying if Carolyn knew Tony had quit, then De would have to— that was De's promise! One word and he'd fling him into the rose bushes. De was funny, but he meant it.

Just before Kelley's seventy-fourth birthday, much of the Valley experienced the Northridge earthquake at four-thirty A.M. Greenleaf was about as close to the action as one could get. The Bermans, Don Smith, Sammye Beron, and the Kelleys were thrown from their beds. In Encino, Kris Smith and Deaken knew it was a big one. For miles around, the world lurched from below, and people struggled to lie flat without being tossed around or crushed, never mind trying to stand in a doorway. Finally, it stopped. Beron recalls people took to the street with their cell phones to check on one another in the darkness. The earth had heaved so violently that the water had sloshed out of their swimming pools. Chimneys and brick walls came down. The Kelleys stayed out just long enough to see that everyone was in one piece and then went inside their home and closed the door.

Once he had checked on the family and the house, Rick Berman and his wife, Liz, made their way across the street to see about the Kelleys. He knocked at the door, and De came to answer it. Berman felt a little embarrassed. "We were completely freaked out. His chimney had fallen down, I believe. Our house had gotten a tremendous amount of damage." And the Kelleys had gone to bed. "His calmness was such that I felt bad I had woken him up by ringing the doorbell after a 6.9 earthquake." The houses were full of wreckage. Kitchen contents were everywhere. Glass was shattered inside and out. Many of Carolyn's collections were lost. Don Smith's unique cases and furniture pitched over, antiques and heirlooms destroyed. Yet the Kelleys had gone back to bed.[16]

Tony Kirk drove his Jeep from his Antelope Valley home down into the San Fernando Valley. He brought water and supplies. The Kelleys were reluctant to accept any help at all. Kris Smith and the Kelley girls had picked themselves up off the floor, looked around, and called to check in. "We're fine" was the gist of the Kelley response; they told the gals not to come, to take care of their own, to take care of Deaken. Nerves were shattered everywhere, shock and grief and loss of life surrounded them, and the Kelleys burrowed deeper into their sanctuary.

They were unharmed, yet their home had been wounded; indeed, something was traumatized. One could repair a house with tools and brick and mortar, but an extension of De himself had been shaken right to the core—and workmen could not repair it. As Carolyn knew so well, the outer world was chaos. Now the front sidewalk was broken and pitched. The trees listed, and there were cracks in the walls; one had tumbled to the ground, and something changed in De-Forest.

Tony Kirk let no harm come to DeForest or Carolyn, but he could not have shielded them from this; now he stood by, their son and protector, an unconditional strong arm for them to lean on, as much as they would allow themselves to lean on anything.

Like so many in the months after the Northridge quake, Sammye Beron found no rest in the Valley, and she moved to a place where earthquakes didn't haunt her. Rick Berman moved as he had planned to do before the quake, but he drove down Greenleaf whenever he was in the area, hoping to see DeForest, and he often did. Kelley was a warm, lovable man whom Berman found exceptional, without a bad word to say about anybody. Dressed in jeans, thin, fit, and vigorous, to Rick De held his own.

But something had changed. The winding of nerves, uncertainty, and frustrated outbursts could be traced to the shaking of the earth and the crumbling of the sanctuary wall. Before the quake, there was a sense of humor about the tribulations of an old-fashioned home-owner. Now, the humor was not there. Their Turtlehalla had been violated. Not by prying eyes, crime, or even death but by the very earth and forces beyond DeForest's ability to negotiate. Balance, control, predictability, the rightness of things had been taken from his hands. Tony Kirk recalls the mounting anxieties and loss of patience. Kelley sounded like McCoy when he was teed off: damned air conditioner, damned thermostat. "One day, he was so angry. 'You've gotta be Mr. Spock to figure this out! . . . What kind have you got? This is a god-damned Honeywell!' " He was fit to be tied. Repairmen for heating and plumbing were always there. "I really worried about De, because he was overreacting, breathing heavy. 'You gotta watch every move they make. They're no damn good.' " Every flaw was magnified as the workmen attempted to rebuild the garden wall of De's sanctuary. "I thought he'd have a heart attack; the workmen and De drove each other nuts."

The Kelleys did not have to be on their own. A line of people would have assembled to do anything for them—visit, drive, shop, repair, confide, and console—if the Kelleys would have allowed it. They did not. The Kelleys' world of geographically close and meaningful friendships was very small. Neighbors Don Smith and Rick Berman, young Tony Kirk, and Phil Wayland crossed the threshold at Greenleaf rarely; only John Walton, Aileen Pickering, and the old gang came into the house as friends to lounge away the day and shoot the breeze.

Kelley spoke of Nimoy so warmly that for years Tony Kirk was sure that Nimoy had keys to Greenleaf. But no actor, not even Nimoy, was invited to cross the threshold. In fact, since before the television series in 1966, the Kelley home had welcomed very few guests and no actors. Tom Drake had long since passed away from his addictions. R. G. Armstrong visited in the 1960s. That was it. The *Star Trek* crew and associates never got past the door. Was the reluctance to associate with actors part of the Kelleys' deep need for balance and peace? Was it a distrust of the wiles of the acting profession at large, of the contagion of ego and aggressive desires? Was it Carolyn's reluctance to socialize and reciprocate with Hollywood society? Yes to all of that.

For Carolyn, friendship meant do-or-die trust and nothing less. The Kelley circle stayed essentially the same in membership from 1955, before anyone had a reason to treat De and Carolyn as something other than regular people. In some very private way, time was frozen in matters of trust and intimacy. So when times became difficult, it simply was unnatural to them to reach out for help. Carolyn searched for and found a top attorney who specialized in elder care and provisions and trusts. They were going to tough it out together in that house as long as they lived.

There was no one left of that earlier generation once the last of them, the unsinkable Billee, Anne Jolly's mother, died at home with as much laughter and party time as the Jolly women could muster. All around De, he saw his own contemporaries felled by illness. His brother, Casey, had passed years ago. The year of 1995 was one of inner walls crumbling, seemingly endless sickness for De. He had wretched nausea almost every day, and the pain began. He seemed to resign himself to a course of refined aging, if that could be managed.

On the side of new life, every now and again he got word that someone had named a child DeForest, though the last name was generally more popular. One of Anne Jolly's own granddaughters was named Kelley. And there were all those fans, many now in their thirties, forties, and fifties, but also in their teens and twenties.

For decades, Dr. McCoy went out to get what De wanted. McCoy had the fear, but he also had commitment and action. When De sent sketches, cards, and notes, he would use images of the doctor, and in certain situations, he would cloak himself in McCoy, but now even the alter ego did no good. Laughter is the best medicine, but De found nothing funny in the aftermath of the Northridge quake. The redoubled efforts of Kris and the Kelley girls were more important than they could have known or have allowed themselves to think.

It was the Kelley gals who gave Carolyn and De the fresh and surprising laughter that so many of the elderly cherish in their relationships with young family members. It was Kris Smith and the rowdy fans who were the bright stars in their reclusive nights. Solicitous, compassionate, obedient, these were their children.

8 The conventions fed his soul, and he delighted in watching the reception of the audience, their movement with him, the love and release they gave him, but conventions were rare as the Kelley's health declined.

DeForest did go to the big Trek 30 convention in Pasadena, as German fan Anja Schilling called it. Back in 1991, she had sent Kelley a fan letter and told him about her beloved horse that she had saved from the slaughterhouse. Some days later, she received an autographed photo. A few days after that, she received another one, this time for her *and* the horse. She was a goner then for sure. She searched out every piece of biographical material she could find, every video available. No German reference to Kelley or McCoy escaped her. There was no equivalent in German for "Bones," so he was called "Pill," apropos of the crustier side of McCoy. He had never gone to Germany, so she decided that she had to come to him.

In 1994, Anja and her girlfriend went to the big show in Pasadena and left most of their money at the dealers' tables. Then she saw De, Bill, and Leonard onstage together. She wrote: "When I think back today, I have another look for their performance. Today I think it was a well-studied show. Kelley was wonderful. He told all his favorite stories, and he was as charming as I thought he would be. But the show of the three was a lot of acting, I guess. However, when the moment was there, we were all out of control. It was like magic! To see De live in front of me, only six rows away, was the biggest and greatest dream I had. And when De and Bill hugged each other—so cute—we were driven to tears. That hugging they shared—I think that was real friendship and love. They hold each other so strong when they stand up there together."

That day, she wrote a letter, got a chocolate bar, a little turtle, a rose, and some other small gifts. The German girls took a taxi to Greenleaf. "It was my first visit at the Kelleys' home. And it touched me so deeply. There I stood in front of that cute house, looking to the orange trees and the bushes of roses all around. And I felt this unexplainable deep longing. The wish to stay. Just to sit down on the grass of De's front yard and stay there forever. . . . I just laid down my present at his front door and made some pictures. Then I left, and my heart was still there."

DeForest and Carolyn found the gifts from the intrepid Germans. Rather than feeling violated, he sat down and wrote a letter to the young lady who had rescued the horse, who had flown over the Atlantic to see him. "Wishing you happiness," he wrote, and it became a mantra for her heart. She couldn't believe his kindness.[17]

Back home in Germany, Anja Schilling wrote her fan stories about that day in Sherman Oaks the year before and remembered every detail. Then she fictionalized it and wrote about what it must have been like to be Carolyn and DeForest watching these crazy girls, especially Anja, from their little windows facing the street. She got Myrtle into her story and even brought back Fancy. Her friend thought it all so wonderful and funny that she wrote Kelley a letter about it. He promptly sent a picture of Myrtle and one of himself holding that fancy dog. His example made her aware of her own good fortune, her own good place in the world.

In mid-August, De and Carolyn joined Kris Smith and Deaken for a photo shoot at Kris's Encino home. Kris had made the point that there were no really good photos of De and Carolyn together. She engaged a wildlife photographer to do the work, which De and Carolyn really appreciated; they thought of it as a compliment. Actually, the wildlife photographer was there for Deaken, but he worked well with humans, too. He took pictures of the Kelleys and Deaken in the backyard and once caught DeForest unaware—his face had fallen, and he was looking inward, worried and sick. When he addressed the camera again, all that had vanished. They were cut-ups as the photographer used squeaky toys to get Deaken's attention, and they posed a number of times, blowing a few shots because of their laughter. They told Kris to jump in with them. She ran and got on a sweater that went with their clothing, then picked up Deaken's companion, a domestic kitten named Popcorn. It was a very good day. Now they had some lovely portraits to share with friends, and Kris had a very special memento of their friendship.

Chapter XX
The Stardust

"I went home and cried."
—TONY KIRK, 2000

For years, Kris Smith's parents had wondered about Kris's fixation with the Kelleys and often worried that something was amiss. She was beside herself with joy when Carolyn and DeForest met with her parents, Dorothea and Jack, on their trip to California. The elder Smiths became devoted Kelley fans in a single afternoon. As illnesses came and went and as the months passed, the Kelleys and the Smiths maintained an agreeable and fond relationship, mostly through the conduit of Kris's effervescent phone calls and letters. Now Dorothea and Jack made another trip to see the condominium unit their daughter had purchased not far from Warner Brothers and Hollywood Way.

The Kelleys were also proud of Kris's accomplishments. They knew of her great love for her mother, her great difficulties with her father. On March 27, 1996, Kris's world sat in her living room. The four most significant people in her life enjoyed a last few hours together. Dorothea was fighting for her life. Her face was haggard from aggressive treatments for brain cancer. She used colorful turbans to cover her baldness and the indentations in her skull where surgeons had done their work.

They talked casually about little things. Dorothea was so comfortable with the Kelleys that she undid her turban. DeForest rose to examine the patient, and they met in a hug in the middle of the room. He told her she was beautiful and held her a long time—and then De knew something deep down in his private heart, something he kept to himself. He and Dorothea had some understanding; some exchange took place in the long embrace as the others looked on, warmed by the moment. He knew as he held Dorothea that he would have to fight just as she was fighting and that her fate was his fate.

Their generation was fading from view, their stories disappearing by the tens and by the hundreds every day. One morning, De proudly put himself together. He wore his soft denim double-pocketed shirt and selected the roadrunner pin. His hair was just right. He found a few old photographs and left the house. He went down to Gregory Orr Productions to be interviewed for a documentary about the First Motion Picture Unit, to be called *Hollywood Commandos*. He offered and they used a picture of him in his uniform with the Clark Gable mustache, with Carolyn on V-J Day. The old actor was radiant and humble. He made them laugh out loud. He was one of the very few left to tell the tale.

Then he was off to Bill Shatner's horse show, which DeForest had made a habit of attending. Bill was a generous man and pulled a lot of attention toward his cause of a ranch devoted to a therapy horse program for challenged children. De couldn't resist things like that. A few weeks later, De's health took another bad turn, and he did the impossible. He stopped smoking, cold turkey, just as Carolyn had. Her physical ailments were chronic, but De was being whittled away. He just had to last as long as she did, so the smoking stopped.

Now they were out of time, too elderly and their health too much compromised to do anything different. They were in effect one person, one animate being, completing each other, finishing each other's thoughts, each other's sentences. This union, this sufficiency, was so beautiful and yet so all encompassing that it was as if he could not exist without Carolyn. Aileen remembers, "He was afraid to drive. Carolyn drove, [because] she was a hell of a back seat driver." Nor was Aileen spared those admonitions from the back seat: "Jesus Christ, I've flown around the world! I think I can get to the store and back!" One day she was wheeling a cart out of a local grocer's when she saw DeForest. He was so very happy to see her. So happy it made her kind of heartsick. He was so thin, and she loved him so dearly. There was a moment, a look in the eye, that Aileen just couldn't ever find the words for. He was still that handsome fellow whose innocence and intimacy just captured a heart and never really let go. Something so entrancing about it that did not dissipate with the years. Carolyn's osteoporosis and rheumatoid arthritis became a course in suffering, she endured; but became forgetful. The Kelleys made a routine of the smallest details, worked out charts and reminders for such things as cleaning windows, changing batteries, balancing the books. They kept chaos at bay by streamlining the household and applying a Zen-like approach to their days. They held on tight, and occasionally DeForest went out among the fans.

Larry Nemecek fell willingly to the charms of Kelley when he caught up with him at the thirtieth-anniversary convention at Huntsville, Alabama, in 1996. Larry had become a writer and an associate of Dan Madsen's Official Fan Club. For most of his life, he had watched this DeForest, and now Larry was in a pressroom full of yahoos who didn't seem to know a tribble from a Tiberian bat. A disinterested bunch of hacks not sure if they wanted to be there and Larry watched in delight and disbelief as DeForest and Nichelle stood in the pressroom unrecognized.

Thirty years of *Star Trek* had come and gone, no more movies, the original crew facing the final frontier. Everything De could ever say through the character of Dr. McCoy was done, but people just couldn't get enough.

Now, when Larry looks back on DeForest Kelley, another icon comes to mind: Will Rogers. At Huntsville, DeForest proved "that *Star Trek* was something constant, such as the sea"—as he once wrote, constant as the American spirit. Larry and his kind knew it was so in their hearts. But now it was over.

DeForest occasionally wore a T-shirt that read, "Look Who's Dead Now, Jim." Captain Kirk was dead, having met his end in *Star Trek VII*. Phil Weyland had climbed one too many mountains in the shattering high desert heat and nearly died himself as Bill's stand-in. Phil found other distractions in safer environments, such as *Beverly Hills 90210*. But for Phil nothing was ever like *Star Trek*. The original series fans held on, but for some it was filial duty that kept them, their devotion to the family that endured. It was difficult to feel the magic anymore, except now and then when one of the big three took the stage.

2 Kris Smith could not attend the big thirtieth-anniversary bash. She was at home tending to the final needs of her serval cat, Deaken. Just a few days after their return to Sherman Oaks, De and Carolyn soothed their young friend on September 11, 1996, when Deaken was put to sleep in her arms. Carolyn and DeForest made a gift of the wild one's cremation so Kris might always have the ashes.

Fans remained a light and delight in their lives. DeForest received a letter from Anja's friend in Germany in which she explained Anja's incandescent wish to return to Sherman Oaks and Greenleaf. How she dreamed of sitting on the lawn in peace forever. Anja's friend suggested a little something, and DeForest complied. He went out and dug some earth from his front yard and sent it to Anja. "I swear [to] you, I was nearly losing my mind when I got this! I put it in a glass and I carry it like the precious treasure of the world."

Through 1997, De had done a convention or two, but the sickness deep inside wouldn't let loose. In the summer, there was another surgery and some home care. This was done very quietly. Phone calls filled the gaps and kept the information controlled. Kris's workdays were punctuated by calls from Carolyn, to Carolyn, around Carolyn, with DeForest in the background, often laughing over something. Much of their concern was for Dorothea Smith and for Jack, who also was enduring a number of chronic health problems.

For this reason and because of their extreme privacy, they did not let Kris know that DeForest had received his own diagnosis. By late June 1997, he knew his cancer was terminal. A few weeks later, Kris was in Tacoma preparing the eternal way for her mother. DeForest only alluded to his own condition once during their phone calls from Sherman Oaks to Tacoma, telling her, "I'm too mean and stubborn to die."

Tony Kirk knows when he was diagnosed. "Carolyn came to the door; she was taking it hard, flipped out. She said De had cancer. She said they said he might live one to ten years. Then De came to the door. He called me aside. 'You know I been to the doctor. I know I don't have to tell you to keep it to yourself. I have cancer, and I have a spot on my liver where they are going to laser it. If they do that, it will buy me more time . . . it's a slow-moving cancer. I could live maybe another year, another year and a half.' He was fine. I went home and cried."

Later on, De told Tony that the worst part of that day of his diagnosis was the drive home as he tried to think how to tell Carolyn. He confided, "And then I can't take care of Carolyn, I can't lift her if she falls, I don't have the strength." Tony remembers days when Carolyn would come to him and say "De," and just cry.

Just before his seventy-eighth birthday, Anne Jolly called. She read him Barney Girard's obituary from the *Los Angeles Times*. Anne says he cried like a child. Even though their lives had become very different, that didn't mean they didn't love each other anymore. DeForest could not have become all that he was without the loyalty and talents of Barney Girard.

During Easter week in 1998, De had gone out. When he came back, he found Carolyn on the floor, with a fracturing of those fragile bones. To the hospital they went, where it was determined that complex surgeries and further reconstruction would not be possible. The mending would be incremental if at all, months and months. De knew Carolyn would not accept someone else in the house to help. They opted for the Motion Picture and Television Fund Country Home and Hospital. It was one of the greatest achievements of the industry. The list of famous persons who were served by the facility was long and impressive. So was the list of people whose names are not known— grips, cameramen, writers, and now the wife of an actor, Carolyn Kelley. The Kelleys could pay, and they donated as well, so a lovely room was found for her on the first floor of the hospital, with abundant light and greenery and a small patio. So many years before, DeForest drove toward the sunrise on Ventura Boulevard to greet his destiny. Now, every morning, he drove on Ventura toward the sunset to fulfill it.

Dr. Kaaren Douglas was Carolyn Kelley's patient advocate. When she was in medical school, her best friend would spout *Star Trek* stuff about Bones and Jim. She encountered McCoy as an icon, an image to be emulated in the early and mid-1970s. "In all honesty, he really was in many ways the Role Model," she says. And though she herself was not a *Star Trek* viewer, she felt that McCoy surrounded her through her friends. He was a working part of her medical training. When De-Forest was there, they might have a talk, and many talks went by as the days and weeks rolled on.

Dr. Douglas liked to bring in her dog, Sammy, for the patients to see, and on the first day DeForest met Sammy, he just had to pull his wallet from his pocket and show her a picture of his Fancy. The doctor was really touched; the animal had been dead almost nine years, and he showed her the picture proudly and loved to tell stories about Fancy and about Cheers. He had such sweetness. As DeForest became more frail, Dr. Douglas asked if he would like some help, offering to assist him. He politely turned her down.

He was living alone for the first time in more than fifty-five years. Many people would have pulled in the old friends, made new ones, changed the quality and tenor of relationships. He did not. In August 1998, he was still determined to get to Carolyn regularly, come hell or high water, pain or fatigue. One day, he drove the Lexus when he simply was not up to it. The police pulled him over for erratic driving. The cops were sympathetic when they realized he was sick and in pain. Did they recognize this straw man, the name on the license, Jackson D. Kelley? Maybe not, but they took him to the hospital. Don Smith and John Walton came to the rescue. By then, Walton was ill with his own terminal cancer, but Smith, it seemed, would become one of his favorite science-fiction characters, Dr. Methuselah, whom he thought De should play in another time, a better life. The guys took care of De and in a few days had him home again.

Once recovered, with meds adjusted, he resumed his routine. Tony Kirk offered help, as did others. He put up a noble fight. As a treat, sometimes he'd go alone to a few restaurants close by. Tony recalls sadly, "They would give him muffins to take home—free—because he was scrawny and needed to be fed. One night, he was up all night thinking what a no-good bastard Toby Jack was—'to establish how bad I really was, I turned and shot a dog. Too much. I think about Toby Jack.' He asked me to get a copy of *Apache Uprising,* so I got him a copy. The last year was very difficult." Tony says, they became closer in those months than in all the thirty years he had walked the route.

From all over the world, fans sent him stuff, especially chocolate to fatten him up, to show their love. He tried to get anyone who did come into the house to carry some away. Beautiful stuff, he felt bad he couldn't use it. Sick as he was, he was so worried about the needs and expectations of the fans, he could get depressed and anxious about it. Twice it happened, huge boxes, like moving van boxes, of mail from Paramount—Tony muscled in the delivery and De about lost his mind. What could he do about this? He couldn't possibly read even a fraction of it. Couldn't throw it away. Tony told him to rest easy; he'd pick it up and let the postal workers at the office take care of it. "Overtime Baby!"

In October and November 1998, Dorothea passed through all the stages of dying with dignity and vision. Kris was at her side in the last weeks and days. Upon Dorothea's passing, DeForest wrote a letter, a kind of congratulations to Kris, for the fine care she had given her mother, for the devotion and courage Kris had demonstrated. Kris was touched beyond words, and still in the dark about DeForest's own journey.

In early 1999, Tony says, "I remember seeing the veins in his head, hands and arms purple, but up until February he seemed okay." At the very end of February, Tony came to the door and overheard DeForest making arrangements with the Neptune Society. Spread his ashes on the surface of the Pacific; cast them into the brilliant salted air off the coast of Southern California. Oh God—Tony was carried along, a single witness to this determined courage that some souls demonstrate when terminally ill. De had always loved the ocean and lived there—beloved Long Beach. Then the Laguna years, and that long-gone little area other actors called Kelley's Cove a half-century ago. The Kelleys didn't do funerals; he would not do his own. Cremation and release—literally dust to dust—appealed to Kelley's sense of order, the rightness of things.

Of course his arrangement with the Neptune Society completely avoided the morbid line that would constantly appear scrawled on his tombstone if he allowed himself to be interred at Forest Lawn. You know the one.

Tony Kirk had been their guardian for thirty years. For the past six years, five and six days a week, he drove out of his valley and into theirs for their sake and for his. His rounds were explosive; he charged one house after another. It was loud, energizing, a sight to behold. These days, he'd glance up from his mail to see DeForest, a ball cap jammed down over his eyes, creeping down the street to meet him. Always the heart leapt, and then it wept. "One day he was waiting for me, on the corner, I kind of cried and held on to him as we walked. . . . It just—oh God."

Don Smith, Tony Kirk, John Walton, the guys who lived right around him could see—but the guys wouldn't challenge him—they wouldn't want to be challenged. He kept Kris apprised of what he wanted her to know, calling her frequently but turning down her consistent offers of help, to run errands, do chores, bring groceries. He simply wouldn't have it any other way.

No one would breach those walls or the rules of DeForest, except, of course, Aileen Pickering. She drove up to the curb in her candy-apple-red Mustang convertible, the one with Air-Racer plates. She was a tiny spitfire, with her hair cropped short and blown back. Even standing still, she had the look of speed. "Saw him at the house—and for the last time . . . upright." He was going out to see Carolyn; "he was nervous he would be late and she would scold him." The cycle of illness and nerves had him down to 104 pounds, and "he had been in trouble for years. Oh God." Even she had to let things take their course. It was simply too late to pull up.

3 The sawdust trail of the father was the son's stardust trail. Their worlds and times were very different, but the message was the same. Through his sermon notes, Reverend Kelley can still be heard: "Caleb was a man of all heart, he put heart in people, stilled the people. Sent them out with a conquering spirit; he lifted and vibrated with Christian enthusiasm. The work is full of good advice, the trouble is not infidelity [but perplexity]. Caleb as an old man hadn't lost his vision of the Promised Land. . . . There will be bridges over the chasms."

As Gene dreamed, his co-creators lifted those dreams, those stories of the future, to the level of myth. Gene's dreams arising from his heart and his soul were fulfilled in DeForest—the future man. DeForest would live out the mythology, in real time, in the real world, tragically, beautifully. To be valued, mythology must be integrated into life, to take shape and form and to bring us closer to what is in ourselves, sacred.

Gene's message was clear: *You are better than you think you are.* DeForest's message was also clear: *You are more beloved than you think you are.* Gene lived and fought so that when the future arrives, there will be humans in it. DeForest lived and endured so that when the future arrives, it will be humane. From beginning to end, DeForest lived his message and became at one with it for thirty-three years—our Empath.

So, to answer Nick Meyer's question: Was he an actor, really? The answer must be no; at least, after 1969 he was not. He tried with *Beginner's Luck* to find life as an actor again but could not. He became *Star Trek*'s healer and conscience. He was not the best actor that ever came down the pike, but he was indeed one of the best ministers of our generation.

He had been shaped from early childhood to put his talents to work in ministering; through entertainment and by example, he had indeed become his father's son. His reflective life had its own course of adventure, discovery, and expression, and now in so many ways it was time to prove his faith. The wreckage his father had preached about—the broken pieces of life—were no fault of his own. It was the gauntlet of old age, the natural course of the human transition.

In March, the guys had to step in; he couldn't take any more. John Walton came and got him and drove him to the local hospital. DeForest was so engulfed with pain that he could hardly follow what was happening.

They gave him morphine. That was far worse than the dope the doctor had given him back in Tucson, after he fell wrong and Kirk Douglas dragged him. De thought he was dying now, in a horrible, suffocating hallucination that might never end. Somehow the call went out. De asked for the man who knew how to handle everything, the unflappable showman A. C. Lyles. Ace came to him in no time at all. De woke to find Ace at his side, distraught. De was the kind of man to find a way to ease another's pain, and he apparently entertained Lyles with a weak-voiced soliloquy on the visions he had of Roddenberry and the great enterprise beyond which the great minds in heaven were calling him onward. What whisperings were in his heart and mind may or may not have come close, but it eased Lyles's pain, and that was what mattered. They visited, they commiserated, and Lyles performed his duty as a major producer in DeForest's life. Only now he faced the task of orchestrating De's final scenes. Lyles had a place of authority in DeForest's life, and now he used it. There had to be some changes, there had to be some planning, the script could not be fixed, but this production could be mightily improved. Obviously, this one-man show had come to an end. De needed help, but the only woman he could trust had just come from helping her own mother die. In doing so, she had proven herself, as she had with Deaken and her friendship with Carolyn. But he couldn't ask. She had just lost her own mother; how could he ask now? But Lyles could and did on March 14, 1999: "Kris, I need your help. De is dying." Kris did a little dying then and there. Her life as she knew it slammed to a halt. It is hard to know where and when a mythology begins or ends, but she had once had a portrait done of De as Dr. McCoy and she as the Empath—a long time ago. It was there on her living room wall. But the image and the meaning didn't enter her head. She could only focus and listen hard to what was being said and try not to pass out from the shock of Lyles's words.

It was entirely understood that everything must be confidential, in the way of Hollywood, in the way of the Kelleys. Lyles continued: "De and Carolyn would be most appreciative. De has a key here at this room to the house. I know he'd like to say hello to you." Somehow she managed to speak to him, take information, and get into the car and drive. At the hospital room, she found a man she could not recognize, a living skeleton. Lyles and Kris hugged; DeForest got to work making them feel better, healing the pain in the room. He joked with them, and Kris began her caring work. She applied all that her mother's journey had taught her. She began her own ministry.

As DeForest recovered his strength, Kris took the role of personal assistant, the first he had ever had. She tended to the house, messages, banking, the run between DeForest and Carolyn. DeForest so appreciated each errand, favor, and report. The world had become a series of small concrete challenges and achievements—the foundation of peace that would allow them to face whatever might be coming.

He was rather worried about taking Kris away from her professional work; she had endured so much and was finally happy with her role at Warner Brothers. She decided, with DeForest's okay, to tell her boss what was going on. "He said I had carte blanche to do whatever I needed for De for as long as he needs me, that he would hold my job until I got back." Warner Brothers had come to the rescue of a Paramount man.

Kris recalled the results of a new series of tests, including a CAT scan. The cancer had certainly spread to the liver, and DeForest determined that it was best to move to the hospital in Calabassas, where he could be with Carolyn. The old-timers simply referred to the Motion Picture and Television Fund hospital as "Calabassas," where rich and poor would be cared for with dignity.

Up on the hill in the cottages where folks lived independently was Bob Cornthwait. Because of the hospital's policy of secrecy, he didn't know that the young man from the Community Playhouse was just down the hill. The man who did the fundraising for the hospital and the lion's share of visiting of celebrities and industry professionals was actor Bill Campbell, who had turned his Hollywood panache to the service of the hospital and the people it tended to.

Taking care of his beloved wife, who had suffered from Parkinson's since 1950, was Bill Welsh, who had been the property man for Paramount for decades. Welsh was a daily visitor, as DeForest had been. He came to his Doris for the afternoons and evenings to make sure she was well fed, cared for, and loved. They had married in 1937. "Years ago, I made an agreement with the Almighty. I said, 'If you'll keep me healthy long enough, I'll promise my life to her.' I can't imagine anything more magnificent than having the opportunity to take care of her every day." That was devotion DeForest knew and understood, and while Welsh seemed to have his prayers answered, DeForest's time was running through his fingers.

Through the hallways, current stars and comedians visited and put on shows for the joy of it. John Ford's little white chapel sat up on the ridge. Kirk Douglas sponsored the Alzheimer's unit that Barney Girard had lived in. De never knew he was there.

Kris brought Don Smith over to the hospital in the Lexus, giving the vehicle some air. Don and DeForest did some yaking while Carolyn stayed lost in her thoughts. An assisted shower, a therapeutic walk down the corridors, could exhaust De. He was always cold, and the showers had him shivering like a puppy. He weighed ninety-eight pounds.

There were the hard realities of the hospital routines, the spilled blood, the sickening sounds, the loneliness of other patients. De did a lot of reminiscing as things and names came up in conversation. He confessed that he had been drinking Maalox for years and that he had high-blood pressure since signing with Paramount—in 1946. Amazing considering his laidback style, but style it was. The stresses of Hollywood and the competing forces within kept his blood pressure and metabolism on the high side.

He had been preparing for some time, and he wanted to be remembered. He told Kris where she could find his archives when he was gone, where the letters from Jake Ehrlich were, the scrapbooks and the photographs. He told her, "I'm going to tell you where, in the garage, my history is. So, enough about me, what do you think of my career?" They would get misty and soon learned to skirt the painful subject, because, as Kris wrote, "We were discussing his legacy and trying not to talk about his dying."

In caring for her mother, Kris lifted and carried her weight; now she did the same for DeForest, and he weighed a lot less. They recalled Dorothea fondly, and Clora, and they wished those good women could just let them know that they were all right on the other side and that they were still loved by those sacred hearts.

Sometimes for a little stretch of time, the old DeForest returned, with a funny McCoy monologue on things that kind of annoyed him, a little good-natured abuse, a characterization, a joke. There was business, and he continued to take charge. His need for rest became deeper, yet he continued signing autographs and kept Lyles informed. The Kelleys' attorney was by their side, preparing, because they all knew now that Carolyn would survive him and that Carolyn's people were notoriously long-lived. He would fight to live as long as he could to love her—the furies or the angels would have to come get him—but he prepared the Kelley Trust for her security.

He seemed to rally in April. Carolyn seemed to collapse. Ever a realist, she tried to prepare, to illuminate, to comprehend, but life meant DeForest. Who could resist being loved so? She had been the very earth to him, but he had been her heaven, and he was being taken from her. Kris simply didn't know how Carolyn might survive it.

Easter Sunday, 1999, marked one year of hospitalization for Carolyn. What does an environment of one room and a hallway do to a person? She was feisty. She gave them holy hell, and she gave them the most delightful smiles. Her words of encouragement and her warm, deep-blue eyes were a wonder. Her moments of grief were heartbreaking to behold. DeForest wouldn't let the old gals—Anne, Bette, or Aileen—come see him. He told Aileen he didn't want her to see him in the hospital, not as he had become. She let him have his way.

Word came through one of his doctors that UCLA had an experimental treatment for his spreading cancer. He had refused all radiation and chemotherapy, but the UCLA idea was intriguing. Still, he didn't feel up to any kind of challenge at that moment.

Kris and DeForest managed to get back to Greenleaf after a visit to a doctor. He wanted time alone to behold the view beyond his glass house, out into the yard with St. Francis looking back at him. Kris tried to busy herself within earshot. He was her responsibility now, a fragile vessel of all he had been and all he had meant to the world, in her hands now. His private musings were brief. He allowed her to guide him to the car, exhausted, defeated. The exhaustion seemed to take hold, and it was harder for him to waken, harder to attend to the details of each day. Again, UCLA kindly offered an open door to the experimental program they thought might extend his life.

DeForest had made a courageous series of commitments before the cancer overtook him. He was determined to keep everything as normal as possible, to live till he died and do the things he loved. He had a convention within weeks, and it was a bitter dose of reality that he would not be able to attend.

He began to tell Kris about his mother's sweet presence, the way she called him to come in from playing—"De-For-est!" And about Sandy Kelley, the dog that escorted him back and forth to school. So little time, and yet there was so much time to be filled, minute by minute, limited drops out of a glass. One had to do something other than await the end in darkness. To shed a little hope for the future, they talked about moving Carolyn and DeForest home with round-the-clock care. That flittered away in the breeze.

They talked about Dorothea and how DeForest knew he would be following her; he sensed he would be dying the same way. They were all involved in some kind of dance, and he had felt his fate and hers when he hugged her that day at Kris's new home.

He apologized for keeping Kris at a distance, but she had been through so much that he wanted to spare her this. He regretted that he had not been honest, all those times she had called to check on them, on him, her offers of help, her worry. He was sorry he had done that. It might have been easier for everyone if this had been a gradual course of events. "I love you for protecting me so long. I know you did it out of concern for me."

A gift comes as the wave approaches to carry off the soul, a gift comes, the shining face, the rebounded energy, and the clarity to do in the end what needs to be done. It began April 8. DeForest was alive to the world. It made folks hopeful that he might be able to go home to Greenleaf for a while or that he might offer himself for UCLA's experimental treatment. But suddenly, he was firmly resolved about declining the UCLA alternative. A little while before, there had been a storm of controversy about Mickey Mantle and the kind of priority treatment he had received. DeForest suspected he was getting the celebrity treatment, that he might in effect take someone else's opportunity to live longer. In the end, he refused all treatment short of the medication designed to slow the growth of his cancer and the drugs for the pain. Resolved to face his end and at the same time disbelieving that it would come, his heart moved toward the transcendent, and his mind made chore lists for Greenleaf's spring maintenance. Kris brought De and Carolyn roses from Greenleaf.

Ace called; he and DeForest discussed the first night Ace had come to him, the horrible fear when De thought he was dying, scared out of his mind. Kris saw his agitation, the fright returning to his eyes. She called on her memories, her faith, and her mother's example. She explained: "It wasn't your time to go. When it is, it won't be like that. It wasn't for Mom. That isn't the way it happens, De." He seemed to settle in, but the memory stayed with him, that horrible waking and feeling as if he was going to die. Where Kris found the words, the courage, the strength to comfort him like that is an issue for the angels to contemplate.

The time had come. He asked Kris to get his phone book out of her bags. Call Bill. He got hold of Bill's assistant and told her about the cancer. Bill had known but told no one. De's privacy being legend, Bill respected it. Bill wasn't expected back in town for a few days, so his assistant took a message. Kris recalled that De expressed his wonder about Bill, so much life, so much fear of illness and dying. Ace couldn't handle it either. De's compassionate response to their discomfort was to also ignore the approaching departure. Bill had called his assistant right back—he was coming, let De know. De was pleased. When Bill called a few days later to finalize his plans, De was glad of it. Kris remembers he said, "That would be great. I love you, Bill." Kris took Shatner's day off to ensure that they had all the privacy they needed. De told Kris later that they spoke about ideas for original cast movies and such things; De kept the future at arm's length to have his present minutes with Bill unshadowed.

De's weight was about 112 and his outlook brightened when he learned that John Walton's cancer was considered in remission. He dared to hope. Bill Campbell's fundraiser for the hospital, called Fantasticon, was planned for the last weekend in July. DeForest wanted to go, if at all possible, and donate his appearance fees to Campbell's cause.

Then De had some uncomfortable symptoms and trouble breathing. He rallied for Nichelle Nichols. He joked with her about her great gams and said that she still rang his bell.

Then he was ready to visit his home. DeForest could see Kris was very worried. Through the process Kris protected herself one small degree by allowing in some brighter moments that this man was DeForest Kelley; but he was also an elderly, dependent, dying man. He thought he could calm her fears. She remembers he said, "If ever I should happen to die while I'm at the house with you, I don't want you to feel guilty about it. That's where I'd prefer to die, anyway." They pulled their stuff together and went to the parking lot of the hospital.

De got into the car and let the door stay open to let some of the heat escape. Then a young fellow, a very ill man, came up to the car and told DeForest how much De had meant in his life. Kelley asked him about his illness and they talked a little while. De wept and told the young man that he was grateful for his kind words. To Kris, he said, "I wish I could have thought of something more helpful to say to that young man." Kris reassured him that he had been very help-ful. They never saw that fellow again.

They went to the doctor and then on to Greenleaf. De called John Walton, who decided to rush over and have a visit and give De a hair-cut. Then they discovered Myrtle emerging from hibernation, right then and there. DeForest was so pleased to see her. Kris made her fruit salad. De made some phone calls. Don Smith arrived. After the visits, De had a shower in his own place, and a nap on his own bed. He got back to the hospital refreshed. Another round of hope swirled past as doctors offered a few alternative treatments to prolong his life. It seems he gazed at them with an increasing detachment and let them float away in favor of peace and acceptance.

4 Anja Schilling and her friend made a return trip to Southern Cal-ifornia to attend another grand convention. She innocently stopped by Greenleaf and left a box with sweets, a letter, and a photo of the big three from the 1995 convention, asking Kelley to sign it for her. Then Anja saw an orange on the lawn under the tree beyond the rose bushes. All at once, she decided to be brave, and she quickly got the orange. Then they were ready to go to Pasadena and have some fun.

Anja was in shock when she found out about Kelley's cancellation. She found Sue Keenan, who assured her that he would be all right. Then she was brought to near fury by some fans' dismissal of his ab-sence. Bill Shatner had requested and received a Kelley poem to read on his behalf at the convention. Brent Spiner stood in for Kelley, but Shatner read "Yellow Balloon," a poem of Kelley's about a yellow bal-loon that descended into his yard one day. There was a note attached, a lonely girl wanting to play. It was a sample of Kelley's shining inno-cence. Anja wrote, "Well I have to thank Bill Shatner, because he was very kind when he told us about DeForest, and read one of his poems (even though I had never heard someone reading such a long poem in such a short time). Bill said that he visited De at the hospital and told him, 'De, don't die! But if you die—give me your hair!' That's very typical for Bill. He hides his sorrow behind jokes. I learned to know Bill . . . to know him is as hard as to like him. . . . Sometimes it's too difficult to get him. He's a man with a thousand faces. But we saw his sorrow, and we heard it through the jokes he made. And later when we got our autographs from him, we saw it in his eyes."

At the hospital, Kris met a few fans who had found out where De-Forest and Carolyn were when they attended the big convention. She was surprised they had gotten in but not surprised that they had come. German fans were devoted, and a little adventurous. Anja got a small glimpse of the dying man. "I never loved him more than in that moment. I wished I could send him that strong feeling of love, to give him power. I wanted to beam my love over to him."

Kris took custody of the plants they had meant for him. Then Anja was worried about the little parcel she had left at Greenleaf, and said that surely there was no need to sign the photo. Kris realized this was the German girl who had left a gift for De the day before. She assured Anja that De had signed the photo and it was already on its way to Germany. "My heart was crying . . . the thousand things . . . I wanted to hug him . . . only one time touch his hand." Anja thanked Kris and respectfully turned and left the hospital just a few feet from where her Dr. McCoy lay, sick, medicated, or sleeping. She knew now she would never meet him, and she would never see him again. "But in my heart he will always remain as a friend, a gentleman who sent me pictures, letters, and earth of his garden."

DeForest appreciated the miniature roses the German girls had brought. He was touched but glad Kris had kept them out of the room. He didn't look or feel like the man they had known. He could not have been what they needed him to be. Hospital security was notified that fans knew where he was.

A little later, his nurse explained that there was lung involvement, and De admitted he could feel it. Dr. Douglas recalls her patient's husband as "very cheerful, respectful." He called her "doctor" and never anything else. He held her hand while they talked. He had radiance and peace, and it was not a profound personal revelation, rather a "transcendent intimacy," and through it she knew he truly cared. No recrimination, no doubts or fear. She was taken with his laughter, and there were no regrets.

Then Kris and DeForest cried as they watched coverage of the Littleton, Colorado, shootings on April 22, 1999. What an emptying, staggering horror that was, and all there was to do was weep.

A few visitors more, a few more misadventures in the world of hospitals, and a shadow seemed to descend on DeForest and Carolyn. She was out of sorts, and he was feeling very tired and sick, sick and tired. The will to try, to battle, and to hope somehow turned to dust in their grasp—the weeks of blessed rallying were over.

Bill Campbell remembers: "I've seen with DeForest and some others who have passed at the hospital the absolute courage toward the end of their lives. They know they have not burdened others." He observes: "Particularly actors, they don't want to look vulnerable. Now, sometimes Kelley looked terrific, and on others—that's what takes place. You can see the mind close to the precious few they want with them." Campbell knew death, could talk about it, hold its hand, and still enjoy the person who was departing.

De and Kris went again to his doctor, and they had a meeting that finalized his refusal of any further treatment. Then, Kris remembers, "De asked how he would die." The doctor assured him that he was dying right now and that the smooth decline, the lessening of life, the devolving of will was the dying. The doctor promised the most painless and comfortable process possible. Satisfied, De proceeded to say good-bye to the nurses and thanked them for their concern.

They moved on to Greenleaf. He had, they thought, about six weeks or a little more to live, but today was as good as it was going to get. The maintenance fellow showed up, and De directed him about the work he wanted done. Then Tony Kirk came. De told some cowboy stories.

John Walton visited, as did others, but De's sleeping became the rhythm of the days as the middle of May came and went. His own condition was sometimes anxiety provoking, but usually a new realization was met with quiet surprise or a comment to Kris, like, "This is going to look good in your book, Angel." They had resolved to call the book *From Sawdust to Stardust: or How I Got from Hell and Damnation to* Star Trek *and the Federation.*

Then he mentioned to Kris that he was going to call Ma. Oh? But then Kris discovered that Ma was a friend of his youth, now a very elderly lady. Oh, good.

With everything he had left, he made the call, and upon hearing Grace Hartung's tiny voice, he announced, "DeForest Kelley here!" They had a good conversation, and Grace thought he was hopeful, strong, that he believed he was going to beat this thing. It was a fine piece of acting. She had no idea that he was wishing her farewell. She never suspected that De was saying good-bye.

He got home one more time, on June 1, 1999. Tony Kirk, Don Smith, and John Walton came to visit. Kris gave the guys their privacy. She cleaned in the kitchen. De sat in his little chair directly across the narrow living room from the old television. He could glance past the box and see St. Francis looking back. He held court just a bit. At one point, he said to Tony, "Let me see your hands." He took them into his own and began rubbing lotion into them. Tony was a good Catholic boy, a faithful man, and so many images rushed into his mind as De-Forest cared for his hands that he was overwhelmed. De was healing the loss that was yet to come. "He told me how he loved me by cleansing and rubbing my hands, every little bit. And he rallied enough to say good-bye to me." Indeed, DeForest had a son, the "real Captain Kirk," and a daughter, Kris Smith.

His healing kindness was all he really had to leave with them.

Kris spent a few evenings at the hospital, sleeping on the floor beside his bed, his hand down in the darkness where she could reach up and hold it if he felt uneasy. He had become too thin even to wear his mother's ring; there was nothing left but Bones. Once during the darkest hours, he sat up, startled, fearful, distraught. She held him in an embrace of strength and heartbreak, and he said, "Take me home, Kris. Take me home."

———————

And for all the world the stars shot through the heavens and into the room that night. The mythology and the man transcended themselves and came to the end of the voyage. Ten days later, DeForest lay in ever-deepening sleep as Carolyn spoke to him, telling him she was cared for, that she loved him, that it was all right to go. Kris saw that with each small story of the sweet days of their marriage, Carolyn's soft, throaty voice re-

leased him further, relaxing his body, lifting the soul. The murmur of her laughter spread warmly. Somewhere the Lord's Prayer and the 23rd Psalm were said. The sunshine was on the inside. The very Earth offered him up, and he arose until he was stardust.

The day after DeForest Kelley died, Anja Schilling observed a tiny sprout from the Greenleaf orange's seed that she had planted in the special earth he had sent her. "And I know that he is somewhere around . . . waiting for his beloved wife, and maybe he's watching over me and my little daughter."

Dr. Kaaren Douglas attended the commencement of a new class of physicians, and in their keynote speech all the usual invocations were made. Dr. Leonard McCoy was called upon as an icon of what it meant to be a physician. This happens all the time.

"The needs of the many outweigh the needs of the few, or the one," said Nicholas Meyer. "Biography is not for the dead, but for the living."

"Of all the souls I have encountered in my travels, his was the most human," Harve Bennett concluded.

Kris Smith believes that DeForest Kelley was the kind of man God had in mind when he created Adam. She went to work on her account, DeForest Kelley: A Harvest of Memories.

In August 2000, Carolyn Kelley returned home. An extraordinary Jamaican lady by the name of Amy Kelley made Carolyn's return possible. Myrtle Kelley moved across the street; the world turns slowly on her back.

And Carolyn found an embroidered pillow left as a message from her husband for her to find. He knew she would come home; like the Earth itself, she would endure. His message: "Real Love Stories Never Have Endings."

And she directed that nice gal to use it as the dedication for the biography, the love story about her husband of fifty-five years.

Note on the Sources

Most of the research was done in private collections in homes. These included photographs, audio and video tape, and private journals. The key participants worked with the author over the course of months and years and welcomed her into their lives.

Some of the stories DeForest Kelley enjoyed telling were written down by friends, recorded, or told to fans, at public appearances. Transcriptions were made by fans, and they proved to be a great help in assembling the stories. These stories changed slightly with each telling, but Kelley was a lively and consistent source on himself. When one story was told a number of times, an edited version was created to get the best of the tale.

Kelley assisted in this biography as he collected and archived what he wanted a researcher to find.

Thanks always to Carolyn and Kris for opening the doors to DeForest's wishes about his story. Friends, professional colleagues, and loved ones donated many hours of interview time and hospitality to the author and so created an ensemble biography.

The participants were: Carolyn Kelley, Anne Jolly, Kristine Smith, Aileen Pickering, Bette Ireland, Joe Laden, Grace Griffin, Tony LaFata, Tony Kirk, Don Smith, Tom Doyle, Irving Ravetch, R. G. Armstrong, Grace Kelley, Erskine Davis, Peter, Chris and Linda Girard, Bill

Weigel, Bill Welsh, Robert Cornthwait, A. C. Lyles, Phil Weyland,
L. Q. Jones, Morgan Woodward, William Campbell, Nicholas Meyer,
Harve Bennett, Nichelle Nichols, Bob Justman, Charles Washburn,
D. C. Fontana, Leonard Nimoy, Richard Arnold, Sammye Kay Beron,
Larry Nemecek, Peggie Dunn, Harlan Ellison, La Nelle and Stan Fos-
holdt, J. G. Hertzler, Catherine Hicks, Roy Knott, Peggy Latimer, Sue
Keenan, Jackie Edwards, Rolf T. Larsen, Dan Madsen, Stephen
Collins, Bill and Phyllis Daniels, Larry Dobkin, Ralph Winter, Grace
Lee Whitney, Laurence Luckinbill, Marianne Tyler.

The Private Sources:
DC—Doyle Collection, GA.
   Small collection of photographs and clippings pertaining to De-
   Forest Kelley, childhood friend of Tom Doyle, Conyers, GA.
GHA—Girard Collections, CA.
   Unorganized multiple-family collection. Family remembrances,
   news clippings, letters, scripts, magazine articles, and documents
   concerning Bernard Girard, friend of DeForest Kelley, 1941–1997.
GKC—Grace Kelley Collection, FL.
   Small collection of photographs, letters, and clippings pertaining
   to her cousin DeForest Kelley.
IHA—Ireland Home Archive, CA.
   Unorganized, informal, private collection. Photographs and bits
   and pieces about DeForest and Carolyn Kelley by Bette Ireland,
   friend, 1943–present.
JHA—Jolly Home Archives, CA.
   *Organized private collection. Compiled in volumes and largely con-
   cerned with DeForest Kelley's life on Long Beach, theater, and radio.
   Biographical notes, original poetry, photographs, letters, telegrams,
   tapes, magazine articles, and newspaper clippings. Extensive refer-
   ences about DeForest and Carolyn Kelley by Anne Jolly, friend,
   1939–present.*
KHA—Kelley Home Archives, CA.
   Unorganized collection put together by DeForest Kelley. Scrapbooks, manuscripts, telegrams, newspaper clippings, magazine articles, fan letters and gifts, contracts, scripts, letters, poetry,
   extensive personal and professional photographs, artwork, ex-

pense accounts, tickets, meal stubs, and identification cards. Included are DeForest Kelley's collections about his wife, Carolyn, and significant friends, including William H. Daniels and Gene Roddenberry. Scope 1920–1999. The collection has been used as a master guide for research by the author.

KLA—Kelley Legacy Archives, CA.

Active and growing private collection intended to preserve DeForest Kelley material.

LC—LaFata Collection, CA.

Photographs of Carolyn and DeForest Kelley and Olive LaFata, courtesy of Tony LaFata, godson of Carolyn Kelley, 1940–present.

PHA—Pickering Home Archives, CA.

Unorganized private collection. Photographs, scripts, news clippings, letters, and telegrams. By Aileen Pickering, friend, 1943–present.

SHA—Smith Home Archives, CA.

Informal private collection. Extensive and thorough regarding Kelley's professional career, from movie reviews to rare photos. Personal letters, gifts, diaries, journal collections concerning DeForest and Carolyn Kelley, by Kristine Smith, a young fan who became a protégé and friend, 1968–present.

WC—Weyland Collection, CA.

Informal private collection. Photographs and letters of DeForest and Carolyn Kelley at work during *Beginner's Luck* and the *Star Trek* movie productions, courtesy of Phil Weyland, director of *Beginner's Luck* and stand-in for DeForest Kelley, stand-in and dialogue coach for William Shatner 1979–1994, friend of DeForest Kelley 1974–present.

The Public Sources

AMPAS—Herrick Library, Academy of Motion Picture Arts and Sciences, Los Angeles, CA.

LBCPA—Long Beach Community Playhouse Archives, Long Beach, CA.

M-UI—University of Iowa. For the Nicholas Meyer Papers.

R-UCLA—University of California, Los Angeles. For the Roddenberry Papers.

WB-USC—University of Southern California, Los Angeles. For the Warner Brothers Collection.

A constant note of gratitude must be declared for all the friends, neighbors, and professional people who have gone out of their way to make DeForest Kelley's story possible. From New York to Texas and Arizona—in New Orleans and Los Angeles, I thank you all.

Thanks always to DeForest Kelley, the man in the mist, who led me everywhere I needed to go.

And special thanks to Marianne Tyler—I could not have gone on without you. You are more beloved than you think you are.

Notes

I. The Preacher's Son

1. Family archives and photos in *KHA;* Ernest D. Kelley, research file by and courtesy of Arlette Copeland, Mercer University, Georgia.
2. Kelley family genealogy; E. D. Kelley file, Mercer University.
3. Family archives and photos, *KHA;* "Where Is the Welcome Mat?" *TV Guide*, 1968.
4. Family archives and photos, *KHA.*
5. Family archives and photos, *KHA;* Kris Smith, working ms. for *A Harvest of Memories.*
6. Smith, *Harvest;* photos, *KHA.*
7. Erskine Davis, letter to author, November 1999; family archives and photos, *KHA.*
8. Smith, *Harvest.*
9. DeForest Kelley, speech in Seattle, Washington, 1990; Smith, *Harvest.*
10. Smith, *Harvest;* Davis, letter; original oil painting of Emma Banks by DeForest Kelley, Anne Jolly collection, *JHA.*
11. Smith, *Harvest.*
12. Davis, letter.
13. Family archives and photos, *KHA.*
14. Tom Doyle, letter and interview with author, 1999.
15. Ibid.
16. Ibid.
17. DeForest Kelley, letter to Grace Kelley, August 2, 1981; July 5, 1986; August 13, 1996, courtesy of Grace Kelley.
18. Photos, *KHA;* DeForest Kelley, speech in New York, undated.
19. "Where's the Welcome Mat?" *TV Guide,* Aug 24, 1968.

20. Flier, Conyers Baptist Church, *KHA*.
21. Brenda Marshall, "DeForest Kelley's Hidden Youth," *KHA;* Bette Ireland interview with author, January 2000.
22. Davis, letter.
23. Family archives and photos, *KHA;* Davis, letter.
24. Ibid.
25. Marshall, "Hidden Youth."
26. DeForest Kelley, speech in Denver, Colorado, 1988.
27. Scraps and photos, *KHA;* Marshall, "Hidden Youth."
28. Ibid.
29. Ibid.
30. Roger Elwood, "DeForest Kelley, Never Out on a Limb," *TV Star Parade*, February 1968.
31. Items in *KHA*.
32. Items in *KHA;* Davis, letter.
33. Marshall, "Hidden Youth"; Elwood, "Never Out on a Limb"; Bette Ireland; items, work stubs, and tickets, *KHA*.
34. Marshall, "Hidden Youth."
35. Smith, *Harvest*.
36. Marshall, "Hidden Youth"; Anne Jolly interview with author, January 2000; DeForest Kelley, speech in Chicago, Illinois, 1991; DeForest Kelley, speech, November 1991; speech in Los Angeles, California, 1990.
37. Marshall, "Hidden Youth"; Anne Jolly, interviews with author, 2000–2002.
38. Items, postcard, and photos, *KHA*.
39. Elwood, "Never Out on a Limb"; Brenda Marshall, "DeForest Kelley's Strong Arm," ms., *KHA;* Smith, TS.
40. Smith, *Harvest*.

II. The Young Artist

1. Items, scrapbook, *KHA;* the date of his permanent return to California is based on dated evidence such as pay stubs and bus tickets.
2. Grace Griffin, interviews with author, 1999–2002.
3. Griffin, interviews; DeForest Kelley, speech in Chicago, Illinois, July 1991.
4. Griffin, interviews.
5. Ibid.
6. Items and scrapbooks, *KHA;* DeForest Kelley in Paramount Public Relations files, Herrick Library, *AMPAS,* Beverly Hills, California.
7. Jolly, interview.
8. Files in Long Beach Playhouse Collection of Reviews, Long Beach, California; Joe Laden, interview with author, January 2000.
9. Laden, interview.
10. Ibid.
11. Items, personal notes, *KHA*.

12. Marshall, "Hidden Youth."
13. Griffin, interview; Laden, interview.
14. La Nelle and Stan Fosholdt, interviews with author, January 2000.
15. Fosholdt, interview; William Stull, "Ray Fosholdt Built a Movie Maker's Dream Home," *American Cinematographer*, August 1941.
16. Fosholdt, interview; scrapbooks, *KHA;* the original *Susanna* donated to *KLA*.
17. Fosholdt, interview.
18. *Chronicle of the 20th Century*, Clifton Daniel, editor. (Mount Kisco, N.Y.: Chronicle Publications, 1987), pp. 514–17.
19. Laden, interview; Anne Jolly, interview; Robert Cornthwait, interview with author, September, 1999.
20. Jolly, interviews; items, scrapbooks, *JHA*.
21. Scrapbooks and items, Long Beach Community Players, as described in *KHA* and *JHA*.
22. Cornthwait, interview; Anne Jolly, ms. essays, *JHA;* review files, Long Beach Playhouse, *LBCPA*.
23. Scrapbooks, *JHA*.
24. Linda Girard, interview with author, December 2000.
25. Items, Long Beach Cinema Club, newsletters, 1941, *KHA*.
26. Items, *LBCPA;* photos, *KHA;* Olive Ann Burns, "How 'Cinderella Boy' Crashed the Movies," *Atlanta Journal Magazine*, October 12, 1947, *KHA*.
27. Marshall, "DeForest Kelley's"; Jolly, interviews.
28. Production files, *This Gun for Hire*, *AMPAS*.
29. Items, scrapbooks, *KHA;* production files, *This Gun for Hire*, *AMPAS;* A. C. Lyles, speaking at the Golden Boot Awards in memory of DeForest Kelley, August 1999, private video.
30. "Alan Ladd," *CMG Worldwide*, August 22, 2000, online.
31. "Where Is the Welcome Mat?" *TV Guide*.
32. R. G. Armstrong, interview with author, April 2001; production files, *This Gun for Hire*, *AMPAS;* items, scrapbook, *KHA;* Burns, "How 'Cinderella Boy.' "
33. Production files, *This Gun for Hire*, *AMPAS;* "Alan Ladd," vertical files, *AMPAS;* http://yorty.sonoma.edu/filmfrog, online.
34. Items, scrapbooks, *KHA*.
35. Items, *Calship Journal,* and notes, *JHA*.
36. *Chronicle of the 20th Century*, pp. 522–27
37. Cornthwait, interview.
38. Items, scrapbook, *KHA;* Kahn file, *AMPAS;* original Ivan Kahn talent report—special thanks to Doug Johnson for uncovering this and some other crucial primary sources in the Herrick Library, *AMPAS*.
39. Items, Community Playhouse files, *LBCPA;* items, scraps, *KHA*.
40. Items, *KHA*.
41. Burns, "How 'Cinderella Boy.' "
42. Scrapbook, *KHA;* Kahn file, *AMPAS*.

43. Griffin, interview, February 2001; Jolly, interviews.
44. Jolly and Don Crews, interviews.
45. Jolly, interviews.
46. Ibid.

III. Her Innocent Young Man

1. Items, playbills, scrapbooks, *JHA*.
2. Items, play reviews, *JHA*.
3. Jolly, interviews; Griffin, interviews.
4. Griffin, interviews; Kelley, Denver, 1988; Carolyn Kelley, interviews with author, 1999–2002.
5. Items, playbill, *JHA;* items, scrapbooks, *KHA;* Jolly, interviews; Carolyn Kelley, interviews.
6. Items, scraps, *KHA.* The extent of Carolyn Kelley's background, training, and accomplishments is based on the evidence in the archives assembled by DeForest Kelley.
7. Anne Jolly, *JHA;* Irving Ravetch, interview with author, November 2000.
8. Laden, interview.
9. Laden, interview; photos, *KHA;* Altoni Place and Atlantic photos, Clora's photos in summer 1942, scrapbook, *KHA.*
10. "Two More Local Draft Groups Are Headed for Army," news clipping, *JHA;* Burns, "How 'Cinderella Boy' "; Bette Ireland Collection.
11. Ibid. *Starlog,* June 1999.
12. "Two More Local Draft Groups" *JHA.*
13. Jolly, interviews; Griffin, interviews.
14. Kelley told Anne the full story of how Walter had died in 1985.
15. *Los Angeles Times,* June 14, 1943, *JHA.*
16. Jolly, *JHA;* items, *KHA.*
17. Military records and discharge papers, *KHA;* Marianne Tyler, interview with author, September 2000; Jolly, interview; Laden, interview.
18. Linda Girard interviews, 2002; "Aerial Traffic Cops," Roswell clipping, scrapbooks, *KHA.*
19. "Specifications for Military Occupational Specialties," National Personnel Records Center; public relations clippings, *KHA.*
20. Roswell mission details from Yvonne Kinkaid, AF/HO, Pentagon, Washington, D.C., November 2, 2000.
21. R. G. Armstrong, interview with author.
22. Scrapbook, *KHA.*
23. Ibid.
24. Ibid.
25. Carolyn Kelley; Jolly; item, *Calship Log,* 1943, *JHA.*
26. Scrapbooks, Girard letter to Jolly, July 18, 1943, *JHA.*
27. Carolyn Kelley; Jolly; *KHA; JHA.*

28. Items, papers, *KHA*.
29. Jolly, *JHA*.
30. Ibid.
31. Items, scrapbook, *KHA*.
32. Scrapbook, *KHA*.
33. Girard letter to Jolly, September 24, 1943, *JHA*.
34. Armstrong, interview.
35. Original program, *JHA; Salvo*, Roswell Army Field, October 1, 1943, *JHA;* Roy Knott, letter to author, October 2000.
36. Items, telegrams, December 25, 1943, and December 29, 1943, *KHA*.
37. *Salvo*, October 1, 1943, *JHA*.
38. Jolly, interviews, *JHA*.
39. Ibid.
40. *Los Angeles Times,* March 19, 1944; *Edisonian*, April 15, 1944, *KHA;* Aileen Pickering, *JHA*.
41. Pickering.
42. Ibid.
43. Ibid.
44. Anne Jolly, collection of poems; Laurence Hope, *The Teak Forest and Indian Love and Song Lyrics,* undated; items, scrapbooks, *KHA*.
45. Unidentified poem, full length, in possession of Anne Jolly, *JHA*.
46. Telegram, *JHA*.
47. Bette Ireland, interview.
48. Ireland, interview; Carolyn Kelley, interview.
49. Ireland, interview.
50. Jolly, *JHA*.
51. Ireland, interview.
52. As told to Kris Smith. See her memoir.
53. Linda Girard, interviews and correspondence.
54. Laden, interview.
55. Ibid.
56. Recollections as told to Tony Kirk, Kris Smith, Joe Laden; Kelley, Denver, 1988.
57. Meiklejohn to Kelley, *KHA; Hollywood Commandoes*, AMC/Gregory Orr Productions, 1997, with commentary by DeForest Kelley.

IV. Cinderella Boy

1. Owen Crump oral history, ms., Douglas Bell for the Academy Foundation, *AMPAS,* Beverly Hills, California, 1991–1992, 1, 73–75, 109.
2. *Hollywood Commandoes*, Gregory Orr Productions.
3. "Model Target," *Air Force*, November 1945, pp. 22–23, in J. A. Schlein Collection, *AMPAS;* Aileen Pickering interviews; *Hollywood Commandoes; Chronicle of the 20th Century*, p. 586.

4. DeForest Kelley, vertical file, *AMPAS;* A. C. Lyles, interview with author, September 1999.
5. Ivan Kahn file, Lew Schreiber reports, *AMPAS;* Rolf Larsen, interview with author, April 2000.
6. First Motion Picture Unit, folder 13, Jay A. Schlein Collection, *AMPAS.*
7. "Trail Blazers," ms. regimental history, April 28, 1946, *KHA.*
8. Pickering, interviews.
9. Jolly, Ireland, Pickering, Laden, and many others confirm, *KHA.*
10. "Specifications for Military Occupational Specialties," National Personnel Records Center; "Tower Men Are Aerial Traffic Cops," clipping, photographs, scrapbook, *KHA;* Owen Crump oral history, 128–30, 143–45, *AMPAS.*
11. Kelley, Denver, 1988; Walt Faulconer, correspondence with the author, 2001.
12. Ibid.
13. Jackson D. Kelley WD AGO Form 53–55, *KHA.*
14. Laden, interview.
15. DeForest Kelley vertical file, includes A. C. Lyles original typescripts and other public relations pieces, *AMPAS.*
16. *Fear in the Night* is available through Sinister Cinema; see Web page.
17. A. C. Lyles, interview with author, September 1999; A. C. Lyles vertical file, *AMPAS.*
18. Griffin, interviews.
19. Fred D. Moon, "Atlanta Parents See Son Star on Screen," undated clipping, *Atlanta Journal, KHA.*
20. Smith photocopied review collection, *SHA;* Harve Bennett, interview with author and Smith, December 2000.
21. Bennett, interview.
22. *Screen Romances,* February 1947, *JHA.*
23. DeForest Kelley, original contract, *AMPAS; Fear in the Night* publicity collections, in *JHA, KHA.*
24. Phil Weyland, conversations with the author, 2000–2002.
25. This account varies. In "Where Is the Welcome Mat?" an article in *TV Guide* in 1968, the palm reader is an old man at a party; in other accounts, it is a palm reader on the Santa Monica pier.
26. *Daily News,* film review, October 9, 1947, *KSA.*
27. "Doctor DeForest Kelley Can't Aid Ailing Series," *Philadelphia Inquirer,* June 1, 1969.
28. Production file, *Variety Girl, AMPAS;* Scott, *Los Angeles Times, KSA.*
29. DeForest Kelley, vertical file, *AMPAS.*
30. Carolyn Kelley to Aileen Pickering, letter, January 7, 1947, *PHA.*
31. Alice Meyers, letters and photographs, *KHA.*
32. Smith, *KSA.*
33. Ibid.
34. Ireland, interview.

35. Jolly, interviews.

36. Jolly, interviews; Tom Drake, vertical file, *AMPAS*.

37. Bill Campbell, interview with author and Smith, September 1999.

38. Thomas Shatz, *Boom and Bust: American Cinema in the 1940s* (Los Angeles: University of California Press, 1999) pp. 286, 290–307; Laden, interview.

39. Larsen, interview.

40. Larsen, interview.

41. Larsen, interview.

V. The Cold Hunger

1. *Sealed Verdict*, production file, *AMPAS*.

2. Jolly, interview.

3. Shatz, *Boom and Bust*, pp. 318, 333–78

4. Jan Alan Henderson, *Speeding Bullet: The Life and Bizarre Death of George Reeves* (Grand Rapids, Mich.: Bifulco, 1999), pp. 21–29, 39; Pickering, interviews; Carolyn Kelley, interviews.

5. Items, scrapbooks, Kelley film reviews, *SHA*.

6. Shatz, *Boom and Bust*, p. 438.

7. Carolyn Kelley, interviews; "My Real-life Encounter with a UFO," *National Enquirer,* January 13, 1987. Carolyn Kelley and friends corroborate the story, and the *Enquirer* was accurate.

8. Carolyn Kelley, interviews.

9. DeForest Kelley film reviews, *SHA*. For DeForest Kelley career credits, research largely conducted by Sue Keenan, longtime president of the DeForest Kelley Fan Club and friend of the Kelleys. Her credit list was reviewed by DeForest Kelley and found to be very complete. Other resources have surfaced and have been used when applicable.

10. Scrapbooks, *KHA;* DeForest Kelley, speech in New York, New York, November 1990.

11. Peggy Benoit Dunn, interview with author, December 1999.

12. Kelley, New York, 1990.

13. "Tobacco Road" review in *The Record American* September 6, 1950. Original program donated to the Kelley Legacy Project, courtesy of Peggy Benoit Dunn.

14. Kelley, New York, 1990.

15. Carolyn Kelley, letter from Cherie, October 14, 1951, *KHA*.

16. Marshall, "Strong Arm," TS, *KHA*.

VI. DeForest Lawn

1. Tony LaFata, interviews with author, 2000–2002.

2. Items, "Telepix Review," and others from 1953, *KSA*.

3. Tom Doyle, letter to author, November 15, 1999.

4. Carolyn Kelley, interviews; "George Reeves," *A&E Biography*, September 25, 2000.

5. Ibid; Kelley, Denver, March, 1988. Special thanks to Phil Weyland, actor, director, and dialogue coach, for his referrals and observations about Reeves, Kelley, and the nature of celebrity.

6. Walter Ames, "History TV Series Director Catches Up with Worst Subject," *Los Angeles Times,* April 17, 1955.

7. Larry Dobkin, interview with author, March 2001.

8. Linda Girard, interviews and correspondence; items, credit lists, *KHA.* In four years of *You Are There,* Kelley appeared in twelve episodes.

9. Pickering, interviews.

10. *Illegal,* Warner Brothers Archives, University of Southern California, Los Angeles, California.

11. *Gunfight at the OK Corral*, production file, *AMPAS.*

12. DeForest Kelley; author's edited composite of this very popular story.

VII. **The Reel Cowboy**

1. Smith, *Harvest*; some sources remain anonymous.

2. Don Smith and Aileen Pickering, conversations with author, separately and together, 1999–2002; items, *KHA.* For the significance of wearing a mother's ring, Kris Smith, Nicholas Meyer.

3. Tom Doyle.

4. Items, Carolyn Kelley, correspondence with Phyllis and Bill Daniels, *KHA.*

5. Antoni Gronowics with Richard Schikel, *Garbo: Her Story* (New York: Simon and Schuster, 1990), pp. 183, 186, 196, 285.

6. *The Law and Jake Wade*, production file; John Sturges Collection; MGM wardrobe files, all in *AMPAS.*

7. DeForest Kelley, speech in Chicago, Illinois, 1991.

8. Harry Carey, Jr., *Company of Heroes: My Life As an Actor in the John Ford Stock Company* (New York: Madison Brooks, 1994), pp. 180–89.

9. DeForest Kelley, speech in Denver, Colorado, 1992; items, *KHA;* Dr. Lee DeForest vertical file, *AMPAS.*

10. Reviews collection, *KSA;* Bill Campbell, interview.

11. Kelley credit lists, *KHA;* Grace Lee Whitney, interview with author, March 2001; see also Grace Lee Whitney, *The Longest Trek: My Tour of the Galaxy* (Clovis Calif.: Quill Driver Books, 1998).

12. Tom Drake, vertical file; *Warlock,* production file; William Gordon Collection, all in *AMPAS.*

13. DeForest Kelley; author's edited compilation of this popular story.

14. Ibid.

15. Carolyn Kelley, interviews, *KHA.*

16. Smith, *Harvest.*

17. Ibid.

VIII. Playing the Heavy

1. DeForest Kelley credit lists, *KHA;* Whitney, interview; Whitney, *Longest Trek.*
2. Carey, Jr., *Company of Heroes,* pp. 158–61.
3. Smith, *Harvest.*
4. Ibid.
5. DeForest Kelley, speech in Phoenix, Arizonia, March 1996.
6. DeForest Kelley, speech in St. Petersburg, Florida, November 1991.
7. Items, Jake Ehrlich collection, *KHA.*
8. Ibid.; *Oakland Tribune,* February 9, 1960; *San Francisco Chronicle,* February 11, 1960, in *KHA.*
9. David Alexander, *Star Trek Creator: The Authorized Biography of Gene Roddenberry* (New York: ROC Dutton Signet, 1994).
10. Jake Ehrlich, letters to DeForest Kelley, *KHA; Daily Variety,* June 13, 1960.
11. Kelley, Los Angeles, 1990; speech in St. Petersburg, Florida, November 1991.
12. R. G. Armstrong, interview.
13. DeForest Kelley letter to Sam Peckinpah, Sam Peckinpah collection, *AMPAS.*
14. DeForest Kelley, speech in Baltimore, Maryland, July 1985.
15. Kelley, Denver, 1988.
16. Whitney, interview.
17. Pickering, interviews.
18. Carolyn Kelley, interviews.
19. Jolly, interview.
20. Ireland, interview.
21. *Where Love Has Gone,* production file, *AMPAS.*
22. A. C. Lyles, vertical file, *AMPAS.*
23. The actual development of the *Star Trek* series is something different from a biographical accounting based on the oral histories of people involved in DeForest Kelley's life. For a focus on *Star Trek,* see the various autobiographies and Stephen Whitfield and Gene Roddenberry, *The Making of Star Trek* (New York: Ballantine Books, 1968), and especially Herbert F. Solow and Robert H. Justman, *Inside Star Trek: The Real Story* (New York: Pocket Books, 1996); D.C. Fontana, interview with author, May 2000.
24. Kelley, Baltimore, 1985.
25. Solow and Justman, *Inside Star Trek,* pp. 37–38.
26. Kelley, Los Angeles, 1990; Denver, 1991.
27. *Marriage on the Rocks,* production files, Warner Brothers Archives, USC; Kelley, Denver, 1988.
28. DeForest Kelley, author's composite.
29. Kelley, Denver, 1988.
30. Kelley, Baltimore, 1985; Kelley and Lyles, Los Angeles, 1990.
31. Reviews collection, Smith, *SHA;* Tony Kirk, interview with author and Smith, January 2000.
32. Fontana, interview.

33. Solow and Justman, *Inside Star Trek*, p. 75.
34. Fontana, interview; Whitney, *Longest Trek*, pp. 70–71; Harry Harris, "Kelley," *Philadelphia Inquirer*, June 1, 1969; Robert Justman, interview with author and Smith, January, 2000.
35. *Waco*, production files, *AMPAS;* Kelley credits, *KHA*.
36. Kelley, Baltimore, 1985; Harris, "Kelley"; Fontana, interview; Solow and Justman, *Inside Star Trek*, p. 84.

IX. Starlight

1. Items in *KHA;* Pickering, interviews; DeForest Kelley, speech in Denver, Colorado, 1991.
2. Pickering, interviews.
3. Consensus with author, Carolyn Kelley, Anne Jolly, Linda Girard, Irving Ravetch. See also Internet Movie Database (www.imdb.com) for Ravetch and Girard.
4. *Star Trek: The Magazine*, October 1999, 23.
5. Fontana, interview.
6. Roddenberry's position on Christianity is well known. For an exploration of his humanism, deism, and pantheistic inner life, see Yvonne Fern, *Gene Roddenberry: The Last Conversation* (New York: Pocket Books, 1996).
7. Kelley, Denver, 1991; Chicago, 1991.
8. Fontana, interview.
9. Alexander, *Star Trek Creator*, p. 233.
10. *Star Trek Communicator*, June 1999.
11. "I'll Never Forgive Nimoy and Shatner," *TV Picture Life*, March 1968; Alexander, *Star Trek Creator*, p. 232.
12. Kelley, Denver, 1988.
13. Solow and Justman, *Inside Star Trek*, pp. 117, 119.
14. Roddenberry papers, R-UCLA.
15. *Star Trek Communicator*, June 1999.
16. *Telepix Review,* September 8, 1966, *SHA*.
17. Solow and Justman, *Inside Star Trek*, pp. 132, 133.
18. David Gerrold, *The World of Star Trek*, p. 64.
19. Kelley, Baltimore, 1985.
20. Kelly, Los Angeles, 1990.
21. Nichelle Nichols, interview with author, September 2000.
22. Items in *KHA*.
23. Elwood, *"Never Out on a Limb."*
24. Robert Justman, interview.
25. Roddenberry collection, Box 28, UCLA.
26. Marshall, "Strong Arm," *KHA*.
27. Gerrold, *World of Star Trek*, 66; Pamela Roller, "DeForest Kelley: Memories from the Real McCoy," *Star Trek Communicator* 111 (March–April 1997) 14.

X. Dammit, Jim

1. Harve Bennett, interview with author, January 2000.
2. Leonard Nimoy, interview with author, November 2000.
3. Kelley, Baltimore, 1985.
4. Kelley, Denver, 1988; Solow and Justman, *Inside Star Trek*, pp. 286, 287.
5. Alexander, *Star Trek Creator,* pp. 296–301; Solow and Justman, *Inside Star Trek*, pp. 293–95.
6. Rolf Larsen, interview.
7. Fontana, interview.
8. Thanks to Laura Guyer for counting.
9. Alexander, *Star Trek Creator,* pp. 275–87; Roddenberry papers, April 1967, R-UCLA.
10. Solow and Justman, *Inside Star Trek*, pp. 318, 319.
11. Roddenberry papers, R-UCLA.
12. Solow and Justman, *Inside Star Trek*, pp. 240–41.
13. Fontana, interview; Leonard Nimoy, *I Am Spock* (New York: Hyperion, 1995), pp. 67, 68. See Nimoy's autobiography for the authoritive account of the world of *Star Trek*.
14. Nimoy, *I Am Spock*, pp. 59, 60, 64.
15. See the autobiographies of *Star Trek* actors.
16. Solow, quoted in David Kronke, "Calendar: *Star Trek*," *Los Angeles Times,* September 8, 1996.
17. Nimoy, interview.
18. Gerrold, *World of Star Trek,* pp. 62–63.
19. Items in *KHA*.
20. Nimoy, interview.
21. Ibid.
22. Kelley, Baltimore, 1985.
23. Gerrold, *World of Star Trek,* pp. 62–63.
24. Kelley, Denver, 1988.
25. Ireland, interview.
26. George Eres, "DeForest Kelley: A New Image in '*Star Trek*,'" *Independent Press-Telegram*, June 4, 1967, *IHA*.
27. Solow and Justman, *Inside Star Trek*, pp. 240–41.
28. Bill Campbell, interview; Solow and Justman, *Inside Star Trek*, p. 349.
29. Charles Washburn, interview with author, May 2000.
30. Kelley, Denver, 1988.
31. Washburn, interview.
32. Gerrold, *World of Star Trek,* pp. 64–65.
33. Kelley, New York, 1990.

XI. Rising Star

1. Roddenberry collection, Box 28, R-UCLA.
2. Kelley, Denver, 1991.
3. Alexander, *Star Trek Creator*, pp. 314–15; Solow and Justman, p. 389.
4. Ibid., 319.
5. Robert Justman, review of manuscript, October, 2001.
6. Alexander, *Star Trek Creator*, pp. 315–17.
7. Ibid.
8. Kelley, Seattle, 1990; Denver, 1988.
9. Kristine Smith, *Harvest*. Extended quotation of material courtesy of Kris Smith. Her friendship and journey with DeForest Kelley is now available in print from First Books. *DeForest Kelley: A Harvest of Memories* is recommended for a very personal look at friendship, trust, and the remarkable transformation that is inherent in the care of the terminally ill.
10. Alexander, *Star Trek Creator*, pp. 356–57.
11. Solow and Justman, *Inside Star Trek*, p. 395.
12. "Where Is the Welcome Mat?"
13. Alexander, *Star Trek Creator*, pp. 364–65.
14. Roddenberry collection, R-UCLA.
15. Marshall, "Strong Arm"; Gene Roddenberry, 1967 Paramount news release, July 6, Box 28, UCLA.
16. Ibid.
17. "I'll Never Forgive."
18. "Where Is the Welcome Mat?"
19. Roddenberry collection, R-UCLA.
20. Alexander, *Star Trek Creator*, pp. 364, 365; Harris, "Kelley."
21. Jacqueline Lichtenberg, Sondra Marshak, and Joan Winston, *Star Trek Lives!* (London: Corgi Books, 1975), pp. 184–85.
22. Ibid., pp. 192–99.
23. Carolyn Kelley, letter to Anne, *JHA*.
24. Kelley, Seattle, 1990; Alexander, *Star Trek Creator*, p. 365; Solow and Justman, *Inside Star Trek*, pp. 414–15.
25. Pickering, interviews; Carolyn Kelley, interviews.

XII. DeForest Lawn Revisited

1. Kronke, "Calender."
2. Armstrong, interview.
3. Carolyn Kelley, interviews; Phyllis and Bill Daniels, correspondence with author.
4. Tony Kirk, interview with Smith and the author, January 2000.
5. Karen E. Willson, "A Candid Conversation with a 'Simple Country Doctor' DeForest Kelley," *Starlog*, September 1980; Phil Weyland, interviews with the author, 2000–2002.

6. Don Smith, conversations with Smith and the author, September 1999–2002. He has opened his home and his heart to us when we needed it most.
7. *Star Trek Communicator*, June 1999.
8. Richard Arnold, interview with the author, January 2001.
9. Richard Arnold, "Convention Memories of De," *Star Trek Communicator*, June 1999.
10. Lichtenberg, Marshak, and Winston, *Star Trek Lives!* pp. 213–14; as gleaned from reviewing convention appearances and talking to fans, 1999–2002.
11. Kronke, "Calendar."
12. Nichelle Nichols, *Beyond Uhura* (New York: G. P. Putnam's Sons, 1994). p. 205; *Starlog*, September 1991.
13. Willson, "Candid Conversation."
14. Kelley's desire to keep the boy's name private is honored.

XIII. Beginner's Luck

1. J. G. Hertzler, interview with author, May 2000; Dan Madsen, interviews with author, 1999–2000.
2. Larry Nemecek, interviews with author, 2000–2002; Hertzler, interview.
3. Kelley, Denver, 1988.
4. The author would like to thank Phil Weyland for his many hours of assistance with the research.
5. Kelley, Denver, 1988.
6. Jane Ann Dixon, correspondence with author, January 2001.
7. Kelley, Chicago, 1991.
8. Kelley, Denver, 1988; Chicago 1991; St. Petersburg, 1991.
9. Phil Weyland, correspondence with author, 2000–2001.
10. Willson, "Candid Conversation."
11. Alexander, *Star Trek Creator*, p. 430–31.

XIV. I Must Be McCoy

1. *New York Hotline*, 1978, SHA.
2. Weyland, interviews and correspondence.
3. Willson, "Candid Conversation."
4. Stephen Collins, interview with author, September 2000.
5. Weyland, interviews.
6. Nimoy, *I Am Spock*, p. 168.
7. Weyland, interviews.
8. Collins, interview; Nimoy, interview.
9. Collins, interview.
10. Willson, "Candid Conversation."
11. Weyland, interviews.
12. Items, *KHA*.
13. Ralph Winter, interview with author, 2001.

14. Collins, interview.
15. Items, *KHA;* Pickering, interview.
16. Willson, "Candid Conversation."
17. Ibid.
18. Jolly, interviews; *JHA.*
19. Pickering, interview; *PHA.*
20. Madsen, interview.
21. Pickering interview; Grace Kelley, correspondence with author, 2000.
22. Tony Kirk, interview; items in *KHA;* Pickering, interview.

XV. "Someone suggested they get Harve Bennett, *Rich Man Poor Man*—fix it in a minute."

1. DeForest Kelley, "The Dream Goes On," ms., 1984; Harve Bennett, interview, January 2000.
2. The veracity of Bennett's statement about working with Roddenberry is borne out by Roddenberry's missives over the course of screenplay development. Most of his objections were addressed, and much of his advice was taken and used by Bennett and Meyer. Items in Meyer collection, University of Iowa. Bennett states that "Gene was, from the beginning, opposed to the story . . . some of his advice was taken and used and all of his objections were addressed."
3. Randy and Jean-Marc Lofficier and Julius Fabrini, "DeForest Kelley: He's an Actor, not a Doctor," *Starlog,* November 1984.
4. Ibid.
5. Troy Yeary, www.filmfrontier.com.
6. Nicholas Meyer biography, nmeyer.pxl.net; Nicholas Meyer, interview and correspondence with author, 2001–2002.
7. Lofficier and Fabrini, "He's an Actor."
8. Ibid.
9. Ibid; Meyer collection, University of Iowa.
10. Weyland, interview; Yeary, www.filmfrontier.com.
11. Bennett, interviews; Winter, interview.
12. Meyer, interview, May 2000.
13. Kelley, Chicago, 1991.
14. Bennett, correspondence; Meyer, correspondence; Weyland, correspondence, all with author.
15. Nimoy, 207–10.
16. Bennett, correspondence; Nimoy, 211–15.
17. Lofficier and Fabrini, "He's an Actor."
18. Ibid.; items in Meyer collection, University of Iowa.
19. Yeary, www.filmfrontier.com. Selections from the Yeary compilation have been very valuable.
20. Ibid.
21. Bennett, interview, January, 2000.

XVI. That Green-Blooded Son of a Bitch

1. DeForest Kelley, "The Dream Goes On"; Kirk, interview.
2. Nimoy, p. 217.
3. Yeary, www.filmfrontier.com.
4. Ibid.
5. Ibid.; Bennett, interview.
6. Weyland, interview.
7. Kelley, Baltimore, 1985.
8. Ibid.
9. Nimoy, pp. 222, 228–31.
10. *Variety*, May 25, 1984; items, *SHA.*
11. DeForest Kelley, speech at SpaceTrek III, *SHA.*
12. Kelley, Baltimore, 1985.

XVII. Any Problems, Just Call Me

1. Dan Madsen, "Ralph Winter: Overseeing the Voyage Home, Part II," *Star Trek: The Official Fan Club* 54 (February/March 1987); original AMA article, *SHA.*
2. Nimoy, pp. 264–65; Yeary, www.filmfrontier.com.
3. Madsen, "Overseeing."
4. Bennett, interview.
5. Catherine Hicks, interview with author, September 2000.
6. Yeary, www.filmfrontier.com.
7. Madsen, "Overseeing."
8. Ibid.
9. Yeary, www.filmfrontier.com.; Bennett, interview.
10. Madsen, "Overseeing."
11. Smith, *Harvest.*
12. Arnold, interview.
13. Sammye K. Beron, interview with author, April 2000.
14. DeForest Kelley, speech at TrekCruise, 1987; Walter Koenig, Kelley Hollywood Star Ceremony, 1991, fan tape.
15. Julia Woodson Jackson, letter to author, January 2000.
16. Dan Madsen, "DeForest Kelley: Still the Real McCoy," *Star Trek: the Official Fan Club,* (December–January 1988).
17. Don Smith, interview; items, *KHA;* Justman, interview.
18. Lyles, interview.
19. A number of friends tell the Elizabeth Taylor story independently; Lyles, interview.
20. Item, NSAL newsletters, *KHA.*
21. Marge Stien, interview with author, August 2001; contact NSAL on the Internet for more information.
22. Mike Arms, interview with author, August 2001.
23. Madsen, "Overseeing."
24. Ibid.

XVIII. Don't Say I Didn't Warn Ya

1. Rick Berman, interview with author, September 2001.
2. Yeary, www.filmfrontier.com.
3. Lisabeth Shatner, *Captain's Log: William Shatner's Personal Account of the Making of Star Trek V: The Final Frontier* (New York: Pocket Books), p. 69.
4. Winter, interview.
5. Yeary, www.filmfrontier.com.
6. Bennett, interview.
7. Yeary, www.filmfrontier.com.
8. DeForest Kelley, speech in Baltimore, Maryland, 1992.
9. Laurence Luckinbill, interview with author, January 2002.
10. Shatner, *Captain's Log*, p. 180.
11. Kelley, "The Dream Goes On and On . . .and On . . .," self-published, 1990 and 1993.
12. Yeary, www.filmfrontier.com.
13. Smith, *Harvest*.
14. Peggy Latimer, letter to author, January 2000.

XIX. The Last Best Hope in the Universe for Peace

1. Kelley, "The Dream Goes On and On . . .and On. . . ."
2. Kirk, interview; Kris Smith; *SHA*.
3. Nimoy, *I Am Spock*, pp. 325–33; Yeary, www.filmfrontier.com.
4. Yeary, www.filmfrontier.com.; Winter, interview.
5. Lynne Stephens, Marc Shapiro, and Ian Spelling, "Beloved Doctor," *Starlog*, yearbook 1991, p. 35.
6. Kelley, speech at Vulkon, 1991.
7. Kelley, "The Dream Goes On and On . . .and On . . .," 1993.
8. Kirk, interview Kelley, Vulkon, 1991.
9. Yeary, www.filmfrontier.com.
10. Kelley, Vulkon, 1991.
11. Meyer, correspondence.
12. Yeary, www.filmfrontier.com.
13. Kelley, Vulkon, 1991.
14. Kelley, ceremony tape, *KSA*.
15. Harry Haun, "The Good Doctor McCoy," *The Daily News*, December 1991.
16. Beron, interview.
17. Anja Schilling, letter to Smith, 2000.

ABOUT THE AUTHOR

Terry Lee Rioux lives in New Orleans and works with the
National D-Day Museum and the National Park Service.
   A portion of royalties from this book will be donated
to the North Shore Animal League in honor of Carolyn and
DeForest Kelley.